SHADOW OF THE SITH

STAR WARS

SHADOW OF THE SITH

ADAM CHRISTOPHER

RANDOM HOUSE

WORLDS

NEW YORK

2023 Random House Worlds Trade Paperback Edition

Published in the United States by Random House Worlds, an imprint of Random House, a division of Penguin Random House LLC, New York.

RANDOM HOUSE is a registered trademark, and RANDOM HOUSE WORLDS and colophon are trademarks of Penguin Random House LLC.

Originally published in hardcover in the United States by Del Rey, an imprint of Random House, a division of Penguin Random House LLC, in 2022.

ISBN 978-0-593-35862-7
Ebook ISBN 978-0-593-35861-0

Printed in the United States of America on acid-free paper

randomhousebooks.com

1st Printing

Book design by Elizabeth A. D. Eno

For Sandra, always.
To Mum and Dad. Love you heaps.

THE STAR WARS NOVELS TIMELINE

THE HIGH REPUBLIC

Convergence
The Battle of Jedha
Cataclysm

Light of the Jedi
The Rising Storm
Tempest Runner
The Fallen Star

Dooku: Jedi Lost
Master and Apprentice

I THE PHANTOM MENACE

II ATTACK OF THE CLONES

Brotherhood
The Thrawn Ascendancy Trilogy
Dark Disciple: A Clone Wars Novel

III REVENGE OF THE SITH

Inquisitor: Rise of the Red Blade
Catalyst: A Rogue One Novel
Lords of the Sith
Tarkin
Jedi: Battle Scars

SOLO

Thrawn
A New Dawn: A Rebels Novel
Thrawn: Alliances
Thrawn: Treason

ROGUE ONE

IV A NEW HOPE

Battlefront II: Inferno Squad
Heir to the Jedi
Doctor Aphra
Battlefront: Twilight Company

V THE EMPIRE STRIKES BACK

VI RETURN OF THE JEDI

The Princess and the Scoundrel
The Alphabet Squadron Trilogy
The Aftermath Trilogy
Last Shot

Shadow of the Sith
Bloodline
Phasma
Canto Bight

VII THE FORCE AWAKENS

VIII THE LAST JEDI

Resistance Reborn
Galaxy's Edge: Black Spire

IX THE RISE OF SKYWALKER

A long time ago in a galaxy far, far away. . . .

And in the end, you cannot touch the shadow.
In the end, you do not even want to.
In the end, the shadow is all you have left.
Because the shadow understands you.
The shadow forgives you.
The shadow gathers you unto itself.
And within your furnace heart, you burn in your own flame.

—A warning from a darker time

SHADOW OF THE SITH

It is a time of peace. As the ashes of the evil Galactic Empire cool, the New Republic works to establish a new era of freedom and cooperation, while Jedi Master LUKE SKYWALKER trains the next generation of younglings at his temple.

But there is a dark shadow growing in the Force. As former Rebel Alliance general LANDO CALRISSIAN continues his search for his kidnapped daughter, cultists from the hidden world of EXEGOL work to enact plans a generation in the making.

Meanwhile, in the depths of Wild Space, a terrified young family makes a desperate journey, fleeing agents of an evil presence the galaxy has long thought dead. . . .

CHAPTER I

WILD SPACE, COORDINATES UNKNOWN
NOW

A t first, there was nothing but empty space. And then the ship appeared, mass and form and structure. Here to there, crossing boundless gulfs of space, as easy as pulling a lever. It was almost magical in its simplicity.

Right then, however, the ship's overheating navicomputer begged to differ.

For a moment, the battered old freighter just floated, hanging in space, like a garu-bear coming out of a long hibernation, taking stock of its surroundings.

And then the ship shuddered and began listing to port, carving a long, slow spiral that was suddenly accelerated as an aft impulse stabilizer failed in a shower of white sparks. The ship's nose dipped even further, the starboard engine now sputtering, a loose cover plate revealing a dangerous red glow from beneath.

For the pilot and her two passengers, the situation had just gone from bad, to worse.

Two days. That was all they'd managed. Two days out from Jakku, limping along in a ship that shouldn't be flying at all, but was the only hulk they'd managed to jack from Unkar Plutt's scrapyard outside of Niima Outpost. And it didn't look like they were going to make it much farther.

Just a few hours earlier, they dared to think that maybe . . . they'd made it? They'd gotten out of their homestead, their all-purpose house droid, handcrafted from more scrap and salvage, sacrificing itself as it led the hunters astray. Then they found the ship (truth be told, they had long ago earmarked it for such a day—a day they hoped would never come). Launched it, just themselves, a bag with toys and books and a blanket, a handful of credits, the clothes on their backs. Pointed the navicomputer along a vector that would take them *way* out of range (so they hoped). And buckled in for the ride.

But now? The ship had barely survived the initial trip. Escaping to Wild Space had been a desperate move, but was far from the endgame. It was supposed to be where they could hide, just for a while, take the time to *make a plan* and *plot a course.*

Those options now seemed decidedly more limited as they floated adrift. They'd escaped Jakku, only to . . . what? Die in the cold reaches of space, the old freighter now nothing but a tomb for the three of them, lost forever on the outskirts of the galaxy, their passing unmourned, their names unremembered.

Dathan, Miramir.

Rey.

The freighter's interior was as old and battered as the exterior—the flight deck was cramped and functional, the old-fashioned design requiring not just pilot and copilot but navigator, the third seat at the back of the cabin, facing away from the forward viewports. For this trip, they'd had to make do with a crew of just two.

The pilot's seat was occupied by a young woman, her long blond hair corralled loosely with a blue tie that matched the color of her cloak, the sleeves of her cream tunic rolled up as she leaned over the control console in front of her, one hand gripping the uncooperative yoke, the other flying over buttons and switches as she fought to control the shuddering ship. The forward view, as seen through the angled, heavily scratched transparisteel viewport, showed the starscape ahead sliding diagonally as the freighter's spin accelerated.

Behind her, a young man, his dark hair short, the beginnings of a beard over his jaw, knelt on the decking behind the navigator's seat. His arms were wrapped around it and its small occupant, the child cradled in a padded nest formed out of a bright, multicolored blanket, a stark contrast with the drab, greasy gunmetal of the flight deck.

The man craned his neck around as he watched his wife wrestle with the controls, then he stood and leaned down to kiss the head of the six-year-old girl strapped securely in the seat, a large pair of navigator's sound-deadening headphones over her ears. In front of the girl, the ancient navigation panel—a square matrix of hundreds of individual tiny square lights—flashed in multicolored patterns of moving shapes, a simple game the girl's mother had loaded into the auxiliary computer to keep her daughter occupied on the long journey.

The man looked up at the game board, but the girl had stopped playing. He moved around to the front of the chair and saw she had her eyes screwed tightly shut. He leaned in, embracing his daughter.

"I've got you," Dathan whispered to Rey. "We're all right. I've got you."

There was a bang; Dathan felt it as much as he heard it as another part of the strained engines gave up, the small explosion reverberating through the ship. A tear ran down from Rey's closed eyes. Dathan wiped it away, and closed his own eyes, wishing that, for once, a little good luck would come their way.

"Okay, there we go!" Miramir yelled, following her statement with a *whoop* of triumph. The ship jolted once, and then the steady shaking stopped. Through the forward viewports, the stars were now completely still.

Despite himself, despite their situation, Dathan found himself smiling. He couldn't help it. His wife was a genius and he loved her. He didn't know *where* she got it from, but she was a natural, like it was genetic. She could fly anything, had been—and still was—a self-taught engineer and inventor. Tinkering, Miramir called it, as though it were nothing, as though she didn't realize just how special her talents were. In the years that he had known her, Dathan had often asked where this gift had come from, but Miramir would just shrug and say her grandmother was a wonderful woman. Dathan knew that to be true—he had met her, several times, before Miramir gave up her life in the twilight forest of Hyperkarn to travel with Dathan. But then . . . where had her *grandmother* learned it all?

Dathan wanted to know, but over time he'd learned not to ask any further. Miramir missed her grandmother. She missed her home.

That was something else Dathan had tried to understand. To be *homesick*, to miss something that you could never return to—that was something unknown to him. Oh sure, he could *understand* it. And yes, he felt something for his days on Hyperkarn, even the years on Jakku, but he wasn't sure it was the same. Neither of those places had been truly *home*.

He did have a home, a place he could legitimately say he came from. It was a place he revisited a lot, in dreams.

Dreams . . . and nightmares.

"That will hold for a while," said Miramir, releasing the yoke and reaching up to flick a series of heavy switches in the angled panel above the pilot's position. "I've rerouted reserve power into the starboard impulse stabilizer, and then pushed the angle of the field *way* beyond point-seven, but that's fine because—"

She stopped as Dathan dropped into the copilot's seat and looked at her, one eyebrow raised.

"I don't know what any of that means," he said, "except that we're safe, right?"

Miramir sat back, her slight form dwarfed by the pilot's seat. She grinned and nodded.

Dathan felt his own grin growing. Miramir's happiness—her relief—was infectious. Maybe they *would* get out of this after all.

"The stabilizers will hold until the hyperdrive resets," said Miramir. "The motivator overheats every time we make a jump, but it's still working for the moment. We should be good for another couple of jumps." She paused, then wrinkled her nose. "But we do need to find another ship. Which means . . ." She gestured at the viewports, to the infinite emptiness that was Wild Space.

Dathan nodded. "Which means heading back to the Outer Rim."

At that, Miramir unclipped her seat restraints and headed over to Rey. Kneeling by the navigator's seat, she gently lifted the headphones off her daughter's head, then unclipped the seat restraints. As soon as she was freed, Rey sprang out of the seat and tackled her mother, arms and legs wrapped around Miramir, her head buried in her chest. Rey was perhaps small for a six-year-old, but Miramir didn't mind her daughter's desire for closeness, knowing the girl would soon grow out of it. Miramir turned and sank gently into the navigator's seat, still cradling Rey, and kicked the seat around so she was facing Dathan.

"I know it's dangerous," said Miramir, "but this ship was in Plutt's scrap heap for a reason. We've managed one long jump, and look what happened. It'll be worse each time."

Dathan sighed and gave his wife a nod. "We don't have a choice," he said. "I know."

Miramir lowered her face to Rey's hair, burying her nose in the brunette plait, her eyes focused somewhere on the floor.

Dathan knew that look. He'd seen it plenty of times over the last two days. It pained him to see Miramir like this. His wife, his love, the smartest and most beautiful and best person he had ever met. Certainly the most capable, far better at most things than he was, no matter how hard he tried.

And he knew something else, too.

This was *all* his fault.

But there would be time for that later. Right now, they were out of options, and only one path was open to them.

"Hey," said Dathan. He forced the smile back onto his face.

Miramir looked up but didn't speak.

"Hey, come on, now," said Dathan.

Miramir looked at him, her big eyes beginning to water.

"Mum, I'm hungry."

Miramir looked down at Rey, and—

She laughed. Dathan grinned, then found himself unable to stop himself from joining in.

Rey unraveled herself from her mother's arms and turned to look at her dad.

"You guys are silly," she said. And then she pointed at the front viewport. "Who's that?"

No sooner had the child spoken than an alarm sounded. Dathan toggled a switch to clear it, then turned around to look at what Rey had spotted. The alarm began to sound again.

"What is that?" asked Miramir.

"We've got company," said Dathan, watching as in the distance three stars moved and began growing in size.

Three ships, flying in formation.

Coming right for them.

CHAPTER 2

WILD SPACE, COORDINATES UNKNOWN
NOW

"They've found us," Dathan whispered. "How did they find us?" He looked down at the controls in front of them, nearly every one a complete mystery. "Miramir, we have to get out of here."

"Take Rey," said his wife, "let me handle this." As they swapped positions, there was a flash and a roar, the pair ducking instinctively as the trio of pursuing ships split right on the freighter's nose, two disappearing port and starboard, the third flying directly over the top. Lights flashed on the consoles around them as the freighter's antique computer systems kicked into life, tracking the other ships.

"They're turning," said Dathan, looking at a readout on the navigator's console. The display was poor—the freighter should have been in a museum, not lost in Wild Space—but against the burnt-orange grid, three fuzzy markers indicating the other craft crawled over the screen as they looped around and headed back toward them.

"Are we sure it's them?" asked Miramir, her focus on the flight systems. "How did they track us?"

Dathan shrugged. "How did they track us the first time? They're not going to give up, Miramir. They're *never* going to give up. How long until we can make the jump?"

Miramir toggled another readout and blew out her cheeks. "A few minutes. The hyperdrive motivator is still too hot, and if I touch the impulse stabilizers it'll be too hard to get an escape vector anyway."

There was a screeching sound from somewhere far away. Dathan looked up at the flight deck ceiling, alive with dancing indicators. Then there was a bang and the freighter rocked from side to side. Ahead, the blackness of space flashed green as the attacking ships, now back in a new formation, screamed overhead, firing warning shots over their bow. Dathan watched as the ships receded from view, then split and turned back around, careening toward them, another salvo of what had to have been deliberately wide shots lighting up the flight deck.

Heart racing, Dathan turned his attention to Rey. She was back in the navigator's seat, eyes closed, her small hands clutching the edges of the blanket beneath her, the one piece of the only home the girl had ever known that they had been able to bring with them. Dathan felt a tightening in his chest, his love for the child so profound, so real, that it was all he could do to keep breathing as he grabbed the navigator's headphones and slipped them over Rey's ears, buckling her into the seat.

The ship rocked again as another shot streaked almost too close to their hull. Dathan made his way back to the copilot's seat and strapped himself in.

Miramir frowned, reading something on a panel above her. "Maybe I can kick the hyperdrive in manually, bypassing the motivator . . ." She trailed off, then glanced at Dathan. "Might be a rough ride."

Dathan nodded. "How long do you need?"

"Three minutes."

Dathan nodded. "Then three minutes you shall have. Hold tight."

He grabbed the copilot's control yoke, the twin of the one at Miramir's station, and disengaged the autos, about the only control he recognized. Immediately the freighter bucked, then dipped into a steep dive as the overloaded starboard impulse stabilizer blew, unable to compensate now for its already inactive counterpart on the opposite side of the ship. In front of them, the attacking fighters vanished from sight as the freighter's course abruptly changed. Space flashed green, but in silence, the warning shots now distant.

Dathan gritted his teeth. Beneath his grip, the yoke shuddered and shook, the whole ship fighting him as he tried to steer it away from their attackers. He didn't know what he was doing—he couldn't fly *anything* and had never wanted to try—but even the most basic, instinctive maneuvering would give them time while Miramir worked on her new plan.

The attackers were small, were agile, and, as Dathan had suspected, were making fast tracks toward them. As they swung into view, he pulled back and to the left, lifting the nose as the freighter spun on its axis, corkscrewing the much larger ship straight through the center of the attackers' formation, forcing them to take evasive action of their own.

"One minute," said Miramir.

Dathan nodded in acknowledgment, not taking his eyes from the forward viewports, now trying to keep the freighter level. The attackers had regrouped and sped in for yet another frontal approach, but they were still careful with their shots—they wanted the freighter crippled, not destroyed, and were slowly closing the warning blasts in, banking, perhaps, on the shock waves disabling the already damaged craft. Dathan used their caution to his advantage, accelerating again toward the group. As the fighters split once more, he jerked the yoke to port, swinging the freighter directly into the path of one of the other ships.

The freighter rocked as more blasterfire streaked past. Dathan knew he couldn't keep this up forever. He just hoped the ship would hold together for a little while longer.

"Okay, nearly done, nearly done," said Miramir, now standing at the pilot's position, her blue cloak falling behind her as she focused her attention on the multitude of control panels above her. "We just need to set the navicomputer to null coordinates and we can make a jump. Not a long one, but it should be enough to lose them."

That was when there was another blinding flash from the forward viewports, another dull thud of an explosion from somewhere at the rear, the ship rocking hard enough to throw Miramir to the floor. Behind them, Rey cried out in surprise and fear.

Miramir pulled herself back into the pilot's seat. "We're okay, Rey, we're right here," she said, perhaps more for her own benefit than her daughter's, given Rey couldn't hear her with the headphones on. "Not long now. Just hold tight." But as she strapped herself in, she looked back over her shoulder with a terrible, anguished expression on her face that Dathan hated to see. He craned his neck around and followed her gaze, to where their daughter sat, her head buried in her blanket.

"Okay, here we go," said Miramir. She grabbed the pilot's master control yoke, and Dathan felt his own yoke pull away from his grip. He let go.

Far ahead, the three attack ships regrouped again, their ion engines leaving glowing trails across the stars as they flew in a tight arc back toward them.

This was it. They were done playing. They were coming in for a final run, ready to knock the ship out of commission permanently and make their collection.

The ships approached, fast.

"We're not going to make it," said Dathan.

"Yes, we are."

"Not enough time or space, Miramir. They'll box us in. We can't jump with them right in front of us."

"I can do it."

"You know what?"

Miramir didn't pause, didn't look up from the controls, as she kept her eyes fixed on the hyperdrive readout. From his position, Dathan could see data scrolling, almost too fast to read. "What?"

"I love you," said Dathan.

Miramir glanced at her husband, and for Dathan, time seemed to stop, again. She looked like she was going to say something, but instead, she just . . . smiled that smile, a smile he knew so well, a smile he loved, a smile he'd cross the galaxy for, a smile that could light up even this nameless reach of empty space, the smile of his wife, the mother of his child, the smile of Miramir—

There was another flash; this time it was blue. The ship rocked again, but the movement was gentle, the battered freighter not knocked by a shock wave but riding the crest of an energy pulse. Dathan and Miramir turned to watch as the central fighter in the trio flying toward them evaporated in a flash of ionized particles, sending its two companion craft into desperate escape headings.

They were fast, but not fast enough. A second fighter exploded into an expanding cloud of glowing gas, that cloud pierced by the sleek lines of a new ship that spun through the debris.

This new arrival was long, sleek, a finely sculpted nose cone leading a narrow, arrowlike fuselage, engines at the rear, and from the side, four wings with long, spearlike cannons mounted at the ends, the flight surfaces locked into a distinct shape known across the whole galaxy.

"An X-wing," said Miramir, blinking, as though she could scarcely believe their luck. "We're nowhere near New Republic space. What are they doing here?" She turned to Dathan, her eyes wide, now alert to the possibility that maybe, just maybe, they were somewhere safe.

But Dathan shook his head. "Don't know, don't care." He looked down at the copilot's console, wishing he knew more about the ship's systems. "We ready to jump again or what?"

Miramir's eyes were wide. "What are you talking about?" She gestured to the forward viewports. "We don't need to jump again. The New Republic will help us."

Even as she said that, there was another blue flash from outside. The last remaining attacker had peeled away, trying to find room to make a jump to lightspeed. But the pursuing X-wing was faster and more heavily armed, the pilot sending their ship into a tight spiral as all four cannons opened up, sending a blazing corkscrew of blasterfire after its quarry.

No, not one X-wing. Two—three. The other two fighters came into view from underneath the freighter, racing away from them to join the first. While Dathan and Miramir watched, their S-foils opened out into attack position and their quad engines flared as they accelerated away.

The attacker didn't stand a chance. The craft spun on its axis, then dived up and then sharply down, the pilot making a vain attempt to break target locks before it could punch the hyperdrive.

Dathan watched as the three X-wings fell into a tight formation and closed the distance behind their target, but he took no satisfaction in seeing the last hunter destroyed. They'd been saved this time, out of sheer luck—what *was* the New Republic doing out here?—but as he knew all too well, there were more hunters where those had come from, their prize far too valuable to give up on.

"Make the jump," he said quietly. Miramir looked at him again, and the two locked eyes. Dathan hoped she would understand, they'd talked about it often enough—hell, she knew *exactly* what he was thinking.

And then, to his relief, she nodded.

They could trust nobody. Not even the New Republic.

They were on their own. Always had been, always would be.

As Miramir refocused on the controls, Dathan looked around again at the navigator's seat, but Rey was simply a huddled mass under the blanket, only the fingers of one hand visible as she clutched at the seat beneath her.

That was when the ship-wide comms crackled into life.

"Attention, unknown craft. Clear your navicomputer and stand by for inspection."

Dathan once again looked at the ceiling. Inspection, by . . . three X-wings? That didn't make any sense.

And then a fourth ship appeared, pulling in close over the top of the freighter, a huge slab of ash-gray metal, the surface studded with antennas, hatchways, sensor blocks, and gun emplacements.

A New Republic gunship. Dathan didn't know what kind, but it didn't matter. Even as he watched the gunship's hull blot out the entire starscape, he felt the slight shudder as tractor beams were locked on and they were pulled slowly to the glowing blue opening of the hangar that now appeared in view.

Dathan sat back, his face behind his hands. He shook his head, and then he felt Miramir's hands on his. He opened his eyes, letting his hands, still held by Miramir's, drop into his lap.

He looked at the viewport as the hangar grew larger and larger. Beside them, two of the escorting X-wings pulled in ahead of them and made soft touchdowns. Then the blue shimmer vanished as the freighter passed through the magnetic shield.

"This is it," Dathan said, with a sigh. "The end of the road."

"We don't know that," said Miramir.

Perhaps she was right. Perhaps he was being too cautious—too *cynical.*

The comms barked again.

"Attention, unknown craft. Proceed to your exit ramp. Please follow our directions."

Miramir unclipped her restraint and stood.

"Well," she said, giving a weak shrug. "At least they said 'please.' "

Dathan stood stock-still, his heart pounding. He felt Rey wriggling her hand in his, trying to break free. He glanced down at her.

"You're holding too tight, Daddy."

Dathan almost laughed, but he did relax his grip, then looked up and watched as Miramir talked to one of the X-wing pilots, the officer still in his blue flight suit, his helmet under one arm. Next to him stood one of the other pilots, her helmet hanging from one hand.

They were standing in the hangar, by their freighter's exit ramp. So far, all the New Republic officers had done was motion them to stay where they were, and when they started asking questions, it was Miramir who volunteered herself to answer them.

She was good with people, Dathan knew that, but it didn't make him feel much better. The fact was they had no identification, no licenses or permits, no official documentation of any kind, and their ship had no ID tags or transponder or . . . anything. Dathan could only hope that Miramir was working her charm on the officers, because he—and Miramir—knew that while the New Republic claimed control of a large section of the galaxy, there were regions that lived happily outside their borders, peaceably, but unwilling, or unconvinced, to join the glorious cause. It had been seventeen years since the second Death Star had been destroyed over Endor, seventeen long years since Dathan's father—even now, he felt the chill, felt the hollow, almost light-headed sensation as he thought of Palpatine—had fallen, the Empire over which he ruled shattered. A long time, to be sure, but the galaxy was big and the fledgling new authority had a lot of ground, both literally and figuratively, to reclaim. To Dathan, watching, *willing* the old order to be replaced with the new, it sometimes seemed that the New Republic had done nothing at all.

But right now, it was all academic, anyway. They were in Wild Space, a literal no-being's-land. Even the New Republic couldn't claim authority here.

Could they?

Miramir glanced back at Dathan, her mouth twisted in an *I have no idea what's going on* expression. She walked back to join him and Rey, followed by the two X-wing pilots. The male pilot stood tall, his back ramrod-straight—the senior officer, Dathan guessed. The pilot looked at Dathan and then at Rey with an expression that wasn't one of distaste, but it wasn't far off. The female pilot looked far friendlier and, crucially, far more relaxed.

The senior officer sniffed, glanced at Miramir, then looked at Dathan again.

"I understand you have no identification of any kind?"

Dathan gave the man a smile that was not returned. "You understand correctly."

The officer's mouth twitched. The other pilot moved to his shoulder, the smile on her face apparently quite genuine.

"We're sorry to have to do this," she said, "but we do need to ask what you're doing out here."

"I could ask you the same question," said Dathan. Beside him, Miramir frowned and gave a slight shake of her head. The male officer didn't react, except to cast his cold gaze at Dathan.

"I am Lieutenant Zaycker Asheron. This is my flight sergeant, Dina Dipurl. You are aboard the *Starheart*, the command ship of Halo Squadron." He lifted his chin, as though it could go any higher. "You are in a very dangerous part of the galaxy, young man."

Dathan nodded. "As we discovered. And also," he added, "a part of the galaxy a long way from the Galactic Core." He spread his hands. "Thank you for the rescue, but we're just travelers. We're not part of your republic, nor do we wish to be."

Asheron bristled but said nothing.

"Then consider this a routine check," said Flight Sergeant Dipurl. "Being attacked by pirates is no small thing." She smiled and dropped into a crouch so she was the same height as Rey. She smiled at the child, then looked up at her parents. "Is everyone all right? Your ship doesn't look in the best shape."

"Our hyperdrive is temperamental," said Miramir. "We were waiting for the motivator to cool before we attempted another jump. That's when we were attacked."

"And do you have any reason to have been attacked?" asked Asheron, sharply. At this, Dipurl stood and shook her head.

"Sir, with all due respect, do pirates and marauders ever need a reason to attack? That's why we're out here, after all."

Asheron raised an eyebrow. "Our objectives are classified, Sergeant." Then, satisfied at his subordinate's downcast glance, he turned back to the others.

"So where are you going?"

"Just passing through," muttered Dathan.

Asheron's expression soured. He was clearly a man who needed things right and proper, to be done according to the rule book. "But to *where*, exactly?"

Dathan and Miramir exchanged a look, then Miramir said, "We don't know."

"Are you some kind of space vagrants?" Asheron sniffed again. "Where did you come from?"

Dathan was about to give an answer, but Miramir got in first.

"Jakku," she said.

"Never heard of it."

He was lying. Dathan knew it—the way Asheron had answered so quickly, showing again the superiority of his position, the power he had over them at this moment. The Battle of Jakku had been sixteen years ago, but everybody over a certain age would remember the name, and Asheron certainly fit the bill.

"We're in danger," said Miramir. "We need help."

"Really?" Asheron's tone indicated he had little to no interest in their immediate plight, only answers to his own pointless questions. He turned to the other pilot. "Sergeant, I'll leave you to wrap this up. This little diversion has cost us too much time already."

Miramir and Dathan looked at each other. Asheron adjusted his helmet under his arm and turned to leave, but Miramir stepped forward and pulled on his arm. He stopped and just looked down at her hand.

"Don't you understand?" she asked. "We need help. Isn't the New Republic supposed to help people?" Exasperated, Miramir reached down the front of her tunic and pulled out a thin silver chain. She held it up, showing the amulet that hung on it—it was stylized, daggerlike, the symbol somehow . . . sinister. "We are being hunted by the Sith."

Dathan felt his stomach drop. The amulet—the hex charm—was his. He'd carried it all his life, even when he fled home . . . he had kept it with him, a symbol of everything he hated and everything he was determined never to be. Kept it with him—but had been unable to stomach wearing it. Years ago, Miramir had taken the hex charm from him and promised to keep it close to her own heart, a symbol now of the way their love could overcome any evil.

Asheron looked at her and smiled, a thin, tight line completely devoid of warmth, or interest.

"Is that so?"

Dathan blinked. Was Asheron really *that* ignorant? He hadn't expected to get any help from the New Republic, but did this senior officer really not even know what the Sith were?

Then again . . . perhaps he didn't. Perhaps he thought they were long dead, as most other people in the galaxy did.

If only that were the truth. Dathan glanced at Miramir, but she was now just shaking her head as she looked down at the amulet in her hands. He wanted to punch the New Republic officer, very, very hard, but he knew exactly where that would land the three of them. He let his fist unclench at his side.

"The New Republic helps its *citizens,* yes," Asheron continued, glancing sideways at Dathan before returning his gaze to Miramir. "But as you have said, you live outside its bounds." His expression softened, and he sighed. "Might I suggest," he continued, quietly, "that you clear this region, find your way to somewhere a little closer to the Core. You might find your travels a little safer." Then he turned on his heel. "Flight Sergeant Dipurl, we will debrief in ten minutes." He marched away, heading toward the main doors on the other side of the hangar.

Miramir and Dathan looked at each other. Dathan felt Rey's hand squeeze his, and he dropped down, bringing her in for a hug. He glanced up at the underside of their ship. It looked exactly like what it was— a pile of junk.

"You have to help us," he said, turning back to the sergeant. Miramir moved to join him, reaching down to take Rey's other hand. "You said it yourself," Dathan continued. "This ship isn't going to get far at all."

Dipurl looked at them with a sigh. "Okay, let me take a look," she said, placing her flight helmet down on the deck next to the freighter's ramp, and gesturing for them all to go aboard. "But this has to be fast. I'll see if there's anything I can patch quickly." She paused. "I think I have somewhere you can reach from here. I have a contact who owes me one—someone who worked with my father, back in the days of the Rebel Alliance. They might be able to take you in, at least until you can get any major repairs taken care of." She waved the family aboard ahead of her. "And I'm sorry, I really am," she said, following them up into the ship. "All I can do is file a report. You can tell me about this Sith and that amulet, and I'll log it all. It might make a difference to someone."

CHAPTER 3

THE SEPULCHRE, COORDINATES UNKNOWN
NOW

Something moves in the darkness—a shadow, cast long, crawling through the abyssal night. The shadow is a thing apart: neither alive nor dead.

It is a relic. It is an . . . echo. A presence from an older time, a malignancy that somehow survived, somehow found a way.

Found a *path*.

She can see it now. Black and blacker still, moving, always moving. An intelligence, yes. A mind, but one without form or substance.

But here—*present*—nonetheless.

She closes her eyes. It makes no difference. There is nothing to see but a gulf, a nothing, where the shadow lives.

Where the shadow thrives.

In the darkness, in the forever night inside her head.

And the void is not silent. It is anything but. It is a cacophony, a sound so loud it lights up every nerve fiber of her entire being, even though she knows there is nothing to hear, physically.

It is the sound of pain. The sound of death. The sound of a thousand thousand thousand souls crying out in sorrow and agony before they are snuffed out in an instant. Brothers and sisters. Sons and daughters.

Mothers and fathers. Podlings, branchlings, kithkin. Sporechilds and denmothers; space fathers and their brethren, and their gene-clusters and their shoots. Spawn, and offspring. Children.

Entire generations of the living, consumed, their dying cries absorbed and left to reflect forever, trapped inside a dark vessel crafted centuries ago by a power uncommon, inhuman.

By a darkness.

By a shadow, cast long.

And there is another sound. A voice, from the ancient past. It is far distant, a call echoing across a huge valley of space and time.

The voice is terrible.

The voice is as familiar as her own.

SOON.

She opens her golden eyes. The room is bright and, mercifully, silent. Her ears ring like a bell, the sudden absence of screams almost as painful, the echo of the voice still reverberating in her mind.

Slowly, slowly, she remembers where she is. As she lies on the floor and blinks the world into existence around her, she pulls up a hand and touches her face. It is warm, and wet, the blood on her fingertips the bright blue of the Pantoran sky.

The place is lit by flickering flame, and the flickering flame lights the plinth of meteoric iron, and beside the plinth lies the mask made of the same starstuff. The mask faces away from her. It rocks, gently, like it has just been thrown.

She stares at the back of it, the curve of nothing, of darkness, of deep shadow.

And she hears the voice again.

SOON.

SOON.

She closes her eyes, and she sleeps, exchanging one nightmare for another, in the dead of night, in the dead of space.

She wakes to another sound, one technological, modern. She lifts herself from her nest, ignoring the throbbing in her head, the ache of her limbs.

Because she can't keep them waiting. They are patient, yes. Infuriatingly so.

But they are also quick to anger, and if there is one thing she dares not do, it is make them angry.

She agreed to help them. They agreed to show her the way.

This is how it was.

And she would do nothing to jeopardize that.

Standing, she activates the communicator, and her nest is lit in the sudden electric blue of a hologram. The image shimmers and pulses, tinged with the same static and interference that protects the caller's point of origin.

She kneels before the figure, cloaked in darkness, the hood barely concealing a face that is wrapped tightly in heavy black bandages, in the manner all cultists of the Sith Eternal hide their features.

She doesn't know why. She doesn't care.

But she does obey.

"What is thy bidding, my Master," she intones, repeating the litany that echoed through time like the screams inside the mask she knew she would have to put on again, soon.

The looming figure speaks, and she listens, and she wonders whether this will be the last time or whether they will ever honor their promise.

Perhaps one day, they will ask too much.

CHAPTER 4

THE JEDI TEMPLE OF
MASTER LUKE SKYWALKER, OSSUS
NOW

"Luke? Uncle?"

Luke Skywalker opened his eyes and looked up from where he was sitting cross-legged in the middle of the stone-flagged floor. The teenager who had called him was standing half in, half out of Luke's hut, the look on his face both expectant and clearly embarrassed that he had accidentally interrupted Luke's meditation.

Luke sighed but didn't move from his position. The fact was, he was glad of the disturbance. His meditation had been . . . difficult.

Again.

"Ben, I've told you before."

Ben Solo ran a hand through his mop of black hair. "I . . . ah, yes, I'm sorry . . . *Master* Skywalker."

"The ways of the Jedi are many," said Luke, "and they include discipline and control."

"Of course, Master."

"And that includes knocking before entering," added Luke, with a smile that was soft and friendly.

Ben smiled back, but the expression was fleeting. He shuffled a little and looked around the stone hut. The small building was no different from any other in the temple grounds, but Luke knew the look on Ben's face.

Luke told himself to go easy, but not just because his Padawan was his nephew. Far from it—family ties had little to do with the teachings of the Jedi Order that Luke had worked hard to reestablish. Detachment and distance were required for the pure focus the Jedi constantly strove to achieve, and for Luke, there was a simple satisfaction in adhering to those tenets.

But Ben was trying his best, and Luke knew it wasn't easy for him, being out here in the forests of Ossus. The land was picturesque, the temple calm and ordered, the life of the Padawans one of training, with little time for leisure and, even when their schedules allowed, few facilities for it.

Ossus was *exactly* the kind of place a sixteen-year-old like Ben Solo would find crushingly dull, the studious life perhaps nice in theory but boring in practice.

But Ben was trying. More than that, he was good—even now, as Ben just stood in the doorway, leaning one shoulder casually against the frame as he ran his hand through his hair yet again, Luke could feel the power in him. It was a beautiful flower, growing inside his Padawan, waiting to blossom into something wonderful. Sometimes Luke thought Ben would one day be as powerful as he was.

The Skywalker legacy ran deep.

Luke raised an eyebrow, then laughed, the growing silence in the hut clearly making Ben even more uncomfortable. That wasn't something Luke had expected in his nephew—he was a fine boy, but there was an edge to him, a slow anxiety that simmered just below the surface. Luke put it down to an eagerness to please him, as the temple's Jedi Master. But it was also reflective of an internal struggle, Jedi versus family, nephew versus uncle, Padawan versus Master. Luke knew it couldn't be easy for Ben, no matter how hard he tried to hide it.

And sometimes he tried to hide it too well.

"So what is it, Ben? You want me for something?"

At this, Ben snapped into focus, even composing himself enough to give his Master a small bow.

"Sorry, Master. You have a visitor."

"A visitor? I wasn't expecting anyone."

"I didn't think I had to ask your permission to see an old friend."

Ben turned at the new voice as another man entered the hut.

Luke pushed himself to his feet to greet the new arrival.

"Of course not," said Luke. The Jedi and the visitor clasped their hands around each other's forearms. "It's good to see you, Lor."

Lor San Tekka released Luke's arm and stepped back to give the Jedi Master a more formal bow. Then he stood and clapped a hand on Luke's shoulder.

"I never take an audience with a Jedi Master for granted," said Lor. He turned to Ben. "Young Ben Solo, you look well. How goes the training?"

Ben gave the older man a stiff bow. "Greetings, sir," he said. "And . . . uh . . ."

Luke laughed. "He's doing fine. In fact, I couldn't hope for a better student."

"I am very glad to hear that," said Lor, before turning back to Luke. "I have some information you might be interested in, Luke, if—"

Now it was Luke's turn to lay a hand on his friend's shoulder. "I'm always interested." He glanced at his Padawan. "And you should be studying, Ben. Lor and I have a lot to discuss."

Ben looked at the pair of them and bowed again, but Luke noticed the frown on his face. "At once, Master." Then he stood tall and, giving a look to Lor, left the hut.

Luke wandered to the doorway and watched his nephew stalk away down the grassy slope. Over by the other cluster of temple buildings, an orange-skinned Twi'lek woman, Enyo, was leading a class of younglings through a series of exercises with training blades.

Luke turned and headed back inside, guiding his friend by the arm. "Actually, I'm glad you're here," he said, stopping in the center of the stone hut.

"They're still happening, aren't they?" asked Lor, facing Luke's back.

Luke nodded, then turned around. "And they're getting worse."

"Worse? Or stronger?" Lor cocked his head. "There's a difference, Luke. You just need to listen to the Force, it will guide you."

Luke's lips twitched in amusement—but the expression was mirrored by Lor San Tekka. He raised a hand.

"I know, I know, an adherent of the Church of the Force dares to instruct a Jedi Master." Lor gave a quiet chuckle. "Maybe I'll learn one day, but I'm an old man with old habits." He folded his arms. "Do you know where your vision takes you?"

Luke fixed his gaze on the old man. "That's where I want your help."

Lor frowned. "I am always happy to guide, Master Skywalker, but only for one willing to follow." He spread his hands. "The Force itself remains a mystery to me. I'm not sure what you think I can do."

Luke stroked his beard. "I want to try something." Luke folded himself down into a cross-legged position again in the middle of the room.

Lor stayed right where he was. "Luke, are you sure this is a good idea?"

Luke glanced up. "I need to find out what these visions mean. If I meditate, try to describe what I'm seeing as I see it—"

"Luke, I'm serious." Lor lowered himself to his knees in front of his friend. "I'm not a Jedi. You know that. There must be someone else in the temple who can assist. Ben, perhaps?"

But Luke shook his head. "You're the only person who knows about the visions, and I want to keep it that way."

Lor lifted his hands, his jaw working as he tried to work up some kind of protest, but in the end he just sighed.

"Very well," he said. "I will stand vigil. Tell me what you see and perhaps the Force will guide me as it guides you."

Luke nodded. "Thank you." He lifted his chin, and closed his eyes, and—

In another world, he opened them, and looked around, and saw—

Nothing. Darkness. A . . . void, empty of anything, a space without limits or dimensions, a place that didn't even exist outside of the confines of his own mind.

And yet a *place* nonetheless.

Luke took a step forward, not really feeling anything beneath his feet, because there was nothing there. His footfalls made no sound, and took him no distance. He looked around, straining to see, even while knowing there was nothing to see, no light, no energy, no anything.

The suddenness of this vision startled him. He had been visiting this place in his meditations for weeks now, but the strange dark world usually took a while to appear, Luke's consciousness drifting away from reality as he focused his mind and body on the meditation. And then, as though falling from a great height, he succumbed to a dark gravity he couldn't escape, and he was there.

Over the years, his meditations had gotten deeper and deeper, as he delved into the recesses of his mind, not just to unlock the potential he knew was there, just out of reach, but to try to commune with the galaxy around him. The Force, he knew, was a living thing, in the crudest terms an energy field that bound the universe together. The Force was not a power, not something to be wielded, or used, or manipulated. Rather, it was something that allowed others to share in it—a thing vast and alive and yet not sentient.

In that respect, his friend Lor San Tekka was right. Adherents to the Church of the Force were not Force-sensitive, but that didn't mean they didn't understand it, or those who could tap into the field that underlined the very fabric of being.

But this time, it was different. He had closed his eyes and suddenly he was *here*. Luke knew that without his own iron grip on his emotions, he would be afraid now, and rightly so. But instead he turned that feeling that even now grew inside him into something else, using it as fuel for his senses, heightening his awareness of his surroundings.

And the void, he realized, was somehow . . . *aware* of him, of this visitor, this intruder from elsewhere.

Luke concentrated.

Yes, he felt it now. It had come and gone before, in previous visions, but whether the presence of Lor San Tekka really was doing something or not, it didn't matter, because it was stronger now.

A presence.

The void was not empty.

He concentrated.

It was dark, but it was different from the black awfulness he had felt in the Emperor's presence, even in the presence of his own father, so many years ago. That was something he could understand. He knew where it came from, knew how the light could be corrupted and twisted, turned to darkness, that darkness wrenched and abused into a tool of power that had no place in the light of the Force.

This void was not a part of that, but it was still alive, and Luke was not alone.

Then the void changed, becoming a reality, not an abstract.

Luke was somewhere ancient, somewhere distant.

Somewhere . . . hidden.

Black ground. Black sky. Both flat, cold, like metal. Lightning flashes, electrical discharges that snapped from sky to ground in great pillars of energy, illuminating gray dust that formed low, suffocating clouds, like the sky itself was pressing down on the ground, the world between it squeezed until it cracked.

Desolation. That was the word for it. The landscape, the place, was blasted, by eons of time, the air dry and charged with a dangerous electricity that danced over a ground of black basalt that was already immeasurably ancient.

And then, he—

"Well?"

Luke opened his eyes. He was sitting on the floor. Lor San Tekka was kneeling in front of him, hands pressed down on his knees. It didn't look comfortable.

Luke pursed his lips, surprised that his vision had gone just as fast as it had arrived.

"Tell me what you saw, Luke," said Lor. "Describe it to me."

Luke stared into the middle distance as he brought the memories back to the front of his mind. He described the void, and the blackened landscape—and the dark presence he sensed.

Lor listened carefully, then he stood and began a slow pace of the hut, stretching out his legs, his knees clicking loudly, each accompanied by a wince.

Luke watched him. "Does any of that mean anything to you?"

Lor stopped pacing and pursed his lips. "We've been to a lot of places, Luke. We've seen a lot of things."

Luke nodded. That was quite true—the two had spent a lot of time in each other's company since the death of the Emperor and the fall of the Empire. Luke was driven by a desire to reestablish the Jedi Order from, essentially, absolutely nothing. It was to Lor that he had come, eager for the old explorer's help in hunting down relics and artifacts that had a connection with the Force. Together they followed the star compass Luke had uncovered from Pilio, mapping out the network of Jedi temples that were scattered across the galaxy—perhaps half of them not even remembered after the Empire's purge of the Order four decades before.

Their voyages had been largely fruitful, too. Luke had amassed quite a collection of antiquities at his own fledgling Jedi temple—books, tomes, papers, and data cards; ritual items, sigils and symbols of power; technology, including lightsabers, the star compass, and more. All of which Luke and Lor had studied, the older man's deep knowledge of the Jedi Order a boon to Luke, who was eager not only to learn but also to *understand* as he tried to rebuild the Jedi.

"I sense a *but* coming," said Luke.

Lor began to pace again. "It could be a real place, or it may just be what it is—a vision, a representation of the darkness that must always exist where there is light."

"But why now? I've never had visions like this before."

"The influence of some artifact, perhaps? We have collected and studied many products of the dark arts, Luke."

The suggestion was plausible, but it didn't feel right to Luke. Truth was, his focus had drifted over the last few weeks, his daily rituals and training with the younglings—a strict, unwavering routine—suddenly became disrupted. Luke had handed basic responsibilities to his senior pupils—Ben included—while he holed himself up in his quarters, trying to understand the visions. But he hadn't handled any Sith relics in a long time. He knew full well the danger such artifacts could pose.

"I'm sorry," said Luke, unfolding himself from his position and standing up. He brushed down his cream-colored robes and ran his cybernetic hand through his mop of ash-brown hair. "I don't know what I thought this would achieve." He paused, shaking his head. "But this . . . place, whatever it is. I'm seeing it for a reason, Lor. I can feel it."

"Oh," said Lor, clapping a hand on his friend's shoulder. "Of that, Luke, I have no doubt. No doubt at all. I just wish I could help you in some way. Research, fieldwork—the search!—there, I feel like I can be of use. But standing vigil over a Jedi who is looking into his own mind?" He clicked his tongue. "I'm a little out of my depth."

Luke laughed softly, relaxing again in the company of his old friend. "Perhaps you're right," he said. "But why did you come to Ossus, anyway? You said you'd found some information?"

"Well," began Lor, "it's going to sound a little . . . anticlimactic, shall we say, after all that."

"Go on," said Luke. "I'm interested."

Lor nodded. "You ever heard of a planet called Yoturba?"

Luke frowned. "I don't think so."

"Mid Rim, nothing remarkable," said Lor, "but the Lerct Historical Institute is running an archaeological dig out there."

Luke felt his eyebrows going up as his interest was piqued. "Have they found something?"

"No," said Lor. "Not yet, anyway. But they have uncovered a large settlement. I couldn't find any record of the Jedi having a temple on Yoturba, but the period is correct. I thought we should take a look. If, of course, you can spare the time from your own temple."

Luke stroked his beard in thought, then he nodded.

"Of course," he said. "We should go. I could use some time to think, anyway."

He stepped past Lor and walked out of the hut. Standing at the top of the small hill on which it stood, he looked out and saw Ben had taken the place of Enyo in leading the training session.

Luke lifted his hand, catching Ben's attention. The young man nodded in acknowledgment and began to bring the training session to an end.

"He's going to make a fine Jedi one day, Luke," said Lor, joining his friend at the door. "And learning the responsibilities of the temple while his Master is away will do him a world of good."

Luke nodded, then patting his friend on the shoulder, turned, and headed back inside to prepare himself for the expedition ahead.

CHAPTER 5

THE JUNKYARD, SOMEWHERE NEAR THE INNER RIM
NOW

If the moon had a name, he didn't know what it was. Nor did he much care, about the moon, about anything.

Not anymore.

As far as he knew, he was alone, although he hadn't bothered to explore much beyond the confines of the junkyard in which he had made his home. The moon, like so many others in this sector, was the size of a planet—standard mass, standard gravity, standard atmosphere—and while it was cold it was livable, and that was all that mattered.

And he called it . . . actually, he didn't call it anything. He didn't need to. He knew the coordinates, yes—he did *occasionally* venture beyond the moon's gravity well, but never far. He was happy right where he was. There was nothing out there for him.

So the moon was simply the moon and the junkyard was just that, a junkyard. Hardly poetic, but then he'd never had a taste for literature.

Whose junkyard, again, he didn't know, and he didn't care, and he had made no attempt to learn in all the time he had been here. Oh, it was old, that much was obvious. The debris here sat in strata like a geologic landscape, layer upon layer upon layer of metallic and ceramic refuse, the decayed remnants of starships from long-forgotten civilizations, empires, republics. On the surface, the material had been ground down by the pervasive wind—wind that howled and moaned, and at night seemed to *sing* among the ruins, like it was a life-form all of its own—into a kind of rough, silver sand. From this top layer protruded larger fragments, some more intact than others, some even recognizable, despite their age and antique design. Thruster pods, their innards long since collapsed, formed great tubes, some of which stretched for hundreds of meters across the junkyard dunes, looking like casings from some giant, metal-eating worms that lived perpetually below the surface. There were other parts, too, all skeletal, all ancient—superstructures and frameworks, cockpits and engine housings, and if he dug below the surface, kilometers and kilometers of plastoid cabling, some of it in shockingly bright colors, reds and yellows and blues, the tough substance infinitely less susceptible to centuries of rot and decay than the rest of whatever ship it was that'd had these wires and conduits as its nervous and circulatory system.

He didn't know where any of it came from, and he didn't care, because he wasn't here for salvage. There was absolutely nothing of use in this former dumping ground, abandoned in ages past, and that was precisely why he had picked it, because that meant there was no reason for anyone else to come here, either. Perhaps, one day, the junkyard moon would be the target for element hunters, equipped with the tools and knowledge to extract pure, raw minerals, metals, metalloids. Or maybe that had already happened and this was what was left.

It didn't matter. The only thing that did was that he was alone, and nobody came to visit the moon, and—perhaps most important of all—nobody even knew he was here.

The only thing that mattered was that the name of Ochi of Bestoon would be slowly forgotten.

Good. Because his current mission required the help of no one, and if he was going to find what he was looking for, he needed to be alone and undisturbed.

"Master!"

Well . . . while his existence was solitary, he was not, strictly speaking, *alone*.

"Master!" came the high-pitched, quavering voice of his droid again. "M-m-m-master."

Ochi paused and gave a sigh, the sound amplified and echoed through his respirator. Yes, the atmosphere was breathable, but he suspected that inhaling the silver sand wasn't the best thing to be doing over the long term, and he certainly hadn't come here to die. Far from it, in fact.

Ochi pulled back the hood of his cloak and knelt down by his droid, a small unit that consisted of two main pieces—a single wheel with a rubberized tread and a flat-nosed, cone-shaped head—connected by an articulated arm, with three long green slots that formed the droid's optical array. As Ochi crouched beside it, the droid rolled a little in the silver sand, the three short antennas on the back of its head quivering, as though it were afraid of being so close to its owner.

"What is it, Dee-Oh?"

"I-I-I-"

"Spit it out," said Ochi, "or I'll leave you outside again tonight. See how your lubricant likes the cold again, eh?"

At this, D-O rolled to the top of the silver dune the pair were trekking up, then stopped. There, its head shook, like it was trying to get Ochi to take a look over the crest, beyond which lay their encampment.

Ochi followed the droid up the slope—the machine was nothing more than a low-intelligence data storage and retrieval unit, but Ochi had been impressed by the sensitivity of its sensors in the past. If D-O dared get Ochi's attention, there was usually a good reason for it.

Usually. Because right now, as he scanned the encampment, careful to keep his head low, Ochi couldn't see anything he wasn't expecting to see.

He sighed again, stood tall, and turned on the droid. From his belt he slipped a short piece of dull-black pipework, one of the few useful bits of scrap he'd picked up when he'd first arrived. He wasn't sure what it was made of—it was black and polished, more like stone than metal, but it had a slight kink in it—nor did he know what it had been made for, originally.

But whatever it was, it did everything he needed now.

Ochi swung the pipe, clipping the back of D-O's head, sending the

droid sliding forward and knocking its nose into the sand. As the machine burbled in fear, Ochi put his boot on the back of the droid's head
and held it down. D-O's wheel spun uselessly, kicking up a silver plume
as it tried to free itself.

"Maybe one day you'll learn not to waste my time, *droid*," said Ochi,
whispering the last word like it was an insult. Then he lifted his foot and
gave the back of D-O's wheel a kick. The droid rolled down the slope a
little and managed to pull its head from the sand before coming to a
sliding stop. It shook its head, trying to dislodge sand from its workings.

"Sorry, master. S-s-s-sorry, master. Sorry."

"Shut up," said Ochi. "What was it that you couldn't just spit out and
say?"

The droid twitched, and it turned its cone-shaped head up to look at
its master.

"Movement. Master. Movement. Movement."

Ochi looked down at D-O, then turned and walked back up the slope.
He looked down at his encampment for anything unusual, out of place.

In his time on the moon, he'd made himself quite comfortable. In the
center of the flat area sat his ship, the *Bestoon Legacy*. The main ramp
was open, but Ochi had built a temporary extension onto it with maintenance scaffold pipework and a heavy plastoid tarp, expanding his
available space while keeping the sand out of the ship itself. Behind the
tarp screens he had dragged equipment crates and other bits of the *Legacy*'s interior fittings to make himself a proper work space.

But Ochi couldn't see or hear anything out of the ordinary. One corner of the tarp flapped as the wind picked up, the moonsong growing
louder as dusk approached. He'd have to fix that corner, he thought,
before taking a step down the slope, his boots sinking heel-first into the
dune. Behind him, D-O shivered and made a squawking sound, like its
vocabulator was finally about to short out completely. Ochi paused and
glanced down at the droid.

As much as he hated it, despising the stupid machine as the only
company he had on this wrecked moon, he *did* trust it.

If D-O had detected movement, then there was movement.

Ochi dropped down onto one knee and, reaching under his cloak, extracted a battered set of quadnocs. Flicking the cloak clear of his shoulders, he pulled his hood down and put the quadnocs up to the goggles of his respirator. As he adjusted the device, his vision filled with a scratchy but enhanced view of the area below, his ship, the workshop, and the debris around it crawling with data and tracking lines as the quadnocs ran an analysis, presenting the user with a mess of data that Ochi supposed would be useful, if he'd ever figured out how to interpret it properly.

He scanned carefully, slowly, left to right. The wind continued to pick up, spinning the silver sand into eddies, the air humming through it. The quadnocs locked onto the shifting particles, giving Ochi range, degrees of movement, any number of reference points that were of no use at all.

And that was the problem. The metallic sand played havoc with sensor readings. It was another reason why nobody came to this moon, why any ship flying on even a low pass was unlikely to spot his ship, parked out in a clearing in the junkyard. D-O had learned how to adapt and filter this interference, but now, as Ochi felt the quadnocs growing warm through his gloves while the device tried to process what it was pointed at, he wondered if even his little droid was reaching the end of its usefulness.

He lowered the quadnocs and looked ahead. A dust devil had spun up near his ship, the miniature twister rising up, dragging the glittering silver sand into it, before dissipating just as quickly as it had formed. Then the wind shifted again, blowing Ochi's cloak across his mask before he pushed it away, and then, for a moment, everything was still.

There was nothing down there.

"Time to adjust your sensor array," Ochi muttered to his droid, as he stood and headed down the dune. "Or I'll adjust it for you."

Behind him, D-O shivered again, muttering to itself, then it followed its master at a safe distance.

The inside of Ochi's makeshift work space was cluttered but, despite the loose side of tarp, mercifully free of sand. Once inside, with D-O shooting in behind him, he secured the entrance flap, then went to the corner to fix the loose tie. Satisfied with his work, he stood, unclipped his cloak at the throat, and tossed it over an equipment crate before brushing any lingering sand off himself and making his way up the ramp and into the *Bestoon Legacy.*

The craft's interior was spacious but crammed with more of the plastoid crates, stacks of them piled up against the walls, more dragged out into the open, their sealed tops popped to reveal their contents. Several crates were also arranged as a table, another as a stool. On top of the table, the contents of several more now empty crates were spread out.

There were books, and charts, and even papers, most of them ancient and brown, written on the processed pulp of trees or the finely prepared hides of animals—rarities of some considerable value simply as objects, regardless of the information inscribed or printed on them. There were some newer documents, their synthetic sheets bright and shiny compared with their ancient counterparts. Balanced on a stack of two crates all on its own was one large tome, its spine broken long ago, the pages stained and crooked and mostly separating from the binding. On top of the open page was a large-format datapad with a stylus.

Ochi walked to the table while D-O scooted off into a corner, where it had made a nest out of discarded papers, a cozy, almost hidden spot next to its recharge port.

Ochi looked down at his work—his *research*—for one minute, two minutes, three minutes, then hissed in annoyance. His only routine was a daily five-kilometer trek around the junkyard, and it was supposed to clear his head, allowing his subconscious to work out problems and puzzles while he just focused on putting one foot in front of another.

Today his subconscious hadn't done much at all. It was tired, like its conscious counterpart. Ochi had been studying the books for a long time.

Probably far too long.

He sat heavily on a crate and took off his gloves, then his respirator, dropping both into an open crate full of more ancient documents that sat at his side. He rubbed his bald scalp, the yellowish skin tight with burn scars, the lights on the cybernetic implant that wrapped around the back of his skull and covered both ears winking softly. He leaned over the table, the two circular, black, cybernetic eyes embedded in his smooth face focusing on the text he had not yet been able to translate. He reached for his datapad, a pale tongue running over his lipless mouth, as he got back to work.

He would crack the text, and he would find that place, that blasted planet that was both cursed and blessed.

Exegol.

He was close. He knew it. He could *feel* it.

At least that's what he told himself, like he could just wish it to be true. Because Ochi of Bestoon had been looking for Exegol for a long, long time, and however hopeless a part of him knew his task was, he refused to give up.

He'd been there once. He was going to get there again.

But Exegol wasn't just in an unknown region of space; the ancient planet was deliberately *hidden*, screened off from the rest of the galaxy, whether by design or by some by-product of an arcane ritual, Ochi didn't know. But . . . he'd made it before, he could make it again. He'd crossed the Red Honeycomb Zone, that murderous expanse of crimson chaos that shielded the planet of the Sith. He'd reached it. Exegol. He'd *been there*. He knew what secrets the dark planet kept. Secrets that would be his. The things he'd seen, the things he'd learned, on his short visit all those years ago. Secrets the Emperor had whispered in his ear, secrets Darth Vader had hinted at.

And Ochi knew that was just the start of it, a merest fraction of the power that lay slumbering below the cracked black surface of that dead planet.

Power? Ochi laughed. Oh yes, he'd wanted power, once. Power, and riches. But he had never wanted to use those spoils to rule—because, look, ruling a galaxy? What was the point? He supposed if you did rule a galaxy, you'd have . . . what, staff? Servants? Minions? Drones, who did all the actual work while you sat back on your ebonite throne and reaped the rewards?

No. That wasn't for him. Maybe it hadn't been then, either, but it certainly wasn't what he wanted now. Power came in many forms, and the kind he wanted now was entirely different in scope.

What Ochi of Bestoon wanted was the power to live, to heal, to become . . . himself, again.

Ochi had lost track of time, but it had been years now since he had crossed the nightmare gulfs of the Red Honeycomb Zone with Darth Vader himself, Ochi an unwilling companion to the Dark Lord of the Sith as he investigated the Emperor's secret works. There, on a planet hidden from the galaxy, they discovered the vast fleet the cultists and their enslaved workers were slowly building—Star Destroyers, hundreds of them, each a thousand times more powerful than those commanded by the Imperial Navy. The ships were equipped with huge cannons, their power matching that of the Death Star's own planet-destroying armament, the energy channeled and concentrated by shards of kyber crystal, those pieces cleaved from a huge mountain of the stuff amassed at the heart of the cultists' fortress-temple.

It was this kyber mountain that had scarred Ochi. As he watched the crystals being ripped from their formations, they had screamed out in pain, releasing a burst of energy that seared the skin from his skull and burned his eyes from their sockets. And still, the Sith Eternal tortured the crystal hoard even as they divided it, imbuing the kyber—so they believed—with even greater power for the fleet's mighty weapons.

Ochi remembered the pain. He remembered the darkness. And he remembered the voice of Emperor Palpatine, deep and melodic and almost soothing, as the Sith Eternal repaired him, replaced his eyes, gave him the cybernetic head unit to compensate for the damaged parts of his brain.

But to be repaired was not the same as being healed. After the accident, Ochi wasn't the same, not just because of his injuries but because of something else, deep inside him, that had changed.

He had seen the light of Exegol, and it was beautiful. Powerful—the power to destroy, but the power to heal. To renew. To make whole again.

True enough, he had survived. He had left Exegol, returned to the service of one master or another—Vader once more, Lady Qi'ra and the Crimson Dawn, others—all the while the voice of the Emperor echoing in the dark corners of his mind as the memory of the hidden planet of the Sith shone ever brighter.

It did so now, brighter and hotter than ever, a burning red light like the heart of a screaming, tortured kyber crystal. Ochi was older now, and yet he felt like he was only just getting started, getting things together, embarking on his real purpose, the real reason he'd been placed in this Sithforsaken existence in the first place. What he needed was time. What he needed was life.

What he *needed* was to be himself again. To be whole again.

Healed, not just repaired.

And Exegol was the answer. The Sith Eternal could grant him those wishes, and if they refused, he would take their power and do it himself.

Only problem was, he couldn't get there.

Nobody could. The Red Honeycomb Zone was vast and unnavigable, a nebulous hellspace nobody would dare cross without the correct navigational tool, shielding Exegol as though the planet didn't even exist.

What Ochi needed was a Sith wayfinder.

He didn't know how they worked, and that didn't matter. He'd seen Vader's in action—you just . . . well, you just plugged it into your navicomputer, and the wayfinder handled the rest.

Ochi flipped back a few digital pages in his datapad and cast a cybernetic eye over the diagrams he'd managed to cobble together. A wayfinder was a strange thing, more a piece of art than an advanced technological device; a sculpture in iron and glass, trapping a magical fire within. He didn't quite know who or what the Sith actually were—the Emperor was scary as anything but he paid well and Vader was . . .

Well, Vader was a weirdo was what he was, but Ochi had seen what he'd been capable of, had glimpsed the power he seemed to have at his beck and call, a dark reflection of the Force that the Jedi whom Ochi had hunted back in his glory days of the Clone Wars had wielded.

Ochi didn't much understand or care then, and he still didn't now. But a wayfinder? Now, that was something real, a tool to be used.

Of course there were complications. There were only two of them, because . . . of course there were only two of them. Something the Sith had come up with, an ancient rite or belief or whatever they thought, because the Sith were the Sith. So fine, two wayfinders. Vader had one, Ochi assumed the Emperor had the other.

Problem was, Vader was dead and so was Palpatine. Did that mean the wayfinders were destroyed?

Or were they just lost?

Ochi believed the latter to be the case.

Or at least . . . that's what he told himself. And all he had to do now was find one—a small, pyramidal relic you could hold in one hand, somewhere out there in a galaxy that was very, very big.

Ochi was nothing if not determined. He'd spent too long on this chase to give up now. Years of research, and he wasn't done.

Because he'd found clues. The Sith wayfinders were written about in the ancient texts he had amassed as part of his relic collection. Sith Lords, Masters, and apprentices rose and fell in a cycle over time that was almost mathematical, and those who served them came and went as well. The Sith wayfinders, the keys to Exegol? No, they would not be lost or destroyed so easily. There was a way to find them, and Ochi was close.

The book was old, the pages brittle and burned at the edges, like the tome had been snatched from a burning starship just in the nick of time. Some pages were more badly damaged than others, which made the painstaking task of translation even more difficult. That was why he had D-O. The data storage and retrieval droid had belonged to some scholar Ochi had killed on Primus Cabru when he raided the library there, and the damn thing had actually begged for its electronic life after it had seen its master die. Ochi had seen its utility—D-O was programmed not just with hundreds of languages, but with complex algorithms that enabled fast textual analysis and comparison with other materials stored in its surprisingly large databank. Exactly what Ochi needed.

Ochi put the datapad down and looked around, wondering where the stupid droid was. He felt his anger flare, and he stood, reaching for the black metal rod.

"Dee-Oh? Dee-Oh! Droid! Come here, I need you." Ochi's cracked voice echoed around the interior of the *Bestoon Legacy*. He stood from the makeshift seat, puzzled at the droid's lack of reply.

Truth was, he had come to hate that droid. It was small and stupid, programmed with a personality that seemed rodentlike, barely even sentient. It was timid, and weak, and constantly afraid. Sometimes, as he lay in his bunk at night, listening to the singing sands, wishing he had a drink or two or three or four, Ochi thought he should wipe its central processor and start over from scratch.

An empty threat, and he knew it. Because, as irritating as it was, the droid now contained the sum total of his research, and thanks to its analysis algorithms had even come up with a potential, although only partial, navigational chart for Exegol. Ochi would still need a wayfinder, but at the back of his mind he always knew he had the option to just blast his way through the Red Honeycomb Zone and take his chances. It was likely suicide, but then again, you should always die doing what you loved, right?

This was why Ochi hated D-O. The droid's data was both essential and useless, a constant reminder of Ochi's own failures, his research painstaking yet thoroughly incomplete and, as a result, unusable.

"Droid!"

There was a noise, a fluttering, like a stack of old, precious papers had been knocked from its precarious balance on the edge of one of the crates. Outside, the wind sang through the silver sands, a mournful wail.

Ochi's cybernetic eyes flipped through to infrared as he tried to detect the heat signature of the droid. Shaking his head, he turned—

—And fell back onto the decking in surprise as he came face-to-face with an intruder.

"What the—?"

The intruder was tall and thin, clad entirely in a long black cloak, with a long, narrow hood. From his position on the floor, Ochi could see, under the edge of the hood, the face of the intruder. It was a face he had seen before.

Or rather, *hadn't* seen. The intruder's head was entirely wrapped in tight black bandages, thick swaths of them, around and around, with no visible holes for eyes, or nose, or mouth.

"You!" Ochi scrambled backward on the decking, then stopped as his backward-reaching hand connected with something behind him. He felt around, his fingers sliding on the silver sand that dusted the boot of the person standing behind him.

Turning on the floor, he looked up at another robed figure, identical to the first. And then, from behind this second intruder, stepped two more.

"How did you get in here?" Ochi asked, as he looked at the circle of cultists of the Sith Eternal who had somehow materialized in his ship. His heart thundered in his chest as he felt—

What, exactly? Fear? Surely not. Ochi was afraid of no one (he told himself). But . . . yes, it was fear. Fear that he'd been caught, that the Cult of the Sith Eternal had been watching him, had seen what he was reading, what he was studying, had worked out what he was trying to do, and had come out of the red nebula in person to stop him.

So yes, he was afraid.

"Get up."

Ochi jerked his head around at the voice, but it wasn't the first cultist who had spoken. They had been joined by yet another new arrival. This person—a woman—was also dressed in black, but not in the robes of a cultist. Instead she wore a long, close-fitting outfit, part tunic, part cloak, that flared out to form a tattered, scalloped edge that swept around her boots, the whole thing looking old and worn. Her hands partially bare, the thumb looped through the ends of her sleeves revealed the woman's blue skin. In one of her hands, she held a cylinder of black metal about thirty centimeters long. She wore a mask of burnished bronze, which was framed by a cascade of long, dirty deep-blue hair.

It was the mask that Ochi couldn't tear his gaze from. It frightened him, more so than the sudden presence of the cultists. It made him . . . feel things, in ways he didn't understand, in ways he couldn't describe, like merely *looking* at the mask triggered something deep inside his mind, some primal urge to scream and run and to never stop running.

The mask looked old. The surface was dull and scratched, pitted with divots. The eyes were two catlike angles of black glass that glinted in the light of the flight deck even as the rest of the mask seemed to absorb light. There was no nose, and the mouth was indicated by a line of black rivets, forming a downturned grimace. The mask was strange, somehow industrial and protective but also a work of art, a carefully sculpted thing from a culture long extinct. It was beautiful, and it was terrible.

"Get up," said the woman again. Even her voice made Ochi involuntarily flinch. It was definitely female, albeit processed through the strange mask, giving it a grating, metallic edge. But there was something else in the voice, too—it was like there was someone else speaking at the same time, matching the woman's words exactly, but this voice was male and it was somehow distant, a relic of somewhere or sometime else, echoing perhaps not in Ochi's cybernetically enhanced ears but somewhere inside his mind.

Ochi pushed himself to his feet. He looked around, not able to see D-O, suddenly wanting the stupid droid by his side, the feeling entirely irrational but still comforting. Then he drew himself up to his full height, which was not quite to the eyeline of the black mask. He took a breath and sighed. If this was it, then . . . this was it. He was outnumbered. He just hoped it would be quick.

"Okay, get it over with," he said. "I'm not going to beg or plead or grovel. I'm tired and I'm old but for what it's worth, I'm not sorry. Not now, not ever. You can't blame me for trying."

The cultists were still and silent in the circle that surrounded him. Ochi turned on his heel, casting his gaze over the group. They were all the same, black hooded robes, their features hidden behind the tight weave of black bandages.

Except the one who had spoken.

He turned back to the leader and looked her up and down. Now that the shock of their arrival had passed—now that he was resigned to his fate—Ochi found his fear evaporating. He no longer had anything to lose.

Ochi nodded at the woman. "I haven't seen you before. What are you, some kind of a priestess or something?" He waved his hand. "No, I don't care." He turned to the book on the crate. "I guess you want these back, too. Fine, take them, I'm not going to need them anymore, am I?"

The woman didn't speak, and the cultists didn't move. Ochi idly leafed through the book, then, glancing around the group, turned to face their leader again.

"Well?"

"Exegol."

Ochi's cybernetic optics adjusted themselves. "What about it?"

"You seek Exegol."

Ochi glanced around again. "Yes. You know I do. That's why you're here, isn't it?"

"We can show you the way," said the woman in the black mask. "We can give you the path through Red Space. We can give you what you seek."

Ochi licked his lipless mouth again. "What?" he asked, after a pause of several seconds. "You're just going to, what, take me there? Why would you do that? The path to Exegol is a secret—your secret."

"A secret indeed," said the metallic, grating voice of the woman in the mask. "A secret we can share with you." She tilted her head ever so slightly to one side, as though Ochi was an interesting specimen to be studied. "Once you have earned it."

Ochi stared at the woman—and then, despite himself, burst out laughing. He doubled over, taking great whoops of air as he lost control. He could feel the skin around his cybernetic eyes stretch, his whole face beginning to ache as the scar tissue was pulled tight.

"Exegol!" he managed, between gasps of breath, his arms folded across his middle as he laughed again. "You're just going to *take* me to Exegol? A personal escort to a hidden planet?" He paused. "Oh, wait, wait, no, not an escort. You said you'll give me the secret. Right, the secret. Don't tell me, a wayfinder! You're just going to hand one over. Is that it? After all these years, all my work, you finally decided I was, what, worthy enough?" He drew himself up to his full height and was almost ready to spit on the tattered edge of the woman's black cloak when her arm shot up, bringing the metal cylinder up in front of Ochi's scarred face. He gasped and stumbled backward.

That cylinder. He knew what it was. Vader's wasn't identical, but he knew exactly what it was and what was about to happen.

This was it.

Afraid again, Ochi did the only thing he could. He turned to run and—

Darkness. *Nothingness.* He found himself looking into a void so complete, so absolute, so pure, it was like looking into the heart of a black hole.

He turned around. The darkness was all around him, enveloping him. He could see nothing. The cabin of the *Bestoon Legacy* had vanished, along with the cultists and their leader, replaced with this pure void.

His cybernetic head implant took a moment to process what was going on, then gave him a simple systems report.

His eyes had been turned off.

Yelling in rage, Ochi spun around again, his arms outstretched. He took a step forward then reached down to feel, but somehow there was nothing around him, not the crates, not the decking, not the intruders. He stopped where he was and felt his face, his fingertips running around the hard rims of the electronic optics embedded in his eye sockets.

"What have you done?" he asked the darkness. "I can't see. What have you done!"

And then he felt it, a presence, a form looming over his shoulder, so close he could almost feel the breath against his skin. He flinched, ducking down as though to avoid someone approaching him from behind, but as soon as he moved, it was there again, at his shoulder, leaning in, invisible, intangible, but a presence nonetheless. It felt huge and cold and . . .

It felt wrong.

OCHI OF BESTOON.

That voice. By all the gods, that *voice.* A deep bass rumble, the enunciation so clipped, so perfect, so deliberate. Slow and low, a voice Ochi knew well but had never imagined he would hear again.

"No," he whispered. "No, it's not possible."

The voice chuckled, softly, the sound just enough to turn Ochi's insides to ice water.

ALL THINGS ARE POSSIBLE, OCHI OF BESTOON.

It was the voice of Emperor Palpatine. The *dead* Emperor Palpatine.

YOU HAVE BEEN CHOSEN.

The voice was now echoing from all around the darkness. Ochi looked up, shaking his head, and then he fell to his knees, his head bowed.

What nightmare was this?

I HAVE A TASK FOR YOU TO PERFORM.

The Emperor's voice now moved, left to right, right to left, above, below, around.

YOU WERE ONCE A HUNTER. SO YOU SHALL HUNT AGAIN.

Ochi stammered, unable to find his own voice.

YOU WILL FIND THE GIRL. YOU WILL BRING HER TO ME.

Every word the dead Emperor spoke was a threat, every syllable dagger-sharp and dripping with poison.

Ochi wished the cultists had come to kill him after all. He shook his head.

"I don't understand," he said. "I don't understand."

MY DISCIPLES WILL TEACH YOU. COMPLETE THIS TASK, AND YOU SHALL HAVE YOUR REWARD. YOU SHALL HAVE THE PATH TO EXEGOL.

And then the voice changed to one tinged with sadness, regret, the voice of a frail old man, a soul long lost. If anything, this just made Ochi even more afraid.

YOU HAVE FAILED ME BEFORE. DO NOT FAIL ME AGAIN, OCHI OF BESTOON.

Before Ochi could respond, there was a searing roar, sounding in the infinite darkness like a mighty electrical storm unleashing its fury. The darkness around him flared with a brilliant red light, and instantly he could smell ozone and could feel a sharp tang on the back of his tongue. As his optics adjusted to the glare, he found himself looking directly at the point of a long blade of red energy, buzzing like a trapped and angry insect, the core brilliant, almost white, surrounded by a perfect halo of deepest scarlet.

Ochi fell backward and knocked into his worktop, sending the crates toppling over, taking the ancient Sith text with them. He hit the deck and looked up, his eyes now operational again, and found himself looking up at the woman's black mask as she held her lightsaber a scant few centimeters from his face.

"You have your task," said the woman, and suddenly the blade wasn't there, the lightsaber deactivated.

Ochi let out a breath and looked around. The cultists remained as still as statues, and now the woman in the black mask was sliding her lightsaber back onto her belt.

"I . . . I do," said Ochi. He pushed himself up again, using a toppled crate behind him for support. As he stood, the crate shifted and he fell again onto his knees, catching the edge of a kneecap on the decking. Pain shot up his leg. He winced, then moved to rise again, slower this time.

"But I don't understand," said Ochi, through gritted teeth. "He told me to find the girl. What girl? I don't know what he was talking about." He paused. "How is he even alive? The Emperor is dead. Everybody knows that."

"You are a hunter, Ochi of Bestoon," said the woman, ignoring his question. "Once you were the greatest in the galaxy." She cocked her head again, the mask exaggerating the movement. "Or so you claimed. I hope our Lord was not mistaken in choosing you for reactivation."

"Reactivation? Is that what you want to call it?"

The woman did not answer.

Ochi shook his head. "I still don't understand. The Emperor said you would . . . teach me something?"

At this, the woman in the mask nodded and one of the robed cultists stepped forward. From beneath their long robe they produced a dagger. They held it out in front of them, by the handle, the blade pointed at Ochi.

Ochi looked down at it. Like the Sith wayfinders, like the weird mask the leader of the cultists was wearing, the dagger looked like the product of another age entirely. The weapon was a dull silver, and while the blade was straight, it was lobed, shaped with two bulbous sections separated by a short, squarish serrated portion. The edges of the weapon were bright, like they were freshly machined. The blade itself was plain, the hilt a short, thick curve of metal.

Ochi looked up at the cultist's bandage-wrapped face.

"What is this?"

The cultist did not speak, but they held the dagger forward.

Ochi looked at the masked woman. "Is this for me?"

The black mask inclined in acknowledgment. "Take the blade."

Ochi shrugged and reached for the weapon, expecting the cultist to hand it over by the handle. Instead, they moved the weapon again so the blade remained pointing at Ochi.

"Take the blade," said the woman.

"Yes, but, I don't understand—"

"You will. Take the blade."

Ochi found himself cowering under the commanding order. He reached forward, both hands carefully taking hold of the blade, mindful to keep the cutting edges clear of his palms.

That was when the cultist pulled the knife back and up, toward themselves. Ochi cried out, first in surprise, then in pain as he realized what the cultist had done. He collapsed onto his knees, cradling his cut hands, curling them into fists to try to stop the blood that was now beginning to ooze out between his closed fingers.

"What did you do that for?" he yelled up at the woman in the mask. "You've nearly crippled me."

"Your wounds will heal," said the woman, "and this blade will tell."

She gestured to the cultist. Ochi turned to watch, his injured hands still pressed tightly against his chest.

The cultist held the dagger out, tilting the blade down so it caught the light.

As Ochi watched, the blade began to glow, softly at first, but then with a light that deepened to a red—the same red as the woman's lightsaber. The light spiraled then began to coalesce, almost like particles of dust spinning around the blade. The light was sucked in toward the blade, and then a pulse traveled along the blade, Ochi's blood vanishing, like it was absorbed by the metal itself as the light slowly moved along it, leaving in its wake lines of densely packed symbols, intricate and delicate, the light engraving them in the surface from hilt to tip. When the light reached the point, it flashed and was gone, leaving the dagger's blade smoking slightly in the air.

Ochi dipped his head, the agony of his injured hands refusing to

abate. He closed the irises of his cybernetic eyes, this time thankful for
the peaceful darkness, and shook his head.

"What must I do?" he asked, finally.

"Find the girl," said the woman. "Bring her to Exegol. There the Sith
Eternal will guide the galaxy to its destiny and you shall find that which
you seek."

Ochi shook his head. "Even if I find this girl, how do I get to Exegol?
I need to know. You need to tell me. Show me the path. Give me the
coordinates, or a beacon, or something. Give me a wayfinder."

"When the time is right," said the woman, "the blade will tell. Keep it
with you, always. The blade is your key."

Ochi opened his eyes.

He was alone.

He stood, letting his hands fall to his sides, the blood continuing to
drip onto the decking. As he looked around, he heard a hissing sound
and detected the faint rise of steam.

He looked down. The blood from his hands was dripping down onto
the dagger, which lay on the decking. As each drop hit the blade, it
hissed, like the dagger was white-hot, the blood vanishing as it evaporated.

No, it wasn't evaporating. The blade was absorbing it.

He bent down and grimaced against the pain as he opened his hand
and picked the weapon up, by the handle this time, which was pleasantly cool against his burning hands. The blade was clean, the engraving
on it looking as old as the weapon itself, like it was part of the original
design. He recognized the script. He'd only seen scraps of it in his texts,
and he'd never been able to translate it, but he knew what language it
was.

Ur-Kittât. The old tongue of the Sith, forbidden since the days of the
Old Republic, inscribed in the unique runic alphabet that Ochi had also
seen engraved on the walls of the Sith Citadel on Exegol.

As he held the dagger, Ochi felt . . . something. Not a presence as
such, but something smaller, if just as malevolent. The feeling was, he
realized, coming from the dagger itself, like the relic was somehow . . .
alive.

Alive, and hungry. For blood. For death.

For killing.

Find the girl. Bring her to Exegol.

The blade will tell.

Ochi laughed. *Now* he understood.

Because the Emperor had done it. He'd used the secrets of Exegol and had overcome death itself. That was all Ochi needed, proof enough that Exegol was the answer to all his prayers.

Palpatine was back, and Ochi of Bestoon had work to do.

CHAPTER 6

BOXER POINT STATION, JANX SYSTEM
NOW

The galaxy was a big place, full of magic and full of wonders and bright centers of life and love, civilization, spreading from the Deep Core to the Outer Rim, bringing cooperation, compassion, understanding. Bringing hope.

But where there was light, there was darkness. There were some corners of the galaxy in which shadows bred, where hope was lost and where darkness prevailed, smothering the dreams of peace and goodwill.

And within that darkness, there was danger. There were some places in the galaxy only fools would dare tread, perhaps determined to make a change, take a stand against evil. A place to make their mark, or even their fortune.

Or . . . to just have a good time.

Sennifer's Beam and Balance was just such a place.

And Lando Balthazar Calrissian was in his element.

Tucked into a corner booth, he looked around the circular table that separated him from the other players in this epic game of sabacc, then dropped his eyes to the cards in his hand, spreading them with his fingers just enough so he could double-check what he thought he was holding. He'd been playing for . . . well, okay, he wasn't sure how long. Sennifer's was a place you could lose yourself in, and that was exactly why he was here.

The greasy drinking establishment was located right at the heart of Boxer Point Station, a huge, multipurpose port facility in high orbit over the gas giant Janx II. Boxer Point was located rather close to the Inner Rim, but in a convenient gap between the major hyperspace lanes that made it awkward to get to and, therefore, largely free of most mainstream traffic. It was because of this that Boxer Point had developed something of a reputation as a free port, a place where business could be carried out without much in the way of interruption, official or otherwise.

Boxer Point Station itself consisted of two toroids, linked by a central spoke. The bottom section was devoted to heavy industrial shipping, mostly of dangerous goods, and the large-scale movement of other materials that the traders were keen to keep out of reach of official inspection, while the upper ring was more commercial—Boxer Point *was* a legitimate enterprise, after all—offering standard spaceport facilities to anyone who found themselves in need of them, and no questions asked.

Sennifer's Beam and Balance was positioned exactly in the middle of the stalk that connected the upper and lower rings, making it the ideal place where spacefarers from either section could mix and mingle, two very different kinds of customers sharing an equal desire for rest and relaxation, maybe a chance to do some deals, to share information, to talk, gossip, and relax. Maybe . . . play a game or two. Place a bet, win—or lose—a fortune. Sabacc, Crystallo, even Pontonese Subrakahn tables could be found running in some of the darker corners of the establishment, where life-forms from a hundred different planets sat, eyes—human, compound, electronic—glittering along with their drinks as hushed business and pleasure went on through the infinite night.

And for Lando, the concentration demanded by the game was exactly what he needed. It was almost a form of meditation, a way to clear his mind of all thought and distraction, to remove himself from his troubles and his woes—of which he had many.

Too many.

He'd been doing okay in the game. More than okay—so far, he'd trebled his stake. Not an amazing play, but not terrible. His opponents had stuck with it, their supply of credits seemingly endless. But Lando was playing the long game. If he could keep his luck running high, then at least part of him would be happy that he hadn't wasted his time. Credits were credits and credits were useful. He sure as hell needed them.

By now, however, the pace of the game had slowed to an irritating crawl. To try to spice it up and give his three opponents something to think about, Lando had upped his bet. The others had matched, but Lando was confident. He'd been playing sabacc for, what, forty years now? He had enough experience and skill, and he knew all the tricks. These guys? They were about to go bust.

He checked his cards again, suppressing every muscle in his face with practiced ease. The hand was—

Well, there was no other way to put it. The hand was bad. Very bad. He'd been counting cards but must have lost track. So far it had been a clean game, and they'd run through enough hands for Lando to know the deck was standard, unadulterated.

Which meant he'd made a mistake.

He slid the cards together into a tight stack and put them facedown in front of him, keeping his hand on top. He looked around the table and grinned, his smile flashing in the gloom around the table.

"Gentlemen," he said, then paused and looked to his left. Sitting there was a large bipedal life-form that looked human but was wearing a close-fitting, oval-shaped space helmet with an opaque visor. Lights on the being's chest unit flickered dimly, casting an ever-changing glow across the checkerboard surface of the table. They hadn't spoken throughout the entire game. On the other side of the table sat a Dressellian with a tight, mean expression and another humanoid wearing a helmet that looked like it had been fashioned from the faceplate of an old BX-series commando droid.

"Ladies?" Lando frowned, his brows momentarily knitting together before he grinned expansively and held both arms out, including the whole table in an embrace of friendship. "*Beings!*" he said. "It's been a pleasure, it really has. A night long remembered, a game that will go down in history as, truly, one of the greats." He dropped his arms and sighed, looking down at the table with a slight shake of the head. "But you know what they say. All good things must come to an end, and this player is most certainly folding."

Lando leaned forward, gathering up the not insubstantial pile of credits that were still his to claim. It was a good haul—not his best, but then this was hardly a dedicated casino like Ferona Vivaros, or the *Errant Venture* (now, there was a good gambling hall). But despite the large bet he'd just forfeited, he'd still made a profit, enough to get the *Lady Luck* fueled and a new catalyzer installed.

But more important, there was enough for a long-awaited and well-deserved drink.

Around the table, the players glanced at one another. Lando watched them, the grin plastered on his face, and it occurred to him that he'd broken the promise to himself never to play life-forms that refused to take off their helmets at the table. It wasn't just that he couldn't see their faces (if they had faces) or read their expressions (if they had expressions), but who knew what was being communicated silently between them via personal encrypted networks.

"Look, no hard feelings," said Lando. "Let me get in another round. Hey, any of you ever tried a Red Dwarf?"

Lando moved to stand but was pulled back to the table by the fur-covered hand of the droid-faced opponent.

"I'll have what you're having," the being growled, somehow managing to form the words in Basic despite them sounding like two rocks banging together underwater. "And you'll leave half your cut here so we know you'll come back."

Lando laughed—nervously, despite himself. "Okay, you really must be thirsty." He raised the hand of the arm trapped on the table by the hairy claw, and the being released him. "I'll be right back."

Lando grabbed a random handful of credits and left his seat in a hurry, happy to be away from the table. As he headed toward the bar, he counted the money in his clutched hand. By luck, he'd picked up some high denominations and had enough to refuel. The catalyzer would have to wait, but that was fine, the *Lady Luck* could make it a few more light-years before that particular component was past its best. He could walk out of Sennifer's right now, and he'd be ahead, despite the money he'd left on the table.

Lando reached the bar and, plotting his exit strategy, glanced behind. He saw the Dressellian and droid-face watching him from across the crowded room. He gave them a little salute. He just had to look like he was placing an order, then perhaps going to hit the restroom, and—

His hand was pinned to the bar, this time by the armored gauntlet of his primary sabacc opponent, the unknown species in the fully sealed environment suit. Lando looked up and grinned at his own reflection in the mirrored curve of the creature's helmet.

Lando gestured to the bar with his free hand, indicating that, yes, he really was going to buy them all drinks, when there came a computerized beep and then a mechanical click. The dome of his opponent's helmet split down the middle and the two sides parted, revealing the suit's occupant.

Lando crinkled his nose, not at the appearance of the being within—hey, the galaxy was a big place, he'd seen it all . . . or so he liked to think, anyway—but at the *smell*. Wisps of a pungent orange gas curled up from the collar of the environment suit, clearing to reveal the face within. It was dark green, wet, the skin smooth but covered in a tiny crosshatch pattern. There was no mouth or nose, but the being did have four eyes, white spheres that bobbed on the end of short tentacles.

Lando clicked his tongue. "What can I get you—"

He stopped and frowned. He sniffed again.

"Do you have a problem, little man?" the being asked, its voice thick and wet and surprisingly high-pitched.

"No, no," said Lando. He frowned. He knew that smell anywhere. "Is that tibanna gas?"

The being nodded, or at least its fleshy head stretched and shrank back again in what Lando assumed was the affirmative. "I am from Muqular," said the being. "What you call tibanna is essential to our life process."

Lando grinned and shook his head. "Muqular? Wow. That's down the Western Reaches, right? I haven't been down there in, oh, a long time now." He grinned and shook his head in surprise. "You guys breathe tibanna? Man, oh man, I wish we'd met twenty years ago. We could have come to a truly symbiotic arrangement."

"Who are you calling *symbiotic*, little man?"

"Oh, hey, no, it was just an expression."

The Muqularan released Lando's arm from the bar. "Double or nothing."

Lando grinned. "Now *that*, my fine friend, is what I call a deal."

The Muqular nodded, and with a hiss and a click the two halves of its helmet dome snapped together, leaving a curl of sickly tibanna gas drifting up into the general miasma of fog that formed a permanent layer under the establishment's ceiling. The being patted Lando's shoulder rather heavily, then lumbered off back to the table.

With the Muqularan gone, Lando grimaced as he rolled his shoulder. He'd been too slow to get out, and was now caught up in at least another round—probably many more—at the sabacc table. As he ordered a round of Red Dwarfs from the female Mon Calamari behind the bar, the mottled blue and white of her skin crisscrossed with an intricate spider's web of silver chains hanging from a multitude of piercings, Lando leaned over the bar and stared at the blurry outline of his reflection in the freshly wiped, and very wet, surface.

Who, exactly, was he looking at? Oh, he recognized himself, all right. In his life, he'd spent enough time admiring his own features. And, to be honest, he still had it. Okay, he was getting a little wider in the jowl, his face somehow squarer than it had been in years gone past. But his thick head of hair was as black as ever, slicked back and looking sharp, as was his neatly shaped mustache.

But even in the distorted reflection, he could see not just the years but his worries sitting heavily on him. There were tight lines around his eyes—once, he would have called them laughter lines, but not anymore. His eyes were bright and sparkled with an inner light that Lando had learned to use as he turned on the charm, the smiles, the pleasantries to get what he invariably wanted.

But there was one thing his charm couldn't get, one problem his sly command of body language, his wiles, and his wit couldn't solve.

He hadn't found his daughter, Kadara.

No, not just Kadara—*Kadara Calrissian*. He made a point of that. Her full name was important, symbolizing not just who she was but where she came from. Symbolizing a family that she would come back to, one day.

It had been six years now, and even as he thought of it, he was surprised to admit to himself that the pain of her loss, that exquisite sharpness in his chest that took his breath away, that made the galaxy go fuzzy at the edges as he tried to keep his balance, had faded over time.

He didn't want it to fade. He wanted to feel it, alive and electric and terrible. He wanted to bring it back to the surface, or to take himself down to meet it. He wanted that experience again, to feel the loss and the hurt so badly he would tear the universe apart with his bare hands just to have her back.

Kadara Calrissian.

But . . . he couldn't. He could lie in his bed aboard the *Lady Luck* all night and stare at the ceiling—and he had, more times than he could remember—searching inside himself for that fire, that spark. But it was gone. The pain of his daughter's loss slept inside him, unable to be stirred, buried too deep now to be roused to what it had once felt like.

Perhaps that was for the best, and then as soon as that thought arrived, he felt angry, both at himself and at the galaxy at large. With that anger came disappointment, and with disappointment came guilt.

He had searched, and he had failed. That search had taken him across the galaxy, had seen him ping every contact, visit every planet and moon and station and base he could think of, and come up with absolutely nothing. As six months turned into one year turned into two, he found himself repeating actions, going back to the same places again, without even realizing it, as he tried to follow a lead, a whisper, a clue as to where his daughter had been taken.

Lando snorted. So many years. Was she really his daughter, now, outside of a basic, biological connection? She was just two years old when she'd been taken. Would she remember him? Would she remember her own name? And, he worried, would *he* even recognize her when he found her?

And that, Lando knew, was the worst part of it all. Years searching fruitlessly, expending all his energy, his time, his rapidly dwindling supply of credits, and at the back of his mind, the stark fact that when he did finally find her, she might not even know who he was.

He was brought out of his reverie by the sharp clatter of glasses on the bar under his nose, his senses immediately assailed by the acidic aroma of the drinks he had ordered. He looked up and found himself face-to-face with the legendary patron of her eponymous drinkery, Lady Sennifer herself. All he could see of her was her black hair, cut into a bob surrounding a heavy-duty industrial respirator. Her blue eyes blinked behind the protective eyepieces.

"Remember to sip 'em slow," she said, her voice echoing tinnily through the cans of her mask. "You'll live longer."

Lando found the corner of his mouth lifting in a grin, despite his sour mood. "It's been years since I had one of these."

"Well you're about to be reminded real quick. That'll be four hundred credits."

Lando's grin froze. He blinked. "Excuse me?"

"Danger money," said Sennifer.

With a sigh and a shake of the head, Lando counted a stack of his winnings in the palm of his hand, then handed it over. Sennifer took the money without a word then disappeared to serve another gaggle of customers.

Lando gathered up the glasses between his hands, then stopped.

Ah yes, there it was. That creeping feeling, the guilt back again to say hello and to stay awhile. He looked down at the noxious drinks, trying to come to some kind of a decision.

He'd come to Boxer Point on a notion that it was exactly the kind of place he might find a lead on his daughter. It had seemed like a good idea, but even as he plotted his course, he knew from bitter experience that he was just trying very hard to convince himself he was doing something productive to further his search. True enough, he hadn't actually been to Boxer Point Station in years, and, yes, the mix of spacefarers, particularly in a place like Sennifer's, *was* the kind of place you could pick up all kinds of information.

But Sennifer's also had, on a good night, anyway, some of the best unregulated gambling you could happen to find, and Lando knew that all too well. What was supposed to be a search could—*would*—be easily derailed by the distraction.

He was using his daughter as an excuse, and he knew it, and, right here, right now, it killed him.

Kadara Calrissian.

He put the glasses back down and took a breath, surprised at his reaction—and then . . . happy, because that was what he wanted, he deserved to be guilty, and he deserved to be—

"Kidnapping? Have you got hyperphasic space worms?"

Lando looked up, shaking his head to clear it, like he'd just been punched in the jaw.

Farther along the curve of the bar, three beings were huddled. The one who had just mentioned kidnapping had his back to Lando, his bulky form clad in scuffed gray plastoid armor that matched the tone of his skin, with a skullcap on his huge, angular head. The second looked identical to the first, only this one was facing Lando, revealing the long, low-slung, flat-nosed snout and wide-set, reptilian eyes.

That second member of the party had his attention fixed on the third being, who seemed to be holding court, his back against the bar, an entire bottle of what looked like Serennian herbal gin cradled in the crook of one arm. This one was wearing a black outfit that looked like a mix of leather and something synthetic, and his flattened face was pale and scarred, like the features had been burned off in some terrible accident. His eyes were perfectly round and black—*electronic optics?* Lando wondered—and a cybernetic headband wrapped around his skull, small red and blue lights winking over the spots where, Lando assumed, the man's ears would be.

"Listen, listen," said the man, his rounded head bobbing, his voice clear but slurred from the expensive gin. "This isn't just some kind of a job, you know. It's not just a job."

The first being grunted a laugh and turned to the bar; Lando could now see the face, confirming that while he didn't recognize the species, the pair could well have been twins. The being lifted a shot glass of something brilliant orange in color—a Rodian Splice—and knocked it back in a single gulp. Then he shook his head and said again, "Kidnapping? You are some piece of work, you know that, right?"

Whoever these three were, they clearly thought they were tough guys, and knowing the clientele of Sennifer's, Lando had to be cautious. The kind of spacefarers who came here for some R&R were unlikely to react well to an eavesdropper.

But . . . kidnapping? Was this it? He'd come here on an excuse to find a clue and had . . . found one?

Lando got a grip on the glasses in front of him again. The others would be waiting for him, but he didn't care. He slid the four drinks carefully a little along the bar, closer to the trio.

Because the being at the bar was right. Okay, so the deals that were done and the jobs that were planned in Sennifer's Beam and Balance often crossed the line from what you might call legal and ethical, but kidnapping was a particularly dirty kind of business, because kidnapping often meant slavery, and slavery was one of the galaxy's true evils, had been for longer than the Empire had ever been around. And sure, that Empire might be gone, but it wasn't like it had evaporated the instant the second Death Star had gone up over Endor. There were pockets of the galaxy where it was like nothing had changed, where, Lando had heard, armies were being built using not clones or volunteers but *the enslaved*, children kidnapped, brainwashed, shaped into mindless minions, cannon fodder for some war that he really hoped would never come.

Lando didn't know if that had happened to his daughter. He also didn't know what this trio was actually talking about.

But it . . . stirred something. That fire he had long forgotten, he felt it begin to smolder once more.

He moved a little closer still.

"You're not going to make any friends over this," said the second being. He was the only one of the group who didn't seem to be drinking, his hands instead on his hips as he balanced on his stool—or, more specifically, one hand on a hip and the other on the butt of the blaster hanging from its holster. "I doubt you'll find anyone on Boxer Point who will want in."

At this comment, the scarred man pushed himself off the bar, bumping into his first companion, whose drink slopped onto the floor.

"Hey, watch it," the first being growled. But the drunk didn't seem to notice, instead turning his full attention to the third member of the group.

"Did Ochi of Bestoon say he wanted help, Bosvarga? Eh? Did he say he needed any?" He then turned his black electric eyes back over to the other being, his fellow drinker. "Ochi of Bestoon made you, Cerensco. I made you. Made both of you. Remember that. You owe me." He stabbed a finger now at Bosvarga. "You both do. Which means you're in and I don't even have to ask, right?"

Bosvarga grinned—or at least opened his small mouth to reveal a set of razor-sharp and entirely false teeth made of shiny metal—and rose off his stool. He was a full head taller than his drunk cohort.

"Ochi," said Bosvarga, clearly trying to calm his friend, "we've always been in. That's why you called us, right? Just like old times, right?" He looked at Cerensco and batted him with the back of one meaty hand.

Cerensco sniggered, the hollow sound echoing through his long snout. "Sure, why not. But maybe let's not call it kidnapping, okay? How about . . . covert procurement?" He seemed pleased with this and laughed louder this time, a deep, wet gurgle. "Just, please, Bosvarga, stop him talking about himself in the third person, okay?"

Cerensco laughed some more. Ochi didn't seem pleased. As Lando watched, Ochi thumped his bottle of gin down on the bar and it tipped over, the expensive contents pouring out. Ochi didn't notice; instead it was Cerensco who quickly righted the bottle, then used it to refill his own spilled tumbler.

"Now, you listen to me, you listen to me," said Ochi of Bestoon, his flash of anger suddenly forgotten in his drunken haze. "This isn't a job. This is a *calling*. I've been chosen, right?" He reached for the gin bottle on the bar, apparently not noticing that his hand closed around empty air, the bottle now safely in Cerensco's care. "They chose me." Ochi puffed out his chest. "I've been . . . *reactivated*."

"Sounds great," said Bosvarga, his eyes rolling melodramatically, then he nodded at Cerensco. "Hey, brother, you still know Pysarian? He was here, wasn't he?"

Cerensco nodded, sipping his drink. "And Anduluuvil. We should put out a call."

"Think I saw Krastan around, too. And his friend, whatever his name was."

"The Balosar? Okay, sure." Cerensco raised his glass to Ochi. "The more, the merrier. Sound okay? Get a crew together, right? Just like old times."

"You know," said Ochi, ignoring his companion, "they sent bounty hunters after them? You know how that went?" He waved a hand. "Hopeless. Chased them into Wild Space and got themselves vaporized by the New Republic." He tapped his own chest. "No wonder they came crawling back to me. I used to hunt Jedi, back in the Clone Wars, did you know that? Ochi of Bestoon was the best hunter in the galaxy. They want the girl? Easy. Ochi will have it done in no time."

Lando watched as Bosvarga shot a glance at his brother, Cerensco, before refocusing on Ochi.

"Wait, the New Republic got them?"

"What?" Ochi's head bobbed around from the effects of his drinking. "No." He waved a hand again. "It was some patrol. Halo something. From what I was told they just blasted the hunters out of space and then sent the family on their way somewhere. I don't know."

Cerensco frowned, and shook his head. "The less I have to do with the New Republic, the better. I'm still wanted in more than ten systems."

Bosvarga hissed and held up a hand. "Eleven."

Cerensco raised his glass. "I'll drink to that!"

Ochi slumped on his stool. "I've got power now," he muttered, his voice almost disappearing in the general hubbub of Sennifer's.

Lando slid just a *little* bit closer and strained his ears. This was a stroke of . . . well, it was luck, pure and simple. Lando didn't pretend he understood the ways of the universe, but neither did he waste any time questioning them. The Jedi had the Force, right? And Lando didn't understand that, either, but he accepted it. So maybe there were other powers at work, not to be understood but to be accepted, and welcomed when they came calling. Hell, maybe *luck* was his version of the Force? It sounded ridiculous even as the thought entered his mind, but Lando willed himself to ignore the doubts. He relied on luck, often too heavily, both in business and in pleasure—the gambling he loved so much was the perfect combination of skill and luck, and often, in the heat of a game, Lando felt like he was master of both—but something itched at the back of his mind whenever he thought about it. He'd spent too many years chasing clues, relying on overheard conversations, intercepted data transmissions, even whispers and rumors and chatter from the backs of spaceports and cantinas and places just like Sennifer's Beam and Balance—all of it, in some form or another, convenient, or coincidental, or just plain lucky. And while none of those roads had led to his daughter, there had been times when Lando had felt he'd made progress, gotten that one step closer. True enough, he hadn't had that feeling much lately, but maybe, just *maybe,* as the wheel of the universe turned once more, it was time for another little piece of luck.

Lando felt a little flutter in his chest. Not hope, exactly, but the unmistakable sense that he had stumbled onto something important.

"I've got secrets, too," Ochi continued.

"Sounds great," said Bosvarga again.

"I do," said Ochi. "They told me. Showed me the way." He looked around, as though he was expecting someone to be eavesdropping at his shoulder, completely unaware Lando was, in fact, eavesdropping from just slightly farther along the bar. "Showed me the *way.*"

Cerensco topped up his glass. "Way to where?"

Ochi turned his black eyes on him. "To Exegol."

Lando frowned. He wasn't familiar with that planet, or system, or whatever it was.

Then Ochi smiled. It was a strange expression. The skin of his face, already stretched tight by the extensive scarring, was pulling even closer against his skull, his lipless mouth nothing but a wide slit. The tip of a white tongue poked out and moistened them.

"The Sith have called me," he said, quietly. "I served them before. And now they have called me again."

While Lando had been straining to hear over the noise of the bar, that single word—"Sith"—had come across loud and clear, like the whole place had suddenly dropped in volume, by pure coincidence.

Sith.

Lando hadn't heard that name spoken in years, but the sudden, unexpected mention was like a gut punch.

Sith? Did they even still exist? Weren't they all dead? Surely they weren't involved with the kidnappings?

Were they?

What the hell had he run across now?

Bosvarga bared his metal teeth at Cerensco. "I ever tell you, I met a Sith Lord once. I ever tell you that? Tall guy, black robe, walked around with the hood so low he was looking at his feet the whole time."

"Wait," said Cerensco, "was that on Ord Mantell?"

"No, it was out near the Orgri. Remember that time we were working out there with Anduluuvil and Cyanox?"

"Do I ever." Cerensco raised the bottle of gin in salute. "Oh, Cyanox. Now, *there* was a mighty fine specimen of opposing chromosomes." He laughed, and his brother laughed with him.

"You compressing the degenerate matter yourself or something?"

Lando turned, startled by the synthesized voice at his shoulder. His Muqularan sabacc opponent was at the bar again, clearly annoyed at the significant delay in getting the drinks. "You're not thinking of skipping out on us, are you? My friends and I have invested a lot in you and we expect the opportunity to get some return on that."

Lando nodded, then turned on a wide smile he most certainly did not feel on the inside. "Skip out on you?" Next he feigned shock, with just a hint of amazement and a dash of horror, the fingers of one hand splayed across his chest in a playful show of offense. "My friend, I wouldn't dream of it. Here." He turned to the bar and slid the drinks across to the being. "Take these back to the table. I'm just waiting on some Bloomspice chasers. Sennifer said she had to bring them out of the polarizer."

If the Muqularan was suspicious, he didn't show it. He gathered the shot glasses up, the three leaf-shaped fingers of his now ungloved hand wrapped around the whole lot, covering the glassware with a thick coating of slime in the process. Lando kept the grin fixed on his face. "Start the shuffle, I'll be there in a—"

Lando didn't finish his sentence, as the breath was knocked out of him when something large and heavy collided with him from behind, shoving his stomach into the edge of the bar and winding him. He turned just in time to duck as the half-empty bottle of Serennian herbal gin sailed through the air and shattered on the back of the flight helmet a pilot was still wearing as he leaned just around the curve of the circular bar.

Wincing, Lando turned and was shoved again, this time as Cerensco backed into him, forearms raised, while Ochi of Bestoon pummeled him with his fists. Bosvarga grabbed Ochi by the back of the neck and swung him around, only to get a fist in the face—this from the pilot who had been accidentally drawn into the fight. Bosvarga grunted in surprise and pushed the pilot away, only for another patron—an Ithorian, clearly a friend of the pilot—to wrap two extremely long and woody arms around him.

Lando moved away, glancing around, realizing all too well that the whole place was about to erupt into a full-scale brawl as more of Sennifer's patrons began to join in, drawn by accident or by a desire to let off some steam in a good old-fashioned bar fight. Reaching the sabacc table, Lando found his playing partners right where he'd left them, apparently happy to sit and enjoy the show.

All except the Muqularan. Lando was about to ask where he was when a slime-coated, three-fingered paw grabbed him by the back of his head. Sliding out of the wet grip, Lando ducked around and turned to face the player. The front of the being's suit was smoking from where the Red Dwarfs had spilled onto it.

"You owe me money, friend. And a new environment suit."

Lando held up his hands. "It's not my fault!"

The Muqularan wasn't interested. He grabbed Lando's upper arm with one hand and raised the other, the three large fingers fanning out like the leaves of a tropical plant. But just as he seemed like he was about to smother Lando's entire face, Lando managed to slide out from his grip, thanks to the liberal amounts of slime that were being excreted by the being's skin.

Lando had to get out—but he also had to learn more about the trio at the bar. He ran back to where he had been standing, then skidded to a halt as he tried to make out what was going on in the fight. It had grown in size—there were at least a dozen beings of various species involved—but at the bar, he could see Sennifer, her respirator now hanging around her neck, talking to two of her burly security staff, a pair of purple-furred, muscle-bound Lasats. Lando watched the duo nod as they received their instructions then leapt over the bar, sending patrons scattering out of their way, before they pushed their way toward the trio who had instigated the whole drama—a trio who had vanished, having apparently decided to evade responsibility by making their own swift exit from the establishment.

Lando felt a huge clamp on his shoulder—the Muqularan again, but, wasting no time, Lando slipped out of its grip and bumped straight into one of the Lasat security. He pointed behind him.

"You want that guy," he said before scooting out of the way, only glancing over his shoulder to see the Lasat cornering his former sabacc opponent. Satisfied, Lando slipped past the struggling mass of patrons and out of Sennifer's, into one of Boxer Point Station's main thoroughfares.

He was too late. Ochi of Bestoon and his pals were now nowhere to be seen. The thoroughfare in both directions was fifty meters wide and filled not only with people and spacefarers and droids but also with a huge variety of cargo carts and transport sleds, some on wheels, some floating on repulsors, as the business of the station continued. Lando stood on his toes, trying to get a look over the crowds, but there was no sign of Ochi or the others.

Lando sighed and moved over to a quiet spot at the side of the thoroughfare. He rolled his shoulder, then grimaced as he felt the slime from the Muqularan on his shirt. With a frown, he ran his fingers through his hair and found it was thick with the stuff as well.

He'd lost his credits, and had possibly made a few enemies around the sabacc table, but now he had something to do. That feeling . . . well, it thrilled him, actually. He had a mystery, and a mission.

First, he needed to get cleaned up. And then he needed to find out just who this Ochi of Bestoon was, and who the hell he was planning to kidnap.

CHAPTER 7

EXEGOL

THEN

The boy watches the pair from the shadows, from the unseen corners of the place where he has learned to live, where he has made his home these last countless years. They don't know he is here. None of them do.

He is good at hiding. He is good at not being seen.

The temple is vast, a citadel of black rock and iron, the two visitors dwarfed by the colossal statuary that surrounds them, the forms cyclopean and impossible, carved not with hands but with dark magic and arcane ritual. The two visitors—he hesitates to call them invaders, as their presence, while perhaps not *welcome,* is not resisted by the robed, bandage-faced cultists as they continue their work—walk on beneath the towering monoliths, toward the center, toward the source of all this power.

He doesn't know who they are. He wants to think he can *sense* the presence of the tall one in black armor, long cape lapping at his heels, his breath echoing and artificial from beneath the cowled helmet that looks like a skull, that looks like it should belong with the statuary, another face of evil to gaze down across the ages at the dark toil of the cultists.

But . . . he's lying to himself, because no matter how hard he tries, he can't sense a thing, and while the figure in black armor looks like he belongs here, looks like his very existence should cause a ripple in the Force, the boy feels nothing. It's the same for the other, the smaller man's red-and-white mask a flash of color in this dark place. As the boy watches, this one seems to be doing his best to irritate his companion, who refuses to rise to the bait. They make a strange pair. The boy doesn't know who they are. Maybe they are more cultists, like the others. Perhaps they wield the Force like the Sith do.

For the boy, the Force is a mystery, a thing he knows exists only because he has been told, and he has only been told because he is a failure, nothing more than rejected matter from the scalpel of creation. He is useless, without power, a genetic strandcast that failed to inherit anything from his father.

He is an abomination.

That's what they call him, in place of a name, because to give him a name would be to *recognize* him, to grant him a life and an existence beyond his own failure. Instead, they called him the Abomination and then they continued with their work, shunning him entirely, pretending he doesn't even exist, but unable to end his life and *recycle* him as they would normally do with failed experiments thanks to the protection granted by his father.

Why his life is protected, he doesn't know, and he isn't entirely sure he wants that protection.

Life on Exegol is no life at all.

But he has survived, and that survival has given him something else.

Hope.

He isn't sure quite what that is, what it means, but he senses something now—not with the Force, of course, but with his own mind—that there might be a way out, there might be a life beyond the Citadel, beyond the shadows.

One day.

He leaves the visitors to their tour. He retreats into the shadowed vaults, ignored by the cultists of the Sith Eternal, enjoying a freedom unknown, he thinks, to anyone else in the Citadel. Because he can go anywhere within its seemingly endless vaults. At first, he was afraid of being caught and punished or—worse—his freedom curtailed as he was sent to join the ranks of the enslaved who served their dark masters in silence.

But he hasn't been caught. Perhaps his luck will run out, one day.

Perhaps, one day, he will get away from this nightmare.

He goes *down*. He has been to the lower levels before, but has never reached their bottom, and he wonders if there really is a bottom. Perhaps the Citadel goes on forever. It feels like it.

But he also wonders if the cultists think that as well, because he isn't the only one interested in finding the hidden foundations of the place. There are cultists here, searching, lighting their way with red lanterns that buzz in his ears as he watches from a distance.

He follows them now, down, and down. There is more statuary, more evidence that the Citadel is older, and perhaps it wasn't even built by the cultists or their ancestors. Perhaps it was built by another people entirely, in another age, long forgotten.

As he follows, he hears again the cultists whisper to one another as they walk in single file, deeper, deeper. Their voices are harsh scratches, but they echo around the funerary vault, the cultist in front leading the others in what sounds like a chant but somehow isn't one.

Plagueis.

(Plagueis, Plagueis, Plagueis)

Revan.

(Revan, Revan, Revan)

Perhaps they are spells. Perhaps they are incantations to the dark side of the Force. He wonders again what the cultists are looking for, and he wonders if they are trying to find the source, the well of black power in the basement of the world, from which the Sith draw their magic.

Noctyss.

(Noctyss, Noctyss, Noctyss)

Sanguis.

(Sanguis, Sanguis, Sanguis)

Kakon.

(Kakon, Kakon, Kakon)

Voord.

(Voord, Voord, Voord)

Shaa.

(Shaa, Shaa, Shaa)

It sounds like they are calling names, he realizes, and sometimes, in the echoing responses from the line of cultists, it sounds like others answer, their whispers emanating from the catacombs of the Citadel.

But it is his imagination. He knows it is.

He also knows something else. It has plagued his mind for a long, long time, but as he has gotten older, it has started to crystallize in his thoughts with terrifying clarity.

He is afraid. Not of the dark, not of the shadows, not of the cultists and their strange bandaged faces, and their ceaseless work in dark laboratories filled with biological horror.

He is afraid of himself. Of what he might become. Of his own curiosity.

He is protected by his father, and this has given him freedom. What if . . .

What if that is the whole point? What if he has been left to live not because he is the only strandcast to have actually survived, developing and growing normally, but because there is some other purpose for him?

What if he discovers that purpose? What if he is meant to follow the cultists? What if he is the one to find whatever they are looking for.

He wants no part of this.

Finally, it is time to leave. As he heads back up to the surface, he realizes his opportunity.

The visitors.

Their ship.

Can he do it?

He doesn't have much time. If he is to do this, he must act fast. And he will need help.

Luckily, he has a friend, of sorts. There is one being on the entire planet who seems to know he exists, who has given him food, showed him where to live and *how* to live in a place devoid of life. A friend, of sorts, who has, if not looked after him, then watched him, at least when he was younger. Perhaps the friend raised him from a babe. He doesn't know, doesn't remember. He does remember the teaching machines, the way his friend smuggled him in and hooked him up and filled his head with knowledge and experience that was impossible to get on Exegol any other way.

But he hasn't spoken to him in a long time. Again, he wonders—is this a part of his dark design, has it all been planned this way, arranged by his father?

He doesn't know. But right now, he has no choice.

He finds his friend among the other captives—a Symeong, older than the others, an administrator, enjoying some measure of autonomy and purpose while still remaining enslaved himself.

It is too easy. At least, that's what it feels like. His friend smuggles him aboard the visitors' ship, sealing him inside a compartment not made for a person. Before the panel is closed, the Symeong lifts the chain and amulet from his own neck and puts it around the boy's.

May the hex charm bring you luck and safety, as it has brought luck and safety to me.

And, he adds, with a chuckle, it will make him invisible. Because if he is really doing this, then he is going to need to be invisible. The galaxy is a big place, as the boy has learned from the teaching machines and is about to discover for himself, but his father is the Emperor Palpatine, who commands not only an Empire but a dark and terrible power.

The boy holds the amulet in his hand, in the darkness of the secret compartment. He holds it all the way on the uncomfortable journey, and still holds it as the compartment is opened and he is smuggled out.

The spaceport is called Koke Frost and it is large and it is dirty, and it is filled with life, a hundred species working on and around a fleet of ships. He hides at first, sticking to the shadows and to the dark corners like he always has, watching and learning, biding his time. The port is busy, serving some heavy industry.

This is it. The moment. The crossroads. The first step to a new life entirely.

He eavesdrops, learns which ships want crews, learns which crews ask questions—and which don't. He picks his opportunity—a sun-scooper needs an engine team and the owner is both desperate and in a hurry to meet his commission.

He hires the boy without a glance, and as the boy is handed the ship's crew register, realizing that his dream is coming true, that he is really going to get away, he also realizes that this is the moment his new life begins.

He looks at the register. The captain tells him to hurry up or he'll have to find another ship. Just sign your name on the line and get to work.

A name.

The boy panics. A name is the one thing he doesn't have. And now, as the captain taps his boot and starts to look at him strangely, he realizes that he needs to make a decision, and fast.

A name. The boy signs the register, borrowing the name of his Symeong friend, the only being who acknowledged his existence. Who raised him, who looked after him, who helped his dream come true.

Dathan signs the register, and his new life begins.

CHAPTER 8

THE *LADY LUCK,*
BOXER POINT STATION, JANX SYSTEM
NOW

An hour later, Lando walked onto the flight deck of his luxury space yacht the *Lady Luck*, the long, blade-shaped craft berthed just a quarter turn around the upper ring of Boxer Point Station. The ship, with its smooth white lines, elegantly sculpted all the way from the twin hyperdrive pods up to the bridge viewports and, farther back, the raised slope of the observation deck, had been Lando's pride and joy longer than any other vessel he'd owned, and as he'd trotted up the entry ramp, it really felt like coming home.

And now, after a scalding-hot shower, he was starting to feel more like himself. To his dismay, the slime from the Muqularan had set like cement, and it had taken him an age just to get the stuff off. He padded around to the main console, a brilliant spectrum-patterned towel wrapped firmly around his middle, another in green with gold edging being used to dry his hair.

Lando checked the computer's security data. Nobody had come knocking while he'd been cleaning himself up. He hadn't expected his erstwhile sabacc players to find him—he hadn't used his real identity in the game, and they would have no idea what his ship was or where it was berthed—but he knew it paid to be cautious nonetheless.

Hair mostly presentable, he neatly folded the green towel and placed it on the copilot's flight seat before he dropped himself into the pilot's. He ran the overheard conversation from Sennifer's back in his mind. A Sith Jedi hunter, hired to kidnap a girl—and Ochi's muttered story of the girl's family being rescued by the New Republic from an earlier kidnap attempt, out in Wild Space? That was a weird one. Ochi had mentioned the word "Halo." Was that a . . . squadron? Maybe. It wasn't a call sign Lando was familiar with, but he hadn't exactly been keeping up with New Republic military matters.

But he needed to know more—and he knew just who to ask.

Settling into the pilot's seat, Lando punched up the comm panel and within a couple of minutes had gotten through to precisely the right person.

"Lando Calrissian, the one and the only," came the gruff male voice over the loudspeaker.

Lando relaxed. It sure was good to hear a familiar voice. "Shriv Suurgav! My man, it has been a minute."

"You're telling me. You still owe me five credits."

Lando sat back in his chair and blinked. "Hey, I used to be a general, you know. You ever heard of a Death Star? I blew it up. That was me, Shriv."

Shriv's sigh came across the comm loud and clear. Lando smiled and stretched out his hands behind his still-damp head.

"But listen, Shriv, I'm afraid this isn't a social call."

"I figured."

"I need you to check in on something for me."

"Officially?"

Lando frowned. "Officially unofficial," he said. "But you get stuck, I can give you my command code. I still hold rank, last time I checked, but I'd rather this be off the books."

"Okay, let me have it," said Shriv. "What do you need?"

Lando leaned forward, took a moment to gather his thoughts, then spoke into the console mic.

. . .

Shriv's search had taken longer than Lando had anticipated, but then again, he trusted his old friend to be discreet, and sometimes being discreet took time. But he was grateful that he'd kept in touch with the Duros, and even if he wasn't entirely sure what his position was, he knew Shriv was deep enough inside the New Republic machine to be a useful contact.

Maybe he should have gone to him before, Lando thought. Shriv was a good man and a good friend. There had been times over the last few years that Lando had needed both, not just at the end of a comm unit but there, by his side.

While he waited, Lando had gotten dressed, a scarlet tunic with a wraparound front, and sharp black trousers with a silver embroidered seam down the side. He combed his hair and his mustache, and slipped on a pair of very comfortable and exquisitely vintage elastic-sided boots. Now *that*, he thought, felt better.

The comm pinged just as he returned to the flight deck.

"Shriv, what have you got?"

"Well, I've found the report," came Shriv's voice. "You know—" he continued, and then he stopped.

Lando frowned. "What is it?"

"This is perhaps a little more sensitive than I bargained for, Lando. The report came from Halo Squadron. Their mission is out in Wild Space, and the folks in charge, they're a little . . . touchy. My search will have left a trail, and there're going to be questions."

"Okay, no problem," said Lando. "Log it with my code, and they can come to me if they want to complain."

"Deal. I'll transmit the report now. Good talking to you, Lando."

"And you."

Lando cut the comm channel, then reached forward as the display showed Shriv's transmission ready to be accepted. Lando hit CONFIRM, then, leaning on his elbows, began to read.

The report was sobering. A family: a mother, father, young daughter, attacked by what the New Republic patrol had classified as pirates, their own ship—a barely serviceable hulk salvaged from the scrapyards of Jakku—in a bad way and able to make only one more jump.

Lando felt his jaw tighten as he read about the poor family—clearly desperate, clearly on the run from something. There was an attachment to the report. Lando hit the button and the holoprojector on the console sprang into life, rendering a three-dimensional image in ghostly blue in the air.

Lando sat back and peered at it, tilting his head as he examined the object. It was an amulet, on the end of a chain—diamond-shaped, almost like a stylized dagger or arrowhead, inside a circle. It was clearly a symbol of some kind, but not one that meant anything to Lando.

With the holoimage still on display, he continued to read, and then—

"What the . . . ?"

The amulet, according to the report, had been presented by the mother, who said it was proof that they were being chased by the Sith.

Lando felt his blood run cold. Everything Ochi had said in the Beam and Balance, despite his drunken haze, had been the truth. He was working for the Sith, and the Sith wanted the girl. *Their* girl.

Lando sat and stared at the holoimage in horror. He thought of this family, out on their own, desperately running from an enemy that Lando suspected would simply not give up. He didn't know who Ochi of Bestoon was, but he'd said he had been in the service of the Sith before. Lando had never even heard of him.

Kadara Calrissian.

Lando's daughter entered his thoughts, his subconscious catastrophizing already. Was that why Lando had never found her, or heard even a wisp of rumor about her? Had she been taken by the Sith? It would mean, if she was still alive, that she was in even greater danger than he had realized.

Lando sighed and sat back again, his face in his hands, as he ran options through his mind.

What was he going to do? This now felt . . . big. Felt *huge.*

Then he sat back up.

Okay, okay. Think, think.

Exegol.

Lando reached forward and brought the *Lady Luck*'s navicomputer online, and began trawling through its database. A few minutes in, and he knew—as he had perhaps suspected—that the world or system was not charted. He spent a few more minutes diving through the rest of the databank, trying different spellings, tangential keyword searches, anything he could think of.

Nothing.

Lando considered. The family needed help—and, sure, even as he thought it, he knew he was using this as a distraction, an excuse to do something to help them when he couldn't do anything to help *himself.*

But he had to help them. Because . . . what if this was *precisely* the clue he had gone to Boxer Point Station to find? What if this was the moment he could crack the whole thing open—a kidnap operation, led by the Sith.

If he could help the family, save their daughter . . . perhaps he could find his own.

Lando checked the report again. The author, one Flight Sergeant Dina Dipurl, had added an addendum, noting that she had sent the family to a safe harbor they could potentially seek refuge in, and that Dipurl herself had sent a transmission ahead to a contact there, requesting assistance on the family's behalf.

Lando clicked his fingers.

Good work, Flight Sergeant. Good work indeed.

Only problem was, the coordinates of the safe harbor were redacted. Halo Squadron, as Shriv had indicated, was on a sensitive mission. It was likely the redaction had been automatic. The data was *there*—it was just that Lando couldn't see it.

But . . . it was a start. And a promising one, at that. The information Lando had gathered was more valuable than he had initially realized, and he couldn't shake the growing feeling he'd stumbled onto something that was perhaps even bigger, more important.

What he needed was help. Lando thought again of Shriv—he did have to get those redacted coordinates, after all, and perhaps a personal visit was in order—but he also rolled around a couple of other words in his mind.

Sith.

Vader.

There was only one man in the galaxy Lando could go to.

With deft movements over the controls, Lando disengaged the hangar lock and sent the Boxer Point Station harbormaster his exit payment—the very last of his available credits—and as the automatic timer to launch came up on the navicomputer, Lando Calrissian set course for the Galactic Core.

It was time to talk to an old friend.

CHAPTER 9

LERCT HISTORICAL INSTITUTE
ARCHAEOLOGICAL EXPEDITION, YOTURBA
NOW

As planets went, Yoturba was not the most interesting, but neither was it the most boring. Its climate was . . . fine. Comfortable, habitable. Maybe slightly too much oxygen, giving you a certain lightheadedness if you worked too hard. There were no hostile life-forms, which was a definite plus. The last planet he'd been to a dig on with the Lerct Historical Institute—Vavarna, and even the name of the place made him shudder—the plant life had tried to eat him, the tendrils of vegetation not even trying to hide themselves as they crept all over the dig site, taking tools and samples, making valiant, but ultimately fruitless, attempts to pull workers away from their tasks.

So sure, Yoturba didn't have that. Problem was, it didn't have much of anything else. Including anything of archaeological interest.

Which was a distinct problem for an archaeologist.

Beaumont Kin lowered his datapad and looked out across the field from his vantage point, standing atop a mound of soft-packed dirt created by his team's initial excavations. Shielding his eyes from the glare of the sun, he watched as his fellow archaeologists busied themselves over the spread of ruins that covered the square kilometer or so of open space that sat in the middle of the dense forest.

Of course, it was a big site, and there were ruins of something large and substantial, and that in itself was intrinsically *archaeological*, but already Beaumont was dreading writing the monograph he would have to prepare on the project.

No. Not "the" project. *His* project. *His* expedition.

His baby.

He smiled at this and lowered his hand. Yes, it was all his. Although Beaumont was only a junior research assistant, his mentor, Professor Re-Bec Arclarka, had clearly seen something in his work. It was that study of Maleinatori tablet inscriptions and their relation to the constellations over Billaron and modern-day star charts. Beaumont nodded, satisfied, at the memory. Not a bad little bit of research, even if he did say so himself. The Hoopaloo professor was notoriously hard to please, and Beaumont had considered winning the professional respect of the prickly academic something of a career achievement.

If only this project would result in a text anything like as interesting. Beaumont doubted it. When he got back to Hosnian Prime he had five thousand words to write and a tight deadline and . . . he wasn't entirely sure what he was going to say.

The Yoturba dig site was massive, but it was also old, so old that the ruins of the settlement, whatever it had been, had eroded to mere rows of buried stone humps, between which the thirty or so archaeologists—a mix of students, researcher assistants like Beaumont, and a handful of older, more experienced academics who had promised to lend a hand, as well as machine help, dig droids as they were called—worked in long trenches.

So far, they'd found . . . nothing. In fact, they'd found so much *nothing* that some of those senior academics had suggested to their team leader that it might be best to wrap it up and get back to Hosnian Prime before Yoturba's legendary rains arrived, which were apparently already overdue. Beaumont, despite their protestations, had told them they were staying. His mentor, Arclarka, who had insisted on coming along, had agreed with him.

But not, Beaumont suspected, because there was any scientific value in staying. On the contrary, Arclarka was more concerned with the honor of the dig having a special visitor.

Two visitors, actually, although Beaumont had hardly seen anything of one of them. Even as he thought about the pair, he turned and saw one of them approaching from the other side of the forest clearing, away from the dig, where the team had established their base camp of prefab huts, spread out in a small area in front of the two spacecraft they had arrived in, a third ship, belonging to the visitors, parked a little farther away.

Beaumont lifted his datapad in greeting as the older man approached. The visitor had about forty years on the young academic, his features chiseled but still warm beneath a crop of tightly buzzed dark-gray hair. Lor San Tekka was no archaeologist, nor even an academic, but his knowledge of ancient myths and stories, cultures, society, and the relics they left behind was recognized even in the highest academic circles. Even the stuffy, by-the-book Arclarka was pleased he was here.

"How goes the dig?"

Beaumont juggled his shoulders and clutched his datapad tight to his chest—rather defensively, he realized, before making himself relax and letting his arms drop to his sides.

"We're nearly done, I think. We could excavate a little deeper, cut in some new trenches and see if we can expand out to the southwest corner"—at this, he indicated with one hand—"but I'm not sure if there's any point. We haven't found anything other than these foundations. No artifacts, not even any rubbish." He glanced at the older man. "Certainly no relics," he said, with a grin, then shook his head. "Certainly nothing with any writing on it."

Lor San Tekka nodded as he looked out over the dig. Beaumont followed his gaze, watching as a trio of white-shirted archaeologists directed a dig droid, which then moved forward and began scanning the area they had finished with a red laser array, the pencil-thin beams dancing as they took a complete and accurate holorecording of their work.

The two men stood in silence. Then Beaumont cleared his throat. "So . . ."

Lor San Tekka smiled. "You want to ask why we're here."

Beaumont glanced sideways at him, feeling his face flush, but he noticed that the older man was smiling, just slightly.

"Actually, yes, I would."

"I was told of your expedition," said Lor San Tekka. "Oh yes," he continued, as Beaumont's forehead creased in confusion. "Your reputation begins to grow, Dr. Kin. I brought Master Skywalker here. The preliminary field report lodged at the institute suggested that this settlement you have uncovered may have had a Jedi temple. There are precious few such sites recorded." He grinned. "I apologize for the intrusion, but I thought it was worth a look."

Beaumont pursed his lips, then nodded and returned his gaze to the field ahead.

That felt . . . rather good, actually. People knew his work? People outside the institute?

Well now.

And then his expression dropped as he remembered what he'd put into that initial field report. He'd been accurate and scientific, certainly, but he might have been a little . . . overenthusiastic in his assessment of the large, but very uninteresting, site.

A few more moments of silence passed, then Beaumont took a breath, adjusted his grip on the datapad again, and turned to Lor San Tekka.

"I'm very gratified by your visit, but I'm just sorry this place is so . . . well." He gestured to the field, then sighed. "I've used an entire semester's research grant for this project." He paused, a sudden thought occurring to him. "I mean, Master Skywalker is a Jedi Knight. If there's any way he could . . . well . . ."

Beaumont trailed off. Lor San Tekka glanced at him.

"Well, what?"

"Well," said Beaumont. "You know." He waved his hand at the dig site. "You *know*."

Lor San Tekka grinned. "Perhaps I do, but that's not how it works."

"Ah, no, of course not," said Beaumont, feeling rather foolish. "Silly me."

Lor San Tekka patted the archaeologist on the shoulder, then turned to survey the view. Looking back at the encampment and landing area, he stopped, a smile growing on his face. "But perhaps," he said, "you can ask him for his own opinion."

Beaumont spun around, his boots sinking into the soft dirt, as a black-robed figure walked up the slope toward them, hands hidden within the voluminous sleeves, hood pulled low. Beaumont watched as the man reached them, his throat suddenly very dry. He opened his mouth to say something just as the man threw back his hood and extended a black-gloved hand.

"Dr. Kin," said Luke Skywalker, "thank you for being so accommodating."

Beaumont stared at the outstretched hand for a moment before pulling himself together. He took a breath, then took the hand.

"Ah, of course, Master Skywalker, it's an honor, really." He felt himself relax under the warm smile of the Jedi, and he chuckled. "I just wish there was more I could show you. So far this dig has been a little, well . . ." Momentarily lost for words, he panicked—just a little—and glanced at Lor San Tekka.

The older man grinned and turned to Luke. "*Disappointing,* I think, is the word Dr. Kin is looking for." Then his smile dropped, and he pointed over Luke's shoulder. Beaumont moved to see past Lor San Tekka's look, a sinking feeling developing somewhere in his stomach.

"Oh," he said, as he watched his supervisor and mentor, Professor Arclarka, clamber up the slope toward the group, his winglike arms flapping, his beak clattering as he seemed to be trying to get Beaumont's attention. "Ah, excuse me, would you?"

Luke gave Beaumont a small bow, while Lor San Tekka nodded and stepped aside. Beaumont slid down the hill, wondering what the professor was in such a fuss about.

Luke watched as the archaeologist almost slid down the slope, and laughed softly.

"No temple, I'm afraid," said Lor.

Luke turned and looked down over the dig site. They'd been here several hours now, mostly leaving the archaeologists to their work. Luke had reviewed their catalog of finds while Lor had taken a more personal approach, asking students about their discoveries and discussing the site with Professor Arclarka.

"No temple, no artifacts," said Luke.

Lor laughed, and gestured back toward where Beaumont and the professor were locked in close conversation. "They are, at least, all very pleased to have us here."

Luke moved past Lor San Tekka and cast an eye over the main dig site. He didn't respond.

Lor looked at him. "What is it? You feel something?"

Luke frowned. "I'm not sure. It feels like you brought me here for a reason."

"I did! I thought it might be interesting."

"No, not that," said Luke. "I didn't want to say anything before, not until I was sure."

"Sure of what?"

Luke cocked his head, then shook it. "There's something—"

"Master Skywalker! Ah, sirs!"

Beaumont's voice caused both Luke and Lor to turn around as the young archaeologist scrambled up the slope.

"What is it?" asked Lor.

"We've found something," said Beaumont.

"There he is."

Luke stopped at the base of the mound as beside him, Beaumont pointed, then waved back to the archaeologist on the other side of the dig who had both arms raised to catch the attention of the group.

"Maybe this dig wasn't a total washout after all, *kwark*," muttered Arclarka. Luke glanced at the Hoopaloo professor, his silky brown plumage hidden under layers of colorful academic robes that he had seen fit to don for his and Lor's visit. Arclarka clacked his large yellow beak a couple of times, then spread a feathered armlike wing. "Shall we, gentlemen?" He turned and led the way, Beaumont, Lor San Tekka, and Luke following behind.

This, Luke knew, was why he was here. The feeling was much stronger now, like a lodestone pulling him in. He didn't know what the archaeologist had uncovered, but he was *certain* it was nothing good. As he walked across the carefully laid-out boards that crisscrossed the dig, he allowed himself a small smile. Oh, how cynical he had become.

As the group approached the site of interest, the archaeologist, a young student, turned from the dig droid and brushed her dirt-caked hands on her already dirt-caked white tunic. She gave the group a big, lopsided grin, and then a more respectful nod of the head to Professor Arclarka.

"Well? Well? What have you found?" squawked Arclarka.

At this, the young student frowned. "Ah, I'm not actually sure. Yet, anyway." She gestured to the dig droid, which beeped like an astromech but in much lower tones, its shiny octagonal body rotating as it hovered evenly a meter from the ground, coming to a smooth halt by the group.

The student pulled gently at the side of the droid, turning it around a little more, until a folded-down panel that formed one of the droid's sides was presented to them, an ideal, portable worktop for an archaeologist to clean and study finds.

The group peered at the object on display, which the student had freed from a large mass of clay. The object was, or had been, a polyhedron of some kind, with a square base and tapering sides that might have come to a point if the object had been undamaged. It was, however, partially crushed, the sides askew, like it had been flattened under a great weight, bending the metal frame that ran along the vertices of the object, holding some kind of semi-translucent, crystalline substance—now reduced to broken shards—that formed the main body of the thing.

Arclarka hummed, his beak vibrating, as he looked at the find.

"Interesting, *kwark*. Most interesting. Theories, Ms. . . . ?"

"Mairi, sir," said the student. "Tee Mairi." She looked at the object and folded her arms. "And none as yet, sir. It looks like a piece of art, rather than anything utilitarian." She frowned. "Although we haven't found anything else that could give it context, so I just don't know." She unfolded her arms and reached to pick the object up. "If you look at the—"

Mairi gasped as Luke grabbed her hand before she could touch it. She looked at him, her eyes wide in surprise, but Luke's attention was only on the object on the tray.

Luke glanced sideways at Lor San Tekka, who met his gaze and gave a tiny, almost imperceptible nod. Luke turned to Mairi and released his grip.

"I'm sorry," he said, "but this is as important as it is dangerous."

Beaumont peered at the object. "It looks familiar, I think. I've seen it in my research." He looked up at Luke. "Do you know what it is?"

Luke nodded. "It's a Sith Holocron," he said quietly. "Or at least, what's left of one."

Arclarka's beak clacked. "A Sith Holocron? Are you sure?"

Luke nodded. He pointed at the thicker metal framework that formed the base of the object, and, with a gloved thumb, gently rubbed the surface to remove more of the dirt, revealing writing in a sharp, angular script that seemed to run all along the edge.

Mairi frowned. "It feels like I should be able to read that."

"That's because you can," Luke said. He picked up the smashed holocron off the tray in one hand and gently pushed the dig droid with his other hand, spinning it around until one of the flat, chromed sides was facing them. Holding the holocron close to the panel, he pointed at the reflection in the droid's casing.

Beaumont Kin moved around to get a better look, peering at the reflective side of the droid so closely that his nose was almost touching the metal.

"Is that . . ."

He paused, glanced at Luke, then turned back to the reflection. "Is that *backward* Aurebesh?"

Luke nodded. "It is."

Beaumont stepped back. "I can recognize the characters, but I can't read it. It looks like a bunch of random letters." He put his hands on his hips. "Why would they bother to engrave something backward when the text is scrambled anyway?"

"It's not scrambled."

Beaumont turned. This was Lor San Tekka. He was staring at the smashed holocron, his hands clasped behind his back, like he was trying to resist the temptation to touch the object.

"The Sith had their own language and script," he continued, "but not all who thought themselves adherents of that misguided path were themselves fluent in it. Some had transcribed their own runic alphabet into Aurebesh, and they adopted a method of writing it in reflected characters."

Beaumont nodded, slowly at first, then with growing speed. As a grin began to spread across his face, he clapped his hands. "This is incredible," he said. "We've dug up nothing of any interest for weeks and weeks, and now we—sorry, *you*, Tee—uncover a genuine Sith relic." He blinked. "I've never seen anything like it." He turned to his supervisor. "Professor Arclarka, we need to take this back to the institute so I can begin work. Just think of the new lines of research this will open up for us." He paused and stood stock-still, his eyes now focused somewhere in the middle distance between himself and the others. He slowly raised a hand and clicked his fingers. "I could change my dissertation." He blinked, bringing himself out of his temporary daydream. "Nobody at the institute is studying the Sith." He gestured at the holocron. "This could be the first artifact of a new collection."

At this, Professor Arclarka held up a clawed hand. He snapped his beak in irritation before speaking quietly. "Beaumont Kin, while I appreciate your enthusiasm, *kwark*, you must not allow your excitement to cloud your judgment. There has been no study of the Sith and their history at the institute for very good reason, young man."

Beaumont shook his head. "But that's what I'm saying, Professor. This can be the beginning. We can start, right now."

Arclarka's feathered crest shook. "Beaumont Kin! The occult and the arcane have no place in the halls of the Lerct Historical Institute. Why, the very thought of it!"

Lor San Tekka and Luke Skywalker exchanged a glance, then Lor indicated with his head that they should give the two academics some space. Laying a gentle hand on Luke's shoulder, he led them a few meters away, turning so they had their backs to the main dig site.

Lor leaned in to Luke. "Is this what you sensed?"

Luke stroked his short beard with the fingers of his human hand. "I'm not certain. A holocron is just a data store, and even if this one held anything important, it's completely smashed."

Lor raised an eyebrow. "So there's something else here?"

"I'm not sure," Luke murmured. "There's . . . something. Here, or very near." He narrowed his eyes and reached out with one hand, concentrating on the feeling that now grew and grew in his mind, chasing it like a tooka-cat would chase a thread.

Then he sighed, heavily, and blew out his cheeks.

"Or maybe not," Luke said with a chuckle.

Lor San Tekka smiled warmly and clapped his friend on the shoulder. He opened his mouth to speak, and that was when the screaming began.

CHAPTER 10

LERCT HISTORICAL INSTITUTE
ARCHAEOLOGICAL EXPEDITION, YOTURBA
NOW

Mico Haswell swore loudly, enjoying the way his voice echoed in the stone chamber. He threw down his tool—an old-fashioned durasteel trowel, traditional archaeology through and through—and also enjoyed the way it clanged against the old stones, the sound sharp and unpleasant, and, he knew, thoroughly annoying to his colleagues working nearby.

Oh, yes. *Colleagues.* Well, wasn't that a joke? Haswell had a whole ten years on all of them—the humans, anyway, he didn't know or much care about the others working on the dig, better they just keep to themselves and not annoy him and the other humans. Okay, so he was still a junior research fellow, but come on, his work was important and difficult and these things took *time,* any fool knew that, which was why his academic progression had been . . . sluggish, at best.

Slow and steady wins the race. That was Mico Haswell's axiom, one he repeated to himself each and every day when he saw old students graduate and the new intakes arrive, all wide-eyed and fresh-faced and completely ignorant of the work that he was doing.

Slow and steady wins the race. And, oh yes, he was going to win, all right. He was going to show all of them. Every last one.

Especially Beaumont Kin. Seriously, *that guy*. He was short and funny looking and who knew where his accent came from. Wasn't a Core World, that's for sure. He probably came from some pathetic backwater, Tatooine or Dantooine, probably had some kind of scholarship, fulfilled some kind of quota so Lerct Historical Institute would look good, something to use in advertising, when Mico Haswell knew full well that the only thing that mattered was *ability*. Which he had. In spades—today, quite literally.

So why he'd been assigned to this dig, he didn't know. Professor Arclarka was an idiot. How was a Hoopaloo even allowed through the institute doors, let alone given a job—a professor's chair! Another quota, probably. Another box checked, another round of gentle applause and a sip of something outrageously expensive in the chancellor's office.

But the fact was—and it didn't take Mico Haswell's vast experience and knowledge of these things to work it out—that this dig was a bust. Yoturba was uninteresting. The ruins were uninteresting. Sure, it was a big site, but they'd found nothing.

Mico sat heavily on the edge of the wall behind him and wiped his brow. The chamber to which he'd been assigned was the partially collapsed shell of a building, one of the few larger structures that was still partially intact, with half of a domed roof still standing. It was, at least, one of the more promising sites among the whole dig for investigation, and Haswell had at least gotten to work on his own trench with some thought and precision.

Because Mico Haswell was no amateur—he knew fieldwork. He knew it a whole lot better than most of the others in this sorry little expedition. While the others knelt in the dirt and sifted through dust and *ooh*ed and *ahh*ed at every little rock they uncovered, loading the trays of their dig droids with worthless bits of dirt, Haswell was going to find something good. Something *important*. It would be him, and everyone would have to acknowledge that and congratulate him on his work. Even Arclarka.

Even Beaumont Kin.

Rolling his neck, he readied himself to get back to work. He looked down and around, trying to see where his thrown trowel had bounced.

After a few seconds, he caught a glimpse of the shining silver durasteel of its blade sticking out from behind a curved block of grayish stone.

He moved over and knelt down, reaching forward to pick up the tool, and then he stopped. He spun around on the ground, eyes scanning the open section of the wall that held up the remains of the roof, the rest of the site stretching out back toward their camp.

Someone had crept up behind him, tickled the back of his neck, he was sure of it.

"Yes, very good," he said, then he frowned. He could see three—no, four students working nearby, out in the open beyond the wall, two dig droids hovering close, one with its trays already laden with finds. None of them, droid or human, was paying him the slightest bit of attention, despite his earlier tantrum.

Typical.

But . . . someone had been playing a trick, hadn't they? Someone had sneaked in behind him, being childish in the extreme.

And then—

Mico.

He spun around. The voice, the *whisper,* had come from right in front of him, which was impossible, because he was kneeling on the ground in front of a huge gray curve of stone, and there was no way there was anyone else in the chamber with him.

Mico Mico Mico Mico Mico Mico Mico.

He found his voice. "Hello?" He sounded a lot weaker than he had expected. But as he spoke, the whispering of his name stopped. The half chamber was still and silent. Mico couldn't even hear the others outside, continuing with their slow work, the hum of hovering dig droids, their low electronic tones burbling at regular intervals. All of it was gone. The silence that enveloped the space was so total, so . . . *whole* . . . that Mico felt like he was being wrapped in a fineweave padding, ready for shipping out in a crate, just another relic recovered from a forgotten ruin on an uninteresting planet at the edge of the Mid Rim.

It was getting dark, too. Mico reached forward, hands groping the air as the light seemed to dim, like a sudden nightfall, or—

Or like a shadow being cast, eclipsing the sun, covering the landscape in a pall of darkness.

That was when he saw it. There, on the ground, next to his silver trowel, the blade of which had scoured the ground to reveal something hidden just below the surface. Something bright, something red, something that shone with a light all of its own in the rapidly gathering gloom.

Mico reached for the object. He'd done it. He'd found . . . something. Something better than what the others had managed to dig up. Something important. Something *valuable*. Treasure! Treasure and

Mico Mico Mico Mico Mico Mico Mico

it was all his. His discovery. His work. His

Mico Mico Mico Mico Mico Mico Mico

fame and his fortune and this was it and

Mico Mico Mico Mico Mico Mico Mico

and he picked the object up. It was both hot and cold, his fingers both numb and on fire as he lifted the relic from the dirt and stared into it.

It was a crystal, or part of one. A large, multi-sided shard. It was deep red in color. One end was a perfect hexagonal crown, the other split and broken. Mico squinted at it, the light it seemed to reflect from somewhere unknown, bright and dazzling. Through the flashing purple streaks in his vision, he could see more pieces of the crystal in the dirt, like it had been one larger piece that had shattered under the collapsing roof of the chamber centuries ago.

And

Mico Mico Mico Mico Mico Mico Mico

he'd found it. He was the one. This was his. Nobody else would have it. Nobody else would even *know* about it. Not yet. Not until he

Mico Mico Mico Mico Mico Mico Mico

was ready.

He had found it.

And *it* had found *him*.

"Hey, what's that?"

Still kneeling on the ground, Mico jolted in place, like the new voice had just delivered him a huge electric shock. He turned his head, willing himself to take his eyes off the crystal shard to see who had dared come into *his* area to interrupt *his* work. But . . . he didn't want to. He wanted to look at the crystal, to study it, to imagine the possibilities. The intruder, how dare they come in here, interrupt him, spoil his moment.

He craned his neck around, the grimace in his face already formed by the time he looked at the intruder. It was a young man, his big hair ridiculously impractical for fieldwork. But that was the thing, wasn't it? These kids, they didn't take it seriously, they didn't know what work was, not like Mico did. He knew more about archaeology and excavations than all of them put together.

"Get out," he snarled.

For a moment, the young man looked shocked, then the expression vanished and he frowned and shook his head and the hair that went with it.

"Oh, suit yourself, Mico," he said. "I thought you'd had an accident or something." He lifted a hand and waved it dismissively at him. "Next time, I won't bother. None of us will, you can trust me on that one."

He turned to leave, his slim form a silhouette against the sky.

Mico Haswell blinked into the daylight, but it was dull, flat, gray; a dead light, not like the spinning red of the crystal, the one he'd found, his treasure, the crystal that

Mico Mico Mico Mico Mico Mico Mico

spoke to him, that knew him, that told him what to

Mico Mico Mico Mico Mico Mico Mico

do, that gave him the power to do it, and all he had to do was—

The young man froze where he was, his outline shaking slightly. Mico stood awkwardly, one hand clutching the crystal shard, squeezing it until the skin of his knuckles was white, the other hand reaching out in front of him, reaching out to the student—Kirs, was it?—holding on to him even though he was out of reach, holding him right where he was, every muscle of the young, strong body under his control.

"Did I say you could leave?" Mico's voice was a harsh whisper, and inside his head it echoed and rasped like the voice of the crystal, like it wasn't him speaking but he was just reciting the words it fed him. Mico's vision clouded, narrowed into a tunnel. But despite this, he saw with a clarity unlike anything he'd experienced before.

He took a step forward. He flexed the fingers of his outstretched hand, then flicked his wrist, and Kirs spun around to face the older man, shoulders bunched up, the student standing on his toes, his balance far too forward, almost as though it was Mico who was holding him upright. Mico wondered if he could lift Kirs up just by thinking about it, and even as he did, Kirs rose in the air, just a few centimeters. Mico's eyes widened in surprise at this . . . what was it, exactly, this feeling?

Control. That was it. For once, Mico felt . . . strong. Powerful, even. He didn't quite know what he was doing, even as a part of his mind screamed at him that this *wasn't* happening, this *couldn't* be happening, *how* was this even happening, but it felt . . .

It felt good.

The young student's eyes were wide, Kirs as surprised as Mico. His mouth was open, and his chest fluttered, like he was gasping for air, because he was, because Mico controlled every muscle in his body, including the ones that let him breathe.

Mico felt something else, then. A . . . warmth. Something comforting, like someone was pleased with him, that he was doing well. He wanted to turn around, to gaze at the presence at his shoulder, the force that was there, guiding him, lifting his hand and wrapping around his fist, the lips whispering in his ear, up close and personal, approving.

The world continued to darken. In front of him, Kirs gasped for breath, held by the invisible force in the air. Mico stared at him, but he was fading, everything was fading, and then—

A flash of light, and then another, and then another, a staccato burst of lightning in a dark sky filled with roiling clouds, a thunderstorm over a landscape so old, so dry, so dead, Mico could feel his skin tighten, his mouth dry, filled with the taste of ash, his eyes gritty with a black dust that spun and whirled in eddies all around him. The lightning flashed and shorted into the hard ground all around him.

And he was there, now. Not in the chamber, not on Yoturba, but in this place, this blasted hellscape, a flat plain of cracked basalt that stretched away in every direction, so vast and wide that it felt claustrophobic, an inescapable prison of open space.

The lightning flashed again. There, on the horizon, a shape, a structure, immense and shadowed, towering into the black clouds, the edges glowing a blue so electric, Mico couldn't tell if it was real or just the afterglow in his eyes as the lightning flashed and flashed and flashed. The building—was it a building? A pyramid . . . no, a ziggurat? Temple? Citadel?—ancient and awful and mathematically precise, seemed to float above the cursed surface of this black world.

He felt it then. That presence, behind him, whispering in his ear, pushing him forward, toward the building. Only . . . he didn't want to go. He didn't want to be here. He didn't even know where here was. He was on Yoturba, at the stupid dig, inside the half-broken chamber, the only place where there was any hope of finding anything interesting—

He lifted his hand. He looked down. He opened his fist, saw the crystal shard, the thing glowing with a light of its own, the brilliant scarlet the only color in Mico Haswell's entire universe and

Mico Mico Mico Mico Mico Mico Mico

he opened his mouth, breathed in a lungful of dust-choked air, and screamed.

Luke spun around at the sound, eyes searching the dig, picking out the individual workers, the floating droids. And he saw—

"What's wrong?"

Lor was at his side, one warm hand on his shoulder again. Luke narrowed his eyes, then glanced at his old friend.

"Didn't you hear that?"

Lor frowned. "Hear what?" he asked. Each man met the other's gaze, and Luke knew immediately that there was no judgment in Lor San Tekka's voice, only concern.

If Luke Skywalker had sensed something—*heard* something?—then there was reason for concern.

Luke turned back to the dig. "I'm not sure. I thought I heard something."

Lor's hand dropped from his shoulder and he walked a tight circle. Beaumont, Professor Arclarka, and Tee Mairi were still huddled in discussion by the dig droid. Around the site, workers continued with their tasks.

Lor turned and looked back up at Luke. "You sensed there was something else here. More than just that holocron."

Luke sighed. "Something's wrong, all right. I just don't know what—"

That was when someone screamed, and this time the sound was very real. Luke heard it, and so did Lor, and so did everyone at the dig, everyone all around stopping and turning, almost in perfect unison, toward the source.

At the far end of the dig, the buildings of the ruined settlement were more complete, the biggest of which was a low dome, half of which was still intact. As Luke watched, he saw something fly out of the side of the building and realized, with horror, that it was a person, thrown bodily with great force.

Luke sprinted down the boardwalks that ran between the archaeological trenches toward the building. As he ran, he half turned, waving back at Lor.

"Stay with the others. Get everyone out of the site."

There was a crash from ahead of him. He turned back around, then skidded to a halt.

A man ran out of the domed building. He was hunched over and off balance. He careened into the trestle tables that were set up outside the building, jolting the tools off the first and knocking the second clean over. As Luke watched, the man leaned over the still-upright table, breathing heavily, his eyes, Luke noticed, screwed firmly shut. Then he threw back his head and screamed, and flipped the light table over with both hands.

At once, the nearest dig droid shot through the air, its entire array of manipulator arms unfolding from its hexagonal body as it prepared to clean up the tools, the machine burbling furiously in its low Binary tones, clearly aggravated at the mess. As it came closer, the man stood tall and, eyes still closed, reached out with one hand. The droid was still two meters away but it stopped in the air and began to spin on its axis, faster and faster, its manipulator arms rising up and out from the centrifugal force.

There was a bang, and a puff of smoke from somewhere inside the droid, and it listed sharply to one side, although it remained hovering. Its spin slowed, and then stopped, and then, lopsided, it drifted away at an angle before finally hitting the ground softly a short distance away.

Luke knew then that he was *supposed* to be here. That feeling had grown and grown, right from when he and Lor had taken off from Ossus. He'd hidden that feeling from his friend, perhaps unwilling to admit that it could simply be the afterglow of his Force vision rather than a real premonition, Luke projecting that feeling onto his friend's invitation to visit the unremarkable archaeological dig.

Whatever the case, Force vision or premonition or just plain coincidence, Luke had been right to come.

Almost on cue, the man straightened and spun around to face Luke, standing tall, although his eyes were still shut tight. Luke licked his lips and braced himself. He didn't know quite what he was facing—he had theories, yes, even fears, but none of that mattered, not right now—and he didn't know how strong the man was. He was dressed like the others, casual Core World fashion underneath a more practical work vest, studded with pockets and pouches, a tool belt hung loosely around his hips, just like all the other archaeologists. The man looked older than most of the other humans on-site. Perhaps a research fellow, rather than a student.

Luke reached out with the Force. He didn't want to hurt the man, but neither did he want the man to hurt others, or himself. Luke narrowed his eyes in concentration, and by his side, his organic hand uncurled from its tight fist and stretched out so the palm was flat against his thigh.

Luke willed the man to be still, gently persuading him through the Force. The man stiffened, caught in the invisible grip.

There was a flash, then another, then another, and the world of Yoturba around Luke and the troubled young man vanished, replaced by a flat desert of black cracked rock, the dark sky overhead filled with clouds that billowed like smoke, lit by the furious, never-ending arcs of lightning.

It was the world of Luke's nightmares. He was back in a vision—only this time, he was not alone, the archaeologist still held by the Force.

"Who are you?" asked Luke, but his voice didn't seem to travel. It didn't matter. The man heard, his head snapped around, his eyes still shut tight. He snarled, a reptilian sound, revealing not human teeth but rows of razor-sharp, pointed fangs, and he leapt for Luke, breaking free of the Force and jumping toward him in a way that Luke knew no human could ever manage, not without a certain kind of assistance.

Luke reacted at once. He lifted his hand, the palm still flat, fingers outstretched, ready to meet the oncoming attacker. He felt it immediately, his own mastery of the Force meeting something equal but opposite, soft but still quite firm, like the two matching poles of a strong magnet coming together and meeting resistance.

The lightning flashed, bright enough that even Luke flinched.

When he opened his eyes, he was back on Yoturba. Around him, the workers from the Lerct Historical Institute kept a safe distance, but all were watching. Out of the corner of his eye, Luke could see three archaeologists kneeling by the crumpled form of the worker who had been thrown across the site, one of them, wearing the green sash of someone assigned as a field medic, already opening a medpac.

Luke looked back in front of him, his arm still outstretched.

The man was frozen in the air, held now by Luke's much stronger grip in the Force. The man struggled, spitting and snarling, but already the malign, mysterious presence Luke had sensed was beginning to fade.

"Luke, are you all right?"

Lor San Tekka arrived at Luke's elbow. He looked at Luke's arm, and then at the archaeologist suspended in the air. He opened his mouth to speak again but was interrupted by a series of loud, agitated squawks and the clatter of Professor Arclarka's heavy bill.

"What is the meaning of this, *kwark*? *Kwark!* What is going on here?" The Hoopaloo professor, angry rather than confused or afraid, approached the archaeologist. He took his eyeglasses from their chain around his neck and held them on the top of his beak as he peered at the man. "Haswell, isn't it? And just what do you think you're doing, *kwark*?" Arclarka gestured to the wrecked tables. "This is no way to be-have on an expedition of mine. There will be an inquiry when we get back to Hosnian Prime. Oh yes. Believe me, there will be."

When Haswell didn't answer, Arclarka looked at Luke. He waved a wing at him, completely unperturbed by the demonstration of Luke's power. "Well? Do you plan on keeping him like that all day?"

As he spoke, Haswell snarled again, forcing Luke to adjust his hold on the man, squeezing just a fraction tighter with his mind. For some-thing that seemed relatively simple, it was, in fact, a difficult task to perform: Such was the well of energy Luke could draw on that the slightest drop in his concentration could kill the man.

Sometimes, powerful was *too* powerful.

Luke jerked his head at the group treating the unconscious student. "Medic! I need you to sedate this man."

The medic looked up, then glanced at Haswell. Even from a distance of a dozen meters, Luke could see the fear on her face. But the woman gulped, and then nodded, turning back to the other two kneeling over the prone form and giving them instructions before taking a silver rod from the medical kit and running over to Haswell. She paused within touching distance, clearly unsure whether it was safe to proceed.

"It's fine," said Luke with a reassuring smile. "I'm holding him. Give him as much as you think is safe. We're going to need him out for a while."

The woman nodded and stepped closer to Haswell. She reached up—he was still being held approximately ten centimeters from the ground—and pulled back the collar of his vest to expose the jugular vein. Holding the collar back, she pressed the end of the silver cylinder against his skin and depressed a hidden button on the back with her thumb.

The effect was instantaneous. Haswell slumped, his head lolling against his chest. Luke could also feel a change—that malignant *other* had now gone altogether. Haswell now felt much lighter, like his mass had somehow been halved.

Luke relaxed his grip, lowering Haswell to the ground. As soon as the toes of Haswell's boots touched the dirt, the medic stepped behind and hooked her hands under his arms, gently lowering him flat on his back.

Luke exchanged a look with Lor, and the two men approached Haswell. Arclarka flapped and went to join them, but Beaumont Kin—wisely, thought Luke—distracted the professor, indicating they should give the others some space.

Luke knelt down by Haswell's supine form. Beside him, the medic moved back a little to give Luke room, but shook her head at him as she did so.

"I don't understand," she said. "I gave him enough to knock out a fathier." On the ground, Haswell writhed a little, held down by two burly archaeologists who had quickly joined the group. As Luke leaned over Haswell, he glanced at each of them and nodded.

"It's okay," he said, quietly. "It's fine. I'll be fine."

The two big men glanced at each other, then released their grip on Haswell's shoulders. They both rocked back on their haunches, close enough to spring into aid if needed.

Mico Haswell rolled his head, then took a huge gasp and opened his eyes. His breathing quickened as he looked around, an expression of pure terror on his face, his lips flecked with white foam.

The two other men moved in, but Luke waved them away. Luke laid his left hand on Haswell's shoulder, gently, not even pressing down. Immediately, the man jolted, then seemed to settle, as his unfocused gaze finally met Luke's.

"I . . . I . . . I . . ."

Luke smiled slightly. "It's okay. You're going to be all right. I'm with you, right here, right now."

At this reassurance, Haswell seemed to relax. He let out a deep sigh and sank back onto the ground. He blinked and licked his lips, sighing again. "I'm sorry," he said. "I'm sorry."

"It's fine, it's fine." Luke lifted his hand and, shifting his weight, moved to sit cross-legged next to Haswell as Haswell got himself up onto one elbow. Luke gestured to the group gathered around them, which was now quite large.

"See? We're all here. We're all with you. Everything's fine."

Luke looked around at those assembled. Everyone was quiet, and calm, feeling nothing but warmth and empathy for the man on the ground. Luke could feel their love, feel its warmth, its comfort. He turned back to Haswell.

"What's your first name?"

"Mico. It's Mico."

"Mico, can you tell me what happened?"

Haswell frowned, then blinked, then wiped the tears out of his eyes with his free hand, only to leave his face streaked with dirt. He didn't seem to notice. He shook his head, his eyes dropping as he tried to remember the events of the last few minutes.

"I . . . I don't know. I'm sorry, I don't know. I—" He looked up and around at the group, then back at Luke. "I don't remember. I was in the chamber, back there, and I dropped my trowel. And then, I think someone came in?" He shook his head. "I don't remember."

Luke nodded. "It'll come back to you. It'll—"

He was interrupted by Haswell's fist, clutching at the front of Luke's robe, pulling him a little closer. "I think I saw something. I . . . I *felt* something."

Luke didn't resist the other man. "What? What did you see, Mico? Tell me what you saw, what you felt." He closed his hand around Haswell's.

Haswell frowned, his grip relaxing. "I saw . . . a place. Darkness, and lightning. It was so *dry*, so old. And . . ." He trailed off, then stiffened. "There was something there," he said, his voice now nothing but a hoarse whisper. "There was *something there*. A . . . person. No. A shape. Like a . . . a shadow. It was . . . on me, I could feel it, I could hear it speaking to me."

Haswell shuddered. He stared at Luke's face. Luke could feel the other man's breath, short and fast and hot, against his own skin. Tears streamed down Haswell's face as he was caught in the grip of some terrible, fearful memory.

"You're fine," said Luke. He squeezed Haswell's hand and placed his other behind the man's head. As Haswell began to hyperventilate, Luke gently lowered him back to the ground, still squeezing his hand.

Luke closed his own eyes, and let the Force flow through him, enveloping the man in a blanket of love and comfort, channeling the emotion of the group around them, and their love and concern for their colleague.

He felt something else, too, and he couldn't resist a small smile, just to himself. He sensed Haswell's anger and resentment, his belief that he was being sidelined by the institute, his work ignored by Professor Arclarka, and others, and beneath all that, the foundation of disappointment, the feeling that his life was passing him by and he wasn't making any progress.

All of that was possibly true, but so was the love and friendship of his colleagues. They put up with his moods, his short temper, knowing that he was not at heart cruel, but merely lonely. They all looked up to him. Luke could feel that, and he used that feeling as he nudged Mico Haswell's consciousness with the power of the Force.

"Sleep, my friend, sleep," murmured Luke, opening his eyes. On the ground, Haswell's eyes were closed once more, but his eyes were still beneath their lids, and his breathing was soft and slow.

Lor San Tekka crouched beside Luke. "Did any of that mean anything to you?"

Luke turned to his old friend and gave a single, small nod.

It certainly meant something. The vision Mico Haswell had described—the place he had spoken of seeing—it was the same place as in Luke's own visions. He was certain of it.

Luke turned to the medic. "He'll sleep for a while. He should be fine when he wakes up, but he might have nightmares. You should get him back to Hosnian Prime and have him monitored for a few days. Make sure he's okay."

"Will do," said the medic. She opened her kit and began rifling through it for something, then reached down to take Haswell's pulse. She paused. "What's he holding?"

Luke looked down. The medic lifted Haswell's wrist. His hand was closed, the fingers curled around something long and thin. Blood trickled from his palm, running down his wrist. The medic went to open Haswell's hand, but Luke stopped her.

"Wait. Don't touch it. Let me."

The medic lowered Haswell's hand and got out of the way again.

Luke reached down and carefully unfolded the unconscious man's fingers.

Inside his fist was a long shard of crystal. It was bright red and vaguely blade-shaped, tapering to a point where it had clearly been sheared off a much larger piece. The split edge of the crystal was razor-sharp and had cut into Haswell's hand, embedding itself in his palm as he held it tight inside his fist.

Luke went to touch the crystal with his left hand, then paused and swapped over, his intuition making him carefully pull the crystal free with his cybernetic right hand.

Luke stood, holding the crystal shard between one mechanical thumb and finger. Again, he felt the presence of Lor San Tekka at his shoulder.

"A kyber crystal?" asked Lor.

Luke nodded and held the object up for them both to see. He turned it over in the light. It was an odd thing to look at, from some angles a brilliant, shining red, from others a dead, awful black.

"It's been bled," said Luke. He turned it again, and frowned. "It's the wrong size and shape for a lightsaber, though." He looked at Lor. "Get Beaumont Kin. Start closing the dig up, move everyone back up toward the mound. They're going to need to stop the dig until I can take a proper look. Professor Arclarka isn't going to like that, but he'll listen if you have Beaumont on your side."

Lor nodded. "Understood. What are you going to do?"

Luke looked at the crystal again then, from his utility belt, pulled out a swatch of the cloth he used for cleaning equipment. He wrapped the crystal shard in it and stowed it away in a pocket deep inside his robe.

"I'm going to take a look in that chamber," said Luke. "The crystal was broken off a larger one. There might be more pieces inside."

Lor nodded and moved back to join the others.

Luke turned back to the chamber. He took a breath and walked in.

The half chamber had been well prepared by Haswell. Although the intact wall portions looked solid enough, props had been installed, their telescopic forms placed at intervals around the edges of the chamber, matching the curve of the partial ceiling. Two more props were placed in the center, supporting—just in case—the remnants of the shattered dome itself. Between the props, rubble was scattered, some of which had been cleared systematically by the archaeologist, who had also set up a grid, the floor crisscrossed by fine lines of green laser to allow the worker to progress systematically, easily mapping the location of any finds as he came across them.

Haswell had been digging at the edge of the chamber, and as Luke moved toward the man's abandoned tools, he saw that the curved wall of the chamber continued down below ground level—the ground not being the original floor at all, but a hard-packed base of dirt accumulated over the centuries.

There was something about the chamber that made Luke feel uneasy. While the town ruins were clearly stone, mostly a light, dun-colored substance like sandstone, the interior of this chamber was a dark gray, almost like the gunmetal of the interior of military starships.

Luke approached the curve of the wall. He laid a gloved hand against it, then he peered closer.

He was right. The chamber wasn't stone, it was metal.

Luke stood back and looked around, gauging the dimensions of the room. Then he looked up. Where the ceiling had collapsed, the exposed edge of the chamber was jagged, but it was also *bent*. Luke looked back toward the chamber's entry point, where the wall had been torn open.

Of course. This wasn't a building. It was a starship, a wreck that had crashed, uncountable years ago.

Luke looked around again. The exposed interior was fairly bare, apart from the rubble. Luke wondered if the packed-dirt floor was protecting control panels and instruments, or whether the only thing left was the durable, outer hull of the ship.

Luke knelt down, picking up Haswell's discarded trowel.

That was when he saw it. Red and shining, a scattering of fragments just under the topmost layer of dirt.

Using the point of the trowel, Luke carefully traced an outline around the spot, then used the tool to dig about a centimeter into the dirt and lever out the first piece.

Like the shard wrapped in his pocket, this was a piece of red crystal, perfect in geometry, aside from the fact that it had been clearly sheared off a larger form.

Luke dug. After a few moments, he had uncovered more shards, the largest of which was only a couple of centimeters long, all of them smaller than the piece Haswell had been holding. Luke arranged them on the ground, trying to judge the size and shape of the original crystal. Then he sat back, gazing down at his find. He could sense the Force warping around the shards, like they were rocks in a river, bending the flow of water around them.

Luke shivered despite himself. Kyber crystals were natural conduits of the Force, but the way these had been manipulated disturbed him. Whoever had possessed the original crystal had turned the power of the Force against it, using arcane rituals to twist it, concentrating it in ways that it wasn't supposed to be channeled.

This was a ritual that had its origins eons ago by the adherents of the dark side, the Lords of the Sith, and had been carried down through the ages by those who followed that dark path. Bleeding a kyber crystal demonstrated the mastery over nature by the Sith Lord, turning the crystal—and the lightsaber it powered—blood red as a symbol of their power.

But these crystals were different. They had been bled, but Luke's initial judgment had been right—they weren't for a lightsaber. The original crystal would have been much larger. Perhaps more of the shards were buried under the dirt.

Taking the wrapped crystal from his robe, he peeled back the cloth, gathered the other shards up, and folded them all together. Once he was sure the bundle was secure, he returned it to his robe. He stood, looking around at the ground. He wanted to stay—the entire chamber needed to be cleared out, any more crystal shards carefully collected. If the dirt had protected the lower portion of the ship, maybe there would be clues as to where it had come from, who had flown in.

But that would take time, and Luke had a better idea. He would ask Lor San Tekka to stay, to supervise as the archaeological expedition focused their efforts on the chamber. It would be dangerous, slow work, but Luke trusted Lor to oversee it. The slightest sign of anything amiss, and Luke would return in an instant.

In the meantime, Luke had much work to do. The smashed holocron, the crashed starship, the shattered crystals—not to mention the malign power that had fallen over Haswell, and Luke's visions of the nightmare world—they were all connected.

Something evil was coming. Luke could sense it.

He needed to examine the crystals and holocron. He needed to know where they had come from, and who they had belonged to—fast.

There was only one place in the galaxy that was going to give him those answers. He left the chamber at a jog, already plotting the coordinates for Tython in his head.

CHAPTER II

MALATHON IX, EXPANSION REGION
THEN

He had been tracking her through the jungle for five days, and he was only just getting started.

He hadn't been to Malathon IX before. It didn't matter. He had his target. He had his mission. The location didn't matter—cityscape, desert, tundra, jungle, he'd worked in them all, adapting to his surroundings and doing so with ease, learning quickly to use the location to his own advantage.

That was why he was so good. That was why his skills had demanded such a high premium even before the war, and that was why he had been called on now to serve a higher power, tasked with hunting the most dangerous of quarries.

Because now Ochi of Bestoon hunted the Jedi themselves.

And so far, he had not failed in his mission.

Malathon IX was an odd planet, but Ochi liked it. Half of it was a scorched, cold desert, like the planet had been blasted by some cosmic catastrophe, then left to cool in space, as lifeless as it was featureless. The other half was rain forest, a dense and lush jungle that stretched from pole to pole, covering both hemispheres, with no apparent variation in temperature, or season, or life-form.

Ochi didn't know why the planet didn't have seasons. He didn't care. Nor did he care that the jungle wasn't green but red and purple, the plant life photosynthesizing with something other than chlorophyll. But, so what. The jungle was dense and that provided good cover, and it was wet and noisy, and that hid his own movements and sounds, and whether it was red or green or multicolored, so what.

What did matter was that he was now close. Very close. Just five days in, five days of tracking the Jedi and her party as they hacked their way through the chaotic undergrowth, and the end was in sight. In just a few hours he'd be up in orbit and plotting his hyperspace vector, ready to report to his master with proof of kill: the head of the Jedi, Depa Billaba.

It was a shame she didn't wear a mask or a helmet. Few of the Jedi did. Ochi sometimes thought he would have liked to take a souvenir from each of his kills, but . . . oh well.

Ochi settled into his nest, high in the jungle canopy, and watched his quarry approach through his quadnocs as the rain poured over his red-and-white helmet.

Here. They. Come.

Just a few more meters, and she'd be in range.

Of course, she could have been in range already. Ochi knew that, and the fact was he *was* expert with a sniper rifle. But while he appreciated the fine art of sharpshooting, he lacked the temperament for such precise, calculated work. Assassination from afar seemed too . . . impersonal? Sure, it was *clean,* but then there was still the issue of collecting proof of kill, and besides, Ochi really liked to use his hands. He liked to get up close, to see the fear in the face of his quarry as they realized they had run out of road, or that despite thinking they'd been perfectly safe, they'd actually been followed, been watched this whole time, completely oblivious to the death that stalked them, to their own rapidly shrinking life span.

He used those five days to study Depa Billaba. She was an athletic human, with dark hair in looped braids, as cool and as calm and as collected as that other Jedi, her Master, who had seen her off on her mission from the scraggly village that passed for a starport on this primitive jungle world. Ochi was just glad that *he* wasn't here—oh, there was a bounty out for him all right, the Separatists having put a price on the head of all of the Order. But Ochi worked strictly on personal commission. He was good at killing Jedi, and he had no doubt of his own particular skill set when it came to hunting, but there were some targets that would be suicidal to think you could take. Ochi was sure many had tried, if only by the steady decline in the number of his drinking buddies back on Boxer Point Station.

And—there, down in the clearing, by a river that ran with water the same red color as that which fell from the sky and saturated Ochi's uniform. His target was with a group of four clone troopers who were now making a camp as Depa Billaba separated herself from the group and went to the river's edge. She was now just three meters from Ochi, hidden in the tree above.

It was almost too easy.

Ochi pulled the deadblade from his back, the short, wickedly sharp weapon of *beskar* steel feather-light in his hand.

Oh, this was going to be a good one.

He jumped from the tree, blade out, ready to cut the Jedi down.

And then there was movement, something else, a rushing shape that hit him, catching him in the air even as he headed toward his target. He splashed into the river and scrambled to the surface from the surprisingly deep water. His boots found the bottom, and he pushed up, his deadblade swinging as he exploded from the river.

"Not today, Sithspawn!"

As he heard the words, his weapon was parried by a buzzing lightsaber, the blade a distinct amethyst color. Ochi could feel the sheer physical strength of the hands that wielded the laser sword as a big, bald man with dark skin pushed Ochi back.

The Jedi Master hadn't left at all. Of course he hadn't. He'd been tracking Ochi even as Ochi tracked his apprentice, Depa Billaba.

Ochi tripped backward, crashing into the water, as above him, Mace Windu lifted his lightsaber and prepared to strike—

. . . .

"Uh, boss?"

The mechanical irises of Ochi's cybernetic eyes spiraled open. Looming over him as he slouched in the pilot's seat of the *Bestoon Legacy* was one of the brothers—which one, Ochi couldn't tell, not until the being opened his mouth again to reveal the metal teeth.

"What is it, Bosvarga?" Ochi snarled, annoyed at being woken—embarrassed at being found asleep by his minion.

"All set, boss." This was Cerensco, now joining his brother's side. "We've got them all ready to go."

Ochi sat up, slowly. The *Bestoon Legacy* spun around him a little. For a moment he remembered a splash of red water, a blaze of purple light, and then the dream was gone.

"Them?"

"Anduluuvil," said Bosvarga, starting to count off the names on his thick fingers as he listed them. "Pysarian, Krastan, the Sphox—and her crew—and Repreever and Stiper."

Ochi paused in thought, then shook his head. "Good," he said. "But not enough."

"Not sure we've got any more favors to call in," said Cerensco. He looked at his brother. "Plo Mandrill?"

"Dead," said Bosvarga.

"Oh, shame. What about—"

"Shut up, both of you!" Ochi pushed himself up from the chair and turned a tight circle on his minions. "We're going to be smart about this."

"Got it, boss," said Cerensco.

Ochi glanced at him, then turned to Bosvarga—the smarter of the two, he thought.

"We post a bounty, get the word out, see if anything shakes loose."

"On it."

Ochi nodded. "I got an idea for some extra hands. I've still got a few names in the databank." He waved the two brothers out of the ship's flight deck. "Now get on with it, and get out of my sight."

The two brothers glanced at each other, then shuffled out. Ochi slammed the flight deck door closed behind them.

"Dee-Oh?"

There was a bleep from a corner of the flight deck. "Master?" burbled the little droid as he rolled out from the corner. "Ready to serve, ready to serve."

Ochi walked back around to the pilot's seat and dropped himself in it. "You still got the encrypted channel code for Zee-Nine City Seven?"

D-O rolled back and forth a little on his single wheel. "Affirmative, master."

"Then plug yourself in," said Ochi, "I have a call to make."

As the droid rolled to the dataport at the base of the flight console, Ochi leaned forward and checked the comm deck, clearing the main channel.

Time, he thought, for a little action.

Time for a little . . . muscle.

CHAPTER 12

THE RUINED TEMPLE, TYTHON
NOW

The fact was, Luke liked coming to Tython. The planet was peaceful and pristine, an entire world of forest and grassland, populated only by birds and small mammals. There was no distraction from technology, no electromagnetic fields, no . . . interference.

Tython was not unique in that regard, however. There were plenty of planets in the galaxy that were uninhabited, or undeveloped, natural, tranquil wonderlands—Ossus was the perfect example, of course. That was why Luke had chosen it for his own temple. But there was something else about Tython, some unique quality that perhaps transcended understanding. That was why the Jedi of ancient times had built the Martyrium of Frozen Tears in the planet's Meridonal ice cap, and here, in a more temperate region, a very special temple indeed.

Hefting the heavy pack taken from his X-wing's cargo bin on his shoulder, Luke stood in the Tythonian morning light in his orange flight suit and looked up at the hill, unable to stop that sense of wonder again as he saw the large stone structure at the apex. He'd been here many times, had spent countless hours researching the site and the Jedi who had built it. But still, every time he saw the temple, he wasn't prepared for both the majesty of its construction, and the intense feeling of peace that came with it—even to a troubled mind like his.

Adjusting his grip on the pack, Luke made his way up the winding path to the Jedi temple and the seeing stone at its center. As he got closer, he looked over the vast stone monoliths, quarried, according to Luke's research, hundreds of kilometers away and carried here by the combined will of the Jedi builders, without any technological help. The seeing stone's origins had, however, proved more elusive. It was made from a different material from the monoliths that surrounded it, and had so far resisted analysis.

Perhaps, Luke thought, that was for the best. There were some things that didn't *need* to be understood by science.

As a Jedi, he had all the knowledge he needed.

At the summit, Luke carefully swung his pack down next to the hemisphere of the seeing stone itself and unzipped his flight suit before rolling it and tucking it underneath the pack. Beneath the flight suit he wore a shorter version of his black Jedi robes, far more comfortable to wear in an X-wing. He knelt by his pack and opened it, and began extracting the ancient tomes he had brought with him, along with a freshly bound parchment book that was already half full of his own notes. The books he laid out in order on the grass below the seeing stone, the notes he opened and balanced on the top of the dome itself.

Then Luke took a breath and reached inside his robes to extract the bundle of kyber crystal shards. This he put on top of his notes before ducking down and taking the final object from his pack, another cloth-wrapped parcel. He unwrapped it on the grass, revealing the slanted, squashed form of the Sith Holocron. He stood and unwrapped the bundle of crystals. As the blood-red shards caught the Tython sun, Luke grimaced, the peace he so loved about the temple now gone. Even the air seemed to cool, although he knew this was probably his imagination.

But still—it felt wrong, bringing these objects here. They might have been old, they might have been broken, but there was no denying their true nature, and the nature of the beings who had created them and who had used them.

They were evil, it was that simple. The holocron and the crystals were possessed of an . . . aura, some manifestation of the dark side, echoing down the ages, casting a shadow on the present. Already Luke could feel a pressure in his mind, the sensation of something large and distant that was approaching slowly, its mass pushing against Luke's thoughts.

Something was coming.

Stretching his stiff muscles, Luke picked up the bundle of crystals and the notes, then jumped up on the seeing stone itself, arranging himself cross-legged on the dome, the notes in his lap, the crystal bundle on the page.

He got to work.

The Tythonian day was long, and Luke was grateful for the extended hours of light as he worked. Already the ground around the seeing stone was littered with the open books Luke had consulted as he followed stories and legends, seeking to understand the nature of his visions, to identify the place he saw in them, and to learn how these connected with the holocron and crystals.

It was actually the holocron that had led to the most interesting discoveries, so far, anyway. Luke was very familiar with Sith Holocrons and their Jedi counterparts. There had been an entire vault of them in the archives of the Jedi Temple on Coruscant, before the purge of Emperor Palpatine. Some from that vault had survived somehow; others, Luke had found and studied, Sith and Jedi alike, now safely locked in his own Jedi temple. The books Luke spent so much time poring over were filled with legends and myths about what were, in all essence, simply data storage units.

Luke turned back a page in his notes to the sketch he had made, imagining the original, intact form of the Sith Holocron from Yoturba—a squat, triangular object, the metal frame engraved with backward Aurebesh holding the data core itself, a solid crystal matrix encoded with the arcane and the mysterious.

Or, perhaps, something far more mundane and ordinary. There was no way of telling now. Whatever information the smashed holocron had held, it was long gone.

Shifting on the stone, Luke placed the notebook to one side, allowing it to float in the air beside him as he reached for one of the older books that lay open on the grass. The tome lifted and swung up toward him; as soon as it was within touching distance, Luke took it in his hands and laid it across his lap.

This book—beautifully handcrafted from real paper, a rare antiquity in itself, regardless of the value of its contents—was a catalog of something called the Eeshaypher Collection, a forbidden gallery of artifacts, relics, and antiques, all of which were related to the dark side of the Force. The catalog was incomplete, and several surviving pages were badly charred and largely unreadable; what pages were left were filled with diagrams of the objects in the collection and dense, flowery descriptions that relied so heavily on metaphor, it took Luke twice as long to decipher any actual meaning.

But what he had read was utterly fascinating. He tapped a finger on the picture next to a block of beautiful flowing script, then looked at his own sketch representing the intact holocron.

The catalog image was also a squat, pyramidal object, although there were differences—it was four-sided, a true pyramid, rather than the three-sided tetrahedron of the holocron. The base was larger, and had another, smaller "foot" underneath. But the similarities were interesting, which gave Luke much to think on.

The object described in the ancient book was referred to as a wayfinder, an ancient Sith device with a single, specific purpose.

Navigation.

And . . . that was it.

It seemed strange to have developed such a relatively bulky device just to hold, presumably, coordinates or star charts, but the similarities between the wayfinder and the Sith Holocrons with which Luke was familiar were striking. If the holocron was a *multipurpose* data store, it seemed likely that it had evolved from the wayfinder, the product of a more primitive, but no less powerful, Sith technology. It was also logical, therefore, that if the holocron could contain multitudes of data, so too, the wayfinder might contain not just coordinates and star charts but entire routes and networks, along with the means to decode them, allowing the user to pilot along plotted routes, paths leading to uncharted regions and hidden parts of space.

Or to one place in particular. The collection catalog was vague, but what Luke deciphered matched up with other texts.

There were, according to his research, only ever two wayfinders in existence, the path they contained too secret, too dangerous for any but the Sith Lord and their apprentice to know.

The path to the hidden world of the Sith, a place of power and also, according to an ancient scribe, Kli the Elder, of eternal life.

Ixigul—or Exegol, in Luke's modern Basic translation.

Luke hadn't heard the name before. As he had sat on the seeing stone, he'd called back to R2-D2 at his X-wing, asking the droid to cross-check contemporary star charts, but without any luck.

Was Exegol truly a hidden world of the Sith? Was it even real—or just a myth? With the Sith, it was hard to know—so much of their lore that Luke had managed to cobble together seemed obscure, if not deliberately obtuse, as the adherents of the dark side worked to hide their machinations not only from the galaxy at large but also from rivals within their own Order.

Again, the arcane interpretation of twisted Jedi lore that the ancient Sith had seemed to delight in baffled Luke.

But . . . it had given him an idea.

First, Luke assumed Exegol was real, and the Sith wayfinder showed the path to the planet. Holocrons—the technological descendants of the wayfinders—could hold any kind of data, including navigational aids. The holocron from Yoturba had been found near the ruins of a crashed starship.

So . . . had the pilot been trying to get to Exegol? If there were two wayfinders and both were hidden, had they tried to plot their own course, perhaps the product of years of research not entirely dissimilar to Luke's own work?

But the legends of the Sith were true. Without the wayfinder, the pilot would have gotten lost and then gotten into trouble. Crashed on Yoturba, taking their secrets to the grave.

Luke looked up from the book and rolled his neck. He'd been working for a long time, but he was used to it. This was his life now. Training his students at the temple by day, and taking every moment he could to continue his research into the ways of the Force. It was fascinating, and . . .

He paused in his own thoughts, pursing his lips.

Exegol.

Luke mulled on the name. Could the Sith really hide an entire planet? Perhaps in the Unknown Regions? True, that slice of the galaxy was largely uncharted, but . . . could you actually *hide* a planet? An entire system? Perhaps behind some kind of barrier—perhaps the core of a nebula, or behind the gravitational lensing of a binary star. There were plenty of candidates that would cause havoc with even the most advanced starship sensor banks.

So yes, it was possible. Exegol might exist. It might be out there.

Did that mean the Sith were out there, too? But they were dead, extinct, the ancient Order dying with Palpatine on the second Death Star above Endor.

But was that the truth? Or just one Luke chose to believe?

Luke took the bundle of kyber crystal shards in one hand, closing his notes with the other and letting the bound volume drift off to one side. Adjusting his position on the center of the seeing stone, he straightened his back, placed his hands on his knees—palms facing the sky—and, as he lifted his chin, closed his eyes.

In front of him, the bundle of crystals rose into the air, hovering in front of Luke's chest.

He concentrated. On the breeze ruffling his hair, his beard, his robes. On the distant call of birds. On the rustle of pages that floated nearby. Behind his closed eyes, he stared at nothing, searching the reddish black for a horizon that wasn't there.

Luke Skywalker took a breath, and held it, and communed with the Force.

It took a moment, and then he felt it, the Force a river, his body a stone. He felt it flow around him, surrounding him, enveloping him. A familiar, and very real, sensation.

This was why he had come to Tython. The temple and the seeing stone it protected had been built by Jedi long ago to commune with one another across the stars, to truly connect with the Force, to see into it, to delve into its secrets and learn. Tython was both a site of sacred ritual and a powerful tool of an older world.

If Luke wanted to find out who had taken the Sith Holocron on a perilous journey that had ended in failure on Yoturba, who the kyber crystal had belonged to—even who had created it, twisting the natural conduits of the Force within it to bleed its power and turn it red—then he might be able to do it via the power of the seeing stone.

He felt the air shift, the breeze cooling and picking up, turning very quickly from the natural winds that rolled around the hilltop to a whirlwind, a cone that was centered on the stone and was centered on himself, his robes now flying out in the air. Behind his eyelids, the world brightened, like someone was shining a hangar light directly into his face. He felt himself being lifted. Not physically—he was still firmly connected to the seeing stone beneath him—but, again, he could only compare it with being in a busy flight hangar at the start of a sortie, the roar of ships taking off and the suction effect of atmospheric engines and turbines all working in an enclosed space. A difference in pressure.

And then—

There was a bang, more like a thunderclap, and everything went black. The breeze dropped, the air still and warm. Luke took a breath and could taste dry dust on his tongue, and then he realized he wasn't sitting on the seeing stone anymore.

He looked down. He was *standing* now on black dirt, hard-packed, cracked, coated with dust that swirled in eddies around his boots.

He looked up. The world was black and dry, the sky dark and filled with roiling black clouds, lit by constant flashes of lightning that shorted directly down into the ground. If it was day or night, Luke couldn't tell—the place was both light and dark at the same time, the vast, flat plain of black stone lit evenly from a sun that wasn't there.

Luke took another breath, the taste getting stronger in his mouth. Already his eyes were drying out, the atmosphere, the ground, the whole place so old, so desiccated.

He knew immediately where he was. He had been here many times recently, this nightmare landscape of his visions.

Only now he knew its name.

This was Exegol, the hidden world of the Sith only whispered about in ancient texts. A place reachable only with a wayfinder.

And . . . by meditation? Luke took a step forward, finding the ground solid and most definitely real under his feet. He walked a small and slow circle, eyes at the horizon. Lightning flashed, lighting the farther reaches of the plain, revealing it to be featureless and dead.

The same place as his visions, yes, but this felt . . . different.

This felt *real*.

Could he have been transported? Luke frowned, his mind racing along with his heart. True enough, he didn't know the full extent of the powers of the seeing stone. He had researched the place for years, but he had never fully used the stone for its ancient purpose, to commune directly with the Force. He knew himself what a powerful Jedi he had become, what untapped potential he still had within himself despite—or perhaps because of—his years of self-directed, Masterless training.

Had he done it? He had the holocron, or what was left of it, and the kyber crystals. Was there enough of the holocron data core left for the seeing stone to have been able to read it, somehow, taking him to where the original owner had failed to reach, all those centuries ago? And what about the kyber crystals? They resonated with the Force, their very structures in a natural, sympathetic vibration with it. Were they the catalyst, making the journey possible? Was that what the original pilot had tried—combining two very different forms of Sith power to overcome their lack of a true wayfinder?

It was then that a far more important question entered Luke's head.

Could he get back to Tython?

Then he spun, ducking instinctively as something brushed past the hood of his robe, strong enough to shift the heavy fabric over his shoulder. There was nobody behind him. He turned the circle again. He was alone on the plain, the air perfectly still, the caustic sour taste growing ever stronger in his mouth.

Again. Something brushing past him, this time with a distinct *whoosh* of the dry air and the sound of someone's feet scraping along the hard ground. Luke ducked out of the way again, moving a few meters from his original position. Looking down he saw his footprints in the dust—it was hardly an impression, but enough for him to see his own tracks.

And the tracks of someone, or something, else. Two large arcs, not footsteps but the signs of something being dragged along the ground, on opposite sides of where Luke had just been standing.

He looked up, turning slowly to see all around him. There was no place to hide—no rocks, no buildings, nothing. Luke could see from horizon to empty horizon.

Lightning flashed and then he saw it, just for an instant as it was lit up by the electrical storm. A figure, a fair distance away, perhaps one hundred meters. And then it was gone, before Luke could register any features or form at all.

"Hello?" he called out, feeling slightly foolish. He tried again. "Who's there?"

Again the sound, louder now, and he felt something physically push his back. He went with the movement to keep his own footing, moved forward farther, then spun around, his hand whipping his lightsaber from his belt and presenting it in one smooth, fluid movement. He paused, feet spread, weight low, the defensive position that was as instinctive, as automatic, for him as breathing.

Luke was surrounded. They were tall, thin. Nine of them. Nothing more than wraiths. Nothing more than shadows. Tall, thin ghosts, their bodies curved and arced in a new wind that had picked up, a wind that gusted across the black plain, changing direction constantly.

Luke adjusted his grip on his lightsaber and thumbed the activator. With a searing *swoosh,* the green blade ignited, illuminating a large circle around Luke and the wraiths, lighting the ashy dust that swirled in the air like a halo.

Luke braced himself. Because these weren't ghosts or shadows or wraiths. They were very real. With each flash of lightning in the dark sky above, the wraiths were lit as solid, three-dimensional figures, black-robed, bandage-faced.

It was disorienting. Luke narrowed his eyes as he focused, the foes surrounding him flashing between translucent billowing shadows and solid humanoid figures.

Then they began to circle him. They kept the same distance from Luke, and from one another, as they moved, all of them keeping their front facing this intruder into their world. Luke, balanced on the balls of his feet, fingers adjusting, readjusting on the grip of his lightsaber, was ready for the attack he knew was coming, all the while his mind racing.

How did I get here . . . and how do I get back?

And then the wraiths, moving in unison as though some unseen, unheard communication had passed among them, reached into robes that were in one instant eddies of ash and in the next flash of lightning a heavy, woven black textile, and pulled out lightsabers of their own.

Luke, with his years of experience, years of learning to master his emotions and control his actions, did not allow the sight of these nine weapons to surprise him. Because . . . of course they had lightsabers. He was on Exegol, the Sith world, the heart of darkness. He had dared to see into the planet with the Force, and was now here, in physical reality, facing nine embodiments of the dark side who clearly wanted their existence to remain hidden.

The wraiths lifted their lightsabers and activated them. Luke didn't so much hear their ignition as feel it inside, the familiar sound somehow high-pitched and distant, a half-forgotten memory rather than an actual physical sensation. The wraiths lifted their blades, ready to meet Luke's, but they were nothing, mere black outlines against the black figures standing on the black ground under a black sky. But when the lightning flashed, the nine blades were inverted, a negative flash of white that made spots dance in Luke's eyes. Dazzled, Luke's control slipped for just a moment, and he took an involuntary half step backward.

It was what the wraiths had been waiting for. They rushed at him in silence, their robes of shadow-ash disintegrating in the wind as they moved, their whole bodies becoming insubstantial, particulate matter that blew away in the breeze. And then the lightning flashed and Luke was surrounded by nine very real, very solid, black-clad figures swinging lightsabers of blinding, impossible light.

Driven by instinct, guided by his connection to the Force, Luke parried the first blows, his lightsaber connecting with his enemies' with a familiar high-energy splash. But with the lightning flashing along with the nine black-white blades of his enemies, Luke soon found that he was, effectively, fighting blind, his vision nothing but purple spots and red smears.

But Luke Skywalker did not panic, did not fear. Deflecting another attack, Luke closed his eyes and let out a breath. He didn't need eyes to see his enemies. All he had to do was look *inward,* to feel the Force flow through him, to feel its connection with himself, and the galaxy, and all the beings that lived within.

I am one with the Force, and the Force is with me.

The next attack was parried with perfection; Luke's riposte was likewise a textbook example of the Jedi form.

But then his blade passed through . . . nothing.

Luke didn't open his eyes, he just bowed his head, spinning on the spot to counter the attacks coming from the other side while he concentrated, trying to enter an almost meditative state so he could press an attack rather than let the Force guide him merely through a passive, automatic defense.

And then he faltered. A frown flickered across his face as he reached out with the Force and . . .

There was nothing. No connection. No feeling. It was as though he was still on Tython, on the seeing stone, at the center of a grace where the Force coalesced around him but not *within* him.

The beings around him, nine shadow wraiths with blades of light and dark, did not exist in the Force—they had no presence, no form.

This was impossible.

The Force connected all life in the galaxy, but it also surrounded and penetrated the inanimate. Objects—rocks, planets, starships, droids, everything—had a presence in the Force, or rather an absence that could be felt, and felt to such a degree that a Force-user could see them and use them.

But the wraiths were nothing. Luke couldn't sense them with the Force.

He turned left, then right, lightsaber swinging up, then down, then out, parrying three more blows. But blinded and unable to even sense his opponents, he was unable to attack. He might as well just be swinging randomly at the air around him.

Which he did. He opened his eyes, squinting against the flashes of lightning and the searing sweeps of the wraith-blades, his own green lightsaber the one thing that was familiar, the only color in his nightmare.

But that faithful lightsaber could do nothing against the wraiths. He blocked a blow—his eyes and brain beginning to adjust, very slightly, to the disorienting world around him—and came in with an attack, high then low, completely avoiding his opponent's blade. But his lightsaber passed through the wraith, dragging a wake of ash behind it, lit in the glowing green of Luke's laser sword.

The wraith didn't even seem to notice. It brought its blade up and Luke parried, parried again, ducked sideways and parried a blow from his left side, swung the lightsaber to the right to counter another, then carved a series of angled attacks that should have cut the three opponents in front of him to ribbons.

His blade met no resistance—on the contrary, the wraith directly in front of him stepped *into* his attack, apparently unaware or unconcerned as to the position of Luke's blade.

Luke didn't stop moving. He dodged the shadow-blade of the wraith even as he passed *through* the being himself, the cloud of ash and dust thick around his face, coating his skin, his tongue, filling his mouth with the taste of hot metal. Now behind the group, he turned and pressed a fresh attack to their rear, swinging his lightsaber left and right and left again, blocking the thrust of a shadow-blade as one wraith turned in a whirlwind of spinning black smoke and brought its weapon to bear. Once again, lightsaber met lightsaber, green light met shadow-blade, and Luke could feel the jolt through the hilt of his own weapon, could see the fizz of energy as his blade slid along the length of his enemy's, before the wraith pulled away in one direction and Luke in the other, both then turning to cut in at a sharp angle. Blade met blade again, this time with a bang of spitting plasma, as though the wraiths were toying with him, one moment their weapons real, the next, a shadowed imitation of reality.

Sensing this change, Luke's next blow was powerful enough to knock the other blade away, and he quickly made his riposte, straight through the neck and torso of the apparition.

Once again, his blade met nothing. The shadow-form parted like smoke, even as lightning flashed again and the being was as solid as Luke's own body.

Luke swung again, and again, and again, sweeping now with his blade with no particular intention or design except to keep the nine wraiths at a distance, his focus now not on the fight but on figuring a way *out*.

The wraiths pressed their attack, Luke's blade passing harmlessly through them. As they got closer and closer, they raised their own lightsabers again, acting together in telepathic union, ready to make their final strike.

Nine blades against one. Luke didn't like the odds, but he braced himself nonetheless.

The wraiths attacked, nine shadow-blades held by shadow-arms cutting down at speed—

And that was when a new light appeared. Not the white flash of lightning, or the wraith-blades as they were lit by the unholy light. Not the green glow of Luke's lightsaber, illuminating the ashy ground like a green flashlight.

No, this light was pale blue. It shimmered in the air, streaking a little as it swept down, throwing the attackers off in one smooth movement.

It was a lightsaber, the blade blue and strong, the hilt—

The hilt was transparent, nothing but a blue glow, held in a transparent blue hand.

Luke fell backward, onto his elbows, and gasped at the pain in his joints and also in sheer surprise at the sight before him.

Standing between himself and the wraiths was another figure— a man in flowing pale robes, his back to Luke, his head hidden under a voluminous hood. The entire figure glowed like soft electricity, bright in this world of endless night. When the lightning flashed, Luke could see the nine solid wraiths through the form of the man who stood between them and their quarry.

Luke's mind raced as he tried to identify the spirit of the Force who had arrived to protect him.

"Ben?"

No, it wasn't Ben—*Obi-Wan*—Kenobi, his old mentor. The robe, the man's form, was different, was—

The spectral being lifted his lightsaber, holding it high above his head, the blade parallel to the ground.

For the first time, the wraiths seemed to take note of their enemy. They backed away, nine forms huddling together, blades lowered. They were screaming from their blank bandaged faces, although Luke wasn't sure whether it was a real sound or just an echo inside his head. It was hard to concentrate on what he was seeing, the way the Force reverberated around the figure in blue. His entire vision seemed to buckle around him.

The wraiths continued to back away, and then they vanished, their shadow-shapes evaporating into dust that spun away on the last eddy of the dying wind.

For a moment, all was still.

Then the blue figure turned around, his lightsaber extinguished.

Luke pushed himself up onto his elbows. He blinked.

It couldn't be.

It *couldn't* be.

The blue figure lifted his hood back to reveal the strong, sharp face of a young man, his gaze intense beneath a furrowed brow that was bisected by a straight, vertical scar. His thick hair was shoulder-length and had a slight wave to it.

Anakin Skywalker reached out his hand.

Luke took it, and everything went white.

CHAPTER 13

THE RUINED TEMPLE, TYTHON

NOW

Luke blinked and looked around. He was lying on the ground, in the shadow of the seeing stone.

He was back on Tython.

If he had ever left.

Smoke billowed around him. Luke reacted instantly, realizing that some of his ancient texts were now on fire. As he stood, he yanked off his robe and threw it over the top of the stone dome, smothering the flames, then swept it off and used it to extinguish the smoldering papers that lay on the grass. In a few moments, the fires were out, his books saved—but on top of the seeing stone was a smeary, oily mess, the almost unrecognizable remains of the smashed Sith Holocron. On top of the stain, however, the wrapped bundle of kyber crystals appeared to be completely untouched.

"The seeing stone can be a powerful tool, but one difficult to master."

Luke looked up.

The glowing blue form of Anakin Skywalker stepped out of the shadow of one of the huge monoliths that orbited the hilltop temple. His hood was down, revealing the face of a man who looked a good two decades younger than Luke himself. Luke wet his lips, his chest feeling like it was trapped in a vise, the very breath being squeezed out of him as he came face-to-face with the echo of his own father.

Luke opened his mouth to say something, but a change came over Anakin—the warm, knowing smile was gone, and his blue form seemed to flash and sheer, like a hologram transmission caught in a reception blind spot.

"Father! What is it? What's happening?"

The look on Anakin's face made Luke's blood run cold. His father looked pained—no, worse, in agony—and Luke didn't know if that was even possible. Anakin was one with the Force now.

And yet . . . he was in trouble.

His spirit flickered, faded, flickered. As Luke watched, another man seemed to appear, between the blinks of an eye, superimposed over the vision of Anakin as a young man, before his fall to the dark side. Someone older, a calm, benign face—the face revealed beneath Vader's mask by Luke, so many years ago on a battle station long since destroyed.

And then it was gone, if it had ever been there and not just another vision in Luke's mind.

"Luke—"

Anakin reached out. Luke took a step closer, then stopped as Anakin appeared to be racked with a new agony. When he looked up at Luke again, his face was dark.

Anakin Skywalker was afraid.

When he spoke again, his voice echoed around the hilltop temple, but Luke wasn't sure if he was hearing it with his ears or feeling it inside his own mind with the Force.

"There is a disturbance in the Force."

Luke nodded. "I have felt it, Father."

"There is—"

Anakin faded out, faded in. He stood tall and grimaced. Luke lifted his own hand, the two men, one alive, one long passed, father and son, reaching toward each other, the flesh-and-blood fingers of Luke's hand just out of reach from the blue glow of Anakin's.

"It is a shadow," said Anakin. He was shouting now, yelling across an infinite gulf of time and space, his voice barely even audible to Luke. "Cast long from an ancient time."

Luke nodded. "I know," he said, and it was the truth. Anakin was putting into words what Luke had felt for weeks now. "I've felt it grow in the Force."

Anakin gasped in silence, his spirit-form now fading at the edges, his whole body a vignette that maybe existed only in the corners of Luke's mind.

"It approaches. You must take care, my son."

"What is it? Where did the seeing stone take me? Was that Exegol?"

"Hell has many names, Luke. The seeing stone took a part of you there. But it has taken all that I can give to bring you back."

Anakin faded again, but when he returned, he was only a dim shape, hardly more than a blue glowing outline against the clear blue sky.

"But what do I do, Father?" asked Luke. "If the shadow grows . . . how do I stop what I can't even see?"

"The Force is a river, my son. It flows through the galaxy, a powerful torrent. But there are some things that can divert its course, and some people who would seek to change it."

Luke shook his head. The advice was so cryptic. He took a step closer. He wanted his father to stay. He wanted them to talk. There was so much he didn't know, so much he wanted to ask, so much he wanted to *understand*.

But he knew that now was not the time. It was taking all of Anakin's will even to appear to him now, to offer a warning that Luke couldn't ignore.

This was his task. His mission. The disturbance in the Force was very real, as was the danger it posed. The shadow, cast long, but cast by . . . what? It was connected to Exegol, Anakin had confirmed that, but there was more to it than that.

The dig on Yoturba had accelerated things with the uncovering of the holocron and the kyber crystals, but Luke had been plagued by the visions for weeks. They had drawn him *to* the dig—Lor's invitation had merely been a part of that vision. It was how it was meant to be.

The Force did indeed move in mysterious ways.

"Remember, my son," said Anakin, his voice so far away, Luke could hardly hear it over the rush of blood in his ears, "no matter how dark the night may grow, you are never alone." Anakin gasped and faded again. "You will know what to do, my son," he said. "Let the Force guide you. Let it flow through you as it flows through me. Use that power, and your instincts, for they are one and the same."

And then he was gone, the blue glow fading into the blue sky behind. Luke blinked in the dazzling daylight.

The roaring sound increased, and then Luke saw something in the sky, and realized the sound wasn't the blood in his ears, it was the sublight engines of a starship on approach.

The ship was clearly a pleasure craft, with an elegantly sculpted mid-sized hull that looked as though it would have been equally at home cruising the waters of some exotic leisure lake as it was cutting across the space lanes. The sun glinted off its white ceramo-metal exterior as the craft made a low pass over the hillside, then banked and disappeared from view, in the direction Luke's X-wing was parked. He listened as the sound of the ship's engines wound down with a whine.

He recognized the ship—but quite what its owner was doing here, he didn't know.

Luke ran out between the temple monoliths, and started down the hillside path. In the hollow below, the newly arrived craft shone in the bright Tython day, and already its owner was making his way up the path toward Luke, his bright red shirt blazing. Over the man's shoulder was tossed a black cape lined in gold, which the man was trailing with one finger looped through the tag at the collar.

"Lando!"

The other man stopped and looked up. He gave a wave.

Luke ran down the slope and skidded to a halt in front of him.

Lando's grin was wide beneath his neatly trimmed mustache. His thick black hair glistened with fresh tonic.

"Luke, old pal, I knew I'd find you here!"

He spread his arms in greeting, his cape still hanging from one finger. But Luke did not come in for a hug. Instead, he lifted his hand and pointed over Lando's shoulder, at his ship, the *Lady Luck*.

"You need to leave, Lando. Right now."

CHAPTER 14

THE SEPULCHRE, COORDINATES UNKNOWN
NOW

Under the vaulted roof, she woke again.

The space was vast, silent save for the steady hum of power and the gentle churn of the droid forge, which lit the chamber with an ever-changing, ever-moving light cast from the furnace room at the back of the vault. This, and the patchwork glow of indicators and readouts from the various controls and systems that studded the walls, was the only light.

It could have been the hangar of a vast starship, once. The space was what she needed. Space for her relics, space for her work, space for her army, space for the meditation chamber that sat in the center of the room, open like a gargantuan clamshell fished from the depths of the Marca Pala Sea on Mon Cala.

In front of the meditation chamber, her army slept. Row upon row of huddled forms—battle droids exhumed from the ruins of wars old and new, repaired and reprogrammed and arranged in the vault to face the meditation chamber, each curled onto their knees, heads bowed in supplication to their new mistress. That the droid army hadn't moved a servo in years didn't matter. They were hers to command when the time was right.

She knelt in the center of the chamber, facing out to her sleeping legion, unconsciously mimicking their posture. She hadn't gone to sleep in that pose, but she had woken in it.

This was not unusual. And now, awareness returning, she bowed her head to the mask that sat on the plinth in front of her, the mask she both loved and hated, unable to resist the power within, unwilling to fight it.

The mask was old. Immeasurably so, a relic of a civilization that had disappeared so long ago that nobody now even remembered its name. If the mask was a work of art, it was born from a mind unlike her own. It was crude but beautiful, a product of a tradition unknown. The mask was burnished bronze, but it had a grain in it, the material having been sliced from raw meteoric metal and fashioned by hand into its final shape. But the surface of the mask, though finely sculpted, was not perfect. There were divots, pockmarks. Evidence, perhaps, of battles fought and won and battles fought and lost.

Two eyes of black glass, angular, insectoid.

No nose. A mouth, of sorts—a row of rivets, drawing a grimacing line.

The woman knelt in front of the mask, staring into the black glass eyes of the thing with her own golden ones, her dark-blue hair hanging lankly around her light-blue face.

As she stared at the mask, her lips moved as she mouthed the words to a song only she could hear, a song that existed only inside her head, a song sung to her by the voice trapped inside the mask. The voice—the *music*—was ancient and awful, a noise, a cacophony, but one she knew all too well. At first, she had only ever heard it when she wore the mask. But now, she heard it all the time, loudest when she was close to the relic.

She was losing herself to it, her will weakening as the mask grew in power. It was feeding off her.

She knew that. She knew that and she couldn't do a thing about it.

Sometimes she had to tell herself who she was. Sometimes she didn't remember. She had served her Master for years. She didn't know how many. She had stopped counting, because it didn't matter. All that mattered was her *purpose*, her *quest*, one she had embarked on at the bidding of a dark and ancient power that had roused from its eons-long slumber.

But sometimes she remembered her name and she remembered who she was, who she had been. And she remembered what the mask was and how she had gotten it and *what it was doing to her.*

It gave her power. Abilities. Knowledge. But it was far from a fair exchange. Because the mask took her life. It had done so, the moment she had first put it on.

She had died so *he* could live.

And now it was time to do his bidding once more, now that the petty task of the Sith Eternal had been fulfilled, the message and relic blade delivered to Ochi of Bestoon. She didn't know who he was or what the Sith Eternal had planned for him, but she obeyed nonetheless. Her alliance with the cultists had been the means to an end. Of course, their promise to share in their power had been a lie, but it was still useful to heed their call, to perform the tasks they assigned her as their agent.

Because those cultists came from Exegol, and Exegol was exactly where she—where the *mask*—wanted to go. And they had other uses.

It was true that they used her. But she also used them.

She looked down. In front of the plinth sat a platter of beaten metal, some ancient table piece taken from a ransacked temple. The platter had a dull sheen, and around the scrolled edge were molded the shapes of wormlike creatures with bristled mouths and long tongues.

On the platter was a large piece of crystal. It was scarlet red, and in the dim light of the meditation chamber it seemed to shine with an internal glow all of its own. One end was perfect in its geometry, the hexagonal facets mathematically precise in a way only nature could manage. But the other was rough and broken, the base angled, cracks running up from it. The large crystal, once perfect, had been broken.

She knew exactly what a kyber crystal was. She had collected many, most of them burned-out husks from broken lightsabers. Those that remained intact she kept in her vault, future replacements for her own collection of weapons. But the piece on the platter, that was something new. It was huge, the form of the unbroken end so perfect she knew it had power, even if she, unable to sense the Force herself, couldn't feel it.

It had taken months of work to locate it, using knowledge gleaned here and there from the unwitting Sith Eternal. Her lightsaber had ended many lives in her quest for the crystal, each death adding to the echoing screams inside the mask, joining the menagerie of the damned.

The crystal was important. The key to the final stage of *his* plan.

The key to Exegol.

WE HAVE MUCH WORK TO DO.

The voice was distant, but loud. Whether it echoed around the vault or echoed only in her head, she didn't know.

Around the walls of the meditation chamber, instruments sprang into life. Lights came on, winking as computer systems rebooted and went through routine checks.

And then switches moved. A lever was depressed, moving all of its own accord.

She looked at the mask, already feeling the pull, the desperate urge—the *desire*—to pick it up and put it on and surrender to the dark power within. She could feel *his* presence, feel the power that radiated from the mask, intelligent and malignant, a soft caress on the back of her neck, a lover's whisper in her ear.

For a moment, she remembered her name.

For a moment, she wanted to run.

She lifted her hand. She didn't remember picking up her lightsaber, but she had it now. She closed her eyes and pressed the activator. The blade spat into life, the hum low and angry, and beneath her closed eyelids she could see its death-red glow.

She opened her eyes and raised the weapon.

One movement. One action. One slice of her lightsaber, and the mask would be cleaved in two. In moments, she could reduce it to molten slag, and her pain would be over, and she would be free.

THERE.

She froze.

THERE.

LISTEN.

She stared at the mask. Her grip on the lightsaber hilt was firm but now every muscle in her body trembled in a kind of paralysis, like she was held in an invisible grip.

Perhaps it was *him*. Or perhaps it was just her imagination.

LISTEN.

She jerked, suddenly released. The lightsaber flew from her hand, propelled by an invisible force as it was smashed against the side of the meditation chamber. There was a bang, and the hilt twisted in a flash of blood-red flame, the weapon ruined.

She turned, went to find her broken weapon, but the same force that had snapped it from her hand now kept her right where she was.

LISTEN.

LISTEN.

She relaxed. It was pointless to fight. As the grip on her faded, she bowed her head and succumbed to the dark power.

"I am listening, my Master."

THERE.

DO YOU HEAR IT?

She looked up, closed her eyes, tilted her head. She listened, and then—

She smiled, just faintly. She moved her head, listening, as though the sound was . . . moving. Swelling.

"I can hear . . ." she whispered. "I can hear . . . music, my Master."

IT IS OUR MUSIC.

IT IS THE DISCORD OF THE FORCE.

Her smile grew, even as she felt herself slipping away, her will finally drained by the mask, her own name forgotten once more.

LISTEN TO THE DISCORD AND WEEP, FOR OUR TIME IS NOW.

She could hear it. The screams of the dead echoed from the mask, and the hurricane wind on which they were carried, the tempest that spun invisibly around her, now carried another sound. It was like a mighty chord, the music of the spheres as planets and moons moved and suns died. Deep, resonant.

Dangerous.

OUR TIME IS NOW.

"Yes, my Master."

LET THE MUSIC GUIDE YOU.

"Yes, my Master."

FOLLOW THE DISCORD. FIND THE CENTER. FIND THE STILL POINT.

"Yes, my Master."

She stood, took a step forward, and bent down to pick the mask up. The hard metal of the thing was cold, so cold it burned her hands. When she lifted it, she could feel the ache in her bones as the mask sucked the energy and life out of her to feed itself.

Her face blank, her breathing slow and deep and calm, she picked up the mask, turned it around, and, with her eyes firmly closed, put it on.

For a moment, there was silence, and darkness. She took a breath, and—

And for one second, she woke, her own mind swimming up to the surface, suddenly aware of who she was and where she was and what she was doing. The fear appeared like a lightning bolt, like it always did.

She screamed, and her screams joined the others, a cacophony of fear and pain and death that echoed inside the mask.

Then her mind cleared, just enough.

"My weapon. My blade. I cannot go unarmed."

IT IS TIME. TAKE THE OTHER. WIELD IT AS I ONCE DID AND REVEL IN ITS GLORY.

She moved across the chamber to where a metal-bound casket sat against the wall. It was ancient, the surface dull bronze, the inscription that crawled across the dirty metal mostly obscured by centuries of ash and wear.

She opened the box. Inside was a lightsaber hilt, longer than the weapon now lost, the one she had used for all these long years since that fateful day in Coronet City. She took it, feeling the weight, feeling the balance. It was as old as the box, as old as the mask she wore.

Slipping the replacement lightsaber onto her belt, she stood. Then she moved, her tattered cloak spinning as she marched out of the chamber, heading for her ship, which sat waiting outside in a space cleared by her droids, their last task before she'd put them to sleep. Outside, she passed the twisted wrecks of a thousand crashed starships surrounding her domain, the entire place lit in a sick red light from the swirling tumult of the nebula, glowing and writhing in the sky above.

Her ship was simple but efficient, highly maneuverable, and well armed, with good hyperspace range; the one-person fighter consisted of a central spherical flight module surrounded by three struts that supported triangular, winglike panels—a TIE Defender, another relic salvaged from an old war. The gunmetal gray of the ship had been painted, slashes of red and purple forming the zigzag angles of mirrored Aurebesh characters.

She climbed the ladder and settled into the cockpit. As she activated the ion engines and the Defender gently lifted from the launchpad, she paused and cocked her head, like she was listening again. In the cockpit, there was nothing but the steady hum of power and the distinctive whine of the fighter's engines.

But behind the mask, against the background of screams, the evil vibration was now a steady note, dark and awful.

She knew where to go. The discord of the Force would lead her there.

She punched the controls and the TIE Defender took off.

CHAPTER 15

THE RUINED TEMPLE, TYTHON
NOW

Luke turned and began to head back up the hill to the ancient temple. Truth was, it was good to see his old friend Lando again—it had been too long, and Luke had to admit he felt guilty about that, no matter how hard he tried to adhere to the Jedi Code of casting personal connections aside—but now was certainly not the time or place for a reunion. Not because it was spoiling the peace and tranquility. That had been well and truly shattered by Luke's experience with Exegol and his father. But there was every chance that Luke's actions were bringing the danger, the shadow, closer. The fewer people around him, right now, the better. For their own sake.

"Well, that's not quite the welcome I was expecting, Luke."

Luke stopped and turned around. Lando was standing, cape over one shoulder, hand on one hip.

Luke sighed. "Lando, I'm pleased to see you, really, but you need to get away from Tython. It's not safe here."

Lando frowned. "Hey, I didn't come for a social call—you took some finding, believe me. I had to ask all over before someone pointed me to a friend of yours, guy called Lor San Tekka. He knew exactly where you were."

Luke raised an eyebrow. "Lor San Tekka told you I was here?" That, in itself, was interesting. Lor wouldn't have revealed Luke's location, even to Lando, without a good reason.

But even so . . .

"He did," said Lando. "So at least hear me out, okay?"

"If it was any other time, yes, but you don't understand," said Luke. "There's a great danger coming, fast. I can face it myself, but I need you to leave, for your own safety." He smiled. "I don't want to see anything happen to an old friend." Luke turned and began walking up the path again. "I'll send you a transmission when its safe."

"It's about the Sith," said Lando.

Luke froze. He stared at the path in front of him, at the dirt and the grass and the flowers that moved in the breeze, the entire hillside glowing under the warm sun.

He didn't see any of it. Didn't feel it. All he felt was a . . . form, a *weight,* in the Force, like he was trying to walk through syrup, like the sky itself was a heavy blanket pushing down, trying to crush him into the ground.

And there, at the horizon of his mind, something moving, something distant, something casting a shadow that was long and dark and ancient and evil.

"I think they're back, Luke," said Lando. "The Sith are back."

Luke closed his eyes. Of course, this was why Lor San Tekka had told Lando where to come.

Very wise.

When Luke opened his eyes, he saw Lando, the charming grin gone, his eyes wide with concern.

A moment passed. Then another. The two old friends looked at each other, then Luke lifted his chin.

"Let's talk," he said.

In the forward lounge of the *Lady Luck,* Lando poured himself another tumbler of Declavian cognac, offering the bottle to Luke before noticing that Luke's own glass remained full and untouched on the table between them. Lando slumped into the couch and stoppered the decanter, lifting his glass and holding it up to the light. He looked at Luke and paused, almost feeling . . . guilty? But then the farmboy smile Lando remembered so well flickered across Luke's features, and Lando found himself grinning, too. "Long day," he said, raising the glass in a one-man toast—then draining it in a single gulp. With a satisfied exhale, Lando reached forward, pressing a button on the side of the table.

A concealed holoprojector sprang into life and projected a ghostly blue image above the table.

Luke leaned forward to take a better look. The slowly rotating image was of an amulet on the end of a fine chain. The amulet itself was geometric in design, diamond-shaped, looking like a stylized dagger symbol, held inside a circle.

Luke recognized it at once. "A hex charm," he said. He looked at Lando. "The family was carrying it?"

Lando nodded. He had filled Luke in on the conversation he'd overheard at Sennifer's Beam and Balance on Boxer Point Station, describing both what the strange man with the scarred face calling himself Ochi of Bestoon had said to his companions, and the results of his subsequent conversation with his New Republic contact, Shriv.

"They said they were being hunted down," said Lando, reaching for the bottle again, then pulling his hand away, perhaps thinking better of it. "By the Sith, and one of them showed the New Republic patrol that amulet as proof. Now, you called it a hex charm?"

Luke nodded. "A symbol of the Sith."

"Well, this Ochi of Bestoon," Lando continued, "he talked about the Sith, said this kidnap job was like some kind of sacred task." Lando shrugged. "He was drunk, but I checked out his story. What he told his friends certainly matched up with this report from Halo Squadron."

Luke sat back and stroked his beard. Lando watched him for a moment. Luke looked older than Lando remembered, the short beard and familiar mop of hair now starting to show a few lines of gray—hell, Lando thought, they were *both* older, there was no antidote to the passage of time—but there was still the kindness in Luke's eyes that Lando knew so well, despite Luke's current concerned expression.

It *was* good to see him again. Lando berated himself for taking so long to see an old friend. There weren't many men in the galaxy that shared their kind of history.

History. It wasn't something Lando dwelled on—not before, certainly not now. He had never understood nostalgia, how people could get so caught up in their own past. Lando had always looked to the future, to a destiny he could control, not a past he would regret.

A future that had been shattered, utterly, by the abduction of his daughter.

Lando felt his temper rise. He tightened his grip on his empty tumbler, then carefully set it down on the table before he cracked the glass in his fist.

"They were planning a *kidnapping*, Luke," said Lando, sinking back into the couch, a sneer entering his voice, one he didn't like to hear, but he couldn't help himself. "That hunter was going to kidnap a child. A young girl." Lando shook his head, the muscles at the back of his jaw bunching as he fought to control his emotions.

Then Lando sat up and leaned forward, looking at Luke through the blue glow of the hologram.

"The galaxy is supposed to be a safe place." He waved a hand through the amulet. "Okay, sure, there're always dark corners and bad places and bad people, I'm not pretending there aren't." He sat back and tapped his own chest. "Hey, sometimes those bad people were me. I'm not trying to hide from that." He sighed and shook his head. There it was again. History. The past, a place Lando didn't want to visit. "But the Empire is gone. Palpatine and Vader have been dead twenty years, and the Sith were supposed to have died with them." He waved a hand. "Oh . . . I don't even know what to think now. Maybe Ochi of Bestoon, whoever he was, was lying. He said he's worked for the Sith before, and now they've reactivated him, whatever that means. The way he was talking, didn't sound like he thought of himself as a Sith, but that they were somewhere out there, pulling his strings."

Luke nodded at the hologram. "This amulet is a Sith artifact," he said. He reached forward to touch the projector controls on his side of the table, and cycled through a selection of close-up images of the amulet from different angles and magnifications. He paused on one in particular—a scan of the amulet's back, large enough to see that there was writing inscribed around the circumference of the circle. "This is a Sith inscription."

Lando frowned and leaned forward to look. "It looks familiar."

"It's Aurebesh, mirrored."

"Mirrored?"

Luke shrugged. "The Sith had their own language, but few knew it. So they substituted. Mirroring Aurebesh was their way of corrupting it."

"So what does the amulet say?"

"Nothing much," said Luke. "It's a Sith proverb. 'The tides of power ebb and flow as the wheel of fate turns.' I've come across it several times in my research. It's an old phrase, but it doesn't mean anything in particular."

"Okay," said Lando, "it's more like, what, a good-luck message?"

"Something like that." Luke pursed his lips. "We were lucky—*you* were lucky, Lando, to put this together."

"Hey," said Lando, spreading his hands, his old grin starting to show again, Luke's company—and the cognac—having a pleasantly calming effect. "You know what they say, right place, right time." His grin faded. "But why them? Why that family? Seems a lot of trouble just to get a girl." Lando stopped, his expression tight, his gaze locking with Luke's.

Luke nodded and gave a soft smile. Right then, Lando could almost sense Luke's thoughts. He didn't know how the Force worked, had never felt it himself, but . . . it was like Luke could feel his pain—he could feel it, right here, right now, radiating from him like the heat from the core of a sun.

"So what about these vision things?" asked Lando, quickly distracting himself from his own thoughts with a wave of a hand and another measure of spirit. "You, what, sense something in the Force? You just sort of, close your eyes and see things? How does it work?"

"I actually don't know," said Luke, "but I don't have to. I've been having the visions for weeks now."

"And they've all been to this planet, Exegol?"

Luke nodded. "The hidden world of the Sith."

Lando raised an eyebrow and gave a low whistle as he contemplated the drink in his glass.

"Wow, a whole planet of them. I have to say that doesn't exactly give me a warm feeling." He sipped his drink, slower this time.

Luke stroked his beard again in thought. "The way to Exegol is encoded in a Sith wayfinder." Seeing Lando's curious expression, Luke continued. "It's a navigational aid, allowing the user to find the planet. Only two were ever made, their locations hidden."

Lando took another sip as he thought. "Ochi said he would know the way to Exegol soon. Okay, so . . ." He paused, his eyes going wide. "Maybe the family has one of these wayfinders?"

"Or knows where one is. Maybe that's why they're being hunted. Maybe that's what Ochi was talking about—he kidnaps the girl for his master, he gets the wayfinder."

The two men sat in silence for a moment. Then Lando placed his glass back on the table with a clack and, slapping both thighs, stood up.

"Well, okay," said Lando. "I'm ready."

Luke blinked. "Ready for what?"

"Hey, hey, we have a job here." Lando gesticulated with his hands as he spoke, a fire growing within him. This time, Lando went with the feeling, letting this new passion grow within him. "We need to find the family. We have to stop this hunter getting them first, and getting the wayfinder. Luke, listen, you said it yourself. There's a disturbance in the Force, a, what did you call it, a *shadow*, and it's coming at us fast." He paused, then sat carefully back down. "We need to find out where the New Republic sent the family. It's the one thing redacted in the report."

Luke looked at Lando. "How good is your contact?"

Lando cocked his head. "Shriv? Solid. Plus, his search for the report was logged with my command code. If I show up, it won't be a surprise to anyone. I still hold rank, technically, and there're still strings I can pull. Maybe we can talk to the flight sergeant, Dina Dipurl, and she can tell us herself. It'd be good to get her read on the family."

Luke nodded and stood. "Listen, Lando. I appreciate you coming to me, but I can handle this alone."

Lando shook his head as he walked around the table. He reached out to Luke, and the pair locked arms.

"I need to do this, Luke. This is the best lead I've had in a long, long time. We're doing this together." He paused, and in that moment Lando felt the shadow again, one cast by memory and regret, and the knowledge that maybe, just maybe, this was the chance he'd been waiting for. He just hoped he didn't look too desperate to his old friend.

Luke knew about Lando's daughter, of course. He'd helped out, they all had—Lando had come to his friends in desperation, but he hadn't had to ask. Lando knew, or at least suspected, that family was a complicated concept for Luke, but he also knew that wouldn't stop his old friend from recognizing the pain and loss Lando had suffered, his life changed in an *instant*.

So they had searched, but as time had gone on, as leads had dried up, so the mission had drifted, along with friendships. Luke had his temple to focus on. Han and Leia had their own lives. Lando didn't blame them. In the end, the problem—the pain—was his to bear. So, Lando had continued his search. Alone.

"No matter how the darkness grows, you are never alone."

Lando looked at Luke. "What?"

Luke smiled. "Just something someone once told me." He tightened his grip on Lando's arm and gave a short, affirmative nod. "I'm glad to have you at my side."

Lando's stomach flipped, the relief almost overwhelming. And he felt his own expression change, a huge, but very genuine, grin now spreading across his face.

"Besides," said Lando, "the *Lady Luck* is a hell of a lot more comfortable than that museum piece you've got parked out there."

Luke laughed. "The T-65 is a classic, my friend," he said in mock offense.

"Then point that classic toward Adelphi. My contact Shriv is stationed out there."

"I'll see you there," said Luke. As he walked away from the table, heading toward the *Lady Luck*'s exit ramp, he glanced at his still-full glass. "Thanks for the drink."

Lando laughed and waved both hands at Luke. "Get out of here, farmboy." And then, to Luke's retreating back, he said, "I'll give you a head start, give you time for Artoo to get that 'classic' of yours warmed up."

Luke waved over his shoulder and was gone.

Lando reached down and picked up Luke's drink and the decanter of cognac. He lifted the glass and was about to pour it back into the bottle when he paused and gave a shrug.

"You know, Luke, you never did know how to appreciate the finer side of life in this big, bad galaxy of ours," he muttered to himself before downing Luke's drink. He gasped for breath, shook his whole body from shoulders to toes, then turned and headed to the flight deck.

CHAPTER 16

NEW REPUBLIC STAGING POST, ADELPHI SYSTEM

NOW

Lando shook his head and sighed. He adjusted his gold cape at the collar and ran an elegant finger along both edges, ensuring the fabric sat just *so* across his shoulders. He puffed up his chest and rolled his neck.

"I was a general of the Rebel Alliance, you know," he said. "I destroyed the second Death Star. You remember that? That was me." He stabbed a finger forward. "You *owe* me."

He looked at the face in front of him. The dark skin, the dark hair swept back from the forehead. The immaculately trimmed mustache.

Then he sighed and turned away from his reflection in the window. He looked around the office and sighed again.

He'd been at the New Republic staging outpost in orbit above Adelphi for a couple of hours now, and while his former position in the Alliance had allowed him easy access to the facility, he'd been shunted around between one officer and another, swapping between ranks high and low, nobody quite sure how to help him, nobody quite willing to tell him what he wanted to know. Finally, he had demanded to see the post commander, and had been shown into a large corner office, where he had been waiting for . . .

Well, for quite a while now.

Lando turned back to the window, which formed the entire corner of the room, stretching up to a ceiling a good four meters high. The staging post was an impressive facility, acting as both a surveillance and a relay station for this sector, as well as being large enough for the New Republic fleet to muster strike forces and other large-scale operations. It was big and it was impressive, and that also applied to the post commander's private office.

Outside, Lando could see nothing but stars, the brightly lit office turning the wall into a rather good mirror. If he looked down, Lando could *just* see the blue-green rim of the planet Adelphi itself. He'd been there a few times. Nice place. There was a little card hall, in a town called Cirimalk, where he and Kaasha had once spent a very nice few days with—

There was a soft chime, and the office door slid open to admit a blue-and-white astromech droid.

Lando grinned at the droid, which whistled and beeped at him in recognition.

"Artoo! Finally, you made it. Where's Luke?"

R2-D2 gave a series of complicated woots and whistles that was clearly a detailed explanation, but just then Luke walked in, followed by a young New Republic officer.

"Thank you," said Luke to the officer, who came to attention and snapped a salute, then walked out. The office door slid shut behind her.

The two friends moved together and shook hands. "What took you so long?" asked Lando. "I knew that T-65 was slow, but . . ."

Luke chuckled and held up a hand. "I thought I'd give *you* a head start." He looked around the office and frowned. "I get the feeling you haven't had much luck."

Lando barked a laugh. "You can say that again." He jerked his chin in the direction of the closed door. "I don't think they like us."

That was when the door swished open. Lando and Luke turned to see another New Republic officer enter, followed by her adjunct. Both were clad in the familiar blue-and-tan uniforms, the female officer in front bearing the rank insignia of commander. The commander gave her two waiting guests a sharp nod, but her adjunct ignored them completely.

It seemed Lando's assessment of the situation had been correct.

"I'm sorry, gentlemen," said the commander as she made her way around the large desk in the corner and sat behind it, her back to the expansive view of space and the planet Adelphi, "but I'm afraid you might have had a wasted journey."

Luke moved to stand in front of the desk. He pursed his lips and looked at the officer. She was a middle-aged woman, with sharp features and a bob of bright white hair tinged with a metallic blue sheen.

Luke smiled, and spread his hands. "We're very sorry for the intrusion, Commander . . . ?"

At this, the adjunct snapped into life. "Commander Xarah Blacwood is in charge of this facility, gentlemen." He looked at Luke, and then at Lando, taking his time, his eyes roving up and down the visitors. "If you will put a request through the official channels, I'm sure we could—"

Commander Blacwood put up a hand and shook her head. "I'm sorry," she said, with a sigh. "My adjunct, Lieutenant Jashei Zigler. He is efficient, but he is also somewhat . . . rule-bound."

Lando joined Luke in front of the desk. "Commander Blacwood, we just need to talk to one of your officers, then we'll be out of your way. Flight Sergeant Dina Dipurl. Seconded to Halo Squadron, but based here at Adelphi."

Commander Blacwood just shrugged. "I'm sorry, I really wish I could help you, but I can't."

Luke smiled softly. "We understand the sensitivity of Halo Squadron's mission, Commander. But our business is as urgent as it is important."

Blacwood didn't answer immediately. Lando saw the hesitation, the look in her eyes, and got a sense of . . . something.

"Flight Sergeant Dipurl is not available."

Luke and Lando exchanged a look, then Luke turned back to Blacwood. "Commander, I urge you to reconsider. If you could see your way to allowing us to contact Flight Sergeant Dipurl, we would be immensely grateful."

Commander Blacwood cocked her head at Luke. "Just what *are* you doing here, Master Skywalker? Don't get me wrong, I'm flattered that

Adelphi is graced by your presence, but I still don't know why you want to talk to a flight officer?"

Luke's expression was tight. Lando wondered how much he was going to say, whether they needed to lay it all out to the commander—it was not necessarily a secret, but Lando had a feeling that they wanted to keep the information they had close, need-to-know, at least for the moment. Word of their visit to Adelphi was bound to get out, and if Luke started talking about what he and Lando had discovered, then—

Then . . . what? What were they doing here, if not to get information? Things were moving and Lando knew they had to get ahead of them. He thought again about the stroke of luck that had landed him at Sennifer's Beam and Balance, how he couldn't just throw that away.

Right place, right time.

"It's the Sith," he said, leaning over the commander's desk. "They're back, and there's something big coming and we're trying to head it off."

Commander Blacwood stared at Lando for a moment, then her eyes moved to Luke.

"The Sith?"

Luke said nothing. He didn't need to.

"The Sith are extinct," said Zigler, sharply. He turned to look down at his CO. "I'm sorry to speak out of turn, ma'am, but this kind of talk is dangerous." He looked at Luke and gave him a thin smile. "While I appreciate the fact that Master Skywalker has seen fit to visit Adelphi, I don't think it would do any good if word of this were to get around."

Lando frowned. "If the Sith are dead, then what does it matter? Why would that scare your crew?"

"*Gentlemen*," said Blacwood. She stood from her desk. "We are engaged in several high-value missions that are classified in nature. Halo Squadron included. Master Skywalker, I know your sister might be a senator, but there are channels to go through, and—"

"Channels?" Lando cut in. "Hey, this man isn't just Leia's brother. He won the war for you." He leaned on the desk. "We both did. So how about a little cooperation, huh?"

Luke shook his head and laid a friendly hand on Lando's shoulder.

"Lando," he said quietly.

Lando stood and took a step back. He held up both hands in apology. "All right, all right, I'm sorry. But you have to understand, this is important."

Commander Blacwood looked at them, then shook her head. "I'm sorry, I can't help you." She glanced at her adjunct.

Zigler snapped his heels in a way that reminded Lando, unpleasantly, of the old Imperial order.

"Gentlemen, this interview has come to a conclusion," said the lieutenant. "You are welcome to make full use of station facilities, but the commander will be in conference for the rest of this cycle."

Lando opened his mouth to say something—something possibly quite loud—but Luke waved him down. He gave Commander Blacwood a deep bow, then turned for the door. As he passed Lando, he placed a guiding hand on his friend's shoulder and firmly maneuvered him out. R2-D2 wheeled silently behind them.

The door swished closed, and they stood in the gleaming white corridor.

Lando gestured to the closed door. "What was that about? The New Republic won't help us because we didn't fill out the right forms?"

Luke glanced up and down the corridor, checking in case anyone was watching. Officers and technicians were moving past in a steady stream of foot traffic, but nobody was paying them the slightest bit of attention. He nudged Lando.

"Time for the unofficial route, then. Did you get in touch with your contact?"

Lando nodded. "I sent a transmission as soon as I entered the system." He lifted his wrist comlink to his lips and pressed a button. "Shriv?"

The wrist speaker clicked. "No luck with the big boys, eh?"

Lando smiled. "That's a negative. Where are you?"

"Hangar seven," came Shriv's voice. "And I think I've got something else for you."

Lando and Luke exchanged a hopeful glance.

"But," said Shriv, "I'm not sure you're going to like it."

"We'll be right down," said Lando, releasing the call button.

Luke nodded. "Let's go," he said, peeling out of the doorway and heading down the corridor, his friend and droid right behind.

It took a moment to find Shriv in hangar seven, the Duros was lurking behind a stack of equipment crates that provided ample cover for a recessed workstation in the rear wall of the hangar. Lando and Shriv shook hands, and Lando introduced Luke.

"So what's going on?" asked Lando. "Everyone seems a little on edge."

Shriv looked around, just to make sure they were out of view, and gave a shrug.

"You know how it is," he said. "There's always something going on. Don't take it personally. But listen, you'll want to see this."

At that, he took a small datastick from the pocket of his tunic and inserted it into the workstation's reader. The small display on the wall flicked into life and showed a starfield, the stars spinning around the long nose of a fighter, their viewpoint from the starboard wing of a fighter.

"That's an X-wing," said Luke, stepping closer to peer at the screen. He looked at Shriv. "You got the flight feed from that patrol?"

Shriv nodded. "Took some favors, but I got it." He looked at Lando. "After I found that report you wanted, I did some digging to get access to the redacted portion. The officers who made that report, Flight Sergeant Dipurl and Lieutenant Asheron?"

"What about them?" asked Lando. He glanced at Luke.

Luke said nothing. He just stared at the screen as the recording from the X-wing's flight cam continued to play. The spinning starfield was now filled with flashes of green and red light as streaks of other light shot across space in front of the fighter.

They were watching a dogfight.

"Seems they found more of the pirates that attacked the family," said Shriv, gesturing to the screen, "only this time, they were outnumbered."

Lando forced himself to watch, but he knew what Shriv was suggesting. The recording on the tiny screen was a blur of motion as the X-wing—Lando didn't know which of the two officers it was in the cockpit—maneuvered around the enemy. Finally, it got behind one and locked on, and Lando got a good look at the pirate craft. It was small, angular, a hemispherical central hull bristling with armaments, with multiple winglets and flight surfaces protruding from it. He didn't recognize the design.

Then there was a flash, and the screen went black.

Luke and Lando turned to Shriv. Shriv sighed.

"Killed in action, both of them." He folded his arms and looked at his feet. "I'm sorry," he said, quietly. "They were good people, and they died trying to fight for the little guys, you know?"

Lando felt the air leave his lungs. Yes, he did know. He knew what it was like to risk your life to protect others, to fly into battle when your odds of survival were a rapidly decreasing percentage. But that was wartime. That was fighting to save the galaxy from cruelty and tyranny.

The war was supposed to be over. The Empire was dead. The New Republic had worked hard to establish a new order of peace, prosperity, friendship, cooperation, across thousands of systems, uniting peoples across the galaxy, as far as they could reach.

Lando knew he was being naïve, of course. Just because the war was over didn't mean the galaxy was safe—he knew that all too well. There was always danger and evil. That was still part of being a pilot in the New Republic. Each and every patrol was still a risk, the odds of survival never 100 percent.

He looked at Luke. His old friend seemed frozen on the spot, staring at the now blank monitor.

R2-D2 beeped, the tone low, questioning. Luke glanced down at the droid, and a small smile appeared on his face. Then he looked at Lando. "We have to find that family and help them." He gestured at the screen. "That was a much larger group of hunters than Halo Squadron had first encountered."

Lando nodded and turned to Shriv. "Did you get the redacted coordinates?"

Shriv pointed at the workstation console. "I've got the full flight record, recordings, the official report, and Dipurl's addendum. It'll be faster if your droid scans through it."

Without waiting for instructions, R2-D2 twittered and rolled toward the workstation. Extending his scomp link, he connected to the computer, the rings of the port coupling rotating as he began sifting through the information Shriv had managed to download.

The three men stood by, waiting patiently as R2-D2 analyzed the data. Lando watched Luke, but he was quiet, his expression unreadable. And in that moment, Lando realized just what it was he was asking of his old friend. Luke was a Jedi Master; he had his own temple to run, a new generation of Jedi to train—his own nephew, Ben, included. And now this, chasing off across the galaxy to find a family.

Like those years ago, when they'd chased off across the galaxy to find Kadara.

They hadn't found her. Would it be different, this time? Was that what Luke was thinking right now?

Lando wanted to say something, but he was suddenly . . . nervous? He almost laughed at that, but yes, he was nervous. It was ridiculous, Luke was a friend, a good one. But Lando also knew that they operated on different . . . frequencies, was perhaps the best way to put it. Which was fine, absolutely. But Lando couldn't help but wonder if that time apart had stretched their camaraderie a little further than he had thought.

R2-D2 bleeped. Lando immediately broke out of his tangled train of thought and knelt down by the droid. He placed one hand on top of R2-D2's dome.

"What have you got, little buddy?"

Shriv peered at the display screen. Screeds of text were now flying by, too fast to make out, as R2-D2 collated the files. Then the scrolling text stopped, the last block of characters flashing.

"Some days I could really use a droid of my own," said Shriv. "I think he's got it."

As Luke cast his eye over the display, Lando stood and joined him. Luke traced the text with his finger.

"These are the coordinates. Dipurl sent them to . . . Nightside?" Luke turned to Lando, and Lando was already nodding to himself, the corner of his mouth threatening to break into one of his trademark grins.

"They're on Nightside. All right, all right. Clever Dina Dipurl."

Luke could only shake his head. "Nightside? Is that a system, or a ship, or . . . ?"

"Mining colony," said Shriv, as he folded his arms and shook his head. "I'm not entirely sure I'd call that good news, Lando."

This only made Lando grin even more. "Shriv, this is great news," he said, batting his friend on the arm. He turned to Luke. "Nightside is a mining operation in the rings of the Therezar system."

"'Operation' is one word for it," said Shriv. "*Cartel* is another."

But Lando shook his head. "What? No. Come on, Shriv. Nightside isn't all bad. I know the administrator—regent-captain, they call it. His name is Zargo Anaximander. He gave a lot of help to the Rebel Alliance back in the day, did some very good things for the cause. And he owes me a favor or two." He tapped the display. "And look, it was good enough for Dipurl. She knew someone there, too, that's why she sent the family there. Right, Shriv?"

The Duros officer shrugged. "It's a well-established facility, certainly. Whoever these people are, they'd be able to get repairs, maybe even get an entirely new ship. If Dipurl's contact was solid."

"Well, *mine* is," said Lando. He knelt back down to R2-D2. "Did you download the whole report?"

R2-D2 bleeped in the affirmative. Lando nodded and stood, and he felt . . . different. Energized, almost impatient, ready for action, bouncing on his feet.

Lando held out his hand to Shriv, and the two men drew in for a combination handshake, hug, and backslap.

"Thanks for everything, Shriv. See you soon, I hope."

"Hey, now *you* owe me one, okay? Now, get the hell out of here, before someone really does get into trouble." Shriv turned to Luke, and held out his hand. "It was a pleasure, Master Skywalker."

Luke took the Duros's hand and shook it warmly. "I hope you don't get into any trouble, helping us like this."

Shriv chuckled. "This conversation never happened." He blinked his huge eyes in mock surprise. "Now, who were you again?"

CHAPTER 17

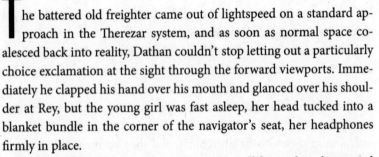

NIGHTSIDE, THEREZAR SYSTEM
NOW

The battered old freighter came out of lightspeed on a standard approach in the Therezar system, and as soon as normal space coalesced back into reality, Dathan couldn't stop letting out a particularly choice exclamation at the sight through the forward viewports. Immediately he clapped his hand over his mouth and glanced over his shoulder at Rey, but the young girl was fast asleep, her head tucked into a blanket bundle in the corner of the navigator's seat, her headphones firmly in place.

"What is it?" asked Miramir, her attention still focused on the myriad controls in front of her, most of which, Dathan could see, were flashing an angry red. He didn't need his wife's knack for technology to know that they had been lucky just to *get* to Therezar. Following Dina Dipurl's suggestion, they'd made the journey in a series of short hops—the long way around, certainly, but each waypoint had been calculated carefully to take them out into the dead space between star systems, and each jump had been short enough for their failing hyperdrive motivator to handle without requiring much time to cool down. The trip had been frustratingly slow, but in the end, Dathan knew that their caution had been worth it. There would have been no point in jumping straight to Therezar only for the stressed engine to explode on their final approach.

When Dathan didn't say anything, Miramir finally looked up at him. He pointed, and she turned to look forward.

Therezar itself was a huge gas giant, filling half the forward view, despite the huge distance that remained between the ship and the planet. Its surface was a mix of swirling colors, like pots of spilled ink—red and blue and yellow and white—either streaking out into long bands that stretched around the entire globe or spinning into vast, eye-shaped storms. That they could sit and watch the striated cloud cover move and change with such speed made Dathan nervous as he contemplated the terrifying force of the storms that must ravage the giant world. The clouds were illuminated by colossal flashes of light, lightning storms with electrical discharges that must have been tens of thousands of kilometers long.

Therezar was a nightmare world, a gas giant tearing itself apart.

Miramir carefully eased the control yoke. As their ship moved up, the ring system of the planet became visible, a huge disk that looked, from their position, entirely solid, shaded by the body of the planet as they approached the dark hemisphere.

Nightside, their actual intended destination, was visible at the far portside horizon of the planet, just where the light from Therezar's sun illuminated the other half of the rings. At first, it looked like a large cuboid, standing upright and penetrating the plane of Therezar's ring, an equal portion of the structure protruding above and below. As they got closer, they could see it was actually two separate structures, a topside cube and an identical station below the rings. In the middle was what looked like a giant skeletal maw, as big as the two solid structures above and below it combined.

Nightside was completely stationary, held in a fixed orbit as the rings passed *through* its skeletal midsection. On the other side of the station there was a bright glow—Dathan thought it was the reflection of the sun on the bright half of the rings, but as Miramir brought them into a parking orbit and the ship swung around, Dathan swore again—a little quieter, this time. He glanced at Miramir, who was looking ahead, her lips parted slightly as she took the sight in with breathless curiosity.

"I've never seen anything like that before," she said, and then her eyes flicked to her husband's, and she grinned. "This is incredible."

Dathan blinked again, and then he shared her smile. He couldn't help it. Miramir found the joy in everything, and he knew already that her mind would be racing with thoughts as she tried to understand what she was looking at and, more specifically, how it *worked*.

Dathan turned back to the view and could only shake his head slowly in awe.

Nightside was eating the band of Therezar's ring system in which it maintained a stationary orbit, the slow turn of the planet bringing the material into the gaping hole of the mining section, where it was pulverized and reduced to component elements, what little waste product remained left to exit the other side as a superhot stream of ionized particles.

Miramir was right. It *was* incredible, not least because of the scale of the operation. Nightside's maw was taking in ring material that was the size of asteroids, with enough mass to have their own gravity.

It was only when they got to docking orbit that the rest of the structure was visible. Because Nightside wasn't just a simple pair of boxes linked by the mine, it was an entire system all of its own.

Surrounding the main structure was a network of smaller constructions—some perfect white cubes like the central superstructure, others elongated platforms bristling with vast, automated machines, both on the topside and underneath, each side floodlit in the darkness of Therezar's night, the gas giant's silhouette punctuated with flashes of light as its storms raged on. Between the outer islands of the Nightside complex, other lights streaked, like the electrical impulses of a vast nervous system, connecting the whole system together.

Dathan leaned forward to get a better look, and as he moved, Miramir reached up and activated a control, dimming the cabin lights so they could get a better look.

The streaks of light were now revealed as transport cars, running along cables that connected all of Nightside's substations together in a vast spider's web.

"Okay," said Miramir, "now I really *haven't* seen anything like that."

Dathan nodded, then he looked down at the comm deck in front of him. "Well, I'm sure we can get the guided tour once we get in." He paused, frowning. "*If* we get in."

Miramir stood and went over to where Rey was sleeping. She knelt by their child and gently stroked her hair as she slept. "Dina gave us the docking code *and* her contact."

Dathan leaned over the console, his head bowed, his eyes closed.

"What?" asked Miramir softly. "You don't think it will work?"

Dathan sighed, loudly, then he sat back into the copilot's seat and spun it around. "I hope it does," he said. "But we can't rely on hope forever."

Miramir turned back to watch the sleeping form of Rey. The child's face was completely serene. Dathan couldn't remember the last time *he* had slept so peacefully.

On Hyperkarn, perhaps. But that was so many, many years ago.

"You don't trust them," said Miramir, not looking at Dathan.

"You know I don't," said Dathan. "We can't afford to. The only people I trust are right here, with me."

Miramir turned to look at her husband. "They've given us a chance, here." She nodded at the forward viewports. "The New Republic might not care, but Dina Dipurl did. I say we give it a shot."

"We don't have a choice, do we?"

Their conversation was interrupted as the comm deck chimed and a rather stern and businesslike female voice echoed loudly in the cabin.

"This is Nightside Flight Control. You are entering a private exclusion zone. Transmit your authorization code now or you will be escorted to neutral territory for questioning."

"Mum?" Rey blinked and looked up at Miramir. "Are we home yet?"

Miramir smiled at her daughter and started stroking her hair again as Rey pushed herself up from the navigator's seat, slipping the headphones off with a clatter as she wrapped her arms around Miramir, snuggling into the crook of her mother's neck.

Miramir hugged Rey, tight. She buried her nose in Rey's hair and breathed in deeply.

As Dathan watched, he could feel a tightness in his chest, his breathing shallow, the pinprick of tears behind his eyes.

Home. Just one simple word. One simple word that meant so much.

"Soon," whispered Miramir into Rey's ear. "Soon, my darling, soon."

The console chimed again. "This is Nightside Flight Control. Transmit your—"

Dathan cut the controller off with the flick of a switch. "Acknowledged, Nightside. Transmitting docking authorization now."

He released the button, then paused, looking down at the controls. He lifted his hand. The datachip Dina Dipurl had given them was tiny, just a square of silver with a tiny port on the side.

He held his breath. He knew he was being irrational, that he was being driven by fear and fatigue and a growing sense of dread. But it wasn't fear for himself. He was afraid for his family. For Miramir. For Rey. They were in this because of him, and they didn't deserve this life.

He had to put it right. He had to make them safe.

So, for the first time in a long time, he decided to trust someone.

Without sparing it another thought, he turned the datachip over in his fingers and inserted it into the comm deck. The light on the reader went green as the key was accepted, then began flickering as the data was transferred to Nightside Flight Control.

Then Dathan sat back and looked at the vast mining colony in front of them, and hoped he had made the right decision.

The code had worked. Flight Sergeant Dipurl had been as good as her word, and Miramir flew their ship into dock 817-4174 in the upper section of the Nightside mining complex with textbook precision.

They hadn't known what to expect after landing. Dathan had braced himself, based on the terse exchange with flight control and their experience with Halo Squadron, for an onslaught of bureaucracy. But as he led them down the ship's ramp, Miramir following hand in hand with Rey, he was surprised to find their arrival had gone, if not unnoticed, then totally ignored.

Dock 817-4174 was vast and gray, and filled with dozens of ships, from small single-pilot hoppers to large bulk freighters. The place was a hive of activity, with people and droids moving everywhere. No sooner had Dathan, Miramir, and Rey stopped at the bottom of their ship's ramp than the craft next to theirs, a roughly circular, midsized trading barge, lifted off with a whine and rotated on its axis before making a leisurely exit.

Dathan looked around, shifting the woven bag on his shoulder that contained all their worldly goods—their money, their blanket, the last of their rations. Miramir picked up Rey—she was getting too big to be carried, but Dathan knew that wouldn't stop his wife from trying—and, balancing her daughter awkwardly on her hip, gazed around the hangar.

"Okay," she said. "Now what?"

"We find our contact."

Miramir nodded. "Zargo Anaximander. Okay." She looked again, Dathan casting his gaze around the opposite direction. There was an exit door nearby. Dathan pointed at it. "First step, we find a comm channel, see if we can raise someone."

He led them the short distance from their ship to the hangar door. Beyond, the corridor was gray durasteel and ceramic, much like the hangar itself. It was functional, industrial, reminding Dathan of his first steps into the galaxy at large, after he'd managed to smuggle himself out of Exegol and found himself in the shipyard of Koke Frost. But he'd found his way then. He would find his way now—for himself, and for his family.

The corridor was as busy as the hangar, and Miramir clutched Rey tightly to her body as the trio made their way through the throng.

"There," said Dathan, pausing only to point, then he speeded up to reach the public comm station, just a few meters down the passage.

The trio huddled around it. Miramir and Dathan looked at each other, then Dathan shrugged and hit the call button for information.

"Nightside Central Control," came the tinny voice, and then it stopped.

"Ah, hello," said Dathan. "I'm looking for Zargo Anaximander."

There was no response. Dathan and Miramir looked at each other, then Dathan pushed the button again. "Hello?"

"Is this some kind of joke?"

"Ah . . . I'm sorry, what?"

"Present your scandocs to the reader, please."

Dathan winced. "We don't have any scandocs. We've just landed in dock 817-4174, and we were told to ask for Zargo Anaximander."

"Who told you?"

"Ah, Dipurl. Dina Dipurl. New Republic, Flight Sergeant."

There was a pause. Dathan released the button and looked at Miramir. She just shook her head, swaying from side to side with Rey slumped over her shoulder.

That was when he saw it. Over Miramir's shoulder, down the busy corridor. Two people in matching uniforms, light-gray tunics with bright-yellow arms, the color scheme matched on their helmets, their faces hidden behind large, mirrored, hemispherical visors. Dathan thought they were human at first, then noticed that their waists were nothing but a narrow column of metal, allowing the upper body to rotate smoothly around the axis as the figures—security droids, Dathan realized—turned to get a lock on the family's position. As he watched, the droids, moving in unison, extended their right hands down, parallel with their upper leg. As they did so, a panel on their legs opened with a snap, presenting the waiting hand with a small blaster.

Thus armed, the droid guards began marching down the corridor toward them.

Miramir reached for the call button again, but Dathan caught her wrist. "We need to get out of here."

Miramir looked at him, then glanced over her shoulder, and saw the guards approaching. She drew Rey's body closer to hers.

"But Zargo Anaximander is supposed to help us," Miramir whispered.

Dathan put his arm around the pair and gently guided them in front of him. "Maybe Dina's contact wasn't as solid as she thought." He propelled Miramir down the corridor, away from the guards and from the hangar door. If they could just lose themselves in the crowd—Nightside wasn't just a factory in space, it was a mining colony—an entire *city*—then perhaps they could find another way back to the ship. All they had to do was hide, wait until the coast was clear, and get out . . . maybe even in another ship. The hangar had been full of them. Miramir could fly anything.

One thing was for certain, though. He wanted to stay as far away from Zargo Anaximander as possible. The reaction from the comm operator, and the appearance of the two droid guards, had told him exactly what he needed to know. Whatever Flight Sergeant Dina Dipurl had known—or *thought* she had known—about the administrator of Nightside, Dathan wasn't prepared to take any more chances.

Trust. No one.

Miramir led them across a passageway junction and down the left-hand corridor, pausing to let Rey down on the ground, then clutching her daughter's hand tight. She glanced behind to see that Dathan was following, then turned—

And ran directly into another droid guard that had appeared in front of her. She yelped in surprise and stepped back, one protective hand on the back of Rey's head.

Dathan was at her side in an instant. Behind him, the first two droid guards had caught up.

Dathan quickly moved closer to Miramir. He put his arm around her and with his other hand drew Rey in close, protecting both mother and daughter with his own body.

The droid guard in front of them turned its opaque visor on the trio. Dathan watched his distorted, fish-eyed reflection in the curved surface.

Then the droid swiveled on its midsection. "You will follow me and obey all instructions," it said, the artificial voice male-sounding and devoid of emotion—not quite a monotone, but not far off.

With that, it moved off, Dathan realizing that the droid guard had multi-jointed legs and symmetrical feet, allowing it to swap direction without turning its lower section around.

There was a gentle shove in the small of his back. Dathan glanced over his shoulder, but again only saw his own tinted reflection.

"You will move now," said the droid guard, its voice identical to the first.

Dathan looked at Miramir, then, one arm around his wife, the other on Rey's shoulder, he let the droid guards escort them down the corridor.

CHAPTER 18

NIGHTSIDE, THEREZAR SYSTEM
NOW

They were led into a holding room that was a square metal chamber that was simply that, an entirely empty metal box, devoid of anything. When the door closed behind them, Dathan hadn't even been able to see its outline in the bare wall.

And . . . they waited.

And waited.

While Dathan focused on assessing their situation and chances of escape, Miramir looked after Rey. As soon as it was clear nobody was going to come and get them anytime soon, she'd taken the bag Dathan was carrying and pulled out the brightly colored woven blanket. She laid it out on the floor, and now she and Rey were sitting on it, sharing a high-density ration bar between them while Dathan restarted his examination of the wall where the door should have been.

After a few more minutes, he stopped and turned around, shaking his head. Miramir looked at him, still chewing her food. Dathan forced a smile onto his face, then joined his family, folding himself down to sit next to Rey. Immediately, the girl offered her father the last part of her ration.

"Hey, thank you very much, Rey!" Dathan took it and broke the chunk in half, handing the remainder back to her. "Here you go. Dessert."

The three sat and ate in silence. Dathan, finishing his mouthful, leaned back, savoring the rough feeling of the blanket underneath his hands. It was heavily textured but soft, a patchwork of warm oranges, browns, red. It had been a farewell gift from Miramir's Baba, her grandmother, woven with her own hands late at night and early in the morning, the kindly old woman fitting it in around her work repairing the droids of the nearby village on Hyperkarn. Dathan had watched the blanket grow over the days and weeks. He remembered the look in the old woman's eyes as she presented it to the couple, folded, tied with the blue ribbon Miramir now tied her long blond hair with.

And now, in the middle of the featureless metal room, the blanket was a familiar burst of color, a reminder of the time before. A reminder of family—not his, but hers, the only family she had ever had, the one she had left behind, the one she had never spoken to again.

The only family *he* had ever known. A glimpse, for just a short while, of what life could be like, free of fear, and pain, and the desperate, crushing inevitability of a fate that was not yours to decide.

But despite this, leaving Hyperkarn had actually been an easy decision. Miramir knew who Dathan was and she accepted the fact that they had to leave, and very likely would never be able to go back. Because she knew it wasn't just the safety of herself and Dathan and Rey that was at stake, it was the safety of Baba, of the villagers she had known since childhood and who had been as much family to her as her own blood.

Right now, Dathan hoped that Hyperkarn was as it always had been, that Baba was safe and well, and was repairing droids and was weaving a new blanket, the one she had promised to have ready for her granddaughter's return.

Dathan hoped that day would come, and maybe it really was possible to go back, one day when they weren't hiding, when they weren't running, when they weren't being hunted.

One day, when they were safe.

That was when the door opened, the sudden loud hum of the hidden mechanism producing an opening in the featureless wall. As Dathan straightened up, Miramir stood, placing herself squarely between Rey and the door.

A mother, ready to defend her family, come what may.

A droid guard entered, followed by another. The pair moved to stand on either side of the door as someone else came in—this time, a living being.

He was a large man, nearly as bulky as the droid guards, a slab of muscle in a long black coat that looked like leather but had a moving, oily sheen, the surface covered with tiny scales. The left sleeve was metallic gold, which was matched by the metallic gold of the man's right trouser leg. Underneath the coat, the man wore a perfectly white shirt with a wide, open collar revealing a generous portion of his upper chest, his magenta skin revealing him to be Zeltron. That same skin was covered in an intricate metallic silver-and-red tattoo that continued up his neck and over his face, and which, Dathan realized, was moving, the serpentine forms slowly slithering around one another. His hair, like his shirt, was white, and cut into a sharp, geometric angle. His eyes were hidden behind a single thick bar of mirrored material that matched the reflective domes of the droid guards.

And then the man smiled and gave a deep, almost theatrical bow, his gold-clad arm across his stomach. When he stood back upright and smiled, Dathan could see several gems embedded in the man's teeth—red, green, blue—and surrounded by fine traceries of gold and silver.

"Friends, I'm sorry to have kept you waiting. And I'm sorry for having you locked up in here like this." He glanced at the two droid guards and gave a slight shake of the head. "My staff are perhaps a little too efficient sometimes. I think it might be time to update their master protocols." He turned back to the family and bowed again. "My name is Zargo Anaximander. I am the regent-captain of Nightside, and I've been looking forward to meeting you." He stood to one side and gestured at the door. "Please, allow me to show you to quarters that are rather more comfortable."

Dathan felt Miramir's hand in his. They looked at each other, then Dathan felt Rey tugging at the leg of his pants. Unhooking his hand from Miramir's, he crouched down by his daughter.

"Come on, Rey," he whispered. "We're going to go somewhere a whole lot nicer than this."

As Miramir bent down to fold up the blanket, Rey gave her father a hug and whispered in his ear.

"I don't like him."

Anaximander barked a laugh and bent down, his hands on his knees. "Now then, that's one cute kid. I like kids. I got lots of my own, of course. But come on, let's get you settled. Follow me."

Miramir and Dathan exchanged a look again, then Miramir began to fold the blanket. One of the droid guards picked up her backpack and turned its blank face to stare down into the open top.

"Thank you," said Miramir, almost snatching it from the droid's hands. The droid's arm went with the movement, allowing Miramir to clutch the pack close to her body, but it didn't let go. Dathan went to pull the bag out of its grip, but Anaximander waved a big hand, and the droid released it.

"Sorry about that," said the regent-captain. "Like I said, they're a little . . . efficient. Come on, this way."

Miramir slipped the folded blanket into the pack and slid the strap over one shoulder—exchanging a look with her husband as she did. Dathan raised an eyebrow in return, then took her hand in his and reached down to take Rey's in his other.

Together, the three of them followed the regent-captain through the door.

Zargo Anaximander's quarters couldn't have been more different from the rest of Nightside. Behind a huge reinforced door that looked like it was going to lead into another greasy, industrial section of the city was a corridor, gleaming and bright and entirely—floor, walls, ceiling— mirrored gold.

The regent-captain led them down this corridor. Miramir glanced at

Dathan and pulled a face that was either surprise or disgust, he wasn't entirely sure. Rey, meanwhile, laughed as she pointed at the walls.

Dathan followed his family down the corridor, wondering what was *really* happening, not allowing himself to believe that . . . maybe they were going to be all right? That Zargo Anaximander, the flamboyant regent-captain of Nightside, was actually true to his word, that their less-than-salubrious arrival had been a mistake and that he was going to make it up to them? Perhaps Flight Sergeant Dina Dipurl really had saved their lives.

The corridor ended in another door, made of what looked like a black, grained material. Wood, perhaps? The door slid open as Anaximander approached, and he stepped through. Dathan, Miramir, and Rey followed.

The room beyond was vast, but with a low ceiling that made it feel somehow homey. It was living quarters, certainly—the opulent, luxurious living quarters of someone who had so many credits that they ceased to have any meaning at all.

This room was white, but the brilliant gold of the entrance corridor continued across the ceiling, which undulated gently, like the quiet, silken swell of a lake. The motion was smooth and, actually, relaxing. Dathan guessed that was the point.

The room was elliptical, the two white walls curving around to a point at the far end. In the middle, furnishings were scattered—multicolored couches and sofas, low tables, and cabinets, set with drinks, entertainment devices, datapads, each little grouping forming its own space in the open-plan layout. The two curved walls were inset with shelves and cabinets, their contents—endless rows of fat data cards, and spaced between them sculptures and statuettes of a dozen different forms, styles, and cultures—on proud display, elegantly lit by hidden spotlights.

Dathan noted that there didn't appear to be another door.

"My friends, my friends," said Anaximander, giving another bow, this one not quite as low as before. He spread his arms, then turned and walked into the middle of the room. "Welcome to my humble abode." He stopped and laughed, his amusement so intense he actually doubled over. He waved at his guests. "I'm sorry, who am I trying to fool? I've worked hard to get where I am, and if I have to live in the middle of the biggest ice-processing factory this side of the Core, I'm damn well going to do it in style."

Miramir smiled at him. "Thank you for your hospitality," she said, still looking around. "It looks very..." She shrugged, but it was Rey who completed her description.

"It's very incredible," she said.

At this, Anaximander clicked the fingers of both hands. "Very incredible! You know, I think I like that. So thank you, thank you very much indeed. Very incredible. Why, yes, I think it is very incredible. This whole operation is." Anaximander turned a half circle, looking around the room, as though his apartment was somehow just an ordinary corner of the factory.

Then he stopped and turned back to them, still smiling, but his expression somehow fixed. He was clearly wanting them to ask about his operation.

Dathan had another question on his mind.

"We were told you could help us."

Anaximander turned his frozen expression on Dathan, then brought his hands together in front of him and steepled his fingers on his chest.

"You're a businessman. Okay, I like that, I like that. You want to get down to business. That's fine. I'm a businessman, too." He separated his hands and, without taking his visored gaze off Dathan, pointed to one side, clicking the fingers of that hand. "But first, refreshments."

Dathan and Miramir turned to look. Two droids had appeared out of nowhere, and in silence: protocol-like units, one with a mirror-finish copper casing, the other a bluish silver, equally shiny. The copper droid held a tray of tall, thin glasses and a matching bottle filled with a light-blue liquid, while the blue-silver droid held a platter of fruit, on which was also a stack of small glass bowls.

Dathan stepped up to Anaximander, ignoring the invitation. He still didn't trust this strange man—and he needed the know exactly where they stood.

"We need to get away from here," he said. "I'm sorry, but we do. We need a ship. We need new identities. We were told you would be able to help."

Dathan wanted to see Anaximander's eyes, but his visor was an impenetrable mirror. It didn't look like a cybernetic attachment, but it was hard to tell. Anaximander clearly had enough credits to have a custom piece crafted for him, if he needed an optical aid. But that smile was still fixed on the man's face. All trace of warmth had gone.

The room was silent, and everyone, even Rey, stood as still as the two droids. It was Anaximander who moved first, very slowly lifting an arm and taking a glass of the blue drink from the droid's offered tray. He lifted the flute up, turning the glass, clearly examining the way the light caught the angles of the crystal. Then he put the drink to his lips and tossed it back, draining the entire flute in one gulp. He put the glass back on the tray, picked up a tiny folded napkin from the same tray, and dabbed his lips.

"Okay, businessman," he said. "What have you got?"

Dathan blinked, then he looked at Miramir, then back at Anaximander.

"What have I got?"

"Right," said Anaximander. He clicked his fingers and the copper droid handed him another flute of blue drink. "What have you got?" He drained the second drink, again in a single gulp. After this one, he gasped. "I'm a businessman. You're a businessman, right? So let's do business. You want something I can provide. So, what do *you* have that *I* want?"

Dathan stammered. Miramir stepped forward, one of her hands sliding into his.

"We don't have anything," she said. "Our ship is a wreck. The hyperdrive core nearly burned out just getting here. We can't even leave. We have some credits." She stopped, sighed, and glanced around Anaximander's apartment. "But credits are clearly the last thing you need." She stopped again, shaking her head.

Dathan had turned to look at her as she spoke. She squeezed his hand, and he squeezed back.

"So you ... *don't* have anything I want," said Anaximander.

Dathan tore his gaze from his wife's and looked at Anaximander.

"We were told you could help us," said Dathan, his voice almost a whisper. "A friend of yours sent us here. She said you would help."

"Oh yeah," said Anaximander, with a grin. "Dina Dipurl. She's a great lady. I worked with her father, in another time." His grin vanished. "But things are different now. The galaxy has moved on. I don't owe her anything. I don't owe anyone anything. So if you want something from me, we're going to have to negotiate a price." He moved away, grabbing a bowl from the other droid's tray with one hand and a handful of fruit with the other before he stalked over to one of the bookcases in the middle of the wall behind him. As he approached, the bookcase slowly swung open, revealing another brightly colored corridor—this one a shiny plastoid red—beyond. "I'll leave you to think about it for a while, okay?" Anaximander said, without turning around. "Maybe we can come to some kind of an arrangement. Until we do, make yourself at home, please." And with that, he disappeared through the concealed door, which closed behind him.

Dathan and Miramir stared at the bookcase, then Dathan sighed and rubbed his face. He wanted to scream. But he also knew he had to remain calm.

They'd get out of this.

Somehow.

Dropping his hands, he turned a circle on his heels, then stopped. The two droids were still standing there. He looked down at his daughter and ruffled her hair.

"Hey, you hungry, Rey? Come on, this looks pretty good."

He walked over to the blue-silver droid, took a bowl, and began picking out pieces of fruit from the selection that looked like something Rey would perhaps be willing to try.

Rey looked up at Miramir, who gave her a smile, and gently eased her over to her father. "Go on." Rey reluctantly obeyed, a frown firmly on her face, but as soon as Dathan presented her with a bowl of food, she seemed happy enough. She took the food and went over to one of the low couches, neatly folding herself down onto it in a cross-legged position as she began to eat.

Miramir, meanwhile, slipped over to the door Anaximander had disappeared through. She ran her fingers along the case, experimentally pulling out the data cards, but unless she planned on emptying the whole shelf, Dathan wasn't sure she was going to get anywhere. Clearly reaching the same conclusion, she turned and gave Dathan, who was now sitting with Rey with his own bowl of fruit, a tiny shake of the head.

Dathan nodded to the original door they had entered through. Miramir acknowledged and went over to it, carefully sidestepping the two protocol droids. The droids moved slightly, their servos whirring as they watched Miramir for a moment before returning their attention to Dathan and Rey. Dathan turned on the floor, watching as his wife examined the control panel next to the closed black portal.

"Can you open it?" he asked.

Miramir turned, glancing again at the droids. Dathan followed her gaze, but the machines were still looking at him, not her.

"Yes," she said, then she glanced at the droids—and now they were both looking right at her.

Dathan followed her gaze. Of course, the droids were watching them. Not only that, they were likely recording everything in the room. Anaximander was probably watching the feed right now.

Dathan waved Miramir back over to him. She walked across the room and sat on the soft couch behind Dathan. She leaned forward, and he leaned back. She wrapped her arms around his shoulders.

They didn't speak. Neither of them had to; they knew exactly what the situation was.

Dathan had been right. They could trust no one.

Because now they were prisoners of the man who was supposed to have helped them.

CHAPTER 19

NIGHTSIDE, THEREZAR SYSTEM
NOW

Zargo Anaximander glanced out the window of the cable train as it sped out across its tether, a flashing red firestorm illuminating the dark side of Therezar a hundred thousand kilometers below them. It would be another ten minutes before they reached Station Seven, one of the outermost network platforms of Nightside, home to a high-power auxiliary communications center. Anaximander might have been regent-captain, but he was no fool and he knew he wasn't untouchable—Nightside was an entire city-state, with a population easily larger than several planetside settlements Anaximander could care to name. He was in charge but there were still eyes on him, always, and he didn't want to risk even the slightest chance of his comm channels being sliced and his transmission intercepted.

He turned back to his companions in the cable train cabin—three droids, the same class of protocol unit that served him in his apartment. The cable train was, however, far from the luxurious transport he usually used. This one was standard industrial car, all greasy metal, every crevice caked with black dust. Anaximander was trying very hard not to touch any surface.

The three droids and the regent-captain were standing around a square table in the center of the train cabin, the table itself lit with a brilliant white glow, uplighting the droids and Anaximander in sharp, unflattering angles. Above the table floated a ghostly holographic scan, showing a large bag of woven fabric. Around the bag floated scans of its contents— a blanket, a box of rations, assorted odds and ends that Dathan and Miramir had managed to grab before fleeing their homestead on Jakku.

"Find anything?" asked Anaximander.

The droid directly opposite Anaximander spoke in pleasant, almost melodic tones, a fair approximation of a high-class server from an elevated Core World. "It appears they were telling the truth. They have no identification and negligible credits."

Anaximander folded his arms. "Imperial chain code?"

The second droid spoke. "No chain code available."

Anaximander shook his head. "We need to be sure it's them."

The third droid swiveled its head to look at its master. "We have a ninety percent match on the bounty put out by Ochi of Bestoon."

"I'd like that percentage to be higher."

"Their bioscan came up with some unusual features."

"Such as?"

The first droid touched a control on the side of the table, and the holoprojection changed to images of the family members, each coming up one by one as the droid reviewed them.

"Subject one, human female, twenty-seven standard years of age. DNA analysis reveals some telomere anomalies identifying her as a native of Ko-Longava or Hyperkarn."

Anaximander shrugged. "Irrelevant."

"Subject two," the droid continued as the image changed to that of Rey. "Human female, six standard years. DNA analysis reveals biological offspring of subjects one and three." The image changed again, this time to Dathan. "Subject three, human male, thirty-three standard years of age. DNA analysis reveals several markers characteristic of artificial replication and engineering."

Anaximander studied the three-dimensional image of Dathan's face. "He's a clone?"

"Subject three lacks genetic signatures of accelerated growth. He is thirty-three standard years of age, but analysis shows he is a hybrid strandcast."

Anaximander shook his head. "Explain."

"The strandcast is not a direct cloned replicate of the donor, but is nonetheless created from an engineered template."

Anaximander rubbed his chin. "That's interesting. Could be why they're important. Subject three might be some experiment that got loose. Any maker's marks? Kaminoan imprint? Khomm logo proteins?"

The droid tilted its head. "No manufacturer labels are detected."

There was a loud, resonant clang. Anaximander glanced up at the journey indicator on the upper wall of the cabin, a simple row of lights that showed the cable train's position along its tether.

Station Seven was coming up soon.

He turned back to the table and tapped at the controls. The holoprojection changed, now showing all three subjects, full three-dimensional scans rotating slowly in the air.

He didn't know who they were. It didn't matter. What did matter was the reason they were being hunted—there was no information in Ochi's private bounty, only that they were to be taken alive at all costs. The fact that the father was a genetic construct was interesting. Perhaps whoever had made him wanted him back.

Anaximander wondered if that would give him a little bargaining power.

The family had been telling the truth when they'd said they had nothing, that their ship was a wreck. They had arrived on a wing and a prayer, following nothing more than the word of a stranger.

They were desperate, all right.

Anaximander killed the holo. He looked at the three droids.

"Nobody can know where I am. This information, and the data analysis on the subjects, and their bioscans, is privileged."

The three protocol droids glanced at one another, then all turned to their master and, in unison, gave him a small bow. Anaximander returned the gesture.

"Thank you for your service," he said.

At that, the three droids instantly reached down, their blasters popping out of their concealed leg holsters. In one perfectly orchestrated movement, the droids pointed the weapons at one another's heads and pulled the triggers.

The three simultaneous blaster shots were painfully loud in the confined space of the train cabin, but Anaximander didn't flinch. He watched as the three now headless machines slumped at the waist, their raised gun-arms clacking down on the worktable. As the sparks from their severed necks reflected in Anaximander's visor, there was another metallic clang as the cable train reached its final destination and jerked to a halt. Anaximander went with the movement, using the momentum to head toward the exit door.

The station was well lit, a cavernous space with an arched ceiling crisscrossed with enormous durasteel girders, the station architecture dwarfing the cable train and its single remaining passenger as he stood on the platform.

Anaximander picked his direction and stalked away.

It took Anaximander another ten minutes to reach the communications substation, the control room suspended on a network of gantries below the main antenna relay itself, a vast dish angled sharply away from the flashing clouds of Therezar. The communications relay was designed as a backup to Nightside's standard comm center, far enough away from the central mining hub to be safe from any accident that might disable the city-wide systems. And by coming out here, accessing the main relay's control room directly, the regent-captain would be able to use the relay to send his transmission and then erase the logs before they were synced back to Nightside's central computer.

He was taking no chances. Anaximander had gotten where he was not just because he had a head for business, but because he was a micromanager and a control freak. If he was going to try to improve the deal, then it was going to be on his terms, and he was going to do it personally.

Zargo Anaximander was the master of his own destiny.

The control room was dimly lit, nothing more than a box with a central control console standing free in the middle of the room, a five-sided flower, each tilted petal covered in levers and buttons, readouts and switches. Above, the ceiling was a geometric shell of angled transparisteel panels, providing a view of the underside of the main antenna itself, lit faintly in flashes of light from Therezar's storms.

Standing by the console, Anaximander pulled a long chain from around his neck, at the end of which was a circular medallion with a printed circuitry pattern around the edge. He slotted the medallion into a reader on the console, and immediately the main touch display changed, the system automatically recognizing Anaximander's override authorization.

He operated the controls for a few moments, then glanced up as the relay dish began to realign. Within moments, a string of lights on the console changed from red to green and a blue hologram appeared in the air in front of the regent-captain.

Anaximander gave one of his trademark bows to the shimmering figure before him, then looked up, hiding his distaste at the bald, scarred face in the projection, the black electronic eyes, the lipless slit of a mouth.

"Ochi of Bestoon," said Anaximander. "I believe my droids have already made the preliminary introductions."

Ochi made no indication that he was listening. "You have them?"

Anaximander paused, then grinned, his gemmed teeth glinting in the control room half-light. "I do."

"Have you confirmed their identity?"

Actually, I was hoping you'd do that for me, Anaximander thought. "I'm transmitting their bioscans now," he said. He slipped a datachip from his jacket pocket and inserted it into the reader. In the holoprojection, Ochi's image glanced down as he read the incoming data stream.

"Good," said Ochi. "That's them." He looked up. "You have them secured?"

Anaximander folded his arms, then extracted one hand to waggle an index finger at Ochi's hologram.

"What do you want them for?"

Ochi didn't answer. His face was expressionless—was *incapable* of expression, thought Anaximander—but the regent-captain could sense something in the other man. There was . . . anger there. Simmering just below the surface. Ochi of Bestoon had been known in certain circles from the old days, and what stories Anaximander remembered told him that Ochi had been on a hair trigger, as unpredictable as he was quick to anger. Anaximander was wise to be cautious.

With no response forthcoming, the regent-captain tried for another tack. "Where are you? I can hold them until you arrive."

"I won't be coming personally," said Ochi. "I'm in the Forome system."

Anaximander frowned. "That's a long way out."

"I will send my associates to collect. Expect them imminently." Ochi moved, like he was leaning forward, about to cut off their transmission. Anaximander immediately reached forward and held down a button, forcing the transmission band to stay open. In the holo, Ochi looked up, his frozen face somehow looking even more annoyed.

"And my payment?" said Anaximander. "My droids are superb negotiators, don't you agree?"

Ochi paused, then answered. "Payment as agreed. Have the captives ready for transfer."

Anaximander looked at Ochi for a moment, his finger still on the button. He drew the moment out, enjoying the way that Ochi's temper grew hotter and hotter as the band remained active.

Then Anaximander released the button and the holoprojection vanished. Now, *that* was how you demonstrated control. Zargo Anaximander was in charge of this transaction, and he had made sure this Ochi of Bestoon had known it.

And he wasn't even coming himself, instead sending . . . associates? Anaximander shook his head. This Ochi was such an amateur—overconfident, thinking that his power was measured by the number of minions he had at his beck and call. Anaximander knew full well that if you wanted something done, you did it yourself.

Anaximander considered his options. The bounty for the family was large, but he wanted a better offer—while Anaximander himself had no actual need for the credits, he had devoted himself to their collection, just for the simple pleasure of looking at long-digit numbers and the knowledge that the more he had, the less someone else did.

He thought about the bounty, and compared it with the three visitors locked in his apartment.

A family. They were nobodies. Vagrants. They had nothing.

And yet . . . Ochi of Bestoon was willing to pay *that* much to have them?

The man—Dathan—it had to be him. And perhaps the child, the biological offspring of a genetic construct and a natural-born human.

It was interesting, from a scientific point of view. Anaximander was no scientist, but even he found the concepts fascinating.

The family was certainly worth more than was being offered. A lot more.

Anaximander deactivated the relay station, wiping the entire control room's memory banks before extracting his regent-captain's medallion. Nobody would know he had even been here, nobody would be able to trace the communication with Ochi.

On his way back to the cable train station, Anaximander pulled a comm stick from inside his jacket and brought it to his lips.

"Dee Eighty-Five," he said. "Move our guests to the *Goldstone*. Our partners are on their way. The renegotiations and transfer will take place in my private hangar. See to it."

Anaximander clicked off the comm without waiting for a response, then stepped into the cabin of the waiting cable train and punched the control for the central hub.

In Anaximander's private apartment, the copper protocol droid lowered the communicator, then stepped forward. Dathan, Miramir, and Rey were sitting together on the low couch. As the droid approached, Miramir stood to meet it.

The droid's servos whirred as it looked among the humans, then it half turned and gestured with one crooked arm to the wall hiding the concealed door, which now swung silently open.

"Please follow me," said the droid.

Dathan stood and joined his wife. "Where are we going?"

"And where's Zargo?" asked Miramir.

The droid turned back around and gesticulated with its arms as it spoke, each movement of its copper limbs apparently matching each syllable of its speech.

"The regent-captain requests the honor of your presence in his private yacht."

Dathan frowned. "His . . . what?"

D-85 gave a slight bow. "Arrangements have been made for your safe transit to a secure site, along with fresh identities and transport." He straightened up and gestured again to the open door.

Neither Dathan nor Miramir moved. D-85 paused and looked from one human to the other, his neck servos whirring, almost like the custom-built protocol droid was irritated with their lack of instant compliance. "This is what you wanted. Everything has been prepared," said the droid. "This way please."

Miramir went to gather the colored blanket up from where it still lay, spread out on the floor, but found the silver-blue droid now standing in her way. She ignored it and made to move around, but the droid was fast. It grabbed her arm, then pushed Miramir away, toward the door.

"Hey!"

The droid released her and was joined by D-85. With both droids occupied, Dathan skipped around them both and scooped up their belongings, quickly stuffing them in the bag before moving to his wife's side. He took her hand and gave it a reassuring squeeze. "Better do as they say," he said, quietly.

With a reluctant glance at Dathan, Miramir have a small nod. Then she clasped Rey's hand tightly before following Dathan and the copper droid through the door.

CHAPTER 20

NIGHTSIDE, THEREZAR SYSTEM
NOW

Luke and Lando had been walking around the endless passageways of Nightside for what felt like hours. The clearance code Zargo Anaximander had given Lando all those years ago still worked, allowing the *Lady Luck* to dock in a VIP hangar bay, a team of service droids already swarming around the craft for a full systems check and valet. Luke had watched them get to work while Lando used the hangar's arrival terminal to try to contact his friend.

That was hours ago. Having been told that the regent-captain was unavailable, Lando had gotten sick of waiting and had led Luke and R2-D2 into the complex itself, determined to pay a visit to Anaximander's personal quarters.

Which . . . they were still looking for. After consulting numerous confusing maps of the complex, they'd finally navigated their way out of the ports and hangars and found themselves in a commercial zone, a vast, multi-level space of high-end consumer stores, restaurants, and leisure zones, linked with moving walkways and escalators. As they paused to get their bearings, R2-D2 let out a low, warbling tone that was unmistakably the sound of the droid getting fed up with their lack of progress, and trundled over to a public computer terminal over in a corner of the atrium.

Lando, hands on hips, turned a circle, taking in the sights, then looked at Luke. He whistled. "Nightside seems to be doing well."

Luke frowned. "I thought this was supposed to be a mining colony?"

"Oh, it is," said Lando, "but old Zargo has scaled things up since I was last here." He cast a look around again. "He was always a businessman, but back when I first met him, this place was hardly more than a simple droid-operated processing plant. I knew he was a supplier for the Rebel Alliance, too, but back then I tried to stay, well . . ."

Luke's eyebrow went up along with the corner of his mouth. "*Uninvolved?*" he asked, his grin spreading.

Lando held up his hands in mock apology. "Hey, we all know how that went, okay," he said, his own smile growing. He dropped his hands and gazed around again. "Zargo was always someone you could go to if you needed something. Looks like he's turned this place into a real city, catering to a high-class market these days." He shrugged. "The ice mine was always profitable, so good for him." He sniffed, his mustache twitching. "I was getting there with Cloud City, but I guess the market for water is infinitely larger than for tibanna gas."

"Well," said Luke, "Zargo seemed to be reliable enough for Flight Sergeant Dipurl to send the family here. I assume she knew him from the days of the Rebellion, too." He looked around. The place was filled with people of dozens of different species, but all of them had one thing in common—they were rich. And with all of this wealth on display—and being exchanged in the hundreds of stores—it was no surprise that the place was heavily guarded. Gray and yellow droids of a kind Luke hadn't seen before patrolled through the crowds of biological beings, as well as being stationed at various strategic points around the atrium and the other levels. "Your friend sure likes droids," said Luke. "Even the hangar crew were droids."

Lando nodded. "Yeah, hobby of his. They're all custom, too. I mean, he's not an engineer himself, but he can afford to hire the best. They're all designed and fabricated here."

R2-D2 bleeped again, his dome turning. Luke glanced over and saw that the little astromech had already connected his scomp link to the terminal without having to be told.

"Hey, hey!" said Lando, rushing over. "We need to be careful what we try to slice into." He glanced at Luke. "This droid of yours has a mind of its own."

Luke couldn't resist a grin. "I should hope so, too." He moved closer and, checking over his shoulder, stepped next to R2-D2 so his left leg was touching the droid, then adjusted his short black robe so it screened the terminal from the view of passersby.

"What have you got, Artoo?"

R2-D2 bleeped and twittered, his dome turning along with the ring around the dataport as he accessed Nightside's central computer. The terminal screen flashed into life. Luke peered at it.

"What is it?" asked Lando, looking at the screen. He shook his head. "I don't know what I'm looking at."

Luke tapped the screen. "Artoo's found the family's ship. Hangar 817, landing pad 4174."

Lando pursed his lips. "If I remember those maps we saw, that'll be down several levels, toward the factory zone, where the industrial port is."

R2-D2 bleeped again. The readout on the display changed. Lando looked at it and frowned, then looked at Luke. "Am I reading that right? That landing pad is on lockdown?"

Luke nodded, stroking his beard in thought. "Could be standard procedure," he murmured, almost to himself. Then he said, "Artoo?"

The dataport spun and the readout changed again, the text now scrolling too fast for Luke or Lando to read. R2-D2 whistled away to himself, then gave a double bleep. The text on screen paused. Luke and Lando looked it over.

"Not standard then," said Lando. "Only two ships in the entire facility are on locked pads." He wrinkled his nose. "The other is Zargo's personal yacht, the *Goldstone*?"

Luke continued to read. "This looks like traffic logs for the two hangars. Nothing here that indicates why the two ships should be locked down." He paused. "Artoo, can you patch us into the hangar security feeds from here?"

Lando leaned in to whisper to his old friend. "Hey, Luke, wait a second here. As much as I trust Artoo, someone is going to notice us snooping around in the central register." He glanced over his shoulder, back into the atrium. "This place is full of security. One alert and we could be in trouble."

"I thought you said Zargo Anaximander was a friend of yours?"

"Oh, sure," said Lando. "But look, that was a long time ago. Time passes, things change. People, too." He drew closer to Luke and gestured with both hands, patting the air in front of him like he was trying to calm the ever-calm Jedi Master. "All I'm saying is we just need to be careful. Zargo's here somewhere, but until we find him, we should probably try not to draw any attention to ourselves. We don't want to get stuck here trying to explain ourselves to his security while the family is in danger."

Luke nodded. Lando made a good point. They needed to make good use of every available moment they had, and not get sidetracked or delayed unnecessarily.

But so far, they were on the right track. They might not have had the audience with Zargo that they expected, but they'd confirmed the family was still here.

R2-D2 whistled softly, and the display changed the security feed for the lower hangar levels. The droid cycled through them and finally reached pad 4174, hangar 817.

"That's their ship, all right," said Lando, looking closely. He pointed at the screen. "The drive stabilizers are totally gone. I'm amazed they got this far. Think we should go down and check it?"

Luke shook his head. There was something not quite right—he could feel it.

He closed his eyes, calling to the Force.

There.

He opened his eyes and looked at Lando. "That ship is empty."

Lando blinked. "What? How do you . . . ?" He paused. "Oh."

"Artoo," said Luke, his voice hushed, "bring up the other locked pad. The *Goldstone*."

R2-D2 didn't reply, but his dome twitched and the display flickered to show another part of Nightside. This hangar was in stark contrast with the lower decks, having the same pristine white-and-yellow decor and smooth, curved design as the VIP hangar that the *Lady Luck* had entered.

Lando whistled softly. "Now, that's what I call a ship."

The regent-captain's personal yacht was sleek, the wide, sculpted shape a deliberate homage to the classic starship design of several decades earlier. The hull was a delta wing of curved golden metal, the pointed nose cones of two atmospheric engine intakes only just visible under each side of the fuselage from their viewing angle. The only viewports on the simple but elegant craft were at the front, in the cockpit, giving the flight crew an expansive 180-degree view.

There were people inside. One was sitting at a flight position, the other pacing back and forth behind.

"They getting ready for takeoff?" asked Lando.

But Luke wasn't so sure. There was something about the figures.

"Artoo, can you get a closer look?"

The image immediately flipped, showing a grainy, zoomed version of the same shot. The figures were now clearly visible—sitting at the controls was a young woman with blond hair, the hood of a blue cloak bunched behind her shoulders. Behind her, pacing, was a young man in a brown-and-cream tunic and matching pants.

"It's them," breathed Lando.

There was a third person in the cockpit. They couldn't see them clearly, but they were small, hidden by the angle of the pilot's and copilot's seats. The young man was holding her hand.

It was a child. *The* child.

"What are they doing?" asked Lando, his eyes fixed to the screen.

Luke just shook his head, but he could hear his friend's breath quicken. Lando's question was a good one. Why *were* they in the cockpit of Zargo's yacht? The woman was unmoving, staring at the controls. They were talking, Luke could see that, but there was no audio available.

Lando stood tall. "Maybe Zargo is going to take them out in his ship."

But as the pair watched, the young woman leaned forward, and was momentarily out of view of the security feed. There was a flash of light through the *Goldstone*'s viewports, and she sat back in the pilot's seat, a bunch of frayed cables now in her hand.

"Wait," said Lando. "Are they trying to *steal* that ship?"

Luke and Lando looked at each other. Luke didn't speak, but Lando wrinkled his nose and began smoothing down his mustache with a thumb and forefinger as he thought. "I don't like how this looks or feels, Luke. I'm starting to think they're not in that ship by their own choice."

"Agreed," said Luke. "Your friend is either keeping them hidden—"

Lando cut in. "Or keeping them prisoner." He sighed. "So maybe Zargo Anaximander isn't quite the 'friend' I remembered."

"We need to get down there," said Luke. "Artoo, show us a map and plot the most direct route to that hangar. We—"

There was a chime from the computer station, and R2-D2 let out a shrill alarm.

Lando looked down at the droid. "What is it?"

R2-D2 chortled a string of complex tones. Lando winced in frustration. "Have we tripped an alarm?"

Luke was looking back at the screen. "No," he said. "Lando, look at this."

Lando leaned over the screen, which now showed a schematic of the Therezar system as a whole, the Nightside complex dead center, the surrounding platforms highlighted and clearly labeled.

As were the incoming ships. Thirteen of them, coming in from different vectors, all of them converging on Nightside.

"Visitors?"

"There's a security alert," said Luke, reading the data on the screen. "Whoever they are, they are not expected. Artoo, can you identify them?"

R2-D2 wailed plaintively, any translation from Binary unnecessary. Lando looked at Luke.

"I don't like the sound of *that*."

That was when a general alarm sounded, the internal security alert registered by R2-D2 now becoming a city-wide situation. The alarm was loud, two alternating tones, interrupted by an automated announcement. Suddenly everyone in the atrium was still, looking up and around as the unseen voice gave its instructions.

"*Attention, attention. Nightside is now at Alert Level Beta. Repeat, Nightside is now at Alert Level Beta. Please make your way to the nearest emergency shelter. Attention, attention. Nightside is now at Alert Level Beta.*"

The crowd, to Luke's surprise, took the alert with a measure of calmness. Everybody began to move, and quickly, but nobody ran, nobody seemed to panic. The droid guards that had been on patrol or stationed around sprang into life and began herding everyone out of the atrium. As a busy—and dangerous—working factory complex, Nightside probably ran through drills for just this kind of alert regularly.

"We can't get caught up in all this," said Lando.

Luke was watching the droid guards. He judged the moment, then said, "It's now or never." He tapped the top of R2-D2's dome. "Lead the way."

R2-D2 turned and sped off down a side corridor, away from the atrium, Luke and Lando sticking close behind. People were moving in every direction, and at speed; in the milieu, the pair of humans and their astromech blended right in.

The trio wove their way through the crowds, the alert still playing over and over again. After a short journey, their surroundings became decidedly less clean and aesthetically pleasing, the retail and commercial zone of the complex transitioning to more functional sections. As R2-D2 trundled in the lead, they started to pass large stretches of transparisteel windows, giving views of space and of the angry gas giant around which Nightside maintained its geostationary orbit.

Then Luke stopped, suddenly. A little ahead, Lando checked behind him and then walked back to his friend.

"Luke, come on, let's go." Lando frowned. "What is it?"

Luke stood stock-still. The alert still sounded, and people were still moving, but now the constant stream of bodies had to part around Luke.

Lando glanced around. So far, they'd blended in, but only when they were moving with the crowd. Farther down the corridor, R2-D2 whistled, then came to a stop and turned around to face the others. He whistled again, his query clear.

"Hey, come on, we have to move—" Lando looked at Luke's face, the words dying in his throat.

Luke had his eyes closed. He breathed gently, and deeply.

He concentrated, isolating himself from his surroundings, from the noise and the movement, listening not to the alert and the sound of hundreds of people seeking shelter. They faded from his senses, replaced with . . .

A sound . . . a musical note—no, a chord . . . no, a—

A *discord*. It wasn't an actual sound, Luke knew that, but he could sense its resonance. It was a presence, and intrusion, not in the physical universe but in that other place that surrounded him.

A disturbance in the Force.

And it was near.

Luke opened his eyes and moved to the side of the passageway, the cascade of bodies brushing and bumping against his. He stopped by the huge transparisteel windows and looked out into space.

The incoming ships were visible. Small and silvery, each one a different shape, angled and spiky, like a swarm of angry insects.

Luke felt Lando by his side, another hand on his shoulder. Then the hand dropped as Lando stepped past Luke to get a better look himself. He pointed.

"It's them," he said. He turned to Luke. "Those are the same kind of ships that were chasing the family, and the ones that attacked Halo Squadron." Lando shook his head. "They must have traced Dipurl's transmission and followed the family here."

Luke stared at the vastness of space. The dark side of Therezar was below them, a black void lit by the spidering crawl of electrical storms in the gas giant's turbulent atmosphere. The ring system wasn't visible from this angle, just the infinite scattering of stars and the strange, evil-looking ships that now encircled the factory. Two of them flew directly past the corridor window, Lando recoiling in surprise. He reached out and pulled on Luke's arm again.

"Okay, we're out of time. We have to get to that hangar."

Luke didn't move. He looked out, not looking at the ships, or the planet, or the stars. There was something else. Something . . . close.

"The dark side," said Luke. "It's here. I can feel it."

Lando stopped pulling on Luke's arm and moved back to stand close to him.

"The Sith are here?" He choked back a gasp and looked out the window. "You're telling me those ships are Sith? All of them?" He looked back out at the view. "They can't be. There're too many."

Luke cocked his head and closed his eyes as he concentrated. He didn't need the Force to sense the fear in Lando's voice. But . . . Lando was right. He opened his eyes and shook his head.

"They aren't Sith."

Lando's shoulders fell and he let out a breath. "Okay. One problem at a time. Let's get the family out of here before it's too late."

Luke spun around to look at Lando. Over his shoulder, he could see R2-D2 waiting down the corridor, the little droid now balanced on his two main feet, tottering sideways in irritation as his human companions dawdled.

Luke nodded toward the astromech. "Go with Artoo. Get the family out of here."

"Wait," said Lando, "you're coming, too."

Luke shook his head. "There's something coming. Something bad. I need to stop it." The corner of his mouth curled up in a grin, and he patted Lando on the arm. "We'll meet at the *Lady Luck*. Go!"

With that, Luke turned on his heel and headed in the opposite direction.

Lando watched his retreating back for a moment, then, not wasting another precious second, turned and headed for R2-D2.

"Come on, little buddy, let's go stage a rescue."

CHAPTER 21

NIGHTSIDE, THEREZAR SYSTEM
NOW

Lando and R2-D2 sped through the crowds. The farther they went, the fewer people they had to weave through as they moved away from the public areas of Nightside and headed back up toward the VIP hangars and the regent-captain's private landing pad.

They turned a corner; Lando heard R2-D2's shrill whistle first, then he bumped straight into the back of the droid. The way ahead was blocked by a huge crowd of people. As Lando glanced around, looking for an alternative route, the air was split by the harsh, high-pitched report of a blaster shot. The crowd surged, panic now finally beginning to set in as they scrambled and screamed, appendages raised along with voices. R2-D2 stayed where he was, Lando behind him, while the crowd moved around them, buffeting the pair as it headed back the way they had just come.

There was another blaster shot and the crowd came to a halt, their retreat now clearly blocked.

Lando looked around, wondering what was going on. They were in a large, open area, more or less like a public square, the transparisteel walls and ceiling giving the illusion of an open space.

The crowd moved again, and Lando and R2-D2 now found themselves at the front. Ahead of them, at the other end of the space, on a raised platform that provided an excellent vantage point, stood a group of droids, covering the entire room with their blasters.

But these were not Zargo Anaximander's custom droid guards. These machines were tall and angular, almost skeletal, with thin articulated arms and legs attached to narrow, streamlined torsos. Their heads were large, almost bulbous, insectoid, with huge optics and craniums studded with stubby antennas.

Raiders, from the thirteen ships that had come into the station. Whoever they were, Lando could see that no two droids were alike. This was no mass-produced army.

The droid at the front stepped forward and fired its blaster at the ceiling again, causing the crowd to flinch and cry out again.

R2-D2 bleeped, his dome turning left and right. Lando glanced down at the astromech, then followed the turn of the dome. R2-D2 was scanning for exits. They couldn't afford this interruption, but getting past the raiders was, at this point, purely wishful thinking.

"You lucky, lucky people," the lead droid said, the androgynous voice amplified over the din of the alarm and the people. "You are in the presence of the Droid Crush Pirates of Bestoon! This day is one that will live long in your history!" The droid lowered its blaster and looked around. "If there is anyone left to read it."

The droids behind it actually chuckled at this. Lando wondered at their programming. It was eccentric, to say the least. Then again, if they were supposed to be pirates, then whoever had built them had done a fine job.

The leader rolled its insectoid head—a very human movement, getting the cricks out, stretching the muscles—and raised its blaster again, pointing it at the front row of people—

Pointing it at Lando.

He stayed calm. Lando knew he was quick on the draw. There was a time he'd taken to practicing in front of the floor-to-ceiling mirrors in his quarters aboard the *Lady Luck*, more often than not with a guest lounging under the covers of the bed behind, watching their lover with delight as he practiced his moves.

Lando blinked away the unexpected memory. With his hands by his side, they were a scant few centimeters away from the blaster on his hip. But he knew it was hopeless. No matter how fast he was, he knew the leader of the Droid Crush would be faster—it was *built* to be. And besides, this wouldn't be a one-on-one shootout. Trying anything would be suicide.

The pirate leader sighed—at least, that's what Lando thought it sounded like—and lifted the blaster a little, taking a better aim.

Lando was ready. Maybe he could take the leader out. Maybe that would be the last thing he ever did.

But at least he would have died trying.

The sound of a blaster rang out. R2-D2 gave a long, ear-piercing electronic wail—

—as the leader of the Droid Crush collapsed, its head a thousand smoking shards that scattered over its gang.

Lando moved his hand away from his untouched weapon, his eyes already scanning around to see where the fateful shot had actually come from. Then the mass of people behind him shifted, first one way, then another, then pandemonium broke out. Lando went with the group as they ran for their lives, parting instinctively around the contingent of Nightside guard droids—the source of the well-aimed blaster bolt—that had entered the room from the rear.

At the edge of the room, Lando pulled away from the crowd, R2-D2 swiveling to a halt just before he smacked into the wall. There was an exit route beside them; Lando ducked down around the corner and risked a look back. The firefight wasn't going to last long—the Droid Crush were good fighters against the methodical, predictable behavior of the Nightside guard droids, but the pirate raiders were outnumbered and uncoordinated.

R2-D2 twittered and burbled, the stream of Binary so fast it made Lando's head spin. He had no idea what the droid was saying, but he got the gist—this was their chance.

Lando tapped R2-D2's dome with his knuckles. "Time to go, little buddy, let's—"

R2-D2 didn't wait. He turned and wheeled down the passageway, bleeping as he went.

Blaster now in his hand, Lando followed at a run.

. . .

Lando and R2-D2 made it to the hangar unscathed, although their route had been circuitous, avoiding more skirmishes between the Droid Crush and Nightside guard droids.

Lando didn't like running from battles. Nightside was home to a lot of people, and they were under attack. Lando felt an obligation to help, almost a pang of guilt as he did nothing but follow R2-D2 through the complex, but while he moved he rationalized his decision. Zargo had built himself an empire all of his own, and he had equipped it well—including his guard droids. What they lacked in tactics, they made up for in sheer numbers. The Droid Crush Pirates of Bestoon—clearly sent in by *Ochi* of Bestoon, Lando thought as he ran—were causing havoc and destruction, but the facility was being defended and the raiders would be repelled.

Which left Lando to focus on the task at hand.

Getting the family out of there.

They came into the regent-captain's private mooring via a maintenance door, R2-D2 making short work of the trilogic lock on the entry panel. The mooring was large, as big as the entire VIP dock the *Lady Luck* was sitting in nearby, but this facility was home to just one ship—the *Goldstone*, the vast, shining delta wing rising up above them on six pairs of landing gear.

Lando saw the problem immediately, and ran underneath the ship, R2-D2 close behind. He stopped at the closest landing gear—the one under the nose of the ship—and knelt to examine it.

It was locked in a fortified infraction restraint, the controls of which winked at him with two red lights. Lando glanced around and saw that all six pairs of landing gears had a restraint in place. R2-D2's readout had been correct—the regent-captain's yacht was locked down and going nowhere.

Lando stood—and from somewhere close came the sounds of a blaster battle. He spun around, trying to gauge direction, distance, but it was impossible. He did know one thing, though—the Droid Crush Pirates were close. Which didn't give him any time at all. His idea to get the family back to the *Lady Luck* was too risky. He couldn't take them back through all that—not with a child.

Lando stood and rubbed his face, then looked up at the shining underside of the *Goldstone*, an idea forming. He thought back to the virtually derelict freighter down in the lower hangar. That they'd managed to get to Nightside in that had been nothing short of a miracle. The *Goldstone* was so far at the other end of the scale of ships that Lando almost had to stifle a laugh at the ridiculousness of it.

With blasterfire echoing even closer, Lando turned to his companion. "Artoo, get to work on the landing restraints. I have an idea."

R2-D2 bleeped an affirmative and rolled to the first landing gear, extended his scomp link, and connected to the restraint's port.

Lando looked around. The private landing pad was as well provisioned as it was immaculate, with every piece of service equipment and ship support system available neatly docked around the walls, ready to cater to every need of Zargo Anaximander's pride and joy.

Lando spotted the trolley—a simple flight controller's console, allowing the user to patch into the ship directly and talk to the crew. A standard piece of kit—and perfect if you didn't want to be overheard on the general comm.

Lando raced over to it and wheeled the trolley to the nose of the *Goldstone*. The trolley itself was articulated, with a small platform at the back for the dock controller to stand on. Lando jumped on the back, activated the platform, and began to rise up until he was within touching distance of the yacht's hull. He pulled a cable from the console and, finding the port concealed under the skin of the ship above them, connected it, then grabbed the headset and pulled it on.

"Hey, hello, can you hear me in there?"

The headset clicked in his ear, but there was no reply. Lando frowned, checking the settings on the trolley console, then he jumped as there came a bang and a shower of sparks somewhere below him.

"Artoo?" He ducked down, peering through the rails of the trolley. R2-D2 was still by the front landing gear, but he was now attacking the restraining bolt with his cutting arm. His dome shifted to look at Lando and he bleeped happily.

"Who is this?"

Lando clutched at the headset and stood, looking up at the curve of the *Goldstone* above him. The voice had been male—the father.

"My name is Lando Calrissian. I'm a friend. I'm going to get you out of this."

"What's going on?"

Lando held his hands out, the gesture invisible to the occupants of the ship but helpful for himself. "Long story. Listen, can you fly this ship?"

A pause. "What?"

"Can you fly this ship?"

There was a scuffing sound in his ears, the distant sound of two people talking, then the next voice that came over the headset was female.

"Yes, I can fly it. I've already cracked the access code. But the ship is physically locked down and—"

"Don't worry about that," said Lando. "You'll be clear to launch." He glanced down at the pad to see that R2-D2 had successfully cut through the first infraction restraint, and was rolling at speed toward the next landing gear.

Blasterfire sounded. It was close.

"What's happening?" asked the woman. "We can hear shooting." In the background, Lando could hear the father talking and—

And then another voice. High and loud, afraid.

The child. The daughter. Calling for her father.

And there, faint but audible, the father telling the daughter that everything would be all right.

Another bang and shower of sparks, and R2-D2 whistled in satisfaction to himself.

Two restraints down, four to go.

Lando screwed his eyes tight, and took a breath, and shook his head, trying to clear his thoughts, trying to control his emotions.

It didn't take long. He might have been older, he might have lost some of his old ways, but he was still Lando Calrissian. A decorated war hero. A general.

A father.

And a man with a plan.

"Okay," he said. "We're nearly there. As soon as your indicator is green, punch it and get the hell out of here."

"Where do we go? We came here for help, we don't have anything. We don't know where to go."

Lando could hear the edge of panic in the woman's voice. "Hey, don't worry. We're here to get you out of this, so all I ask is that you trust me."

More scuffling, and then the man's voice came back.

"Trust you? We don't even know who you are! Are you with Zargo? He locked us in here!"

Lando frowned. Zargo Anaximander had been a business acquaintance rather than a friend, but was someone to be trusted—so Lando had thought, anyway. And so had the late Dina Dipurl. Lando didn't know what her connection with the regent-captain had been, but it was strong enough that the flight sergeant had sent the family here.

But whatever had happened between the man and the family, Lando knew this wasn't the time to start asking questions. If Anaximander had sold them out—Lando really hoped that wasn't the case, but he couldn't ignore the sinking feeling that was rapidly growing in his stomach—then he had his work cut out if he expected them to put their trust in another stranger so soon, someone who was nothing but a voice over a comm.

"Or are you the New Republic?" the man asked. "Those ships out there, are they the New Republic?"

Lando shook his head. "No, they're not. Listen, they're trouble, is what they are." Lando paused, then hissed in frustration. He wasn't good at this kind of thing. He took a breath. Time to take it from the top. If the family was going to listen to a word he was saying, he had to be straight up with them from the start.

"The ships that are coming in now look to be the same kind that attacked you in Wild Space—"

The man's voice cut in almost at once. "How the hell do you know about that?"

"Hey," said Lando, calmly. "I know you were sent here by a New Republic flight sergeant, Dina Dipurl of Halo Squadron. I know she was trying to help you out, and I'm sorry for what's happened. But I'm here to help, and I know I'm asking a lot when I ask you to trust me, but I was an Alliance general and I'm with a Jedi Knight, and together we're going to get you out of this, okay?"

Lando released the comm. There was silence for a moment, punctuated only by a pop as R2-D2 finished off the last restraint. The astro-mech whistled loudly, and Lando turned and raised a hand in acknowledgment. R2-D2 burbled something else, but Lando could only frown as he glanced at the droid, completely unable to even guess what he was trying to tell him without a translator. Ignoring the astromech for now, Lando turned back to the console and punched the call button.

"I know you are frightened," he said, headset mic clutched in one hand. "Believe me, I know. You don't know what's going to happen, and you've just been led from one bad thing to another. I get it. I know what that feels like. But we're really out of time here. The landing restraints are off. If you can fly the ship—or if your partner can—then fly it. Take it out into the rings of Therezar, hole up a moment, and we'll come and get you. Okay? You can do this. It just takes a little faith."

Lando released the button and listened intently for a reply. He counted the seconds, each one somehow feeling longer than the last.

And then the comm popped and this time, the woman spoke.

"Prepping for takeoff. You'd better get off the pad."

Lando grinned and, unable to stop himself, balled one hand into a fist and gave the air a little punch.

"All right!" He glanced down at the console. "I have your transponder ident. Set your receiver to . . . seven-seven-zero. We'll come in on your vector and ping that channel so you'll know it's us."

"Confirmed," said the woman.

"Okay, see you soon." Lando yanked the headset off, buoyed by his success, the adrenaline of a win coursing through him, like he'd just drawn the idiot's array in a game of sabacc and taken the pot. Not both-ering to lower the platform, he vaulted the rail and hit the landing pad in a crouch. Pushing off with the balls of his feet, he sprinted for the safety of the pad's outer ring as the ion engines of the *Goldstone* came to life, R2-D2 already ahead of him. Lando felt the heat of the engines wash over him as he ducked behind a launch shield near the wall, his fingers pressed tight into his ears. As the sound faded, he peered over the shield and saw the glowing engines of the *Goldstone* disappearing into space through the shimmer of the hangar's main entry.

R2-D2 whistled. Lando glanced down at the droid and nodded.

"Time to find Luke and get out of here." From his belt he pulled the short white cylinder of his personal comlink. He pressed the button. "Luke, where are you? The family is away, and we need to go." He released the button, and heard nothing but static.

R2-D2 bleeped and chortled. Lando nodded again, sliding the comlink back into his belt. "Seems like the Droid Crush is jamming transmissions," he said. "Can you trace where Luke is?"

R2-D2 beeped an affirmative and turned, once again leading the way. And once again, Lando followed.

CHAPTER 22

NIGHTSIDE, THEREZAR SYSTEM
NOW

Luke walked with purpose, his mind on one thing, and one thing only:

The darkness.

The *shadow*.

He could sense it, the disturbance in the Force, now transformed into a clear and precise direction, a lodestone, drawing him toward a dark and terrible place Luke wasn't sure he wanted to visit.

But he had to.

This was part of being a Jedi, a commitment to order and progress, and to preserving life.

He moved through the sea of people. Part of him registered the world around him, the way everyone was moving with a purpose—calm, yes, but clearly on edge, ready for anything, as they headed to emergency shelters, chaperoned by the droid guards. Luke didn't know much about Nightside, but given the size of the facility—not to mention the levels of luxury he had seen, all evidence of the regent-captain's leadership and also the vast wealth the mining colony was generating—he wouldn't be surprised if the city-state was *very* well defended.

Which meant he could leave the defense of the colony to those who were dedicated to its protection, and concentrate on his singular task.

Following his feelings, Luke soon arrived on a platform that seemed to float in the dead space above Therezar's rings. The ceiling was a beautifully engineered arc of transparisteel, forming an invisible canopy. At either end of the platform, the faintest glowing line was only just visible where the transparisteel stopped and a magnetic shield began, through which a tether appeared, running the length of the platform and continuing on in the other direction, through the shield on the other side.

It was a cable train station. There was a car at the end of the platform—boxy and industrial, just a single unit locked down, Luke supposed, in the emergency. Moving to the edge of the platform, Luke looked along the length of the tether, following it as it swept up into the network of supporting platforms that surrounded the central hub of Nightside.

The enemy ships were still coming in—spiky orbs with sparking ion jets, one- and two-pilot fighters, some custom, some that looked cobbled together from scrap. There seemed to be more now, passing by on sighting runs. That the forces of Nightside hadn't come out to defend the colony was odd, but suggested to Luke that . . . perhaps the new arrivals *were* expected? Was this something to do with the strange absence of the regent-captain, with even his closest droid-staff unable to locate their master?

It didn't matter. Luke pushed these thoughts and concerns from his mind. The city could look after itself. Lando and R2-D2 would be at the other hangar by now, helping the family. That left Luke free to pursue his own task.

Almost on cue, the ship appeared. It was farther out than the buzzing raiders, looking, from this distance, to be cruising at an almost leisurely pace.

Luke watched it, taking in every detail.

Oh yes, he was in the right place.

The ship was Imperial, a TIE fighter of some kind, but instead of two plate-like wings, this fighter had three, their struts spread evenly around the central hull—yet another variation on the basic TIE design that the

Empire had experimented with in an apparently unending quest for perfection.

Luke's gaze was fixed on the craft as it came in closer. He could almost imagine the sound of its twin ion engines, the hard screech that heralded the incoming storm.

In war, psychology could be as powerful a weapon as a blaster.

The TIE came in to the platform, so close Luke thought it was going to slip through the magnetic shield at the end and make a landing. At the last minute, it pulled up and made a sharp turn to follow the line of cable up into the cluster of platforms. Within seconds, it was gone.

Luke didn't need to see the ship to know where it was. He stood on the platform, a center of calm as the other strange raiders continued to swarm in the space around him.

He felt the presence of the TIE. He reached further, searching for the pilot, and the evil within.

There. Darkness, a powerful, endless night, and—

Different. It felt different.

Luke opened his eyes. He didn't hesitate. He ran to the other end of the platform, to the cable train car. The door was locked, the controls non-responsive; with a split-second flash of green, Luke's lightsaber made short work of the mechanism and he pulled the doors open.

The train car was a featureless box, the controls mounted flat against the front wall. Here, Luke took his time, but the problem wasn't a difficult one. The train car was locked down—so he unlocked it with the manual override, no code or clearance required. A quick glance over the other controls revealed they were just as simple—this was not a high-tech transporter, it was a basic, functionally minimal cargo container.

Luke punched the button, then held the small lever next to it in the FORWARD position. Looking through the forward window of the car, Luke watched as they pulled away from the station, the magnetic shield shimmering as the car pushed through the intangible barrier and out into the vacuum of space.

Ahead was a series of other station platforms, a sequence that looked, from Luke's position, to be stepping up and up, away from Nightside, toward the dark sphere of Therezar. A few platforms ahead, Luke saw the TIE hang for a moment then drop down behind a platform, gone again.

Gritting his teeth, Luke shoved the control lever forward, so hard it banged into its housing. He stared ahead and cleared his mind, prepared for what he knew was coming.

The station platform was the same as all the others Luke had passed, six in total. Functional, and completely deserted. As he exited the car, he looked back. The swarm of raiders looked tiny from here against the huge, cuboid mass of the Nightside central hub. There were fewer now.

The raiders must have landed.

Luke glanced around, getting his bearings. The platform on which he found himself actually consisted of a stack of them, rising in a series connected by ramps to form a kind of low-rise ziggurat, all apparently open to space, although Luke could see the telltale shimmer of the magnetic shields from the corner of his eyes as he moved up each level toward the top. The platforms were clearly cargo loading pads for larger ships, judging by the stacked pods and containers that were lined up in groups on each one, ready for the next shipment to depart.

And at the top of the stack, on the uppermost platform, was the TIE, piloted by a Sith. And Luke knew it *was* Sith—he could feel it now, the ship a blazing beacon in the Force, despite, in reality, being nothing but a silhouette lit by the flashing clouds of Therezar behind.

Luke slowed his approach, keeping his hands loose by his side, the edge of his short cloak cinched back, the silver hilt of his lightsaber glinting under the platform floodlights as he passed beneath them. Luke kept his focus ahead, but he was aware of every movement, every particle around him as he approached the fighter. He could see now that the hull of the TIE had been customized, the surface covered in ragged red characters—the mirror writing of the Sith, applied by a rough hand. He stopped on the platform below and looked up into the ship's crosshatched viewport.

The TIE was quiet, powered down.

For a moment, Luke was alone.

And then he felt it. A movement, in both the real world and the river of the Force. A boulder, rolling gently into place.

Luke turned around.

She stepped out of the deep darkness cast by a stack of cargo pods, but even under the floodlight, she was a shadow herself. She was dressed in black robes not entirely dissimilar to Luke's own. But in her case, while they had once been immaculate and tailored, the long cape that flowed from the shoulders was tattered, a torn, scalloped edge. Her robes were fitted around her upper torso, flaring out from the waist, the bottom hem flowing around black boots as she slowly stepped forward. But they were rough, patchy.

The robes were worn out and old.

Like the mask.

The woman stopped, and Luke stared at her face. It was metal, a burnished bronze, with two black glassy eyes, a row of heavy rivets forming a shape approximating the downturned scowl of a mouth. And it was a true mask, rather than a helmet. The woman's long blue-black hair flared out around it.

And it was the *mask* that was the source of the disturbance. Luke could feel it now, a focal point, the hollow core of a storm in the Force that continued to grow, and grow.

The signature of the dark side was unmistakable. Luke had sensed it in his father, Darth Vader. Vader had been a fire, a twisting sun-dragon that curled in the core of a star about to go nova. The Emperor, Palpatine, had been the exact opposite—he was *ice,* the terrifying cold of the bottom of an endlessly deep ocean, the abyssal plain, where there was no light, no hope; a cold so absolute, so ultimate, that all life withered in its presence.

But this Sith was different, and for a moment, Luke was uncertain. He could feel the darkness radiating from the figure—from the mask— and then . . . it seemed to be coming from *elsewhere,* from a place far distant. The woman in front of him . . . she wasn't a Sith herself, even though she wore the ritual mask of one. The power she wielded wasn't hers; she was merely channeling it.

And for a moment, Luke had the strangest sensation that she was, somehow, standing in the *way* of the true source—an *eclipse* of the Force, a black hole that cast a long shadow across space and time. But as he relaxed his mind and controlled his emotions, his fear—not for himself, but for his friends, for Lando and R2-D2, for the family, for the people of Nightside—and searched for the source, the power of it shocked him with a sudden bout of vertigo.

Luke concentrated, and was once again centered, and the two ancient foes—Jedi and Sith—stood facing each other. Neither moved. Luke imagined that the woman was studying him just as he was studying her, perhaps in silent conversation with the true Sith that cast its shadow long across her life.

Luke's hand found his lightsaber hilt. Without taking his eyes off the Sith, he unhooked it and held it out to one side. He didn't activate it, but it was ready.

The Sith did not move.

Luke lifted his chin and stared her down. "Who are you?"

There was a long, sharp snap, followed by the familiar buzz of a lightsaber igniting. The Sith had been holding her weapon all this time, and the scarlet blade was now alive and angry, angled away from her body. But instead of a straight blade, it curved like a scimitar.

Luke's eyes dropped to the weapon. He had spent years, now, cataloging relics, artifacts, and antiquities, both of the Jedi Order and those of the Sith. Luke and Lor San Tekka had crisscrossed the galaxy in search of any that might have survived the Great Jedi Purge that followed the rise of the Empire—for Lor, this was a holy quest; for Luke, a quest of understanding, of knowing the past so the future could be shaped.

Now, standing before the woman who wasn't a Sith, who wore the mask of one who was, Luke recognized her weapon. It was straight out of myth, a relic that Luke had never quite been sure was even real, the story of it and the Sith Lord who had created it more like a fable from a darker time than a true historical record.

And yet here it was. Unique, unmistakable.

The lightsaber of Darth Noctyss.

Luke adjusted his footing, his eyes now fixed on his opponent's mask. The woman didn't move. Luke thumbed the activator on his own lightsaber, the blade flaring into being, a brilliant and lively green, its warm hum joining that of the Sith weapon.

Luke and Lor San Tekka had once tried to find the relics of Noctyss, years before, following a lead that a group calling itself the Acolytes of the Beyond were amassing their own arsenal of Sith artifacts in some vain attempt to harness their dark power. Instead, Luke and Lor had found the Acolytes to be a splintered, disorganized cabal, enamored more with the idea of the dark side than with learning how to truly wield that power. They may once have been a terror group, led by fanatics, but that had been in the past.

But it had not been a wasted expedition. Luke and Lor San Tekka had retrieved a number of items, including Sith lightsabers—although the weapon of Darth Noctyss had not been among them—and Luke had even been able to help one of the Acolytes free herself from their cultish thrall.

That was then. Now Luke had stumbled onto proof that Noctyss was no mere legend.

Luke mirrored the woman's stance. He was ready to defend himself, but he was deeply curious—and concerned—about his opponent.

The Sith were dead. Everyone knew that.

Except somewhere out in the Unknown Regions their hidden planet spun, and right here, right now, Luke was faced with evidence that their power was far from extinguished.

The mask. The lightsaber.

Luke needed to know where they had come from and, more important, he needed to know who was wielding them.

Finally, the woman moved, stepping sideways and around. Luke matched the movement, the pair now circling an invisible center of the platform, each keeping their distance equal. She remained silent, but the black glass eyes of the mask were fixed on Luke, reflecting both the green glow of his lightsaber, and the red glow of hers.

"Where did you get that lightsaber?" Luke asked. Noctyss, according to the legend, had been a woman, but she would be long dead. Whoever his opponent was, she wasn't her.

At this, the woman stopped. Luke also came to a stop, raising his lightsaber slightly, the warm, familiar buzz of the blade close in his ear.

"This blade is mine," said the woman. Her voice was deep, modulated, no doubt, by the mask. But there was something else there. A sound, or . . . no, a *feeling*. It was like her voice resonated both in Luke's ears and in the Force itself.

Was that even possible?

"Who are you?" Luke demanded. This time, he took one decisive step forward, which made the woman raise her blade.

"I am many things," she said. "I am a hunter. A servant. A master. A collector." At this, she lifted her lightsaber and pointed the curved end at Luke. "And I am here to collect that which is rightfully ours."

Ours? That was it—there was *another* voice, mixed with the woman's own, and it wasn't just the mask's vocalizer altering it.

It was another presence entirely. The blaze of the red lightsaber was bright in Luke's eyes, and when he blinked, he thought he could see—

Yes. He *could* see. There, in the flashing afterimage left on his retinas, someone else was present. Someone behind the woman, standing close, so close the figure could whisper in her ear, the woman merely repeating what the form said. Luke blinked, and the figure flared, like a black shadow streaming out from the . . .

From the mask?

But when Luke blinked again, they were alone on the platform. It was just Luke, and the woman. They circled each other, and now her back was to the TIE, and behind her, the dark globe of Therezar flashed.

And then there was a brighter flash, and multicolored streaks that Luke instantly recognized as ship-to-ship fire.

He glanced up. The swarm of raiders had been engaged by other craft, sleek and uniform in design, marked with the slabs of yellow that were characteristic of Nightside.

The raiders were being routed. Nightside was, despite the strange delay, finally defending itself.

"The crystals. Give them to me."

Luke looked back at his opponent.

That was when he felt the movement inside his robe. The shards of bled kyber crystal were still carefully wrapped in their bundle, safely tucked into the concealed pocket.

That bundle was now moving, just a little, just a gentle tug, like a careless—invisible—pickpocket was making a clumsy but concerted effort to lift it.

"What you found on Yoturba belongs to me. Belongs to us." The woman lifted her empty hand, and Luke realized she wasn't wearing gloves; the sleeves of the tunic under her own tattered robe simply looped around her thumbs. Her hands, naked under the floodlights of the cargo platform, were blue in color.

Was she Pantoran? Wroonian? Luke racked his brain, trying to remember the Acolytes of the Beyond he had met. None came to mind who might have matched his opponent, but he and Lor San Tekka had encountered only a fraction of the group's scattered membership.

Still, whoever she was: Did she know about his discovery on Yoturba, or was she merely sensing the presence of the shattered crystals in the Force?

"The crystals belong to us. *Give them to us!*" The voice echoed strangely again, two voices in one, male and female, one close, as though whispering in Luke's ear, the other far, someone screaming their rage across an endless chasm.

The bundle in Luke's robe moved again.

"Where are the crystals from?" Luke asked. "Who was flying the ship that crashed? Do you know?"

The woman didn't answer. She did, however, take a step toward Luke, but Luke matched the movement, taking a step back as he raised his weapon, the blade humming through the air. At this, his opponent jerked her own curved blade up, ready to fight.

And—there, at the corner of Luke's eye, darkness flared at the woman's shoulder, a darkness that emanated not from her but from her mask. At the same time, he felt the movement in the Force.

Luke was right. There were three of them on the platform.

Himself. The woman.

And a Sith . . . or at the very least, the shadow of one, cast over the woman. How much free will did she even have? Luke knew full well the power that a relic like the Sith mask could have over those who would dare to wear it.

He fell into a defensive pose, two hands on his lightsaber hilt, legs spread, feet planted.

"I can help you," he said. "Join me, and I can free you from the power that has hold of you."

The woman—and the mask—watched Luke.

"I don't want to hurt you," Luke continued, "but I will defend myself."

The woman lifted her lightsaber. The red glow of the blade lit up the mask, lit up the black glass eyes.

Luke braced himself. He knew what he had to do, even if he didn't want to do it.

There was a flash of white over the woman's head. Luke glanced up as two members of Nightside security pursued one of the raiders, the trio heading for the platform. The Nightside ships fired, their shots aligned with perfect timing, and the raiding ship was reduced to boiling gases and burning scrap—scrap that was now falling directly toward the platform on which Luke and his opponent were facing each other.

Luke leapt out of the way, using the Force to both propel himself backward and push his opponent forward, saving her from the rain of debris. He grunted as he hit the deck on his back several meters away, and when he looked up, he had just a moment to shield his eyes as the wreck of the droid raider impacted the platform and exploded. Luke scrambled away, turning his back and curling into a ball as the heat and pressure wave washed over him.

It had been close. Too close. The top platform had been small, and while he had managed to push himself back and down the ramp onto the one below, he didn't know where his opponent had ended up. He turned, covering his face from the burning pyre on the top platform. He couldn't see a thing beyond the white and blue flames and thick, choking smoke. Luke got to his feet and pulled on one sleeve, drawing the fabric of his robes over his mouth and nose in an attempt to protect his lungs from the hot and toxic gases.

Then the smoke billowed in a huge, rolling wave and Luke was pushed back again; this time, he kept his footing, his robe spilling out as he looked up and saw the TIE fighter lifting up, out of the smoke and flame, its thrust blowing back against the platform. The ship hung for a moment, then turned and hurtled into space, the shield of the cargo platform rippling as the fighter crossed its threshold. It sped out toward Nightside, catching the attention of the two circling defense fighters, which began a new pursuit, their twin cannons spitting blue plasma as they attempted to destroy this new craft.

But the TIE was too fast, and within seconds it had vanished into the shadow of Therezar.

The platform shuddered, and there was a deep bass rumble from somewhere below, followed by an even louder double *thud thud* that Luke could feel through the soles of his boots. The platform shuddered again, then tilted sharply at an angle as its repulsorlift failed on one side, tipping the entire structure on a single pivot point, the remaining antigravity units shrieking under the suddenly increased load.

Luke hardly had time to register what was happening before he found himself tumbling down what was now a steep metal incline. Unsecured cargo containers fell past, careening off into empty space, the platform's shield shimmering like the surface of a lake as debris rained through it.

Through gritted teeth, Luke focused, reaching out with both his mind and his right hand, arresting his fall with the Force and then propelling himself back up what was now an almost perpendicular platform. He grabbed at the railing that ran along the edge, grasping it with just his cybernetic hand and using his momentum to swing himself up and onto it, balancing on the precarious structure on the balls of his feet.

Luke outstretched both arms for balance, but it wasn't enough. More muffled bangs from somewhere near signaled the imminent failure of the remaining repulsorlifts.

He looked up just in time to see the webbing that held a stack of small equipment boxes in one corner of the cargo deck fail, the dozen or so human-sized oblong cases falling almost in slow motion toward him.

Luke had no time to think, only to act. He reached his human hand toward the falling cases, bending their inevitable trajectory to his will. For a single second, he could feel all their weight, their mass, their momentum, and then he turned that feeling around, projecting it back toward the falling equipment.

The dozen cases were flung up and away, scattering like they were nothing, and falling safely around Luke.

But that wasn't going to save him. There was a final, huge *thwumph* from what was now the top of the platform, and, looking up, Luke saw a huge ball of fire, a deep orange swell curling with thick gray smoke, erupting from the mangled, twisted lump that had once been an antigrav generator.

The platform shook once more, and then it began to fall.

Luke crouched on the railing, keeping his balance for just a second longer, all the while aware that he was rapidly running out of options.

Then he saw it. The cable train. The tether running past this platform and out to the next—the final one in the chain—had buckled as the platform had torn itself away, but it was still intact, and farther back along, the simple cargo car was still attached, although it now hung from the tether at an angle. Luke didn't know if it was still operational, but it was his only shot.

The superstructure of the platform groaned beneath him as it began to crumple under its own weight and fall. Luke jumped, but his footing on the rail hadn't been as steady as he needed.

Still he made it—just. He took hold of the cable train tether with his cybernetic hand, the serrated edge cutting clean through the leather of his glove; as Luke adjusted his grip, the glove was cut again, and it fell from his hand entirely, exposing the naked mechanism beneath. Luke swung his legs up, locking his ankles around the cable. He looked up, down, getting his bearings, judging how far the train car was.

It looked a long, long way away.

As Luke struggled to get into a better position, the comlink on his belt crackled into life. He grabbed it with his free hand, thumbing the button on the end of the stubby little device as he brought it up to his mouth.

"Lando!"

The first thing Luke heard was R2-D2's whistle, ear-piercingly loud. Then Lando's voice, as clear as a bell.

"Hold on, Luke," he said. "We see you. Coming in below."

With a roar, the *Lady Luck* appeared beneath Luke, the rear end drifting, as though the boat-shaped starship really were riding the waves of a turbulent sea. As the back end of the craft swung in underneath Luke, he saw a maintenance hatch iris open on the top.

There were about twenty meters between the *Lady Luck* and himself. Good enough.

Luke unhooked his feet, and hung for a moment from his mechanical hand. The cable swayed, and Lando's ship moved, the tiny circle of the hatchway circling as Lando tried to keep the alignment.

Luke let go. He dropped straight through the hatch, using the Force to cushion his descent so he didn't break his legs.

Then, as the *Lady Luck* turned and powered away to safety, the cable swung again and then snapped, sending a cascading series of bright electrical explosions along its length until they reached the cable train.

The car exploded, the debris raining down into the clouds of Therezar.

CHAPTER 23

THE *GOLDSTONE,* THEREZAR SYSTEM
NOW

The interior of Zargo Anaximander's yacht was as expensive, as luxurious, as his private apartments on Nightside. In fact, it was hard to know you were on a starship and not merely relaxing in an exclusive, high-end pleasure retreat. Even the flight deck was fitted with finely woven rugs, the patterns of which seemed to move as you watched them, and furniture—not fitted, functional starship equipment, but freestanding, handcrafted items that were, Dathan assumed, either unique art pieces or rare antiques. Either way, the cost of each item was likely to be astronomical.

But right now, none of it mattered to him. He stood on the flight deck, arms tightly folded, lost in thought as Miramir steered the craft through the sea of floating ice that formed the Therezar ring system. Rey sat in the copilot's seat, entranced by the view through the wide forward viewport.

Jedi. That man—Lando Calrissian—had said he was with a Jedi.

And Dathan . . . didn't know what to do. Not now.

A Jedi? The enemy of the Sith, their opposite, paragons of the light. Dathan had thought they were all dead, their light extinguished by his father's Empire. But even as he thought that, he realized that for the rest of the galaxy, the opposite was true—that it was the Sith who were extinct, their evil banished from a galaxy that could now take a moment, take a breath, as it began to rebuild and renew itself after a twenty-year reign of darkness.

So if they had a Jedi on their side?

Maybe, maybe after all this time, all these years—hell, a lifetime—Dathan had finally found someone else he could trust outside of those he held so close to his heart.

Dathan let out a shuddering breath. At the sound, Miramir glanced over her shoulder. Ahead, the ice field had thinned, the remaining bergs at the edge of the ring system now distant asteroid-sized lumps, blue and white against the starscape.

"This should do," said Miramir, setting a control. "We're far enough out from Nightside that we should be screened by the rings. We can wait."

Dathan nodded as he stared out the viewport. But he hadn't been listening, not really. His mind was still reeling, torn by indecision. Still, he did know one thing, a single inescapable truth, as solid as a mathematical constant.

They couldn't run forever.

They'd escaped from Jakku. They'd escaped the attack in Wild Space. They'd fallen into the worst trouble yet at Nightside, but had gotten out of it, helped by a mysterious stranger and an astromech droid. That, Dathan knew, was sheer luck. If this Lando Calrissian hadn't appeared, they'd never have gotten away.

And luck, Dathan knew all too well, was not a commodity that could be predicted or relied upon. But as the old proverb went, a common refrain heard around the somewhat less orthodox starports the galaxy over: You had to be lucky all the time; your opponent only had to be lucky *once*.

"Dathan?"

He jumped, jolted from the dark recesses of his own mind by his wife's voice. In the copilot's seat, Rey turned around, watching her parents in wide-eyed silence.

Dathan took a deep breath. "Sorry," he said, then he nodded. "Good."

Miramir frowned and moved to join her husband. The two came together in the middle of the flight deck and held each other for a moment.

"Do you think this is it?" asked Miramir, her cheek on Dathan's shoulder. "Do you think they're going to help us?"

At Miramir's words, Dathan felt his body tense; Miramir must have sensed it, too, because that was when she broke away from their embrace and looked up into his eyes.

"I . . . don't know," said Dathan, and even as he said it, he cursed his own cynicism, his ingrained distrust of anything and everything. Then again, that distrust had kept them alive, so far. Was now really the time to fight against a lifetime of habit and behavioral programming?

"But, a Jedi," said Miramir, her face lighting up as she spoke the word. "That's good, isn't it? The enemy of my enemy is my friend, isn't that how it's supposed to work?"

"The New Republic wouldn't help us."

"The New Republic wouldn't," said Miramir, "but Dina Dipurl *did*."

"And look how that went."

Miramir took a step back, her expression cooling. "Thanks to her, we have a new ship, and we might just have met the people who really can help us."

Dathan shook his head. "What happened on Nightside could easily have gone another way. We were very fortunate to get out of there."

"Okay, fine, we were very fortunate. That's how it happened. I'm not going to question that now, it is what it is, and this is where we are." Miramir spread her hands. "And it sounds to me like we might finally have some friends."

Dathan opened his mouth to reply, then closed it. Instead, he gave a small nod. Because . . . she was right. Now was not the time to catastrophize—but neither was it the time to celebrate. Between Dathan's pessimism and Miramir's optimism, there was a middle ground Dathan knew they needed to navigate if they were going to make it out of their current situation.

Dathan moved closer to his wife and reached out to squeeze her shoulder. She covered his hand with hers, and he drew her in to kiss her on the forehead.

"The stars are moving."

Dathan and Miramir turned as Rey spoke to find their daughter pointing at the forward viewport. As the icebergs of Therezar lazily tumbled through space, two streaks of light were visible between them.

Miramir glanced down at the console. "We have company. Two ships, fast approach."

"Is it them?"

Miramir pursed her lips and sat in the pilot's position. "I have no idea. They have our transponder ident, so they'll know where we are."

Dathan moved to stand by another console. "Seven-seven-zero, right? They said that was the frequency they'd use." He looked over the controls but shook his head. The *Goldstone* was an advanced ship, the systems far more complex than those of their junk freighter.

"Other panel, left-hand side," Miramir said, waving at her husband. Dathan nodded and moved his hand across. Now he recognized the comm deck controls. He pressed a button, and immediately there came a high-pitched alert. He pulled his hand away and looked at his wife.

"Was that me or them?"

Miramir leaned over her controls as the alert sounded again. "Uh . . . no. Weapons lock. We've been targeted."

Dathan swiftly moved back to the main controls. He scooped Rey up and sat in her seat, then clutched his daughter tightly in his lap. Ahead, the two incoming ships were getting closer, their ion trails sparkling as they cut through the ring system.

"That's not them," said Dathan. "We have to move, fast."

"Wait, wait," said Miramir. She was studying the readouts, her face a mask of concern.

"You know how to make a jump in this thing?" asked Dathan.

"Of course." Miramir toggled a switch. "But we're low on fuel. We can't get far."

"We just need to get out of this system."

Miramir looked up. "But what about the others? We said we'd wait for them."

Dathan clicked his front teeth together as he thought. They were running out of time.

He glanced at the comm deck. "Send a transmission along seven-seven-zero. We'll have to meet them somewhere else."

But Miramir shook her head. "We transmit coordinates, that means those other ships will know where we've gone."

"Only if they're on the same frequency. Seven-seven-zero is an auxiliary channel. Lando picked it for a reason. He'll be listening, but they"—he pointed at the forward view—"won't be."

The other ships were close. The target lock alert sounded again.

Dathan turned to his wife.

"Time to go."

Miramir held his look for a moment, then gave a nod, and got to work on the controls.

CHAPTER 24

NIGHTSIDE, THEREZAR SYSTEM
NOW

It was, to put no finer point on it, a disaster.

Zargo Anaximander stalked along the passageway that connected the cable train station to the auxiliary communications center, the structure having mercifully escaped any damage during the raid. This time, he was accompanied by two guard droids, their armored feet clanking on the hard floor, larger, heavy-duty twin-barreled blasters clutched in each metallic hand. As Anaximander ground his molars in frustration, the twisting coils of his tattoos slithered around one another, the particles beneath his skin reflecting his foul temper.

He'd expected a carefully controlled renegotiation with Ochi's "associates," followed by a discreet hand-over. That was why he'd moved the family to his yacht in the first place—private landing pad, the secure access, no surveillance. The entire domain was under Anaximander's total control—like the business he had intended to conduct.

The last thing he could have predicted was an all-out raid on Nightside. He hadn't even gotten back to his quarters when the first ships came in for the attack. Anaximander delayed Nightside's defensive response as he tried to understand what was going on—a cover? A distraction? Or . . . a genuine attack? Soon enough he realized what was happening and sent his droid defense forces out to clear the raiders from his facility and the ships they had arrived in from his skies, and had immediately headed back to the auxiliary communications center.

The doors of the control room slid open at his approach. Anaximander clicked his front teeth together, trying to control his anger, compose his thoughts before he hailed Ochi.

Lucky he wasn't here himself, Anaximander thought, or he'd have killed him with his bare hands, and to hell with the bounty on the family. Someone else might pay for them, if the genetic construct that was the father was as interesting as he suspected.

Anaximander punched up frequency and waited for a response, but the light on the console remained resolutely red. Odd. Was Ochi even coming? Perhaps, having turned a business exchange into an all-out battle, Ochi simply expected his crazed droid minions to have secured the bounty. Droid Crush? What did that even *mean*? If Anaximander was supposed to be intimidated by their name, it hadn't worked. Nor were there any of the mechanized pirates left to pose further problems.

Anaximander smirked at this thought.

Ochi of Bestoon, oh, you are in for a hell of a surprise.

He stabbed the button again, but there was still no response. Anaximander hissed in annoyance, realizing he was going to have to wait, when two blaster shots rang out in the control room. Anaximander spun around, just in time to see his droid escort—now with smoking holes shot clean through their chest units—fall to their knees, then topple backward to the floor.

Anaximander looked up. Standing in the doorway was a figure dressed in black, flanked by a pair of identical bodyguards clad in light plastoid body armor, their long-snouted features identical. Each held a high-caliber blaster rifle, and they were both pointing them in Anaximander's direction.

Anaximander shook his head and moved toward them, ignoring the threat of the blasters. He stepped right up and stared down at the much shorter Ochi of Bestoon. Zargo grimaced at his appearance—the too-smooth, scarred face and bald head, the empty black electronic eyes—not even trying to hide his distaste.

"Oh, you made a real mistake, coming here, you can trust me on that one," said Anaximander. From the corner of his eye, he could see Ochi's two minions adjusting their footing, ready to protect their master. They were big, powerful, and well armed, but they looked slow.

Good.

Ochi looked up at the regent-captain towering over him.

"You're the one who made a mistake, friend," said Ochi. "Is this how you normally do business? By launching a fleet of fighters? Hell of a welcoming committee for a new business partner."

Anaximander stretched his neck, his tattoos crawling over his jawline. "We had an arrangement, Ochi. A deal. I had the package ready and waiting for you, nice and tight. And you send in an army. What was I supposed to do? Let them walk in and take over?" He clicked his tongue. "*Nuh-uh.* Nightside is my domain. I say what happens here. Your Droid Crush Pirates are gone. Finished." He spread his hands. "You overstepped the mark and you paid the price."

"And you, friend," said Ochi, tilting his head, regarding the regent-captain like a particularly interesting specimen of insect under glass, "let the 'package' escape. In your own ship."

Anaximander froze. He glanced at the other two. He suppressed a grimace as the one on Ochi's left grinned, displaying razor-sharp metal teeth. Anaximander looked back to Ochi.

"What are you talking about?"

Ochi laughed, quietly. "Sorry, didn't you say this was your domain? Don't tell me the regent-captain doesn't even know when his shiny prized yacht gets stolen by a family of vagrants." Ochi's tone changed. "We saw them leave on our approach, but we were too late," he snapped. "They're lost in the rings of this planet, somewhere."

Anaximander stared at Ochi for a moment, his mind racing for ideas. He had no reason to suspect Ochi was lying. Perhaps those "vagrants" were more clever than he thought.

Then he laughed. He folded his arms and walked a tight circle, all under the watchful gaze of Ochi's two minions. He could feel Ochi watching him.

That was more like it. He was in control again.

He had an idea.

Anaximander stopped, his back to Ochi. He looked down at the communications console, his eyes lingering on the flickering blue light on the tracking panel. He tapped at the controls then, without turning, he said, "Did you bring the money?"

"That takes some guts, friend," said Ochi. "We've come a long way for nothing."

Anaximander turned back around and watched as Ochi walked slowly toward him.

"I'm not here to *pay* you," said Ochi, his voice almost a whisper. "I'm here to *kill* you."

Anaximander grinned. Ochi stopped. Behind him, the two minions adjusted their blasters, but Anaximander saw them glance sideways at each other.

Anaximander reached behind and tapped a button. There was a *bleep* as a small data card ejected itself from the console. He took it, then held it up between finger and thumb for Ochi to see.

"I know exactly where they are. I can still give you the package. And I'll have my yacht back in one piece while you're at it, please."

Ochi looked at the data card.

"A simple tracker," said Anaximander, with a casual shrug. "You see, I like to know where all of my assets are, all the time."

Ochi stared at the tracker. He didn't speak.

Anaximander glanced at the two bodyguards, who were still watching in stoic silence, although their blaster rifles were perhaps dipping a little now. Anaximander leaned in ever closer to Ochi, swallowing back his distaste at being so close to the damaged face.

The corner of his mouth curled up in a smile, and the tattoos unwound and receded in response to his changing mood.

Oh yes, thought Zargo Anaximander. *I'm in charge here, Ochi of Bestoon.*

"I propose a new deal," he said quietly. "I have the package exactly where I want them. And you can still have them. But I think the price just went up."

Ochi lifted his head, turning his dead black electronic eyes from the data card to the regent-captain.

Anaximander tapped his knuckles against Ochi's tunic, the sound strangely hollow against the hard black leather. "I'm doing you a favor here, Ochi." He looked up at the two minions. "Your boys came in too hot. I had to defend myself. You would have done the same. But that's nothing money can't fix. You buy yourself a new army, am I right? Because whatever I'm getting for the package is a drop in the Sea of Cantonica compared with your own payday, am I right?" Anaximander sniffed. "Besides," he continued, "you won't need an army, not anymore. I've done you a favor, I really have."

Ochi tilted his head again. Anaximander found himself looking at two tiny, washed-out reflections of himself in Ochi's eyes.

"You have, friend," said Ochi. "More than you can imagine."

Anaximander's grin widened, and he nodded. "So we have an agreement?"

"We do," said Ochi.

There was a sudden movement, Ochi's body jerking spasmodically, and Anaximander felt something hot in his middle. A moment later, he coughed, his heartbeat thundering in his head, in time with the pounding pain in his stomach, in time with the spurts of blood that came from his mouth, and from the abdominal wound Ochi opened up a little more with a blade Anaximander hadn't even noticed the man was carrying.

Anaximander coughed again, the grin fixed on his face, and he took one faltering step backward, pulling the dagger out of himself. He looked down, saw the strange, lobed blade, noticed it had an inscription on it, watched as his blood, thick and red, seemed to move *around* the inscription, like he wasn't just bleeding, it was being sucked out of his body by the strange weapon—the inscription of which seemed to glow as the red liquid flowed around the carved runes.

Damn. Is that dagger drinking my blood?

It was the last thought that the regent-captain of Nightside had, and it didn't matter, because a moment later he fell to the deck. As he gasped for air, Ochi's guard with the metal teeth walked over and reached down, taking the data card from between Anaximander's fingers.

The regent-captain of Nightside took one more breath, and then no more.

. . .

Ochi stormed toward the *Bestoon Legacy,* docked on an auxiliary access platform near the comm station. At the bottom of the *Legacy*'s ramp stood two of the gang Bosvarga and Cerensco had managed to gather from Boxer Point Station—Krastan, a leering Gran in a tight burgundy flight suit, and Stiper, a Balosar man with a huge mane of hair coiffured up to cover his antennapalps. As Ochi and the two brothers approached, Bosvarga gave Krastan a slight shake of the head—and Krastan seemed to hesitate, exchanging a look with Stiper. Cerensco didn't notice, but Bosvarga slowed, his grip tightening on his blaster. Something wasn't right, but then Krastan and Stiper quickly turned and followed Cerensco and their boss up into the ship. Bosvarga held back a moment, then shrugged and headed up the ramp.

Ochi, Sith dagger firmly in his grip, was oblivious to everything. The ancient weapon was clean and dry, having absorbed Anaximander's blood to the very last drop.

The blade hummed in Ochi's mind. As soon as he had stabbed the regent-captain, he knew the first cut had been fatal, that death had been unstoppable. Somehow, the blade knew as well.

It knew . . . and it reveled in the murder.

And this feeling passed back to Ochi. He stood, savoring the moment Anaximander's consciousness winked out of existence, enjoying the blood-warmth of the blade as it took his life force, his essence, and absorbed it. Not becoming stronger—the blade was powerful enough—but instead feeding on his life for the sheer, lustful enjoyment of it.

Ochi liked how this felt. As he swung off the ramp and into the ship proper, he felt light-headed—not drunk, exactly, but buzzing, carefree, and alert, everything around him in pin-sharp focus.

A drink would do very nicely, right now. Very nicely indeed.

"Master! M-m-m-master!"

Ochi looked down at D-O as the data retrieval droid wheeled around in a tight circle, apparently keeping its distance, but still trying to give a warning.

Ochi spun around. At the very rear of the *Legacy*'s main cabin, a squat, snub-nosed speeder was parked, ready to be dropped down on the articulated floor plate and reversed out of the ship's rear cargo doors.

Sitting on the speeder's faring was a gangly, almost skeletal droid. It stood, unfolding limbs that were too long and too thin, until it stretched a full two meters tall, the insectoid head that balanced on the slim, cylindrical body ridiculously out of proportion.

"This was a wipeout, Ochi," said the droid, pulling up its two long arms. In each hand it held a blaster, and as it took aim for Ochi, it spun them around the trigger guards, a display of . . . well, something. Ochi watched, as unimpressed with the droid's gunplay as he was by the droid's entire operation. The buzzing in his head faded, and he felt a little sick, a little empty.

And he didn't like how *that* felt.

Ochi took a step toward the intruder in his ship.

"When I hired the Droid Crush Pirates of Bestoon," Ochi said quietly, "I expected results." He lifted the Sith blade and pointed it at the droid. "You said the Droid Crush was different now. Let bygones be bygones, you said. The Droid Crush Pirates weren't like what they were in the old days. You were professional. Renowned, even. But it seems I made the same mistake as I did all those years ago."

The captain of the Droid Crush stomped his feet.

"Likewise," said the droid. "*I* should have known better. I should have killed you the moment you stepped foot in Zee-Nine City Seven. I guess a droid never learns." The droid's huge eyes glittered as it looked around the interior of the *Bestoon Legacy.* "Got a lotta stuff in here, Ochi. Must be worth a credit or two. Won't make up for the crew I lost today, but perhaps I can find another way to satisfy that particular urge for revenge, eh?" It turned and looked down at the speeder, and tapped the emblem mounted on the front of it, facing the rear cargo door. "Nice ornament. Hex charm, isn't it? Haven't seen one of those for years." It cocked its head and turned back to Ochi. "Say, where's that helmet you used to wear, back in the day?" The droid pointed at its own head with one blaster. "White-and-red thing. Maybe I should nail that to the front of my own speeder. Y'know, to make a point."

Ochi didn't reply. Nobody moved. Seconds stretched.

"Or maybe I could just take your actual head."

The droid spun and raised both blasters. It fired.

The twin bolts never found their targets. With almost impossible speed—perhaps driven partly by the blade itself—Ochi swept the Sith dagger up to protect himself, deflecting the blaster bolts with the blade. One reflected bolt clipped the droid captain's shoulder, causing that arm to fall; the other bolt shorted into the *Legacy*'s decking.

The droid captain fired again with its one remaining weapon.

Again, Ochi deflected the bolts with the blade. He wasn't sure how he was doing it, how he could even be *fast* enough to catch the bolts or *lucky* enough that the blade was in just the right place, at just the right angle, to protect him.

Let alone *defend* him. Three blaster bolts fired in quick succession were returned to the droid just as fast, the blade angling them to hit vulnerable points in the droid's exoskeleton. It fell in a shower of sparks and flame then slid down the side of the speeder and twitched on the floor. Bosvarga and Krastan sprang forward, each firing three shots from their heavy blasters at point-blank range into the droid's insect head, while Cerensco and Stiper fanned out, weapons raised to provide additional cover in case more of the Droid Crush were on their way.

Ochi held the Sith blade in front of him. The hilt was warm again—it wasn't the same as when it had drunk Zargo Anaximander's blood, but it was still comforting, like the blade was pleased.

He stepped over to the destroyed droid and nudged the smoking wreck with the toe of his boot.

"Never trust a droid," he muttered. "I won't make that mistake."

"Again."

Ochi spun around, and looked at Krastan.

"What did you say?"

One of Krastan's eyestalks remained fixed on the remains of the Droid Crush captain, while the other two moved to look at Ochi.

"He said, 'Again.' "

This was Stiper. The Balosar giggled, his laugh irritatingly high-pitched, as he moved to Krastan's side. "You said it yourself. Sounds like they were lousy the first time around, too." He nudged the Gran with the side of his blaster, and laughed again.

Ochi nodded, slowly. He lifted a hand and gently patted Stiper on the arm.

"You know," he said, "you're right. Never trust a droid. In fact—"

He lunged forward, plunging the Sith blade into the man's stomach.

"You can never trust anyone, Stiper. Anyone at all," Ochi whispered into the dying man's ear, his lipless mouth brushing Stiper's teased hair. "You let that thing onto my ship, didn't you? My mistake. I should have known not to employ a Balosar. Your kind is too easy to bribe."

Ochi trailed off as he pushed the dagger into his minion's stomach, right to the hilt again. His hand felt warm as the man's blood gushed out over it, and he leaned forward, resting the side of his face on Stiper's shoulder as his victim shuddered. The two stood like that for a moment, the assassin and his victim locked in a deadly embrace. Krastan backed away silently. He looked over at the twins, who had now retreated a safe distance away. Bosvarga held up a hand, like he was apologizing for something.

Ochi jerked, like he'd just woken up. Krastan jumped, his back bumping into one of the ship's internal support pillars.

With the Sith dagger buried deep inside Stiper, Ochi's mind hummed with white noise, so loud, so thick it was like a physical thing, a comforting blanket that surrounded him, enveloped him, protected him.

He pulled the blade out and stepped to one side. The Balosar's lifeless body hit the deck with a heavy thud. Ochi stood there, holding the blade, swaying slightly on his feet. He didn't look down at the body. He didn't look down at the blade. He just stood, and listened to the white noise in his head, felt the warmth of the blade.

Yes. *Yes.* There it was. It felt good. *I feel good.*

The blade is pleased.

Then Ochi snapped out of it.

Ochi glanced at Bosvarga and Cerensco, then turned his attention to Krastan. The Gran didn't move.

"That's what happens if you cross me," said Ochi. "Do we have an understanding?"

Krastan nodded quickly.

Ochi turned to the twins. "You have the tracking data?"

Bosvarga lifted the data card from his pocket.

"Then get out there after them," Ochi said, turning away from Krastan, who slumped against the pillar, visibly relieved. Ochi pointed to the exit ramp. "Go find Pysarian and Anduluuvil and give them this." Ochi gestured at Krastan, like he wasn't a sentient being but a piece of equipment to be used. "Go."

Without another word, Ochi's three surviving minions left the ship at a jog.

Ochi glanced down at the mess in the *Bestoon Legacy*—one fragmented, smoking droid, the facedown body of Stiper, one leg still twitching as his nervous system signaled one more time before going dark. D-O rolled a careful arc around Ochi and came to a halt by the remains of the Droid Crush captain. It leaned its flat-nosed head down, like it was taking a closer look at the exposed innards of its more sophisticated brethren.

Ochi hissed between his teeth. Yes, the transaction with Zargo Anaximander had been a disaster. The Droid Crush had been hopeless, disobeying his orders for their own glory, not realizing they had more than met their match in Anaximander's own droid defenders.

But Anaximander *had* done well, even if it hadn't been quite what he had planned. That the family had managed to steal his yacht had been fortuitous—if they'd fallen into the hands of the Droid Crush, Ochi wasn't sure they'd be alive, given how the pirates had blatantly disregarded their mission.

But with the tracker, he could follow the family anywhere. They wouldn't stick around in the planetary ring system, but it didn't matter. Bosvarga and Cerensco were smart, and would no doubt tell Pysarian and Anduluuvil what had happened on the *Legacy*. In fact, Ochi counted on it.

But as Ochi looked at Stiper's body again, he sighed. He had a small crew, getting smaller. Paying for help—as he had done with the Droid Crush—was out of the question. What he really needed was a group under his *direct* control, a gang that would obey implicitly, follow orders without question.

Ochi walked into the cockpit and opened the forward blast shields. The shutterlike coverings opened, revealing the landing pad at the rear of Nightside's auxiliary communications platform. He looked at the transparisteel building, and the huge dish towering above it. Anaximander's droids would find his body eventually, and there was no point in hanging around.

Ochi sat at the controls and gently powered the *Legacy* away from the platform, turned, and piloted into the rings of Therezar. Within minutes, the gentle dusty snowstorm outside got thicker and thicker, until he was surrounded by icebergs as big as his own ship. He killed the engines and let the ship drift.

Perfect cover, at least for a short while.

He turned to his comm deck, and—

He hesitated.

They had said he could call them. He had the transponder codes, the hidden frequency, routed through a thousand hyperspace relay beacons, making any transmission as scrambled and untraceable as it could get.

But . . .

He gulped, his mouth dry at the thought of speaking to them again. They represented everything he wanted. They were the Sith Eternal, they were *on* Exegol, for frisk's sake. The very place he had been looking for for *years* since that first visit. The place where everything would become clear, where he would be . . .

Whole again. Healed.

Reborn.

He gulped again, nearly choking as his dry throat closed up. He *really* needed a drink, and then he pushed that thought out of his mind and punched the codes. As the comm channel indicators came to life, he slumped back and waited.

Minutes passed. Outside, the frozen rings of Therezar swept past the shutters. Ochi turned in the flight seat and watched. He was getting cold. The buzzing in his head, that familiar, comforting hum of the blade, had faded again. He snapped the shutters closed and sank into the pilot's seat and the gloom of the cabin.

There was a crackle, and the cabin was lit in the eerie blue glow of a holotransmission. Ochi turned and found himself looking at the bandage-wrapped face of a cultist of the Sith Eternal. Whether it was one who had come to his moon, he couldn't say.

"Ochi of Bestoon," said the cultist, its voice a harsh, sibilant whisper. "Have you succeeded in your sacred quest?"

Ochi shook his head—talk about dramatics. "I'm close," he said, his own voice a dry croak. "I need help."

"Are you not worthy of the blessed task entrusted to you by our Dark Lord, Ochi of Bestoon? You must not fail him."

Ochi sighed. This bandage-wrapped freak was just starting to annoy him. He wondered if they really all talked like that, or if it was just for his benefit.

"And I'm not going to fail him," he said. "I know what I'm doing. That's not the kind of help I'm asking for." He leaned forward. "What I need are *bodies*. A group. A gang. I don't know—troopers. Call them whatever you want. But they need to be biologics. No droids. I need people I can depend upon to obey orders." He paused and cocked his head. "How many of you are there on Exegol, anyway? Must be hundreds. Thousands. You must be able to spare some of the workforce."

The hologram shimmered, pulsing as the signal was routed through beacon after beacon after beacon, the audio crackling with waves of static that matched the white noise in Ochi's head that once more began to rise.

For a moment, he thought this was the sound of Exegol, and he thought he could almost smell the dry dust of the place he'd been to, oh, so many years ago.

And then it was gone. With a snap, the holo stabilized, and the Sith Eternal spoke.

"Go to Basta Core. There you will meet an agent. Steadfast. He will assist."

"What kind of an agent?" asked Ochi. "What kind of assistance? Does he have men for me?"

The hologram flickered and was gone, plunging the *Bestoon Legacy* into sudden gloom.

Ochi reached behind him, grabbed a lever, and opened the blast shutters again. The cold glow of the Therezar ring system washed over him.

Basta Core? That wasn't far. He would have time enough to collect whatever help this "Steadfast" could offer, then rendezvous with Bosvarga, Cerensco, and the others. With any luck, they would have picked up the girl and would be waiting for him, and he wouldn't need this Steadfast's help at all.

But it paid to be ready. To have a contingency. Call it . . . insurance.

Because the family was . . . tricky. They had gotten off Nightside in the regent-captain's own ship, and he didn't think slicing the security protocols of Anaximander's private yacht would have been easy.

Ochi had underestimated them.

He wouldn't make that mistake again.

CHAPTER 25

THE *LADY LUCK*, THEREZAR SYSTEM
NOW

Lando flicked a switch and slammed a fist down on the console in front of him.

"It's no good," he said, gesturing to the panel. "There's too much interference out here. We've got debris from the attack scrambling the sensors, and the ice in the rings is shielding everything else. I can't pick up the vector of the *Goldstone,* and anything I transmit just gets bounced straight back." He shook his head. "And they haven't signaled yet. Hell of a place to get lost in."

Luke paced the flight deck of the *Lady Luck* behind Lando. Like the rest of the ship, it was spacious and opulent, the control consoles, even the flight seats, designed for elegance and comfort as well as function—even the deck was covered with a thin, soft synthetic weave embroidered with subtle interlocking designs. The flooring deadened the sound of Luke's boots.

Lando was right. The icy rings of Therezar were a good place to hide, and his advice to the family to take the regent-captain's ship out into them and wait had been good.

Except the rings were *too* good a place to hide. Lando hadn't counted on the interference from the system, and they could spend hours—days, even—cruising among the bergs, trying to find the luxury yacht by eye and close-range mass detectors. Luke only hoped that their non-arrival wouldn't panic the family and they'd at least stay put for a while as they searched. They seemed quite capable, according to Lando's account from the private hangar. They—or the mother, at least—had been able to slice through the *Goldstone*'s security systems and hijack the ship, after all. And they knew, now, that they had a Jedi on their side. Luke didn't know the family's state of mind, but he hoped that if they knew the Sith, they would also know Luke's Order. That, at least, should have counted for something.

But what he *did* know was that they were frightened, and he knew from personal experience the power that fear could hold, even over the most rational minds.

As he paced around on the *Lady Luck*'s soft decking, Luke couldn't help but be drawn back to his own memories. To be hunted by a Sith, to have the focus of the dark side on you, was a terrible thing. But while he had been unprepared for the discovery of his own place in the galaxy, this family, at least, seemed to know what they faced—they had a hex charm, and, more important, they knew exactly what it was and what it symbolized.

They were no ordinary family, and perhaps one that wasn't quite as helpless as he feared.

And that, Luke thought, felt good.

R2-D2 bleeped. Lando turned in his seat to face the droid, who was plugged into a workstation on the port side of the flight deck. R2-D2 turned his dome to face the others, the large indicator light on his front flicking from red, to blue, to red.

"Keep looking, Artoo," said Lando. "Scan all frequencies and see if you can pick up their transponder code. Any sign, any sign at all."

R2-D2 whistled in the affirmative and turned back to his task. Luke, meanwhile, finally dropped into the copilot's seat. He watched Lando as his old friend fussed over the sensor readouts.

Luke was worried about him—despite his outward appearance, his charisma, his confidence, Lando had spent six years in a personal hell, his life torn apart after the kidnapping of his daughter. And that had changed him. How could it not? Sure, Lando was still the free spirit. He was still immaculately dressed and presented, and when he smiled that smile, Luke could see his old friend in there.

But there was something else, now, just beneath the surface. Again, Luke didn't need to use the Force to sense it. The loss, the pain, the hurt. That Lando was holding it together so well was a testament to his strength and resilience. Lando Calrissian was a self-made man, the great impresario. He would let nothing beat him. Not then.

Certainly not now.

"Lando, we'll find them," said Luke. "Trust me."

"Yes," said Lando, a mere mutter under his breath. "Yes, they'll be fine. We'll find them. We'll get to them." He looked up at the forward view as he spoke, perhaps trying to convince himself that Luke was right, that the family was out there and waiting for a rescue they knew was coming.

Luke laid a hand on Lando's shoulder. Lando relaxed a little, and when he glanced sideways at Luke, he gave a small nod, along with a small smile.

"We'll find them," said Lando, and this time it sounded like he meant it.

As Lando turned and asked R2-D2 for an update, Luke sat back and thought about his encounter on the cargo platform. He ran events over and over again in his mind and, almost subconsciously, reached inside his robes with one hand, feeling for the cloth bundle and the kyber crystal shards secured within.

Lando shifted in his seat, watching as Luke withdrew the bundle from his pocket. "So what happened?" he asked. "That TIE that got out of there. Looked like a Defender to me."

Luke's brow furrowed as he thought. "It was pretty fast for an old Imperial ship. I haven't seen one like that before."

"The Defender was an experimental design," said Lando, "with hyperdrive capability. It never went into mainstream service with the Empire, though." He paused and frowned. "So what was it doing out here? And who was flying it? The Sith, the one chasing the family for their wayfinder?"

Luke looked at Lando in silence, composing his thoughts. But Lando's eyes widened, and he leaned toward his friend.

"You know who it was? Don't tell me, you've met them before?"

"No, I haven't met them before, and I don't know who they are. But I recognized her weapon."

"Her . . . weapon? What, she had a lightsaber, or something?"

Luke nodded. "Yes, but no ordinary lightsaber. It was a relic—one I wasn't sure even existed outside of legend."

Lando frowned. "I *really* don't like the sound of that."

Luke shrugged. "The galaxy is full of relics and artifacts, of the dark side and the light."

"Okay, so if this Sith has this special lightsaber, that gives you an *idea*, at least, of who she is, right?"

"Maybe, but I don't think she was Sith."

"What?" Lando waved his hands around. "You said you could sense the dark side, that the Sith were here!"

"Yes," said Luke. "I did sense the dark side, and a Sith was there, but it wasn't her."

Lando dropped his hands. "Okay, now you've lost me."

Luke turned to face him. "She was channeling the power of the Sith, but she's not a Sith herself. The lightsaber she held belonged to a Sith Lord called Noctyss—at least, according to the story. Lor San Tekka and I once tried to find the weapon, following a lead that a group calling themselves the Acolytes of the Beyond had found it."

Luke filled Lando in on the mission he'd undertaken with Lor San Tekka, and on what he had learned about the Acolytes of the Beyond. Lando listened intently, his brow knitted as he took it all in.

"So they were just kids, really?" he asked.

"Kids and outcasts," said Luke. "People who had lost friends and family and were perhaps looking for answers they couldn't find anywhere else."

"But they *weren't* Sith?"

"No, but they were obsessed with those who were. None of them actually understood anything about the Force, but that didn't mean they weren't dangerous. They murdered a lot of people to get what they wanted."

"Relics and artifacts. Like this lightsaber."

Luke nodded. "She was also wearing a mask. The power I sensed seemed to be coming from that."

"Hey," said Lando, clicking his fingers. "That sounds like something I saw, long time ago now. There was this helmet, supposed to have belonged to a Sith Lord called Momin. Anyone who put it on, it took them over, like Momin was back in the room. Could be something like that maybe?"

"Relics of the dark side can hold a lot of true power," said Luke, "but it would take a particularly adept Sith to be able to escape death itself inside one."

"Seems like there were a lot of them around back in the day, Luke. Too many, by the sound of it, if this is another mask like Momin's." Lando sat back and stroked his mustache. "So she's the one Ochi of Bestoon is working for? Can't be a coincidence, she comes in along with the raiders."

"I'm not sure," said Luke. He placed the cloth bundle on the console in front of him. "She wasn't looking for the family. She was looking for these." Luke tugged on the bundle and unwrapped the crystals. Leaning forward, Lando peered at the dark-red shards.

"She wants the crystals you found on Yoturba?"

"She knew where they'd come from. She said they belonged to her—or to *them*."

Lando's face twisted into a grimace. "The mask is possessing her, like Momin?"

"Directing her maybe, not possessing her. She was still there, and she was aware of the other power. She was doing its bidding."

"But doing it willingly?"

Luke rewrapped the crystals and pocketed the bundle again. "I don't know. These are safe with me, but right now we need to find the family and get them to safety."

"I'm with you there, pal."

R2-D2 burbled in the corner, then gave a long, shrill whistle.

Luke spun around. "You got something, Artoo?"

More warbles, and the panel in front of Lando sprang to life. He leaned over it, taking in the readings. Luke peered over his shoulder.

"All right, there they are, there they are." Lando glanced back at R2-D2. "Good work, little buddy." He unlocked the manual controls, activated the *Lady Luck*'s primary drive, and began steering the ship down into the rings, following the vector on the readout. Blue and green ice swept past the forward viewport as Lando accelerated, his hands dancing over the controls as he navigated through the treacherous regions by pure instinct. Luke watched him, impressed. Lando was still a hell of a pilot.

Moments later, Luke glimpsed a flash of yellow light ahead of them.

"There!" he said, pointing.

"I see it," said Lando.

The *Lady Luck* moved closer, ducking under a massive iceberg that looked as big as Nightside itself. Seconds passed, the wall of ice immense, seemingly only a few meters from the nose of the *Lady Luck* as Lando skillfully slid the ship underneath it.

Then they were in open space. Ahead of them, the *Goldstone* was making a tight turn, its engines flaring as the ship powered up.

"Wait," said Lando. "What are they doing?"

"Get closer," said Luke, waving at the controls. "We can hail them on the frequency you gave them."

"We need to be *real* close for that," said Lando. "Hold on."

But as the *Lady Luck* came in, the *Goldstone* continued to move away. A few seconds later, its nose aligned to a clear gap in the ring system, the yacht's engines flashed and the ship was gone, leaving nothing but a streak of glowing energy as it jumped to lightspeed.

Lando half stood from the pilot's seat. "What the . . . ?"

A second later, two more streaks of light, parallel to the trail left by the *Goldstone*.

Two more ships, in pursuit.

"Artoo!" Luke nearly yelled. "Get a lock on those ships. We've got to get after them. Lando?"

His friend nodded, his fingers flying over the console. "I know, I know, I know!" He looked over the data readouts. "We're too late. I can't get a read."

"Lando, we can't lose them now."

R2-D2 gave a shrill whistle, followed by a long and complicated se-ries of tones and bleeps.

"Wait a minute!" Lando looked down at the translated readout. "Artoo says the ship sent a transmission along the frequency I gave them." He flicked a switch, then slapped the console in frustration. "Only partial coordinates. Too much interference, even at close range."

Luke leaned over to read the message. "That's a start."

"A start?" Lando turned to Luke, his eyes wide. He gestured to the panel. "You know how many systems these partial coordinates could match?"

R2-D2 burbled again, loudly. Lando and Luke both turned instinc-tively to look at the droid as he tottered from side to side, clearly trying to impart some important information.

Lando turned back to the readout—his face now breaking into a grin. "That is one mighty fine astromech you have, Luke. Artoo says he got a full readout on the *Goldstone* when it was docked." Lando clicked his tongue. "Of course, that's what he was trying to tell me." He flicked a switch and pointed to the refreshed display. "The ship's fuel supply is limited, which means we can narrow those partial coordinates down quite a lot."

R2-D2 bleeped, and Lando flicked another switch.

"All right," he said. "Good work, Artoo. Torrenoteer system is a match."

"Let's punch it," said Luke.

"Coordinates set," said Lando, his hands moving over the controls. "Jumping to lightspeed in three . . . two . . . one."

Luke leaned back into the copilot's chair as Lando gripped the chrome lever in the center of the console and pushed it forward. The rings of Therezar flared brightly, and the whole forward view was trans-formed into a streaking, spiraling blue of hyperspace as they gave chase.

Luke only hoped they were fast enough.

CHAPTER 26

THE SEPULCHRE, COORDINATES UNKNOWN
NOW

She opened her eyes. She was lying on the floor. In front of her, some distance away, lay the mask.

She blinked, reaching up, and touched her face. The blood on her upper lip was still tacky. She hadn't been out long. The black interior of the mask was a void, an empty place in space and time. From it she heard the echo of a thousand dead souls.

She went to push herself up, then winced as the bare flesh of her hand pressed into the edge of something hard and sharp. She shuffled around, then rose, and saw she had been lying next to the large fragment of red kyber crystal.

She didn't remember the journey back in the TIE, didn't remember coming back into her vault.

What she *did* remember, however, was her encounter at that space station.

The Jedi!

He had the crystals—the other pieces, the other half of the crystal she herself possessed.

She sat back on her haunches, considering this fact as her head began to clear. If a Jedi had the crystals, was there really any hope of getting them back? She was no Sith. And even if *he* had been, so very long ago, would they really be a match for a foe so powerful?

Her chest tightened, her breathing becoming fast and shallow. Fear took hold of her, and that fear was rapidly becoming panic. Because . . . this was it, wasn't it? The end. Failure. To fight a Jedi was suicide.

They would never reach Exegol.

As though sensing her thoughts, her emotions, the vault was pierced with a scream, long and terrible and primal, the sound of death and agony from centuries past. It was loud enough to blot out everything else. Her head spun and her vision started to dance with black sparks.

She was afraid. She remembered her name and she remembered who *he* was and she was afraid. The sound was the roar of his anger.

Then the scream faded, and she heard another sound—a constant, insistent beeping. Realizing what it was, she knelt back down before the bronze plinth. In front of it was the small nub of a holoprojector. Her head bowed, she accepted the incoming transmission, and the communications device snapped into life as contact was established.

She glanced up at the huge bandaged face of a cultist of the Sith Eternal that loomed in ghastly blue above her, then she returned her gaze to the floor.

"You did not answer the call," came the scratchy, dry voice.

She shifted her position, trying to ignore the ache in her legs, the sickly feeling in her stomach. She cocked her head, her eyes screwed tight shut as she tried to focus, tried to remember.

"I . . . I don't understand," she said, finally. She *had* answered the call—she was speaking to the Sith Eternal now, wasn't she?

"You are our agent." The cultist's voice was a whisper from beneath its tightly wrapped face. "If you wish to receive the reward we have promised, you will obey us in everything, mind and body."

She didn't answer. She could barely concentrate on keeping track of the simple conversation, let alone the riddles the cultists seemed to delight in.

"Ochi of Bestoon called for help. You should have answered him."

Ochi. She had almost forgotten him. His mission for the Sith Eternal had nothing to do with her. She was just the intermediary.

"I am sorry," she said.

"You were not here," said the cultist. It was not a question.

She looked up. The hologram was bright, but ragged at the edges. Lines of interference traced up and down, the whole thing pulsating slightly.

"I am your servant," she said, gritting her teeth. "But I still have free will. I will come and go on my business as I see fit." She stared up at the hologram. The cultist was completely still, completely unreadable.

Moments passed. The hologram fizzed and pulsed.

Then the cultist spoke.

"Be mindful of which master you serve."

And with that, the hologram snapped off. She knelt in the same position for a moment, then gently lay down where she was, curled in a fetal position on her side. Sensing the state of its occupant, the white light of the meditation chamber began to dim, and soon it, and the vault beyond, were lit only by the banks of controls around the vault walls, and the flickering blue-green light of the droid forge, burning low and cool.

And then she heard it. Laughter, far away; a male voice, echoing around the vault, or perhaps just echoing inside her head.

He was close. She could feel it. She was facing away from where the mask lay on the floor, but she could *feel* it, a hot and cold pressure point burrowing into the back of her skull.

MY SERVANT.

MY CHILD.

HEED NOT THE WORDS OF THOSE WHO WOULD DENY US THAT WHICH WE DESERVE.

She opened her eyes. They were wet.

"What do you want?"

WE HAVE WORK TO DO.

YOU AND I.

MUCH WORK.

She pulled herself to her feet. She knew she couldn't resist. There was no point even trying to fight it. Even as her fear grew, she felt again the familiar thrill of excitement, knowing she was going to put the mask on, knowing she was going to give herself to the presence that had haunted the mask for untold ages.

That was how it worked. She knew it. It was an addiction. A drug. She hated it and loved it at the same time.

Before she even knew what she was doing, she found herself kneeling on the floor. She picked up the mask, and she put it on, and at once her head exploded with the wailing cries of the dead, and somewhere else, somewhere far and distant, the deep, terrible laugh.

"What must I do?" she asked, unsure if she had spoken the words or just thought them.

THE CRYSTALS.

WE MUST REFORGE THE PARTS OF THE WHOLE.

ONLY THEN CAN WE REACH EXEGOL.

She shook her head. The heavy bronze mask, crafted from meteoric metal, felt as light as air, as though she wasn't wearing it at all.

"The Jedi has the crystals. I—"

She stopped. The sound of the dead howled, like she was the center of a hurricane, then died down again, and *he* spoke.

DO NOT BE AFRAID.

"The Jedi is too powerful. The crystals are lost."

EXEGOL SHALL BE OURS.

THE CRYSTALS WILL SHOW THE WAY.

"I don't understand, my Master."

Again, the howling wind, the screams, but—

She lifted her head. She could sense that *he* was not angry. Far from it. *He* was pleased.

Very pleased.

THE DISCORD IN THE FORCE HAS FADED.

BUT THERE IS A WAY.

AS THE DARK GEOMETRIES WILL SHOW THE PATH TO EXEGOL, SO THEY WILL SHOW THE PATH UNTO THEMSELVES.

"Master?"

A rumble of thunder, distant, an echo of a storm from another age.

YOU DO NOT NEED TO UNDERSTAND, CHILD.

YOU ONLY NEED TO GIVE YOURSELF TO ME AND IT WILL BE DONE.

She relaxed. It was easier this way.

Why fight the inevitable?

Her head sagged, and then lifted sharply, the black glass eyes of the mask flashing with intent. Quickly, she picked up the kyber crystal and carried it into the droid forge. There she placed the crystal on the electro-anvil, a wide slab of carbonized zersium bedrock that stood in front of the conical furnace itself, blue-green flames lazily licking around the slots in the partially closed shielding. She reached down and picked up a huge silver hammer from the floor beside the furnace. Lifting it high, she brought it down with all her strength.

Under the first blow, the crystal fractured, the screams of pain inside her head changing now, taking on a new timbre, like the crystal was adding its own wail of agony to the great cacophony.

On the second blow, the crystal shattered, breaking along the lines of its structure to produce a collection of long shards, each too big for a lightsaber.

Dropping the hammer, she moved to the forge controls. There was a large and heavy lever set into the floor. Taking it with both hands, she threw it. At once, the cone of the furnace split, the slotted shielding opening like the petals of a hai-ka flower. This unleashed a huge flame, the blue and green turning to white as the temperature increased, the intense light bleaching out the interior of the chamber.

She watched the torchlike blaze for a moment, then turned and walked back into the main vault. She stood in front of the meditation chamber and looked out at the ranks of droids bowed before her.

Then she walked to the first droid and, lifting her leg, heaved as she pushed it over with her boot. The droid fell sideways, hitting the metal floor with a huge clang.

She moved around the fallen droid's head and hooked her hands under its arms. She pulled. The droid began to move—slowly—across the floor as she stepped backward, dragging the heavy machine toward the forge.

At the electro-anvil, she dragged the droid onto a rectangular outline on the floor, then operated a foot pedal next to the main furnace lever. The portion of the floor on which the droid lay rose up and tilted, forming an operating table to allow the droidsmith to get to work.

She picked up a heavy duty magno-wrench and began removing the metal carapace covering the droid's midsection, finally swinging the armored panel off and letting it fall to the floor with a heavy bang.

She got to work. She didn't know much about the droids, only that she had been compelled to collect them. She didn't remember setting them up in the vault, but she didn't question it. And now she let go of herself, and let *him* guide her hands as she worked to make adjustments inside the droid's chest.

That task done, she took one of the kyber crystal shards in a pair of furnace tongs and plunged it into the flames of the forge, holding it there until the ends of the tongs themselves began to glow red. Then she pulled the crystal out and placed it inside the new housing she had built inside the droid's open chest.

Minutes or hours passed, she didn't know. Eventually, her consciousness swam back into being, and she looked down at her work.

The shard of kyber crystal, now capped with metal and connected to a cradle of complex electronics, sat inside the droid.

She picked the droid's breastplate up from the floor, and sealed it back in place. She then took a long probe and inserted it into the side of the droid's neck. She activated a button on the probe, and the droid's eyes came on, first glowing white then darkening to a deep, blood red.

As the droid stood from the table and marched back into the vault, she looked down at the crystal shards aligned on the workbench.

One seeker droid activated, every electron in its system singing with the resonance of the kyber crystal inside it, every cycle of its control systems listening for the call of the crystal's other parts, echoing out across the galaxy.

One seeker droid activated.

Ten more to go.

CHAPTER 27

THE *LADY LUCK*, TORRENOTEER SYSTEM
NOW

"This is it?"

"This is it."

The *Lady Luck* had come out of hyperspace at a fair distance from a pale-yellow planet with three moons. Glancing over the readouts, Luke saw the navicomputer had correctly identified their location as the Torrenoteer system and . . .

"*This* is it?"

Relinquishing control to the autopilot, Lando sat back and looked at Luke, hunched over the data readout. Luke gestured to the small screen.

"Your databank needs updating," said Luke. "There's nothing but a catalog name and an old environment scan."

Lando busied himself studying the long-range sensors. "Sounds like a good place to lie low," he said, not looking up.

R2-D2 bleeped happily by the workstation, rotating his dome from Lando to Luke and back again as he chirped.

"Well, there you go," said Lando. "Artoo agrees with me." He looked out at the planet as it rapidly grew in size in the forward viewports. "It is possible they set short coordinates and then recalculated," Lando continued, gesturing to the planet. "That lady I spoke to, she knew what she was doing." He turned in his seat to Luke. "But they're also ready to accept our help. They'll be waiting for us, if they can."

"I wish I could be as sure as you, Lando."

"Hey," said Lando, "I told them I was a general and you were a Jedi." He grinned. "I think that got their attention."

Luke frowned. "And Therezar?"

Lando shrugged. "They got scared. We saw those other ships closing in. Not sure I can blame them for skipping out, Luke."

"I hope you're right," said Luke, then turned to his droid. "Artoo, see if you can locate any activity down on the surface. If they headed down to the planet, there should at least be some sign of them. Maybe an ion trail."

R2-D2 whistled and turned his dome back to the workstation, his data probe spinning as he accessed the *Lady Luck*'s sensor banks directly. Just a few seconds later, there was a chime, and data began to flow across the pilot's main display.

Lando leaned forward as he read the information presented to him. "Well, something's down there, anyway." He unlocked the autopilot and took manual flight control again. "Let's go take a look."

Luke sat back and Lando brought them in.

Torrenoteer Minor—there didn't seem to be a "major," for reasons the *Lady Luck*'s databank was unable to elaborate on—reminded Luke of Tatooine, but the comparison was, actually, a favorable one. While the planet he had grown up on had seemed to be nothing but endless expanses of yellow sand and ocher mountains, there had been a certain stark beauty to the place that he had come to appreciate only in retrospect.

Torrenoteer Minor was also a desert world. As Lando brought the *Lady Luck* skimming over dunes and mountains, he whistled, apparently to himself, as one geological wonder came into view after another.

The desert sands of the planet were vast, undulating dunes, but they were far from featureless. Instead, the sands were banded in muted colors—reds and oranges, yellows, even blues and greens—showcasing a diverse spread of different mineral compositions. As Lando followed the sensor readings toward what they hoped was the landing spot of the *Goldstone*, the desert began to change into more rocky terrain, outcroppings and tors finally becoming canyons and the foothills of mountains. Here, the banded coloring was more intense, the rock formations literally striped with layer upon layer of contrasting geological features.

It was beautiful. It was also entirely uninhabited, the old databank entry in Lando's ship computer apparently still accurate. Breathable atmosphere, comfortable temperature . . . and not a sign of life anywhere on the whole planet.

Except for the place they were now approaching. As another canyon passed beneath them, Lando swung the *Lady Luck* around, slowing to land behind another tor, this one a multi-layered collection of orange and purple stripes, like an exotic confection concocted by a high-class Coruscant pastry chef.

"Don't want to get too close," said Lando as he shut down the ship's main drive. "If the *Goldstone* is here, then those two other ships might be as well."

Luke nodded. "Good idea. How far out are we?"

Lando checked the reading. "Twenty klicks."

"That's a long way to walk." Luke glanced out at the desert terrain. "Couldn't you get us any closer?"

"Just trying to be careful, Luke." Then Lando stood, a wide grin appearing across his face. "But never let it be said that Lando Calrissian comes unprepared." He headed to the flight deck's bulkhead door, then stopped and turned around. His smile dropped, and he gestured to the door. "Uh, that meant you should follow me."

Raising an eyebrow, and a smile, Luke followed.

The *Lady Luck* was a large ship, and Luke hadn't had the chance—nor, to be perfectly honest, the inclination—to get a guided tour, so he followed Lando through the main living area then down a series of elegantly decorated passageways, their baroque design all speaking of custom-made, high-end luxury. Lando led him down two narrow access stairs, and even those were finely crafted, their handrails, the steps themselves, embellished with scrolled edges and engraved designs. It was almost too much for the eye to take in.

"Here we go, here we go," said Lando, coming to a stop. He turned to Luke, his grin back in place. "What did I tell you?"

They were standing in a miniature hangar. In front of them was a cargo ramp, and sitting in front of that was a large, bulky object covered with a single, huge blue cloth that had the same sheen and shimmer as one of Lando's silken capes.

Lando grabbed the edge of the cloth and pulled it off. Beneath were revealed two speeder bikes. Lando laughed and, ditching the cover to one side, walked along the length of one of the machines, running his hand over the side.

"This, my friend, is a Stacker Polaris Stormwolf, fifty-seven model," said Lando, unable to contain the excitement in his voice. He pointed at the other machine, which looked similar in many ways, but with subtle differences. "And that's the custom Stormwolf twenty-seven." Lando whistled. "You have no idea how long it took me to get one of those. They are collector's items, let me tell you."

Lando had made his way to the front of the machines and now leaned over, resting one hand on each of the speeder's fenders.

To be fair, they *did* look, to Luke, like high-end, high-performance speeder bikes. They were sleek, low-profile machines, their steering vanes and control surfaces a series of angled, matte-finish plates, subtle and pleasing to the eye; Luke could see the enjoyment Lando derived from the machines, and could see the workmanship that had been put into them.

He looked up and noticed that Lando was still talking, reeling off a series of stats about *charge capacity* and *torque-to-antigrav ratio* and—

"Lando."

Lando looked up.

Luke pointed to a speeder—whether it was the fifty-seven or the twenty-seven, Luke didn't know.

"I'll take that one," he said, then he walked to the wall and slammed a fist into the large ramp control button. There was a warning tone, and then the rear doors and ramp began to unfold behind Lando.

Lando shook his head and swung himself into the saddle of the other vehicle.

"Master Luke Skywalker, you are a difficult man to be friends with, sometimes," he said, but the smile was still there. He pointed at Luke's machine. "And for the record," he added, "*that* is the twenty-seven."

With a laugh, Luke got onto his speeder bike, and together they headed out into the sands of Torrenoteer Minor.

"Well, that's not Zargo's yacht, that's for sure."

Lando handed the quadnocs to Luke and ducked down a little behind the ridge. Behind them, farther down the slope, the two speeder bikes sat cooling in Torrenoteer's setting sun. In the sky above, two of the planet's three moons glowed large and green.

On the other side of the ridge was a craterlike hollow, bordered on three sides by the ridge behind which Luke and Lando now hid, and on the other by a series of cliffs into which huge, narrow ravines spread. The hollow was two kilometers across, according to the quadnocs' readout, and as far as Luke could tell their approach hadn't been detected by the occupants of the ship that sat parked below them.

The ship was most certainly *not* the *Goldstone*. This space vehicle was boxy, with two large, externally mounted engines on either side of the rectangular main hull, at the rear of which was a floor-to-ceiling ramp. The ramp was down, and there were two humanoids standing on it, facing away from the ridge. Through the quadnocs, Luke had been able to identify one as a Gran, and Lando had confirmed the other was one of the twins, either Bosvarga or Cerensco, from Boxer Point Station. The pair were discussing something, the Gran pointing to the cliff face and the ravines.

"That's one ship," said Luke, handing the quadnocs back to Lando. He then turned to look down the slope at their speeders and the lands beyond. The *Lady Luck* was well out of sight, and they hadn't seen any other signs of activity. "They must have split up, the other landing farther on. If it's here at all."

"Which means," said Lando, taking another look through the quadnocs, "that they've lost the *Goldstone,* too."

"Perhaps," said Luke. "They were following pretty close, so they would have seen the ship come down. It must be nearby." He rolled back around. "They picked this ravine for the same reason we landed back there."

Lando nodded. "To avoid detection—hold on."

He lifted the quadnocs again as there was movement near the ship. Luke pulled himself closer to the edge of the ridge and looked down. As he did, a faint humming came from the landing site.

Two more people emerged from the rear of the ship, each mounted on a speeder bike—far more utilitarian, not to say *cheaper* models than Lando's Stormwolfs—and each towing another, riderless speeder bike behind them. Both beings were wearing close-fitting utility suits, their heads wrapped in trailing black scarves, their faces covered by heavy goggles, ready for a fast ride across the desert—Weequay, perhaps, but Luke couldn't quite tell.

After a few more moments of discussion among the group, Bosvarga and his Gran companion got aboard the free speeders, and the group split into two pairs, Bosvarga and friend gunning their speeders as they shot up the hollow's gentle incline and out over the top of the ridge almost directly opposite Luke and Lando's position, sending a huge arc of multicolored sand cascading into the cool green sky. The other pair, meanwhile, took a more leisurely approach to the cliff side of the hollow, turning their machines in unison as they picked one of the ravines and disappeared from sight.

Satisfied the coast was clear, Luke patted Lando on the back then stood, allowing his boots to sink heel-first into the sand as he headed back to their speeders. "Follow the first pair along the ridge," said Luke. "I'll take the other two." Reaching his vehicle, he swung a leg over it and settled into the saddle. "Keep your distance, but keep in touch."

Luke twisted the handlebar controls, and the speeder's engine came to life with a pleasantly deep purr.

"Good luck," he said, giving a small salute with one hand as he squeezed the throttle with the other and took off after his quarry.

CHAPTER 28

TORRENOTEER MINOR
NOW

Lando pulled the speeder underneath the cover provided by an over-hang of the ridge and quickly leapt off the machine, leaving it idling quietly. Although this was far from how he had imagined using the speeders, he was glad now to have splashed out on the acceleration compensators and noir-fiber engine baffles. These expensive modifica-tions to what was an already expensive speeder bike made it a quiet, stealthy ride.

If there was one thing Lando didn't like, it was ostentation.

He'd followed the first pair of speeders at a comfortable distance, using the curve of the ridgeline that rose up out of the vast dunes of Tor-renoteer Minor in a gently oscillating wave to keep himself covered as the other two vehicles raced ahead of him, their careless riders not even trying to cover their tracks, the great tail of sand spilling up into the air as the rear stabilizers of their speeders kicked the ground beneath them.

After a little while, the two slowed, then turned and headed up over the ridge, disappearing from view. Slowing his own speeder, Lando cut the engine and drifted on the repulsors, listening intently. The hum of the other vehicles faded, then cut with an abrupt choking sound.

They'd stopped, and close. Lando parked his own speeder, grabbed the quadnocs from the equipment bag on the side, and scrambled up the ridge on hands and knees.

He didn't need the quadnocs. On the other side of the ridge, standing out in a flat, cracked plain that might have once been a lake bed, stood the *Goldstone*, its delta wing reflecting the green light of the planet's moons. The two speeder bikes Lando had been pursuing were stopped nearby, the riders now approaching the luxury yacht on foot, blaster rifles at the ready.

Lando lifted the quadnocs to his eyes and took a closer look, zooming in not on the two bounty hunters but on the *Goldstone* itself. He was searching not only for damage, but for armaments. But he could see neither—the ship looked factory-fresh, the golden metal of the hull almost mirror-perfect. If there were any weapons, they were well concealed.

The two bounty hunters had reached the ship and were now looking up at it, like they were trying to figure out how to break in. From Lando's position, he couldn't see into the *Goldstone*'s cockpit.

What was the family doing? Why had they even landed here—and why out in the open?

And, more important, why didn't they just blast off, leave the hunters for dust?

Lando shuffled on his stomach and reached down to his belt to get his comlink. There was no sign of Luke or the other two hunters he'd set off in pursuit of. Lando—and Lando's quarry—had been the lucky ones.

That was when he heard the very distinctive click of a heavy-duty blaster pistol's safety catch being disengaged, and felt something small and sharp prod him painfully in the back of the head.

"Don't move," said the voice behind him—male, low, modulated into a synthetic growl by the vocalizer in the hunter's helmet.

"Don't worry," said Lando, with a sigh. "I wasn't planning on it."

Then he felt a heavy hand on his collar, and he was wrenched up to his feet, then shoved down the slope of the ridge toward the *Goldstone*.

CHAPTER 29

TORRENOTEER MINOR
NOW

The ravine system Luke found himself traversing was beautiful, an exquisite cross section of the planet's odd geology on proud display, the strata of multicolored layers whizzing past him as he kept pressure on the speeder bike's accelerator. The machine, he had to admit, was a joy to ride, and as Luke wove his way along the largest of the narrow cracks in the planet's crust, he allowed himself a small moment to enjoy the sensation.

So far, however, his pursuit had been a wash. The ravines were as frustrating as they were beautiful, and after just a few minutes' riding it became clear that they represented a vast network of gorges and small valleys, spiderwebbing across this part of the desert plain.

Of his quarry, there was no sign. The Stormwolf twenty-seven was a powerful machine fitted, Luke noticed, with dampeners that helped muffle the low purr of its main drive unit. But in the ravines, even that gentle roar echoed, the sounds far louder than Luke would like. His only comfort was the knowledge that the noise of the two speeders he was looking for was much louder, and would easily disguise any sound of Luke's pursuit.

Luke slowed, allowing the speeder to coast as he used its onboard tracker to get his bearings. The ravine was slowly but surely filling with shadows as dusk began to fall, and Luke knew it would be pointless to keep searching the system once night had fully descended.

That was when he heard it—a roar, rising and falling, the sound of a speeder bike being throttled. Luke brought his own to a complete standstill and looked around, straining his senses as he tried to judge direction.

The sound came again, and—

There.

Luke gunned his own machine, pivoted it ninety degrees, and shot down through another gorge. A second later, one of the two speeders he was chasing slid out from a parallel ravine and took position directly in front, almost close enough to touch.

Luke knew exactly what was going to happen next, and he cursed himself for being so naïve. Of course the bounty hunters knew they were being followed; luring Luke deeper into the tight, winding system of ravines was the perfect way to set a trap.

He glanced over his shoulder as he heard the guttural splutter of the second speeder bike, drifting sideways out from a parallel channel and lining up behind Luke. The rider's face, like the first, was almost invisible behind the oversized goggles, his long scarf streaming out behind him as he squeezed the throttle and accelerated toward Luke.

But Luke was already formulating a plan, one based on hard-earned experience. Checking the gearing, he kicked the pedal under his right foot and yanked up the handlebars. His speeder shot up, the nose of the powerful machine threatening to go full vertical before Luke eased on the power and jammed on the brake. In a split second, the pursuing rider appeared to shoot forward underneath Luke, who switched gears again and dropped back in behind the other rider.

Now, *that* was a better position.

Ahead of him, the other two riders were yelling at each other, both risking quick glances back at Luke while they tried to navigate what was now an increasingly tight sequence of gorges. A fine spray began to kick up underneath the speeder ahead; looking down, Luke saw that the ravine floor was now a shallow creek, one that deepened and widened as the trio sped along.

STAR WARS: SHADOW OF THE SITH

Two blaster shots echoed across the smooth rock walls. Luke ducked instinctively, but the bolts were wide, the rider ahead struggling to take any kind of accurate aim while still keeping his speeder bike from smashing into the walls of the gorge. The rider checked his route then turned and fired again, this time with a little more purpose. Luke swerved his vehicle and narrowly avoided the bolt, only to find himself skidding along the base of the ravine wall, now sending his own plume of spray and dirt up in the air behind him.

The bounty hunter leading their group was clearly a more skilled rider, and Luke could see him standing at full height on his running boards, having locked his throttle to maximum. The speeder's engine whined horribly under the load, but with an ease and confidence Luke didn't much like, the rider took careful aim with his blaster and squeezed the trigger.

Luke's lightsaber blade flashed green and he deflected both shots, which were otherwise right on target. The top edge of the ravine on Luke's left exploded as the bolts found their new home, scattering rock and debris down into the channel.

This, at least, appeared to rattle the bounty hunter directly in front of Luke. He turned and leaned over the handlebars, trying to put some distance between himself and what he now knew to be a Jedi, but his speeder was no match for the power of Lando's custom number. The rider lifted his blaster and randomly fired behind his back, without even turning around. These bolts were, remarkably, almost as well aimed as his more careful shots. As the hunter kept pumping the trigger, Luke deflected bolt after bolt reflexively, then, summoning his focus, he caught the next two and angled his lightsaber just *so,* sending the bolts directly back to their point of origin.

The rider's scream as he was blasted off his speeder echoed around the ravine as Luke, his lightsaber held high, wrenched the handlebars with his other hand, swerving to avoid the inevitable impact with just centimeters to spare. As he cleared the danger zone, there was a sharp bang from behind him, amplified by the echo chamber of the ravine, as the speeder collided with an outcropping and exploded.

One down. One to go. Luke deactivated his lightsaber and slid it home on his belt, well aware that taking out the riders was absolutely *not* going to lead him to the *Goldstone*. He only hoped that Lando was having better luck.

Ahead, the first speeder bike was pulling away, the rider having abandoned his attempt to shoot his pursuer, and was now focused on simply making a clean escape.

He had no chance. Luke's machine outmatched the hunter's for sheer speed and maneuverability. All Luke had to do was jam the throttle and pull up to within melee distance. His plan now was to disable the speeder, saving the rider for interrogation.

Luke concentrated, stretching out the fingers of his living hand as he continued to grip the handlebar with his cybernetic one. He reached out with the Force—just a little—and pulled the speeder—just a little—so he could bring this pursuit to a safe and, he hoped, beneficial conclusion.

And then—

Luke's eyes went wide. The speeder ahead had vanished, the presence of its mass in the Force slipping away from Luke's mind. He blinked, aware that the sound of his quarry's engine had changed dramatically. He lifted himself from the saddle even as he accelerated, trying to figure out what had just happened.

Then his own speeder bike engine roared, and Luke felt his stomach flip as the ground suddenly dropped away from underneath him. He squeezed the brakes, but he'd been traveling at a high velocity, enough for the momentum to carry him straight out of the ravine and into midair above what he realized was a lake. Luke just had time to glance behind, seeing that he had come clean out of the other side of the ravine system, at least a hundred meters up from the surface. Now looking down, he saw the rippling body of water fast approaching, the repulsorlifts of the speeder buzzing angrily as they struggled to compensate for the sudden change in circumstance. The lake itself was large and almost exactly circular, the water colored in brilliant, concentric rings of red and yellow, blue and green, that almost glowed under the ever-lower angle of the planet's sun.

And ahead, cutting a path across the lake, a tail of water rising high behind it, the other speeder was making directly for the shoreline opposite, machine and rider having survived their fall intact.

Luke could do nothing but hold on and brace for impact, but he was once again grateful for Lando not sparing any expense on the speeder. The antigrav compensators were in overdrive, and the dashboard showed several warning lights as the stabilizers tried to prevent the speeder, and its rider, from making a hard impact on the rapidly approaching water. Luke's eventual touchdown was a significant jolt, but he was ready for it. He could only imagine how bone-jarring it must have been for the other rider.

Luke didn't have time to consider further. No sooner had he made his splashdown than red blaster bolts began raining out from the spray of water thrown by the other speeder in front of him. Luke dodged them easily, but his machine's control surfaces struggled to adapt to the liquid beneath it, and the speeder slid out from under Luke with surprising speed as he maneuvered. He regained control just before the vehicle was about to pitch him into the lake, then gunned the engine and shot off in pursuit once more. His approach was now more lateral, and—free of the spray from his quarry—Luke had his eyes firmly fixed on the target.

The plan was the same. He needed to get closer.

He needed to end this.

Luke whipped his lightsaber from his belt, twirling the hilt in his hand as he rode the choppy waters of the lake, the speeder bouncing sharply over the wake of the other.

Again, blasterfire. The other rider—a professional, calm and patient, thought Luke—had taken stock of his enemy and was taking advantage of the clear span of water that now lay between them as Luke approached diagonally. The rider once again was standing on the pedals, and began sending volley after volley of shots toward Luke.

The bounty hunter was capable, but also predictable. Each volley consisted of three shots, followed by three more. After only a few of these, Luke had learned the pattern and had his lightsaber ready. He closed the gap and ignited the blade.

The next three blaster bolts hit the blade directly, and Luke, using both training and the intuition granted him by the Force, sent all three back along the exact same path.

There was a pause, then an explosion as the other speeder bike was destroyed, the rider thrown high into the air as his ride flipped and disintegrated. Luke sped toward the scene, lightsaber deactivated and on his belt once more, as burning debris now rained down into the lake. Of the rider, there was no sign.

Luke pulled up, and, scanning the debris, spotted the rider. He was tangled in the broken struts of his machine's front steering vanes, which had broken off in the crash. Somehow, the rider's legs had become stuck fast between the twisted lengths of metal.

The rider floundered in the water, the weight of the wreck starting to drag him under as Luke eased his speeder alongside, then swung off, dropping into the water. He swam toward the debris then grabbed it, giving it an experimental tug.

It was no good. He couldn't shift it, not while he was treading water. What was left of the speeder was sinking, fast.

Luke let go of the wreck and pushed himself back in the water to get some space. His feet kicking to keep himself upright, he reached out with the Force and began to lift the wreck and the rider, but almost as soon as they shifted in the water, the rider screamed in pain. Luke let go, realizing the man was pinned in position, any movement of the debris just making his situation worse.

Luke swam back to the wreck, trying to reach the rider, whose goggled face now bobbed barely clear of the water. Luke ducked under the surface, his Jedi robes billowing as he scooped an arm around the rider's back, trying to stabilize him while he squinted into the sharp, mineral-rich water, trying to see what he could do. With his free hand he unhooked his lightsaber and activated it underwater.

There was a huge fizz and an eruption of steam as Luke dragged the blade through the water, slicing at the wreck to free the rider's legs. Then he brought the weapon up, out of the water, and, angling the blade awkwardly while still supporting the rider, attempted to dissect some more of the tangled steering vanes from around the rider's trapped legs.

That was when the rider began to struggle. He'd lost his blaster in the crash, but perhaps seeing Luke's weapon activated, he thought he was about to be killed. He began to thrash, his leg still stuck, his struggle pulling Luke's head underwater.

Luke deactivated his lightsaber—it was too dangerous now to use it so close to the struggling rider. He let himself be pulled under, relaxing a little to show he wasn't fighting. But it was too late—the rider landed a solid punch to Luke's face. Luke reeled back, tasting blood.

The rider's motions slowed, then stopped. Luke swam forward and grabbed him around the torso once more, kicking up to bring them to the surface. Gulping a lungful of cool evening air, Luke tried to examine the rider, puzzled as to his sudden change in condition. But as Luke moved the body, something dark began to discolor the water around him. Within moments, Luke found himself swimming in a circle of deep red as the Weequay rider bled out from an injury Luke couldn't see. Luke got a better grip under the rider's arms and kicked back in another attempt to pull him free. But it was no use. The rider was now completely limp, and as Luke looked down at the man's body, he saw that a twisted, blade-like shard of the speeder bike's steering vane had penetrated the Weequay's back, the wound mortal. His final struggle with Luke had been one of sheer desperation, sapping the last of his reserves before he succumbed to the injury.

Luke sighed, and shook his head in frustration, before gently letting the rider's body slide off his own. It sank below the surface, dragged down by the broken front end of the speeder.

Luke looked around, then swam over to the main section of the speeder; detached from the heavy front mechanism, it remained afloat, listing on its side. Luke used his weight to pull the machine back upright, then pulled himself up into the saddle. There he sat, leaning forward on his elbows as he got his breath, feeling the weight of his soaked robes.

Bleet-bleet.

Luke opened his eyes. He was staring down at the speeder's simple console. A green light flashed in time with the alert—an incoming message, according to the readout on the small, square display set into the cowling.

Luke hit the receive button. A line of text quickly drew itself across the screen.

GOT SOMETHING NICE AND JUICY.

On the next line was a grid reference. Luke memorized the coordinates, then gently slid off the speeder and swam over to his own, idling nearby. Pulling himself up, he plugged the coordinates into his own tracker. The display on his speeder plotted the course instantly: ten kilometers, due east.

Flicking the wet hair from his forehead, Luke grabbed the handlebars and paused to take a breath.

So far the excursion to Torrenoteer had resulted in two unnecessary deaths; glancing over his shoulder at the sinking wreck of the bounty hunter's speeder bike, Luke ground his molars.

There should have been another way. All his skill—all his *power*—and it had still resulted in this. And what's more, Lando was out there, facing down the other bounty hunters, on his own.

Luke turned back around to face the front. He closed his eyes, focusing inward, finding his calm, trying to silence the doubt in his mind.

He was a Jedi. His commitment to the ways of the Order ran deep. Yes, it was true he had power, but his connection to the Force was not a thing to covet. He had a responsibility to wield that power with care and restraint, every use of it taking him one step away from the darkness that he knew, despite everything, still lingered in his heart, as perhaps it did in the hearts of all sentient beings.

Every action, one step toward the light.

The death of a foe was not something to rejoice in. Reminding himself that there was always another way, Luke took a breath and opened his eyes. He thought of Lando, his old friend. He thought of the family, one he'd never met. Both were out there. Both needed his help, now.

With fresh clarity of mind and focus on the mission, Luke kicked the speeder bike's release pedal and sped off across the lake.

CHAPTER 30

TORRENOTEER MINOR
NOW

Luke was mostly dry by the time he arrived at the coordinates displayed on the dash of his Stormwolf twenty-seven. Keeping one eye on the course plotter, he had left the lake and headed along the shoreline then, spying the vertebra-like ridgeline he and Lando had followed before, used it to hide his approach as he took a longer, looping route to the reference point sent by the other hunters. Parking in the shadow of the ridge, Luke scrambled up the side of it on his elbows and knees, and peered over the top.

What he saw, he was *not* expecting.

There were two bounty hunters on the salt flat below, their speeders parked facing each other. One was the Gran in his figure-hugging burgundy flight suit, the other another figure in protective headgear, but he wasn't one of the twins from Boxer Point. In front of them stood a compact, two-legged walker. Its body was more or less an inverted cone with a flat bottom, the chassis widening toward the top where a transparent dome protected the single pilot at the front of the boxy upper frame. The machine's spindly legs were mounted high on the sides of the walker's midsection, just behind two long, articulated arms that ended in manipulator claws. A stubby blaster cannon protruded below the pilot's dome, and the whole contraption stood about three meters tall.

The one-person walker looked awkward, top-heavy, but Luke knew how formidable they could be in the right hands—it was a CAP-2, another relic of the Empire, although a weapon little used in wartime. The hunters must have salvaged it. The whole galaxy was littered with junk just like it.

There was no sign of the *Goldstone,* but farther away, behind the CAP-2, was a scorched area where the cracked salt flat had been turned a deep brown, the center glassy—ion burn, the telltale signs of a rushed takeoff.

The family? Had they gotten away?

Luke frowned, unsure of what the message he had intercepted meant. Something "nice and juicy"? Because if the family had escaped . . .

Then the CAP-2 rocked from side to side as it turned on its thin legs, and Luke saw the prize—Lando Calrissian, head lolling in unconscious slumber, was held fast in the walker's prisoner clamp, located at the rear of the boxlike upper chassis.

Luke felt his heart rate kick up a gear even as he willed himself to remain calm. Lando was alive—if he was dead, he'd be on the ground, not held in a prisoner transport. They were about to carry him off to the other ship. Luke didn't recognize the CAP-2's controller through the curve of the dome, and the other being—Bosvarga or Cerensco—wasn't here. All of which meant the second ship belonging to the bounty hunters must have been nearby.

Luke wasted no more time. He jumped, clearing the top of the ridge and sailing down through the air, still-damp robe billowing. The others had seen him—Luke saw one point, then the other turned in his direction, the CAP-2 stomping around to face him as well, the blaster cannon already moving to take aim.

As soon as Luke's boots touched the salt flat, his lightsaber was in his hand and alive with green power. Blade raised at an angle across his body, Luke ran at a full sprint as the hunters unleashed a fusillade of blaster bolts. The salt flat erupted in small explosions around Luke's feet, and the ridge wall behind echoed as bolts connected with it, blowing the colored stone to fragments.

Luke closed the gap, lightsaber moving in sharply controlled angles, deflecting any bolt that was about to hit its mark. The CAP-2 hadn't yet fired; Luke realized the other hunters were actually in the way of its cannon, and it was now crabbing slowly sideways to get a clear shot.

And then he was on them. Knowing he now had no choice, Luke cut down one of the hunters instantly in two clinical movements, then turned to face the other. This hunter—the Gran—brought his blaster up and fired at Luke at point-blank range. Luke held his lightsaber tight, but all he could do was deflect the blaster bolt directly down into the ground between them. The brittle surface of the ground shattered like glass, throwing a cloud of dust and larger fragments into the air.

The Gran cried out and stumbled backward, caught by surprise and by a faceful of dust. As he recovered, two of his three stalked eyes blinking furiously, he lifted the blaster again and let loose. This time, Luke sent the bolts straight back at the shooter, and the hunter collapsed onto the broken ground.

That same ground now shook; Luke spun around as the CAP-2 approached, its single cannon now aimed directly at him. There was a split-second buzz as the weapon charged, then Luke dived to the left, the spot where he was standing now a pool of molten glass.

Luke rolled, got to his feet, then jumped again, this time back to the right, as the CAP-2's pilot trained the cannon on his new position and opened up.

"Luke! Luke! Are you okay?"

It was Lando. As the walker swayed, Luke could just see his friend struggling in the capture claw, the motion of the machine having roused him.

Then the cannon hummed again and Luke jumped into the air, trying to gain enough altitude as he somersaulted backward to avoid the next devastating shot.

"Lando, can you get out of that thing?" Luke yelled, his lightsaber once more up in a defensive stance, the air between him and the CAP-2 now an opaque cloud of dust. As Luke peered through it, drawing on the Force to enhance his own senses, the cloud was illuminated in brilliant yellow as the walker's twin headlights snapped on, and the machine stepped forward, one lurching thud at a time.

"I'm trying, I'm trying! Keep it busy!"

The cannon powered up and fired, but Luke didn't have to move far for it to miss, the walker's pilot clearly operating blind in the dust. It stepped forward again, clearing the cloud, then raised one foot for another step—but put the foot straight back down. Under the transparent dome, Luke saw the pilot turning in his seat to look behind him.

There was a shower of sparks from the rear of the CAP-2, followed by a shout of surprise from Lando as the capture claw opened and he dropped heavily to the ground, the slim tool he'd used to short the claw still in one hand. As he groggily tried to crawl away to safety, the CAP-2 made a half turn, one clawed arm extending out to retake the prisoner.

That was all the distraction Luke needed. He ran forward, blade swinging to sever the barrel of the cannon. Then he sidestepped and swept the lightsaber in an arc parallel to the ground. The blade met no resistance as it cut clean through the machine's left leg.

The CAP-2 began to topple immediately, and there was a groan from the machinery as the walker's automatics tried to compensate for the sudden lack of balance. It pivoted on its one remaining leg, threatening to fall onto the dazed Lando. Seeing this, Luke lowered his lightsaber, raised his other hand, and gave the walker a push with the Force, just enough to send it careening over in the other direction.

No sooner had it hit the ground than the cockpit dome popped off with a bang, the pilot having activated the emergency release before clambering onto the back of the machine, blaster in hand. He only managed to loose one shot, which Luke ably deflected back into him. The pilot cried out and slumped over the hull of his downed machine.

Lightsaber deactivated, Luke spun around and raced for Lando, who was now sitting on the ground, one hand rubbing the back of his head as he winced. Luke dropped to one knee in front of his friend.

"Are you okay?"

Lando frowned. "I'll live." He held up the tool he had used to free himself. "Bottle opener for Azuran steam spirit. Given to me by a rather lovely sommelier on Bothsoliman." He slipped it back into the utility pouch on his belt, then looked at Luke, his still-damp robes now thoroughly disheveled. "They have good tailors on Bothsoliman, too. I can recommend one. What the hell happened to you?"

"Long story," said Luke. Still kneeling, he reached down and picked up a handful of glassy, melted salt from beneath them. "Looks like someone made a fast getaway."

With a nod, Lando got to his feet. He turned and looked up into the deep green of the early-evening sky, already scattered with myriad twinkling stars, Torrenoteer Minor's third moon—this one a bright violet—just beginning to rise.

"It was the *Goldstone*," said Lando. "They'd made it. The bounty hunters I followed led me right to the ship, but it blasted off before they could try to get in. That was when I was captured." Lando sighed, his hands on his hips. "There were more hunters than we thought."

Luke stood. "Come on," he said. "Let's see what we can find."

CHAPTER 31

THE *GOLDSTONE*, COORDINATES UNKNOWN
NOW

"All done," said Miramir, walking into the *Goldstone*'s main living area from the flight deck.

Dathan turned as she entered the cabin—another luxurious example of Zargo Anaximander's wealth and taste, the entire place more like a hyper-expensive apartment in a fashionable quarter of Coruscant's ecumenopolis than the interior of a starship—and raised a questioning eyebrow.

Miramir held up the object in her hand—a small, cross-shaped component that looked like it was made of glass capped with silver.

"The hyperwave transponder." She grinned, and tossed the object to Dathan. He caught it awkwardly and turned it over in his hands. Finally he looked up at Miramir, a frown on his face. She walked over to him and took the component back.

"It took some detective work to find it," she said, looking at the small thing, "but they won't be able to follow us again."

Dathan nodded, finally understanding. They had hoped to wait on Torrenoteer, but the two ships in hot pursuit had found them in the desert quickly—far too quickly for it to have been luck. The *Goldstone* had been transmitting its location all this time.

Now, having made a single short jump into empty space to clear the Torrenoteer system, and with the transponder disabled, they were untraceable and untrackable.

"Okay," said Dathan. "That's good. Is Rey okay?"

"She's asleep on the flight deck," said Miramir. "She's holding up well. It just seems to be tiring her out rather than scaring her."

Dathan couldn't help but smile. He drew Miramir toward himself, wrapping his arms around her middle, and pulled her in for a hug. He reached up with one hand and ran a finger through her long, golden hair. He breathed in her scent and felt, for a moment, that everything might be all right, just so long as they were all together.

Dathan. Miramir. Rey.

He closed his eyes, feeling the weight of Miramir as she leaned back into him, her hands playing over his.

"I'm sorry," he whispered.

She shook her head. "You need to stop saying sorry." Miramir pulled out of his grip and looked her husband in the eye. "You *know* that."

Dathan opened his mouth to apologize again, then stopped and just nodded instead. He was tired and frustrated and angry, and that was when the guilt came back.

All of this was his fault, because of who he was, and where he came from—and who he *belonged* to.

"It's not your legacy that defines you, Dathan," said Miramir quietly. "Or your genetic makeup. We've been through this before, and I know we'll go through it again, and we'll go through it as many times as we need to until the day we die." She smiled and cupped her husband's face in her hands. "You are *you*. You are Dathan. You are defined by your choices. You are defined by your actions. And right now, Rey and I need you, and you're doing a very good job at protecting us." She kissed him lightly on the lips. "We're in this together, Dathan."

Dathan nodded, and the couple parted. Miramir took a step back and cocked her head at her husband. "I know what you're thinking."

Dathan sighed, moving over to one of the couches that was positioned in front of a table that, by the look of the controls along the side, was a high-end entertainment system. As he sat down, the piece of furniture adjusted itself automatically to cradle his body perfectly.

He wasn't entirely sure he liked the sensation.

"We lose the Sith," said Miramir, "means we lose the Jedi." She moved across the cabin to a cabinet set against one wall, laden with abstract sculptures of liquid glass that writhed slowly. She shrugged, her back to Dathan. "But at least we know that someone's looking out for us." She turned around. "And that gives us something, right? Now we might have somewhere to run *to*." She paused. "If they can find us."

"Maybe we can help them find us," said Dathan, an idea already beginning to form in his mind.

Miramir frowned. "You want me to reconnect the hyperwave transponder?"

Dathan stood up. "No, no. But . . . we're low on fuel, right?"

Miramir nodded.

"So we're going to have to stop somewhere."

"To refuel, you mean?" Miramir looked around. "I suppose we could barter for fuel. The stuff in here must be worth a fortune. Maybe we could ditch the ship altogether, buy another?"

At this, Dathan winced. "Lando Calrissian and his friend think we're in the *Goldstone*. And besides, I doubt we'd be able to buy a better one, even if we could barter." Dathan glanced around. "And that might be more difficult than you think, anyway. A lot of this stuff is rare. People will know where it came from. Most of it is probably imprinted as well. Legitimate buyers aren't going to want to touch it. We'd have to find a black market somewhere."

Miramir's shoulders slumped. "Which would take a lot of time."

"Time we don't have," said Dathan. "But that's not the point. I have a better idea."

"I'm listening."

Dathan grinned and looked around the cabin.

Miramir watched him. "What are you looking for?"

Dathan walked to the cabinet at the side of the room. He cast his gaze over the moving, abstract sculptures on it.

"Ships like this carry VIPs. And VIPs don't tend to carry credits."

Miramir raised an eyebrow. "Are you guessing, or are you telling me?"

Dathan waved a hand at her. "Hey, I picked up a lot when I worked the sunscooper. Visited a lot of places, saw a lot of ships. Talked to a lot of people."

"Okay," said Miramir. "So what *are* you looking for?"

Dathan fell into a crouch in front of the cabinet. It was made of a dark-brown material, the surface streaked with a golden filigree. He ran his hands over the front, searching for the opening mechanism.

"Ah!" he said. There was a click, and a tiny red light showed at the top of the door.

Miramir moved to join her husband, kneeling beside him so she could get a look. Dathan rubbed the top of the door with his fingers, then pushed. A small, square panel flipped around, presenting what looked like a circuit board.

Dathan sat back and pointed at the panel. "Think you can slice the lock?"

Miramir peered at it. "Of course." She looked at Dathan. "What do you think is inside?"

Dathan rubbed his stubbled chin, then he pointed again at the cabinet. "Rank medallion."

"Medallion? Is that some kind of currency?"

"No," said Dathan, "it's a data card, like an ID. It identifies the holder, their position, any other relevant information. Zargo is rich and powerful. He'd use a rank medallion for nearly everything. Including refueling his personal yacht."

He turned and grinned at Miramir. "This is a strongbox," he said, pointing again at the cabinet. "My bet is his medallion is inside."

Miramir frowned. "Are you sure? It sounds more like something he'd keep on him."

"Oh, he will. But he'll have several." Dathan pulled himself to his feet. "Let's get this thing open, then I can explain what I want to do."

CHAPTER 32

THE *LADY LUCK*, TORRENOTEER
NOW

Lando paused and rubbed his face, long and hard, then with a dramatic sigh resumed his endless pacing around the *Lady Luck*'s flight deck.

"What are we doing, Luke?" he asked, not pausing in his orbit. "Tell me what we're doing, because I really don't know." He sighed again and shook his head.

Luke watched him, unsure of how to answer, because, to be honest, he didn't know their next move, either—yet, anyway.

Their search of the mercenaries' two ships had been fruitless. The second ship, the one carrying the CAP-2, had been parked not far from where Luke had left his own speeder. The ship itself wasn't particularly interesting, nor did it have any clues or particulars that would have enabled identification of the mercenaries themselves, or any organization they might have been a part of.

As they had searched, Luke had sensed Lando's frustration growing and growing. Perhaps he had expected it to be easy—the gang were Black Sun, or part of the Crymorah syndicate, or mercenaries from Shalankie. Maybe even something smaller, a group working out of former Hutt Clan territory, small-timers looking to make their name with a big job for Ochi of Bestoon.

But the ship was clean. That in itself worried Luke—that the group comprised professionals was not in doubt, but the lengths to which they'd gone to cover their tracks was a little above the average muscle for hire. More than that, the being from Boxer Point Station wasn't among the bodies of the bounty hunters—and the disturbed ground next to the second ship indicated that a third vessel had made a touch-down but was now gone, the pilot no doubt going back to make his report to his boss.

Lando had checked the comms and tried to access the ship's navi-computer, to see if they could get a flight path or some other data that might indicate its point of origin, but he succeeded only in activating a small self-destruct mechanism that thoroughly cooked the ship's systems—including, Luke just had time to see, a data card sticking out of its reader. Luke had yanked it out, but it had already mostly melted; rubbing the charred end of it, Luke recognized part of the gray-and-yellow livery of Nightside. It was a tracker, of some sort, allowing the hunters to locate the *Goldstone*.

It was now completely useless.

On the way back to the *Lady Luck*, Luke had pinged R2-D2, instruct-ing the astromech to head to the hunters' first ship and try to slice the systems, but a few minutes later the droid reported the systems in the other ship were also fried—the same self-destruct activated, no doubt, by their tampering in the second craft.

Now they were back on Lando's ship. Night had fallen on Torreno-teer Minor, and through the ship's forward view, the planet's trio of moons glowed brilliantly in the star-spangled sky.

The *Goldstone* had gone, and with the tracker destroyed, it felt like they were back to square one.

Lando stopped pacing again. "Hey, I'm not hearing any bright ideas here. We need to figure out what to do."

Luke stood and gently laid a hand on Lando's arm. He could feel his old friend shivering under his touch, his whole body alive and electric.

"I know what this means to you," said Luke quietly, but he could feel

Lando's muscles tensing at the same time as he saw Lando's expression darken.

"Means to me?" Lando almost laughed. "What about you, Luke? What does it mean to you?"

The two men stood facing each other, Lando's chest rising and falling rapidly, and Luke could feel his friend's anger wafting off him like a hot wind.

Anger, and fear, and always, ever-present, the pain of loss.

But how to answer Lando's question? What did it mean to Luke, this family, alone against the Sith, pursued across the galaxy? They couldn't carry on forever. Their journey would end, one way or another.

It was up to them—the two of them, Lando Calrissian and Luke Skywalker, the impresario and the farmboy, the general and the Jedi; heroes of the Rebellion, brothers-in-arms.

Luke looked into Lando's eyes. He saw the light in them, the fire, the passion. In Lando's eyes there was anger and fear, but what there wasn't was despair.

There was hope. Despite everything, there was hope.

The moment drew on, seconds passing without either man speaking, Lando still waiting for the answer Luke didn't know how to give.

And then Luke nodded and drew his old friend into a hug. As soon as they made contact, he felt Lando's arms tight around him.

"I'm sorry, Lando," said Luke. "I'm sorry for everything. And of course it means the same to me as it does to you. That family needs us. We might be their only hope."

Luke pulled away and Lando exhaled, long and hot. He wiped his wet eyes and chuckled quietly. "What's this, a Jedi with feelings? I thought that wasn't supposed to happen." He rolled his neck. "Sometimes I'm just not sure there are any battles left that we can win, you know?"

Luke smiled. "These people are important, and we're going to find them."

Lando nodded and moved back to the pilot's seat. He almost fell into it, then leaned over the console on his elbows as he ran his hands through his hair. "They were that close, Luke. *That close!* Twice, and we lost them both times." He sat back and turned to Luke. "But it's not just bounty hunters. They're working for Ochi of Bestoon, and Ochi of Bestoon is working for this—" Lando waved his hands as he tried to work out what he was trying to describe. "—this Sith who isn't a Sith. Feels like we find her, we find Ochi. We cut them off at the top, maybe that gives the family some room to breathe."

Luke pursed his lips. Lando made a good point. The connections among the Sith, Ochi, and the family were important. It was time to find out what, exactly, they were. "I have an idea," he said. "I know someone who can help us find the family, and who can help us identify the Sith."

Lando spread his hands. "Luke, I'm listening."

Luke went over to R2-D2, and crouched down beside the droid. "Artoo, that readout you have on the *Goldstone* . . . did you get a full drive signature?"

The droid whistled.

Lando stood and joined them. He looked down at R2-D2. "Drive signature? Is that useful?"

Luke looked up at Lando and nodded. "When Lor San Tekka and I encountered the Acolytes of the Beyond, I saved one of them, turned her away from a future of darkness."

"Right," said Lando. "I remember you saying that."

"She knows more about the Acolytes than I do," continued Luke, "because she *was* one. She may know who holds the relic mask and lightsaber."

Lando clapped his hands. "Yes, I like the sound of that. But what about the *Goldstone*? You think she can help us find that, too?"

"I do," said Luke. "She was one of their best relic hunters. She was able to intercept the shipments going in and out of black-market auction sites, and she led raids on other ships, ambushing them right out of hyperspace."

Lando *hrmm*ed. "Like she knew exactly where they were? She's got some way of tracking ships, using their drive signatures?"

"I think so."

"That's some fancy technology. You know where this friend is?"

Luke winced. "I'm not exactly sure I'd call her a friend. After I saved her life, she renounced her old ways and went to live a life of solitude, paying penance for her past deeds."

"Starting to sound a little like a long shot, Luke."

Luke stood, one hand resting on R2-D2's dome. "Artoo has all the data we need. This is our best chance to find the family *and* identify who is behind Ochi of Bestoon."

Lando raised both hands and stepped back over to the pilot's position. "Hey, you put it like that, I'm all in. Where are we headed?"

"Aubreeyan Cluster."

Lando blinked. "The Aubreeyan Cluster? That's a long way to chase an idea."

Luke nodded, tugging gently on his beard. "You're right. First stop, Adelphi."

"What? Adelphi? Again?"

"Again," said Luke, with a grin. "If we're going to do this, we're going to need a faster ship."

CHAPTER 33

BASTA CORE
NOW

Ochi looped the *Bestoon Legacy* in on a close orbit, ignoring the warning of the navicomputer that, under his manual control, the coordinates were drifting from true.

Ochi wasn't going to let a computer tell him how to fly his own ship.

He focused his optics on the yellow and blue glare of the planet's surface as it approached at considerable speed. He ran his tongue over his front teeth. His mouth was dry, his throat almost closed up.

He wanted a drink. He *needed* a drink, on a job like this. Chasing across the galaxy to get some backup that *they* should have given him in the first place. Did Ochi of Bestoon have to think of everything himself? Clearly, he did, and all this did was sour his mood even further.

"Altitude, master! Altitude!"

That D-O was his only companion on this particular trip did little to make Ochi feel better, and now a data retrieval droid, of all things, thought it knew about spaceflight? All the ridiculous thing was doing was bleating out the same warning that the navicomputer had started. Stupid machine couldn't even think for itself.

Releasing one hand from the control yoke, Ochi swiped down blindly by the side of his seat with his fist, but only succeeded in clipping one of D-O's antennas. Ochi glanced over his shoulder at the sound of the droid wheeling quickly away, and saw it disappearing behind one of the support pillars and turning sideways to hide.

"You'll have to do better than that, droid," said Ochi. He could see the green end of D-O's nose on one side of the pillar, and the silver cap of his twin antenna on the other. The antenna quivered as the droid shook with . . . what? Fear?

Ochi's thin mouth stretched wide in what passed for a smile.

Good.

The navicomputer blared another warning, louder this time, and Ochi turned back around, just in time to skip the *Legacy* over the crest of a ridge. Warning silenced, he looked out at the bright landscape. Ahead was a mountain range, and from here, Ochi could see the entrance to a large cave. In front of the range was a plateau, which was currently serving as a landing port, with two large transports and several smaller vehicles arranged in a fan. In the center, tiny figures were working, hauling crates from the cave and stacking them in front of the transports.

Ochi skimmed the area, then turned back in a lazy circle to find a place to land.

He just hoped that this "Steadfast" was reliable.

Enric Pryde was hating every single individual *millisecond* of the mission, and he made sure that everyone knew it.

For a start, it shouldn't even have been him here. He was a high colonel. A *high* colonel? A rank befitting his ability, befitting his dedication and drive to ensure the fractured remains of an Empire he knew—he *knew*—was going to rise again.

Maybe he'd only been a captain at the Battle of Jakku, but as one of the last surviving members of his battlegroup, he knew he needed to assert his authority. His men needed leadership, stability. They needed to be, well . . . *impressed,* quite frankly, by their new commander. Elevation to high colonel seemed only logical, and Pryde wasn't aware there was anyone else left to actually authorize the promotion anyway, except . . . well . . .

Except himself.

The problem was, as high colonel, he didn't expect to be *on the ground*, exactly. Of course, everything he did brought the Empire one step closer to its glorious rebirth; every sortie, however small, however minor, was part of a larger machine, the wheels of which sometimes turned in mysterious ways but always, *always*, toward a destiny he knew was coming.

But . . . really? This? Did it have to be *him*, personally? On a mission like this?

He shuddered in the cold and adjusted the fur-lined collar of his greatcoat.

A mission like this, on a planet like Basta Core, embedded on mysterious orders that filtered down from the obscure skeletal command structure that was, at last, forming deep in the scattered Imperial hideouts in the Unknown Regions. True enough, he was pleased with that kind of progress. Structure—order—was what the galaxy needed, now more than ever.

But it did occur to him now that perhaps he should have aimed a little higher. Perhaps high colonel wasn't quite high enough.

Well. One day. He was patient, or at least he told himself that. Although on days like today, standing on a frozen rock, embedded with the Corporate Sector Authority, supervising a mission as inane as it was simplistic . . .

Well.

Really.

He glanced to the man standing a few meters away, the CSA viceprex (*What kind of a rank even is that? Honestly, privateers who think they're a little Empire all their own, eh?*) Coromun who was supposed to be his second in command, but was, in reality leading the expedition.

Which suited Pryde just fine. The less he had to actually do with this stupid business, the better.

Checking that Coromun was looking the other way, Pryde slipped a hand inside his greatcoat and pulled out a silver flask. Turning a little to hide his actions, he quickly unscrewed the flask and took a long, healthy swig.

Ah, Abrax. One last, tiny reminder of civilization, an echo of the comforts he had nobly sacrificed to help with this mission. He savored the spicy aroma of the flask, the warm burn as the aquamarine cognac flowed down his throat.

He wondered what would happen if Coromun saw him with the flask. Pryde sniggered. He was CSA. He'd probably slap a duty on it and invoice Pryde's masters by urgent encrypted transmission.

Taking a second swig, he looked up as a small ship flew across the encampment, flying a little too low and, honestly, a little too fast. Turning to watch it as it came back around for landing, Pryde frowned. It wasn't a CSA ship, and any CSA pilot breaking flight regulations with such a pass would soon enough find him- or herself at the back of a chain gang in a spice mine.

There was the sound of shuffling feet behind him. Pryde quickly secreted the flask once more and turned around to see the viceprex talking to a CSA officer. Pryde wrinkled his nose at their current livery— their dull brown uniforms, and the way the CSA trooper's red helmet clashed with his field armor. The CSA liked to think it had an army, but the soldiers' appearance hardly inspired . . . well, anything.

Now, an Imperial stormtrooper, on the other hand.

"Steadfast."

Pryde sighed, inwardly at least. Ah yes. "Steadfast." He was so glad he'd been saddled with that particular code name, although he did understand the need for the Imperial remnant's cooperation with the CSA to remain covert.

"Yes, Viceprex?" he asked, although he knew what was coming next. That incoming ship hadn't been CSA, but it *had* been expected.

"Your agent has just landed. I'll have him brought over directly."

Pryde snorted, and he didn't try to hide it. "What makes you think he's *my* agent? I have no idea who he is."

The viceprex's jaw tightened. Pryde took some amusement in this.

"The orders were quite clear," said Coromun. "We are to give your agent every assistance. The order comes from the highest level."

Pryde raised an eyebrow. Moff. He should have gone for moff. They were all dead. Nobody would have noticed.

The viceprex frowned at Pryde, then turned and ducked back into the command tent behind him. Pryde watched his back, then took his flask out again—openly, this time—and had another swig.

Basta Core. A beautiful planet, mostly prairie, as far as Pryde had seen, covered entirely in scrubby blue vegetation that basked under no fewer than three suns that seemed to bathe the planet in only the most minimal amount of heat required to sustain life. He squinted, looking out from the rise to the mountain range nearby, and at the cave opening that had been enlarged less than an hour ago by the CSA sappers as they blew their way into the syndicate stronghold. There had been a firefight, which, Pryde had to admit, had been fairly entertaining, the CSA troopers cutting their way through the insurgents with reasonable efficiency. It had been over in minutes. Perhaps the CSA weren't quite as militarily inept as he thought.

But all this for . . . what, exactly? A cache of arms. A *large* cache, certainly, but did that justify the expense of the troopers, and their transports, not to mention the rerouting of the CSA capital ship that was in orbit above the planet? The CSA were not a government, not even a faction. They were a company. They existed for profit, pure and simple.

Which meant, at the moment, the secret funding of the Imperial remnant. But Pryde knew that that deal could turn on a single credit.

Of course, what they had needed for this operation was a fireteam of incinerator stormtroopers. Just three of them would have burned the insurgents out of their cave quickly and efficiently, and there would have been no need for such a . . . *performance* as this.

Alas, and indeed, alack.

Pryde sipped from his flask again. As he returned it to his coat, the command tent opened and a trooper called for him to enter.

Inside, Pryde found himself in front of Coromun's battle table once more, the large surface display a holographic wireframe of the mountain range and a trace of the cave system his troops had penetrated, along with markers showing the position of all other CSA assets in the vicinity. Next to the line of yellow models on the map representing the CSA transports, the newly arrived starship glowed red.

That ship's pilot stood at the table, beside Coromun. He was dressed in hard black leather, complete with a waist-length black cape. He lifted his bald, scarred head up, and looked at Pryde with two black electronic eyes. The lights on the side of his cybernetic headband winked.

Pryde stared at the man, his expression one of undisguised disgust.

"Steadfast," said Coromun. "This is Ochi of Bestoon."

Pryde lifted an eyebrow. "Really? How quaint."

Coromun cleared his throat. "We are to give Ochi full cooperation."

"Fine," said Pryde. He sniffed. "So what do you want, Ochi of . . . *Bestoon*." He frowned. "What exactly is a 'Bestoon'? Is that a planet or a . . . clan? Species?"

Ochi didn't respond. He just stared at Pryde with his blank electronic eyes. Pryde glanced at Coromun.

"Sorry, do we need a droid to translate, or—?"

Ochi stepped around the table. He was a few centimeters shorter than Pryde, who lifted his head and made a point of looking down his nose at the strange man. At Ochi's belt was a dagger with a double-lobed blade. Ochi's fingers played over it, caressing the metal, as he approached the high colonel.

Pryde adjusted his fur collar again. Oh, what he would have done for a death stick right about now.

"I need men," said Ochi. "As many as you have, with their ships and weapons."

Pryde's mouth twitched into a smile. Well now, this was going to be fun. "Oh, is that all?" He looked at Coromun and smiled. "Certainly you may have them," he said, enjoying the way the viceprex had begun to squirm. "My colleague here is in charge of the relevant logistics. Tell him how many you want and he will arrange it."

Ochi tilted his head, like he was listening for something, then turned to Coromun. "All of them."

Coromun spluttered. "All of them? Impossible. That's an entire company. Three platoons."

"Plus transport," said Ochi.

"Unacceptable," said the viceprex.

Pryde took the flask from his coat, not even bothering to hide it now—life, he thought, was too damn short—and watched with some glee as the viceprex visibly fought to control his temper.

"Agreed, Ochi of Bestoon," said Pryde. He took a swig from the flask and then raised it in a toast at Coromun. "You forget that I am your commander, Coromun, at least for the moment." He turned to the strange Ochi and raised the flask again. "To Bestoon!" he said, his tone not quite mocking, but close enough. "Wherever and whatever that may be," he added. He took a sip, then offered the flask to Ochi. "I don't know what they drink on your planet," he said, "if, indeed, it even *is* a planet, but I'll wager it isn't Abrax. To your health, sir, and the health of this new alliance."

Ochi was staring at Pryde—or was he staring at the flask? Those weird black eyes were so empty and lifeless, it was impossible to tell— and then he took it and, rather than taking a mere sip, he tipped the flask into his lipless mouth.

Pryde watched him . . . and watched how many hundreds of credits' worth of Abrax disappeared down Ochi's gullet, and then—

He burst out laughing. And he kept laughing—he laughed so hard he doubled over, his greatcoat was suddenly too hot, the inside of Coromun's sudden command tent too close. Waving his hand in some form of excuse, Pryde pushed the tent's flap open and stepped outside.

The cold air of Basta Core hit him like a slap to the face, and his laugh settled into a quiet—but still barely controllable—chuckle. He adjusted the collar and watched as the CSA troops milled around the cave entrance, transferring the weapons cache they had liberated from the insurgents into large stacks, ready for loading onto a cargo skiff that would take them down the slope to a transport and then up to the capital ship in stationary orbit above them. Little did they know that they were all— men, freshly won weapons, transports—about to be commandeered by the strange man in black leather.

Pryde ran a hand through his greasy, slicked-back hair. He patted his coat where his flask should have been, then was immediately annoyed at himself for giving it to Ochi. He wondered if any of the troopers had an illicit stash of death sticks he could confiscate in the name of the CSA and the unpaid duty (plus tax plus penalty). He'd given them up years ago—it was not fit for an Imperial officer to be seen indulging in such stimulants—but now, well . . . maybe it was time for Pryde to start making his own rules.

The flap of the tent opened behind him and a CSA trooper stepped out, ducking sideways to step around Pryde and run down toward the rest of the men. On his way to deliver the good news, Pryde thought. He watched as the trooper got the attention of a redcap, the two of them in close discussion for a moment, before the trooper turned and headed, not back to the command tent, but over to the landing site—to the squat, twin-engined thing that must have belonged to Ochi.

"Of Bestoon," Pryde muttered to himself, allowing a smirk to crawl along his features. That smirk fell away as he saw the trooper looking around the underside of the spaceship, picking a spot to place a—

A *homing beacon*. Pryde watched, openmouthed, as the trooper then ducked under the ship and ran back toward the command tent. As he passed Pryde, the high colonel turned and watched him disappear behind the tent flap.

"Viceprex Coromun," muttered Pryde, a grin forming on his aquiline features, "you sly old fox." Of course, it made perfect sense—Coromun had to obey orders just like Pryde did, but the CSA were certainly going to keep a close watch on their involuntary investment.

Pulling his coat tighter, tilting the collar up to protect against the harsh chill of Basta Core, Pryde stalked off toward the men, determined to uncover a death stick or two.

Perhaps he would start to enjoy this covert secondment after all.

CHAPTER 34

THE TWILIGHT FOREST OF HYPERKARN, OUTER RIM

THEN

"I actually don't know how you do it," he said with a laugh, and then he stopped and narrowed his eyes. "Actually, yes I do. I know exactly."

The woman looked up from her work, pausing only to brush a lock of her long blond hair back behind her ear with a greasy hand before returning her attention to the exposed innards of the agridroid's primary fuel cell conduit.

"It's magic," said the man. He folded his arms and leaned against the side of the droid, looking up toward the machine's head, a good thirty meters above them.

Thank goodness the problem could be fixed from ground level, he thought.

The woman laughed, and her laugh echoed from inside the conduit housing. The man turned and smiled, watching her, his heart lifting at the sound of her happiness.

And she was happy.

So was he.

He'd been on Hyperkarn for nearly a full season, having finally had enough of the cramped confines of the sunscooper. He'd ditched that crew at Volta, then picked up passage to the Outer Rim with a group of Twi'leks. It was from them he'd learned about the need for agridroid crews on Hyperkarn—he'd never heard of the planet, but the way the Twi'lek captain had talked about it, it sounded like a good bet.

And he hadn't been disappointed. He didn't have the right experience, or qualifications, or anything that made him suitable for the job other than a desire to learn, a desire to work hard . . . and a glib tongue and charming smile that, actually, worked pretty well when it had to. He'd talked his way onto a crew, and had found himself assigned as an engineer for this year's harvest, in charge of just one towering, monolithic agridroid.

And he liked it on Hyperkarn. *Really* liked it. The planet was quiet, covered in blue forests with dense leaf cover that blotted out the sun, casting the woodlands in a warm twilight. He'd been to the city only once and had no intention of visiting again, happy just to look at the shining spires on the far horizon, happy to stay working on the fields, next to the woods in which the girl he had fallen in love with lived with her grandmother, her Baba.

No, not girl. Woman. She was twenty, by her count. He was twenty-six by his, although there were times he felt much older, the weight of his secret heavy on his mind and on his heart, and times when he felt younger as he went out into the galaxy for the first time. Seeing the sights, keeping his head down with hard work, and now, finding . . .

Love?

Yes. Love. This was love.

And it was wonderful. It was, he knew now, what life was all about.

She had never been off Hyperkarn. Her Baba repaired electronics for the nearby village, nestled tight against the woodland border. Her granddaughter helped her during the day, and at night was building her own droid.

At least, that was what she'd told him, almost from the first day they'd met. He hadn't been to their house in the woods. He hadn't yet summoned up the courage to ask to meet Baba.

"There," she said, her upper half emerging once more from the conduit housing. She stood back and kicked the cover closed with a booted foot, then pushed the emergency stop lever next to it with both hands. A pleasant, faint chime sounded from somewhere high over their heads, and the agridroid began to move forward.

The pair stood back, admiring her work. The droid turned and headed back to the harvest, ready to join the one hundred other colossal machines as they crept along the pastures, gathering the crop.

He couldn't believe his luck, actually. Because he wasn't a droid engineer. True enough, he'd picked up a variety of useful skills on the jobs he had taken on the way to Hyperkarn, and operating the agridroid was just a matter of reading the manuals and talking to the other engineers.

But repair? No way. Totally beyond his skill set. And if it hadn't been for the love of his life, he wouldn't even still be here. His droid was temperamental, prone to breakdowns far more often than the others in the fleet, although they were all old and kept running way past their design specifications. At least, according to the other engineers.

She had repaired the droid seven times now. That was how they had met, him despairing as he found himself elbow-deep in mysterious and completely non-operational machinery, her back from delivering some gadgets to the village, having decided—purely on a whim—to walk back along the edge of the fields, to watch the agridroids rumble lazily at their task.

The two stood side by side, both staring at the droid, both trying very hard not to look at each other.

Finally, he spoke.

"So, did you—"

"I brought some—"

They glanced at each other, mouths open. And then they laughed.

"I'm sorry—"

"I'm sorry—"

He held up his hands. "Wait. One at a time. I was going to ask . . ."

He trailed off, his eyes wide as he now realized his carefully planned, extremely casual invitation to share his meager lunch rations was now the star performance, the woman's eyes watching him closely.

"You were going to ask what?" Her grin was as wide as it was infectious. She was enjoying his discomfort just a little too much.

He sighed and turned back to watch the droids.

"The harvest is going to end soon," he said quietly. "I wondered if you wanted to eat with me?"

"I politely decline."

"I . . . what?" He turned to face her.

"Because," she said, her grin ever-widening, "I was going to ask you to eat with me and Baba." She paused. "That is, if you can get away for a while?" She gestured at the droid. "There can't be much left to fail in your droid. She should be happy enough for a couple of hours without her boss."

"Uh . . . *she?*"

"Of course," said the woman with a smile. "G4-G4-G5-XNXX7-G4 is a *she.*"

The man opened his mouth for a moment, then he just nodded. "My mistake."

"So," said the woman. "Are you coming, Dathan?" With that, she held out her hand.

Dathan looked at it, then took it in his own. "I can't think of anything I'd rather do, Miramir."

They turned together and headed off into the forest, each trying to summon the courage to look at the other, each trying to believe that they were really holding hands, the smile on Miramir's face as wide as the one on Dathan's.

Dathan woke with a start. He blinked in the dim, blue light shining in his eyes, thinking at first he was back on Hyperkarn . . . then winced at the crick in his neck and the horrible stiffness of one wrist that had been trapped underneath himself, as he realized he'd fallen asleep in front of the *Goldstone*'s primary control console.

No matter how luxurious the yacht was, the pilot's seat made for a poor bed.

Dathan moved, clenching his fists to get the circulation back into them. Sitting up, he glanced at the copilot's seat. Rey was still fast sleep, almost completely buried under her blanket.

Easing himself up, Dathan silently crept out of the flight deck. In the *Goldstone*'s main cabin, he found Miramir still working on the cabinet lock.

"Still nothing?" he asked, hands on his hips.

"Actually," said Miramir, wiggling a needle-like probe deeper into the lock's exposed circuitry, "I'm almost—"

There was a bleep, and the cabinet doors sprang ajar.

Miramir looked up at Dathan with a grin. "My finest work, I think you'll find." She stood, stretching her limbs, as Dathan moved over and pulled the doors fully open.

"There it is," said Dathan. He reached inside and lifted out the only thing inside the cabinet—a small strongbox made of shiny white plastoid. He placed it on top of the cabinet, and the two of them looked down at it.

"You need me to open that now?" asked Miramir.

"No need." Dathan ran a hand over the top of the strongbox, then curled his fingers and rapped on the lid with his knuckles. There was another electronic warble, similar to the main lock on the cabinet, and the lid of the box cracked open. Dathan lifted it the rest of the way.

"You were right about him having more than one," said Miramir.

The interior of the strongbox was lined with protective foam, into which was slotted a row of small disks. Miramir pulled one out and held it up by the edge. It was like a large coin, the center an opaque silver disk inscribed with a code, the outer rim gold and covered with black lines.

Dathan pulled another medallion from the box. "Can I borrow that probe?"

"Of course." Miramir handed the tool over.

Holding the medallion firmly between finger and thumb, Dathan pressed the probe into its edge. He worked the probe a little, and a moment later the medallion split neatly in two, revealing a tightly packed disk of circuitry within.

Miramir peered at the circuit. "Like you said, the medallion is a data card." She looked back at her husband. "So what's this plan of yours?" she asked.

Dathan paused. He laid the probe and the two halves of the medallion on top of the cabinet. He stared at them but didn't answer the question.

"Dathan?" He felt her hand on his arm. "What's wrong?"

Dathan finally managed to find his voice. "We're going to have to do something," he said.

"You're right," said Miramir. "Stop and refuel, like you said—"

"That's not what I meant," said Dathan. "I meant we are going to have to do something about Rey."

Miramir froze. "What? What about Rey?"

"She needs to be safe, Miramir."

Miramir's eyes widened. "I know. What do you think we're doing?"

"No, I didn't mean that. I mean that it's not fair on her. She's just a girl. She deserves better from her parents."

"We're protecting her, Dathan," said Miramir. She went to fold her arms then, perhaps thinking better of it, let them drop to her sides again. "Of course she deserves better. But what choice do we have?"

Dathan grimaced. "We could hide her."

"*Hide* her? You want to just leave her somewhere?"

"No, not at all," said Dathan. "I mean *hide* her. Somewhere safe. Somewhere she won't be found. And then when we've found Lando and the Jedi, we can go back for her."

Miramir shook her head. "The Jedi is one thing," she said, "but I thought you didn't trust anyone." She paused and raised a pointed finger at her husband. "We can't go back to Hyperkarn. We promised."

"I know," said Dathan, and then his shoulders slumped. "I know. I just . . . I just want to make her safe. She can't fall into his hands."

Miramir nodded, and then she blinked a tear away. As Dathan watched her, he felt the hot, pricking sensation behind his own eyes. He cleared his throat and picked up the medallion halves.

"We're going to use this to refuel," he said, "and then we're going to buy us some time until we can make sure Rey is safe."

Miramir shook her head. "And how are we going to do that?"

"We're going to steal Ochi's ship."

CHAPTER 35

THE *STAR HERALD*, HYPERSPACE
NOW

Luke relaxed a little in the pilot's seat. They were almost there. Next to him, Lando was dozing, his arms folded across his brilliant red shirt, his head nodding against his chest.

It had been smooth running and they had made excellent time—because the *Star Herald* was one fast ship . . . and its owner, Lina Graf, owed Luke a favor.

Graf had risen to the rank of commander in the Rebel Alliance days, and was now a senior officer in New Republic Intelligence, based at Adelphi. She was also a friend of both Luke's and Lor San Tekka's—indeed, it was through Lor that she and Luke had met, the three of them using her long-range experimental scout ship, the *Star Herald*, on an expedition to search for Jedi relics that had taken them right across the Galactic Core. Lina had taken great pride in demonstrating the capabilities of the *Star Herald* on that trip, even saying that she would be happy to place it at Luke's disposal should he ever need something with a little range and speed.

En route to Adelphi station, Luke had called in the favor, and within an hour of landing, Luke, Lando, and R2-D2 piloted the *Star Herald* back into hyperspace, the *Lady Luck* now docked, for the moment, next to Luke's X-wing in a New Republic hangar.

And now, after a short, smooth journey, Luke eased the controls and dropped the *Star Herald* out of hyperspace at long range from their destination planet, which now loomed as a pale sphere in the starfield ahead of them. Luke wasn't entirely sure what to expect—he had never actually visited the Polaar system himself, he only knew that this was where his contact had established her hermitage, the Jedi Knight the only person she would trust with her location.

Luke glanced back at Lando. He'd been quiet on the journey to Adelphi in the *Lady Luck,* and while Luke had organized the use of the *Star Herald* with Lina Graf, Lando had busied himself ensuring the New Republic technicians knew exactly how he wanted the *Lady Luck* treated while they were away. No sooner had they blasted off from the station in their borrowed ship than Lando had fallen into an easy slumber in the seat next to Luke.

Luke watched Lando's chest slowly rise and fall. Lando had been through a lot. More than Luke could imagine. And now this, thrust into a quest with more questions than they had answers, and they hadn't even taken the time to get to know each other again.

After this was over, Luke promised he'd make it up to his old friend. They had a lot of catching up to do, and Luke hoped they could take the opportunity to do so in a far happier time.

Almost as though reading his thoughts, R2-D2 gave a low, uncertain tone, snapping Luke from his reverie. He smiled softly at the astromech, then turned his attention to the flight controls.

They were coming in to land.

Luke only hoped the long journey would be worth it.

Luke brought the *Star Herald* in to land at what he thought was a polite distance from his contact's homestead, taking care to curve in gracefully on the final approach rather than buzz directly overhead. Polaar was cut off from outside communication by impenetrable interference—whether a natural phenomenon or an artificial jamming field, Luke didn't know, but it meant he hadn't been able to make contact prior to their arrival. Looking down, the homestead was a series of curved white sails, their elegant shapes barely standing out against the white ground. Luke eased back on the controls, not wanting to spook the planet's solitary resident.

Lando, now awake, was frowning over the sensor readings.

"Nothing about this makes sense," he said, gesturing at the panel. "One minute I get clear energy readings, the next I get nothing, and then I get something that's more like the readout of a solar corona. There're lifesigns, then there aren't any. I get power readings enough for a whole city, and then I look outside and see nothing but . . . what is that, even? Some kind of grass? It looks frozen . . . but the environment readings are standard. I don't get it."

Luke cut the auxiliary drive, and the *Star Herald* settled down in a field of white grass, the long nose of the scout ship pointing in the direction of the compound.

"That's exactly why she—Komat—picked this planet," said Luke. "That's why we had to come in person. She came here to be alone."

"And alone she is." Lando winced. "You think dropping in on her is such a good idea? You sure she's not going to blast us as soon as we set foot outside? This feels like a hell of a gamble."

"Come on, Lando," said Luke with a grin as he stood and headed for the exit ramp. "I thought you liked gambling?"

"Only when I know I'm going to *win*, Luke."

Luke held up a hand. "Just let me do the talking." With that, he disappeared through the bulkhead door.

Lando looked at R2-D2. The droid's main indicator flashed blue and red, his dome whirring as he seemed to be waiting for Lando's response.

Lando just shook his head and held up a hand.

"Hey, don't look at me, little buddy. This is Luke's roll of the dice, not mine."

He stood and followed his friend.

Luke stood at the bottom of the *Star Herald*'s exit ramp in almost knee-high white grass, the bleached vegetation far from frozen, merely devoid of any color at all. Komat's homestead, a cluster of low buildings shaded by the huge white sails strung on tight cables, was not far away, at the center of the large, open grassland, with a low range of hills rising not far behind. Luke could see paths worn through the grass, desire lines that led out from under the sails and across the fields in several different directions. One path was particularly wide—vehicle tracks, leading up the hillside, then vanishing over the top. Another led, perhaps coincidentally, from the *Star Herald* to the homestead itself.

"The air is kind of funny, don't you think?"

Luke turned as Lando stepped down the ramp. He was looking around, nose wrinkled. "Not a smell but . . . I don't know." He waved his hand, like he was inhaling the aroma of a particularly fine bottle of vintage Toniray. "It's odd."

Luke nodded. It certainly was a strange place—he and Lando had been on many worlds across the galaxy, but Polaar was . . .

Well, it was eerie. That was the only way Luke could describe it. The white grass, under a pale sky. There was not a breath of wind, nor were there the sounds of any kind of wildlife at all. It was a still and silent world, and Lando was right, there was something peculiar about the air. It made the inside of Luke's nose ache, just a little, his chest starting to feel tight. The *Star Herald*'s systems had reported the atmospheric composition to be perfectly acceptable . . . but now Luke wondered if they, too, were affected by the planet's strange interference field.

"Is there even anyone here?" Lando walked a circle around Luke, looking out across the fields before turning his attention to the compound. "Looks deserted to me." He turned to Luke. "How many years has it been since you saw her?"

Luke pursed his lips. "A few."

Lando frowned and had opened his mouth to speak when a beeping noise startled him. He spun around, hand instinctively reaching for the blaster Luke now wished he had told Lando to leave on the ship.

Coming down the worn path in front of them was an Imperial mouse droid, but instead of the customary black casing, this one was scarlet, the color standing out in shocking clarity against the white grass. As it trundled closer, the beeping increased. The little wheeled droid came to a stop in front of Lando, almost touching the toe of his boot. The piercing alarm continued to sound.

Lando peered down. "I'll be honest," he said. "I've never had a mouse droid welcoming committee before."

That was when there came a swooshing sound as something fast and metallic cut the air. Luke sensed the movement and turned around at the last second, raising his cybernetic hand. The metal fingers caught the blade just centimeters from his face.

Standing behind them was a droid, crafted from dark, almost purple alloy. It was humanoid, the main body not entirely unlike that of a protocol droid, with flexible, articulated joints and midsection between hard metal plating. Its head was an angled approximation of human features, but instead of two eyes, the droid's optical unit was a single bright blue line. The droid was armed with a long, narrow metal blade, which curved slightly from the long, guardless hilt in the droid's hand. The droid must have been waiting for them, concealed in the long grass.

Nobody—Luke, Lando, droid—moved. The alarm continued from the mouse droid, which now rolled back and forth a little, like it was trying to get somebody's attention. But Luke's and Lando's was fixed firmly on the humanoid droid that had somehow come up silently behind them.

"Uh, Luke?" asked Lando. He was ready for anything, his hands hovering instinctively over his holster. He wasn't moving, but his eyes roved between the droid and Luke.

"It's okay, Lando," said Luke, not taking his own eyes from the blue visor of the droid. "I think, anyway." He pushed a little at the sword the droid held; it moved without resistance. Luke pulled the blade down, and the droid allowed the motion.

"Welcome to Polaar, travelers."

As the sword-wielding droid lowered its weapon and returned the blade to a short magnetic sheath hanging from its middle, Luke and Lando both turned at the new voice. Behind them, coming down the path from the main compound, was another figure.

She was wearing a long poncho in dark-gray and green layers, the collar decorated with scraps of a brightly colored, patterned textile that looked like it had been salvaged from some once luxurious fashion item. Her legs were wrapped in beige-colored bindings above practical, heavy boots, her knees protected by thick blue pads. Around her head and shoulders she wore a loose, billowing white hood, but her face was entirely hidden behind a flat, featureless chrome mask, the mirrored surface unspoiled by any seam or rivet, respirator or optical unit.

But the mask was not devoid of decoration. As the woman got closer, Luke could see blue markings scrawled across the mirror mask in a thick, waxy substance—it was writing, an alphabet he recognized, but a language he couldn't translate.

"Master Luke Skywalker, last of the Jedi," said the woman as she stopped in front of the pair. Her voice was clear, a vaguely metallic echo added by her mask, her accent marking her origin as somewhere far from the Core Worlds. "Someone I never expected to see again, as long as we both lived."

Luke gave the woman a bow. "Komat," he said. He stood and gestured to his companion. "May I introduce my friend Lando Calrissian."

Lando followed Luke's lead and gave a small bow himself. As he stood back up, the droid with the sword stalked around him, its head fixed as it kept its blue visorlike optics on him. The droid joined its master, one hand never far from the hilt of its weapon.

Komat's mask turned a little toward the droid.

"You can return to your work, Kaybee Sixty-Eight."

The droid spoke, its voice light and female. "You sure?"

Komat nodded.

"Fine," said the droid. "You know where I'll be if you need me." KB-68 turned and walked back to the compound.

The mouse droid continued to emit the alarm, and now it bumped into Lando's boot. He lifted his foot in surprise.

"Hey," he said, then he glanced up at their host. "Ah, cute little thing. Never seen a red one before."

"The red coloration is easier to locate within the fields of snapgrass," said Komat. "Sensors are extremely limited in this environment."

"Komat," said Luke, giving a respectful nod again to the woman's mirrored mask. "We are sorry to disturb your seclusion, but we've come to ask for your help."

"Of course you have, Master Skywalker," said Komat. "You would be here for no other reason." Then she turned and began to walk back to the compound. "I have work to do, but you may accompany me. We can begin our discussions when the task rota is completed." She stopped, and turned back around. "Em-One, here."

The scarlet mouse droid rolled back, executed a three-point turn, then trundled back to Komat, stopping by her boot, its alarm still operational.

"What's with the mouse droid?" asked Lando. "Some kind of intruder alert?"

"No," said Komat. "A danger signal. You are walking on Polaar unprotected."

Lando glanced at Luke, his eyes wide.

"Unprotected?"

Luke moved his head slightly, indicating he knew as much about Komat's statement as Lando did.

Komat walked back toward them. "You are both in the early stages of distronic radiation poisoning. If you do not come with me, you will be dead within the hour."

With that, she turned and headed back to her compound, her mouse droid happily speeding along at her feet.

Lando looked at Luke again, then waved him on.

"Hey, you heard the lady, let's go, let's go!"

Then, without waiting for Luke, Lando set off at a jog toward the receding form of Komat.

Luke, for his part, didn't waste any time following.

CHAPTER 36

KOMAT'S HERMITAGE, POLAAR
NOW

Komat led Luke and Lando through a doorway concealed under the huge white sails, set into the outer wall of a building covered in a rough plaster. It reminded Luke of the architecture of his old home on Tatooine.

Beyond the door was a large room—a workshop, littered with equipment and worktables. Along one long wall sat a row of six tall silver cylinders, each stretching down from the ceiling. At head height, each cylinder ended in a fine point, aligned above brass-colored metal cones that rose up from the floor, leaving a gap of approximately ten centimeters between the two objects. In this gap, a beam of inky blue energy crackled, a constant discharge that buzzed like a shorting dedlanite power cell. At the other end of the room sat a ground vehicle, a small truck with eight large wheels and the most basic of control cabins, simply an open frame with hard seats. The rear of the vehicle was a flat bed, on which was a large rack, welded together from a plain metal framework.

Luke didn't know what Komat did on Polaar, but she certainly hadn't been idle in her years of exile.

"So are we okay in here or what?" asked Lando, looking around. "I don't much like the sound of distronic anything. You got a decontamination pod or something?"

"Now that you are shielded from the energy field, you will recover," said Komat. "But you will need protection if you are to accompany me to the capture grid."

Lando held his hands up. "I think I like it in here just fine," he said. "Nice place. Very tidy."

Komat's mirror mask turned to Lando, and he moved back, just a little.

"You have come here to discuss something of great importance." She turned her mask to Luke. "You would not have made this journey if that were not so. I am prepared to listen to your words, but I also offer you a choice. My work here waits for no one. Either accompany me now or return to your ship and depart my planet."

Luke gave Lando a glance, then turned to Komat. "Thank you," he said, with another short bow. "We will abide by your conditions."

Without saying another word, Komat moved to the wall opposite the metal cylinders and opened a storage locker. Inside hung another set of mirrored masks, these clean, without any of the waxy writing across the front. Below the masks were more of the multi-layered ponchos, although unlike Komat's own, these were more functional, lacking any decorative design, instead a plain, bright metallic gray.

"This protection will suffice for the duration of your exposure," said Komat. With that, she headed over to the truck. She unlocked the straps of the rack on the truck's bed, and then, moving to another part of the workshop, she unstrapped a vertical stack of large circular plates, each about a meter in diameter, and began to roll them, one by one, over to the truck, where she loaded them onto the frame.

While she did that, Luke passed Lando a mirror mask and a poncho from the locker before taking a set of protective clothing for himself.

Lando held the mask in front of him and looked at his own reflection in the curved surface. He moved close to Luke, who was fitting the poncho over his own robes.

"You sure about this, Luke?" Lando kept his voice low. "Because we're using up a whole lot of time here if this plan doesn't work out."

"We can bring her around. What Komat has to offer will give us exactly the head start we need."

Lando sighed and slipped the mask on. He turned to Luke.

"How do I look?" His voice echoed metallically. "I'm pretty sure this is the in thing on Constancia this season."

Luke laughed and slipped his own mask on. As he did so, Komat's truck roared into life.

"Come on," said Luke. "I have a feeling she'd happily leave without us."

The all-terrain vehicle bumped over the ground, and Lando felt every single jolt on his tailbone. Why this Komat person was using a wheeled vehicle was beyond him. A speeder would have been just as good, right?

Perhaps she liked the discomfort. Wasn't part of being a hermit the bizarre need to feel miserable?

Lando had a feeling that on Polaar, feeling miserable would come easily.

Neither Komat nor Luke had spoken on the ride. Luke sat next to her, Komat driving them through the tall white grass that swished against the sides of the truck. Lando sat on a sideways-facing bench just behind the cargo rack in the back, but he wasn't sure he was any less comfortable than the two in front, given they were all just sitting on hard metal seats. Beside Lando's foot, at the side of the truck's bed, M-1 sat, the scarlet mouse droid docked with a charging unit.

They'd driven for maybe twenty minutes, zigzagging up the hillside that had been far steeper than it looked. The sky ahead of them seemed to have a little color, a slight tinge of blue, although Lando wasn't sure whether that was just the filter of his face shield.

Distronic radiation? Lando had never heard of it. He didn't much like the idea of walking around outside in it, whatever it was, but Luke seemed happy enough to trust Komat. Lando, for his part, had yet to make up his mind. The woman's manner had been formal, rather than friendly, but at least she hadn't blasted them.

. . . nor had her droid cut them to pieces with her *sword*.

What kind of person lives on her own on a toxic planet with an old Imperial mouse droid and another droid that carries a sword?

The truck lurched to a stop, Lando bumping his head on the cargo frame, breaking his train of thought. Looking around, he saw they had stopped just below the ridgeline.

The whine of the truck's engine spun down as Komat stepped out of the driver's seat, Luke following. As Lando clambered over the cargo frame, he noticed the mouse droid had managed to undock itself and was already scurrying around Komat's feet. She and Luke were standing on the ridgeline.

Lando went to follow, then froze, half off the truck, as a large creature appeared over the crest of the hill and sauntered over to Komat.

It was a cat, some huge species that stood almost as tall as Komat's shoulder. Its fur was a deep purple, lightening to violet around the belly, darkening to almost black around its thick mane. The creature had a long tail with a tuft at the end, and as it approached Komat, the cat lapped at its own muzzle with a long, forked tongue. Komat reached out to ruffle her hand through its mane. The cat seemed to like this, first looking up at Komat, then turning to look down at Lando. The cat had four eyes; Lando wasn't sure whether he should have been surprised at this or not.

Luke, for his part, was watching Komat and the giant cat, his hands politely clasped in front of him. He turned and gestured to Lando with his mask to join them on the crest.

Lando took a breath and walked up the rise, keeping himself on the opposite side of Komat's ferocious-looking pet. He stopped behind Luke and, once he had finally managed to tear his eyes off the animal, turned to face the view ahead.

He swore behind his mask.

The other two curved mirrored faces turned a little toward him, Lando imagining the smirk on Luke's face.

Lando turned back to the view. He opened his mouth to say something, but he wasn't quite sure *what* he was going to say.

They were standing on the edge of a steep slope that led down to a vast, flat plain. The ground here was free of vegetation, revealing a gray, hard-packed surface. Covering that surface was a huge array of circular plates, each standing on a single pedestal, each pointing straight up to the sky. The plates looked like the same as the ones Komat had loaded into her truck, but instead of white, the surfaces of the ones out in the array were dark blue.

Lando frowned behind his mask. It looked like a simple solar setup, the most basic of energy harvesting technologies. But there was something else on show that suggested to him he was probably looking at an entirely different kind of technology.

On the horizon rose a building. It grew out of the ground, a series of soft, layered elliptical shapes that was somehow familiar to Lando. The building was quite some distance away and looked huge, and—

And then Lando realized what it was. He turned his head sideways, craning his neck to look side-on at what he had originally thought was a building.

He straightened and looked at the others. "That's a starship. A Mon Calamari battle cruiser." He looked back at the horizon. "Wait, did it crash here?"

Komat turned her mask to him, then back out at the horizon. She continued to stroke the head of her cat, which was now sitting neatly beside her.

"During one of the last battles of the Galactic Civil War," she said, "there was a skirmish nearby, and that ship was forced to flee. But its hyperdrive was damaged, and it fell out of lightspeed too close to this world. I believe the crew attempted to jump again, but the coaxium regulator overloaded and sent the starship's fusion core into meltdown. When it crashed, the ship's shields overloaded under the core's power surge. The shields maintained the integrity of the superstructure, but the fusion core's chain reaction continued."

Lando blinked, his mind racing as he tried to understand what Komat was telling him. "So . . . instead of exploding, that ship got stuck in the planet, the fusion core still melting?"

Komat nodded. "Discharging distronic radiation. This entire planet is poisoned. Nothing can live here. The contamination also blinds any sensors, the energy field scrambling any kind of transmission."

"The perfect place to hide," said Luke.

Komat turned her mask to his. "If you think I am hiding, then that is your affair."

Lando pointed at the array of disks.

"So, what are these? Looks like some kind of science experiment."

"The array you see is a particle capture grid," continued Komat. "The decaying starship reactor core emits many rare and exotic elements, and will continue to do so for one thousand years raised to the eighth power."

Lando whistled. "Long time."

"The array holds the fallout in stasis," Komat continued, "so Kaybee Sixty-Eight and I can harvest the particles. Many have a useful function in hyperdrive catalyzers and other advanced drive systems."

"What?" Lando turned his mask back to Komat's. "You're telling me you *farm* radiation? And then, what, sell it?"

Komat inclined her mask in acknowledgment. "There is a market moon in the Pirsen system, seven parsecs distant. Once per quarter, Kaybee Sixty-Eight takes our harvested stock and barters for supplies."

At that, the mouse droid began to emit its warning alarm again. Lando looked down at it, then raised both arms a little to look down at the poncho he was wearing.

"I assume we're safe here?"

"There is nowhere safe on this planet."

Lando shook his head and looked at Luke. "Have I mentioned I have a bad feeling about this yet? Because I can feel it starting to come on."

"We're fine for a while," said Luke.

Lando glanced at the animal next to Komat. "Droids with swords . . . and giant cats?"

"Sekhmet is a targon, Lando Calrissian," said Komat. "I find her presence meditative, and her species is immune to the effects of distronic radiation."

Lando eyed the animal. "Meditative, okay."

Luke turned to Komat. "As I said before, we are here for your help."

As Komat moved back around to the truck, Sekhmet stood and loped off down the hill, toward the grid. Komat, meanwhile, began undoing the straps that held the fresh particle capture plates in place. "You can help with the harvest," she said, "and then we can discuss your situation."

Luke and Lando glanced at each other, then Lando gestured expansively to the truck.

"After you, last of the Jedi."

CHAPTER 37

KOMAT'S HERMITAGE, POLAAR
NOW

They worked for a couple of hours, installing fresh plates on the array and loading the old ones into the truck. Lando assumed that Komat normally used her other droid, KB-68, to help her, as it certainly wasn't a job for one person on their own. While they worked, Sekhmet prowled the perimeter—at a distance that, Lando thought, suited him just fine.

Work complete, they left the targon at the grid and headed back to the workshop. There, the finished plates were unloaded, and, under Komat's instruction, Luke and Lando helped install them in the row of cylindrical particle distillers. She operated the controls, and the next cycle of harvesting began.

Work complete, Komat told them to leave their protective gear on a worktable, then—still clad in her own mask and poncho—she led them through a connecting passage and into her living quarters.

In the doorway, Lando stopped, looked up.

"Wow, okay," he said, with a shake of his head. Beside him, Luke smirked at his reaction, but then he raised both eyebrows, indicating that he, too, was impressed.

The main area of Komat's compound was a long room with a huge arched ceiling. The walls were more of the white plasterwork, but they stopped two meters from the floor. From there, the walls were formed of planks of a warm, deep-brown material—natural wood, Lando realized— that stretched up and then curved over, meeting at a pointed apex.

But that wasn't the only impressive piece of architecture.

The room was filled with plants—hundreds of varieties, apparently no two the same, a wild cacophony of greens and yellows, of trailing tendrils and exotic, brightly colored blooms.

The plants were all growing on the sides of huge, square forms— perhaps three meters across, half as thick again. There were a dozen of the frames floating in the air under the huge arched ceiling at different levels and angles.

It was nothing short of magnificent, a collection worthy of the finest botanical institute in the Core. To find such beauty—such life—on display on such a dead, poisoned world gave Lando an incredible feeling.

It filled him with joy, with hope.

Komat led them into the center of the room, where a low table was positioned, surrounded by colored cushions.

Lando glanced at Luke, who grinned at him, then gestured that he should go first. Lando, his own smile plastered firmly on his face, followed their host.

Komat folded herself onto a cushion. Lando looked around, wondering how his stiff muscles and aching joints were going to like him sitting cross-legged on what was essentially the floor, but there didn't seem to be any alternative. He noticed, then, that Komat's droid KB-68 was standing on a small floating platform, just big enough for one person or droid, and was pruning a plant on one of the floating frames. The droid stopped, apparently aware she was being observed, and turned her blue-light gaze down on him. Lando froze and slowly—painfully—lowered himself onto the cushion next to Luke. He glanced back up at KB-68, who continued to watch him, still and silent.

Lando cleared his throat, then turned to his host.

"Ah . . . nice place."

Komat nodded slowly at Lando, then turned toward the droid floating nearby. "Please prepare refreshment, Kaybee Sixty-Eight."

Lando risked another look at the droid. KB-68 gave a nod of her head, still not looking away from Lando as her platform descended to ground level . . . and she continued to fix him with her electric gaze even as she stepped off the platform and headed over to the side of the room, where a food preparation station was positioned in front of a large rectangular span of transparisteel, giving a clear view of the white grassland and the hillside beyond.

Then Komat pushed back her white hood, and took off her mirror mask, revealing skin a deep-brown color and hair pulled back into a tight bun of dark purple. She had a thick blue line—warpaint or tattoo, Lando couldn't tell—that ran across both high cheekbones and her nose, just under her wide-set, narrow eyes. Lando could see her irises were frost white, circled with a deep blue.

KB-68 returned, carrying an ornate wooden tray, laden with tall green ceramic tumblers and a jug of the same design. The droid folded her legs like scissors and sat with perfect grace at one end of the table. She set down the tray and reached across the table to hand out the tumblers before pouring a thick, steaming brown liquid from the jug into each in turn.

Komat inclined her head, indicating for her guests to drink. Luke sipped his tumbler. Lando glanced down at the contents of his, and then the rich, heady aroma hit him. The drink inside his tumbler was heavy, and as he rolled his cup, it stuck pleasingly to the sides of the ceramic vessel.

He grinned. "Well now, there's something I haven't had in a while." He took a sip, sighed with pleasure, then raised his tumbler in salute to Komat. "And if that isn't the finest hot chocolate outside of the Arc of Eden, I don't know what is."

At this, Komat actually smiled, then sipped from her own tumbler. Luke still didn't say anything, and the trio sat in silence for a few moments, drinking their beverage.

And Lando felt . . .

Actually, he felt *relaxed*, but as soon as he realized that, he felt, once again, guilty. He was tired from the work, and was glad for the refreshment, but . . . what were they doing here, sipping chocolate, admiring the plant collection of someone who lived with a sword-wielding droid on a planet that was, in theory, completely uninhabitable.

And all the while, the clock was ticking. Somewhere out there was a family in danger.

Lando put down his tumbler. He'd just realized that, during all their time out at the particle array, they hadn't even begun to broach the question of Komat's assistance.

This sojourn was getting more and more frustrating. And as he watched Komat and Luke drink, the pair silent, apparently entirely comfortable with that silence, Lando wondered what kind of history these two had, outside of what brief details Luke had given him.

"Okay, okay," he said, lifting a hand in apology, then lowering it and shaking his head as he wondered what the hell he should feel apologetic for. "Look, this is great, and thank you for your hospitality, but Luke and I are on something of an urgent mission here." He turned to Luke. "I apologize if I'm spoiling something, Luke, but the longer we linger, the harder it's going to be to find the family. If they haven't been found already."

Luke nodded, his brow furrowed in thought as he sipped his chocolate. Then, cradling the tumbler with both hands, he turned to Komat.

"Lando's right," he said. "You have skills I had never before encountered, not on all my travels in the galaxy, not before, and not since. I hoped I could convince you to aid us. I'm not asking you to come with us, or to break your vow of solitude. But I'm hoping this isn't such an imposition that you won't consider listening to what we have to say. We have two questions, different, but related."

Komat watched Luke, her own drink held in her hands. She was quiet, and seemed to be listening.

But she didn't reply. Lando sensed something, like he was sitting in on a negotiation, and that Luke, for all his power and experience, was very much *not* the one in charge of the situation.

Komat still didn't speak. Luke reached into his robe and took out a data card from the *Star Herald*. He held it out to Komat; she looked at it but did not move her hands from her tumbler.

"I have all the data here. Full readings of the drive and exhaust signature of the ship we need to find." He paused, then put the card on the table between them and glanced around the room. "I'm hoping you still have the equipment."

"I do not," said Komat.

Luke's shoulders fell, his eyes downcast.

"Wait, what?" Lando spluttered. All this time spent on Polaar and Komat *couldn't* help them?

"And even if I did," Komat continued, ignoring Lando's outburst. "The contamination here is too great. As I said, the energy field emanating from the starship crash site acts as a total electromagnetic blackout, scrambling all sensor readings and communication channels, both incoming and outgoing."

"Great," said Lando, standing from the low table. He paced a circle then looked down at Luke. He ran a hand over his mustache, over and over and over. "Great, just great. I don't even know what she was supposed to do for us, and now she says she can't anyway."

"Lando, wait," said Luke. He turned to Komat. "If you had the equipment, could you do it?" He held the data card out to her.

Komat looked down at it. "You have a full reading of the starship you seek?"

Luke nodded. "Full reading."

"Including ionization rate and cycle frequency of the hyperdrive motivator?"

"All of it."

Komat took the card, then stood and looked at Lando.

"Then I can locate the ship."

Lando pressed his fingertips to his forehead. "What equipment? I'm sorry, but Luke didn't even say what you can do. How can you find a ship from its drive signature? The galaxy's a big place."

Komat's mouth threatened to flicker into a smile again. "When I was a member of the Acolytes of the Beyond, we found a cache of Imperial research, something smuggled out of their data store on Scarif."

Lando lowered his hands. "And that helps us how?"

"The Empire had a number of high-concept research projects running," Komat continued. "It took much time for me to slice the encryption, and the data itself was incomplete, but while my brothers and sisters continued to seek the sigils of power they so craved, I came to understand I had in my possession something far more valuable than mere relics. Analysis of the Imperial research files revealed the ability to track any starship in the galaxy, if the correct data was available."

Lando's eyes went wide. That was a lot to process. He rubbed his face and ran it through his head again. Then he looked at Komat, and then he looked at Luke.

"So we can find the *Goldstone*?"

Komat said nothing, but she inclined her head.

"So what do we need?" asked Lando, carefully lowering himself back onto a cushion by the table. "What kind of equipment are we talking about here?"

Komat turned to Luke. "Your starship appears to have a far more sophisticated long-range scanner and antenna array than my own, Master Skywalker. With your permission, I will pilot it beyond Polaar's energy field, where I will be able to initiate the tracking algorithm using the primary sensor array. If your astromech droid will accompany me on this journey, together we will be able to run the filter algorithm to provide the data you seek."

"Thank you, Komat," said Luke, handing the data card to her.

"That is but the first reason you have come here, Master Skywalker. You have a second question for me."

Luke adjusted his position on the cushion. "I do. A short while ago, I encountered a being—a woman. She wore a reliquary mask, and I believe she wielded the lightsaber of Darth Noctyss."

Komat didn't answer, not immediately. Lando saw her eyes flicker, just briefly, her lips parting in apparent surprise. Lando had a feeling Komat knew exactly who Luke was talking about. "We think she might have been Pantoran," he said.

Komat turned her attention to Lando, and for a moment he had the distinct feeling he was butting into a conversation he had no place in. From the corner of his eye, he saw Luke glance at him, giving him a small nod of encouragement.

"I couldn't see her face," Luke continued as Komat turned back to him. "But I saw her hands."

Still Komat didn't speak. Lando watched as her throat bobbed as she swallowed, and then she quickly stood from the table. Lando went to rise with her, but Luke waved him down as he stood himself.

"Komat?" he asked.

She seemed to compose herself, and then she turned to Luke. "The individual you speak of is Kiza of Corellia. It was she who once led the Acolytes of the Beyond."

Lando nodded. "So you do know who she is?"

Komat gave him a small bow.

"Can you tell us *where* she is?" asked Luke.

"I cannot, Master Skywalker."

Now Lando frowned. "Why not?"

"Because, Lando Calrissian," she said, "Kiza is dead."

CHAPTER 38

THE *GOLDSTONE*,
TAW PROVODE IMPERIAL FUEL FACILITY
NOW

Miramir stared at her own reflection in the *Goldstone*'s forward viewports, but her gaze was unfocused, her thoughts not on the functional, artificial world of the fuel dump in which the ship was now docked, but somewhere else, somewhere on the other side of the galaxy.

Somewhere they had tried to make a home, somewhere they had tried to stay safe. Unnoticed.

Jakku.

It had been the one place she had lived for the longest outside of her home on Hyperkarn—nearly five years in total, bringing with them the infant Rey, born on Hyperkarn and hidden there in the twilight forest with the help of her Baba. But it had been too dangerous to stay. They'd known that from the moment little Rey had come into their world.

Rey.

She was a wonder, she was magic, she was love and she was light.

She was also in danger. Not *imminent* danger, but the longer they stayed, the greater the risk. Easy to hide a baby. Difficult to hide a child. And while Hyperkarn was a pastoral world, it was also close to the major space lanes. The longer they stayed, the more they felt like a target was being drawn on them—and on Miramir's home and the only family she had, her grandmother.

She couldn't remember how they had chosen Jakku, but it was a distant, sparsely populated world. Rough, underdeveloped. Life there would be tough. They both knew it.

But it would also be *possible*. Survival was all that mattered. And besides, with Miramir's skills, there was even the sly hint of potential, although neither Dathan nor Miramir ever dared say it.

Because Jakku was a scavenger's paradise. A great battle had been fought, years ago, in the skies above the planet, and the desert below was littered with ships and wreckage, in some places stretching from horizon to horizon.

Miramir had built their first droid from those scraps, while Dathan built their homestead, creating a moisture farm from the desert so they could make their own life, one not beholden to the junk bosses who governed the scavengers of the world.

One of them came to investigate these new arrivals, who had appeared in the plains on the outskirts of Niima Outpost. Dathan had thought they were far enough away from the settlement, but the junk boss, Unkar Plutt, had clearly thought differently. They had learned, though, that Plutt was a pragmatist as well as a businessman, and so long as there was something in it for him, he would tolerate their presence. Miramir scavenged, selling salvage to Plutt, buying her own parts for her droids and for the equipment to establish the moisture farm. Eventually, Dathan—who had come, if not to friendly terms, then at least respectful ones, with Plutt—would sell that water to Niima Outpost.

Life was simple, and while Miramir would hesitate to call it *good,* it was, at least, a life.

They were safe.

Until they weren't.

The hunters had come by daylight, with no apparent desire for discretion or secrecy. For that, at least, Miramir had been grateful. If they'd come by night, their story would have ended there, on Jakku, a few years of peace bought for nothing.

It was Miramir's droids who gave the warning, alerting Dathan to the approach of the hunters. But they had been prepared for the eventuality—even if he and Miramir had never talked about it openly, they'd prepared an emergency cache of credits and belongings, just enough to get by. Miramir had already sliced into a freighter at the Niima Outpost scrapyard, her periodic visits to the place allowing her to effect the most basic repairs, enough for it to move, if they ever needed it. Miramir suspected Unkar Plutt had known what she was doing, despite her best efforts to hide her work. The fact that he never asked questions—not to mention the fact that somehow he just happened to have just the right part for her, available at a discounted price—was something she was forever grateful for.

Miramir's droids had given the warning and they gave their lives, the simple, homemade agricultural units engaging the hunters in awkward, doomed hand-to-hand combat. But it was enough. It bought them time. It bought them a *window*. Miramir and Dathan and Rey piled into the freighter and took off, their life, their farm, abandoned.

And their hope?

Miramir wasn't sure about that. They'd gotten away, and they were still alive. That was something.

But, she reminded herself, that was, literally, just *days* ago. If they were going to survive—*really* survive, finding a place, forging a new life, probably with new identities, something beyond mere *existence*—then they had to . . . do something.

Dathan was right. They couldn't run forever. And still, a part of her wondered whether relying on the kindness of a stranger, this Lando Calrissian, was really wise. They didn't know who he was. He said he had a Jedi with him. Was that even the truth?

She blinked out of her reverie, and stood, and stretched. A moment later, she heard laughter, high and happy, laughter that filled her heart and made it soar.

And then she thought again about Dathan's plan, to find a place to hide, to keep Rey safe while they . . .

While they *fixed things*.

She cast her eye over the main console. They'd landed at the fuel dump on Taw Provode seven hours ago, but had yet to refuel. The place was entirely automated, on a backwater planet. Nobody knew they were here, and they could, for just a short while, afford to take a much needed rest.

From her pocket, she took the regent-captain's medallion, the two halves now pressed back into place; tapping the medallion against her chin, she followed the sound of her daughter's laugh back into the main cabin.

She found Rey and Dathan sitting together on the floor in the main cabin, facing each other. Between them was one of the moving sculptures from the side cabinet, now disassembled into a dozen pieces that floated in the air between them, whatever field that controlled the sculpture apparently able to cope with its structure being disrupted. Perhaps that was the whole point.

Right now, that structure was being turned into the shape of a—

"No, it's a happabore!" Rey clapped her hands and pointed to her creation, a collection of fluid sculpture parts that looked . . . actually, they looked nothing like a happabore, the parts already beginning to drift apart. Dathan gave a look of mock surprise, then shook his head.

"That's four to you and six to me," he said.

"Only six because you're cheating, Daddy."

"Oh, is that right, Rey?"

Rey gave a very enthusiastic nod.

"Then how much do you think I should have?"

Rey pouted as she considered. "Maybe two."

"Two? More like two *hundred*."

"More like no hundred!"

Miramir laughed; Rey, hearing her mother's voice, looked over her shoulder, then stood and ran over for a hug.

"Mummy!"

"Hi, Rey, hi!" She looked down at her daughter as Rey squeezed her around the middle. "How are you feeling?"

"I had a good sleep," said Rey. "The chairs here are very nice."

"I know, aren't they?" said Miramir.

Rey laughed, then pulled away and went back to the improvised game. Miramir wandered over and nodded at Dathan.

"Looks like fun."

Dathan looked up at her and grinned. "For a fancy starship, it is surprisingly lacking in entertainment options for a six-year-old."

Miramir's grin matched her husband's, and then, seeing that Rey was busy with her new toy, she gestured for Dathan to stand and follow her over to the other side of the cabin.

"Everything okay?" asked Dathan, as they stood together over by a wall, close enough for him to put his hand on her hip. He looked at the medallion that was still in Miramir's hand. "Have you started the refueling yet?"

Miramir looked at the medallion, then shook her head. "There's something I wanted to say first."

"Okay."

"I think you're right."

Dathan's smile twitched into life again. "Sounds good. Keep going."

Miramir couldn't resist smiling herself, but then she shook her head and folded her arms. She glanced away from her husband—body language that did not go unnoticed.

"What is it?"

"I agree with you. I think we should hide Rey. If we know she's out of direct danger, we can face this head-on. Try to find Lando and his friend." She paused, and took a deep breath. "I mean, we don't know who they are, or whether they really are trying to help us, but my point is, if we know Rey is somewhere safe, then that gives us some room to move."

Dathan nodded. "Then we're agreed." He rubbed his stubbled cheek. "Now we just need to find somewhere safe for her."

Miramir looked at her husband. "I know a place. And I know someone we can trust."

Dathan blinked, and dropped his hand. "What? Where? Who?"

Miramir paused before answering. "Unkar Plutt," she said. "We can trust Unkar Plutt."

Dathan's mouth opened, but he didn't speak. He just stared at Miramir, almost frozen in place.

A moment passed, then another. Miramir sighed.

"Dathan, talk to me."

He closed his mouth, then closed his eyes. "You want to take Rey back to Jakku, to . . . Unkar Plutt." He opened his eyes. "Tell me what you're thinking."

Relieved at the hopeful tone of Dathan's voice—and hoping that it wasn't her imagination—Miramir outlined her plan.

"Unkar Plutt is a businessman. We know that. So long as there is something in it for him, he'll help us."

Dathan opened his mouth to speak again, but Miramir cut him off quickly.

"*And*," she said, "it will only be temporary. That'll be part of the deal. He can hide her in Niima Outpost until we come back for her. And, yes, Jakku is . . . Jakku. Trust me, I know exactly what it is. But I also know exactly who Unkar Plutt is. And right now, he's about the only person in the galaxy outside of this starship that we can trust. Not because he's a friend. Not because he's on one side or the other. But because he is who he is. We know that, and I think we can work with it."

Dathan began to rub his cheek again, and then he began to walk a tight circle, eyes downcast, his first hand now joined by his second as he scratched his stubbled chin.

"And," Miramir continued, "the Sith won't go back to Jakku. It's a dead end."

Dathan didn't pause in his pacing. "You don't know that. You can't be sure of that."

Miramir sighed. "Of course not. We can't be sure of anything." She fought to keep her voice low so Rey wouldn't hear. She glanced past her husband to watch as their daughter continued to play with her floating sculpture, her back to her parents.

Miramir's breath caught in her throat, and her heart fluttered.

Her girl, Rey. Her love. She needed protection. And yes, she needed better than this—and she needed better than Unkar Plutt, better than Jakku.

But it was only temporary. It was *only temporary.*

They would be back.

Then Dathan stopped pacing. With his eyes closed, he nodded.

"Yes."

Miramir choked back a sob. This was it. *This was it.* They had made their decision—their heartbreaking, soul-stopping decision—but the decision they had to make.

For Rey.

"We'll have to pay him," said Dathan, coming back to join Miramir. "You said it yourself. Unkar will want something in return."

"Then we pay him."

Dathan gestured around the ship. "But we've been through this. All this stuff will be imprinted. Plutt will check anything we take to him."

"Don't worry," said Miramir. "I know what we can use."

Dathan frowned, then his eyes went wide. He looked at Miramir a moment, then gave a short nod.

"Now," said Miramir, holding up the medallion. "Time for your part of the plan."

"So you agree? We steal Ochi's ship?"

Miramir nodded. "If we're going to take Rey to Jakku," said Miramir, "then she *has* to be safe. That means we can't be followed, we can't be tracked. We take no risks whatsoever. Nobody can know where she is."

"Agreed," said Dathan. "If we can take Ochi's ship and strand him here, we can buy us a lot of time." He took the medallion from her. "All we need is right here."

Miramir blinked. "So how does this work?"

"Follow me," said Dathan. He led the way back into the flight deck. Outside, the gray industrial wasteland of the Taw Provode fuel dump was flatly lit under harsh floodlight towers. He looked down at the main console and ran a finger along the controls until he found what he was looking for, a small slot next to the comm panel. Taking the regent-captain's medallion, he inserted it into the reader. Immediately, the panel next to it lit up, and outside, a series of indicator lights illuminated on what looked like a bank of automated fuel pumps. Dathan watched as the *Goldstone*'s energy cell indicator started to creep up.

Miramir shook her head. "How does that bring Ochi here?"

"It won't," said Dathan. "Yet." He turned to his wife, and leaned forward, giving her a kiss on the forehead. "For that, I'm going to need your help again."

CHAPTER 39

KOMAT'S HERMITAGE, POLAAR

NOW

"Dead? What do you mean, dead?" Lando looked between Komat and Luke. "Luke saw her. She was there, on Nightside. Flew around in a TIE Defender." He waved his hands in the air, motioning the zigzag movement of the high-speed fighter.

"Indeed, Lando Calrissian, it appears my assumption was incorrect." Komat bowed, an action Lando guessed was supposed to convey an apology. She turned to Luke. "You must tell me more of this encounter, Master Skywalker." Lando folded his arms and moved to the window wall to look out at the poisoned white fields of Polaar. It was starting to get dark.

Luke told Komat everything, not just about his encounter with Kiza at Nightside, but also about the crystals and holocron found on Yoturba, and the visions of Exegol he had been experiencing for weeks now. Komat listened in silence, never once taking her icy stare from Luke's face.

When Luke was finished, Komat's gaze fell onto the table and remained there, the enigmatic woman clearly deep in thought.

Lando pushed himself off the window and rejoined the others, lowering himself to lie on his side rather than cross-legged.

"So who is this Kiza?" he asked, quietly. "Why did you think she was dead?"

Komat looked up. "Kiza was an Acolyte of the Beyond. She was born to Pantoran exiles on Corellia. She experienced great hardship during her life."

"Making her an easy mark for the Acolytes," said Luke.

"This is indeed so," said Komat. "She claimed to have experienced visions of the Force before the Acolytes welcomed her to their number, but I am not certain of this truth. But she did indeed become a most fervent adherent of the cult, and her thirst for power through the dark side appeared unquenchable. Soon, all the Acolytes became enthralled to her."

"Yourself included," said Lando.

"*Lando*," whispered Luke, but Komat merely inclined her head.

"Lando Calrissian speaks the truth," she said. "I make no attempt to conceal my past. I was an Acolyte of the Beyond. I considered Kiza to be as a sister to me."

Luke lifted his chin. "Tell me about the mask."

Komat looked at him. "This was a most powerful artifact, a relic that had once belonged to an ancient Lord of the Sith, Exim Panshard. He held the title of viceroy on a planet long forgotten, and legend tells of his tyrannical reign there. The Acolytes of the Beyond sought many such relics, believing they could grant themselves great power through their use."

Lando ran a finger over his mustache. "So Kiza found the mask and put it on, only it turns out that this Exim Panshard is, what, still in it? Like Momin." Lando wagged a finger at Luke. "You said you sensed the presence of a Sith, and that it wasn't Kiza, but was using her."

"Kiza did not find the mask, Lando Calrissian."

Luke turned to her. "Oh?"

"It was gifted to her on Devaron. I was with her when the Acolytes received a visitation from Yupe Tashu. It was he who carried the mask."

Lando froze. "Yupe Tashu?" The name was familiar, but he couldn't place it.

"One of the Emperor's advisers," said Luke. He frowned. "When was this?"

"Fifteen years ago. Yupe Tashu was revealed as the true master of the Acolytes of the Beyond, intending to use them to restore the dark power to the galaxy. It was he who had recruited many of their number, including Kiza. It was possible that it was he who had implanted visions of the Force within her mind, perhaps using another unknown relic of the Sith. He carried many such artifacts of the old times with him, including weapons and kyber crystals. But most important of all was the mask of Viceroy Exim Panshard. It was to Kiza he bequeathed this most powerful of relics."

"She put it on," said Lando, "and Exim Panshard lived again."

Komat nodded slowly once more. "I believe this to be the case, Lando Calrissian. Yupe Tashu planned for this to happen. He craved the dark power of Viceroy Exim Panshard, but he knew he dare not attempt to wield that power himself. What he required was another host, one he could control without losing his own will to the Lord of the Sith."

"Of course," said Luke, tugging on his beard in thought. "With Palpatine dead and the Empire splintered, Yupe Tashu saw his opportunity. He thought he would wield Kiza like a weapon, using her to reestablish his own order in the galaxy."

"Okay," said Lando, "but Komat, you said you thought Kiza was dead. This was all a long time ago. What happened to her and the mask?"

Komat paused before she spoke again.

"Kiza became lost to the mask. I remained by her side always, but she no longer recognized our bond of sisterhood. She spent much time in the presence of Yupe Tashu and away from the other Acolytes. We believed they were searching for more powerful artifacts. Yupe Tashu wanted to turn Kiza into a force unable to be resisted."

"Artifacts like the lightsaber of Darth Noctyss," said Luke.

"This lightsaber," said Komat, "like the mask, was mentioned only in legend. But if the mask existed, then it was possible that so, too, did such a weapon as that ancient blade." She turned back to Lando. "Kiza and Yupe Tashu returned, but Kiza had great difficulty in recognizing people she had previously known well. It was then that I realized the plans of Yupe Tashu, and that Kiza would soon become lost to the mask of Viceroy Exim Panshard forever. When Yupe Tashu was not present, I attempted to take the mask from her, and we engaged in a great battle. It was during this that Yupe Tashu returned, and was killed by Kiza. She fled with the mask and was not seen again. She had been gravely injured in our struggle, and I did not believe she would survive unaided."

"But you didn't stop looking for her, did you?" asked Luke.

Komat turned to him. "I believed that if she lived, she would remain a danger to the galaxy. I sought the Noctyss blade myself, to prevent her from locating it. I failed in my task"—she turned to Lando—"but it was at that time I met Master Luke Skywalker, who guided me to the path of salvation."

"So Kiza is still alive," said Lando, "and she's got the mask and this lightsaber. And now, what, she's working with Ochi of Bestoon—she sent him after the family, to get their wayfinder?"

"If they have a wayfinder," said Luke.

"A wayfinder would be the most powerful Sith relic of all," said Komat. "According to legend only two were ever made."

"And both of them point the way to Exegol," said Lando.

Komat inclined her head. "The hidden world of the Sith. It would be imperative that Kiza and the mask of Viceroy Exim Panshard do not discover the location of this place."

The three of them fell into an uneasy silence. KB-68 appeared, bringing more hot chocolate. Komat and Luke drank theirs slowly, but Lando left his steaming mug untouched.

It was a lot to take in. Lando felt like he'd just walked straight into something that was best left alone, his chance encounter at Boxer Point Station opening a door to something huge and dark and terrifying.

And at the center of it, a young family, with a young child. Fleeing for their life, pursued by an evil even Lando could scarcely comprehend.

"You look tired, Lando."

Lando opened his eyes—he hadn't even realized he'd closed them—to see Luke looking at him, a friendly smile on his face. "I think you need some rest."

"Ah, yes, maybe you're right." Lando sat up and rubbed his face, then went to stand, only to find KB-68 next to him. She held out a copper-plated hand.

"Kaybee Sixty-Eight has prepared quarters for you," said Komat.

Lando looked up. KB-68's electric-blue gaze bored into his eyes. He glanced at Luke, but his old friend gave him a nod. "Go and get some sleep. Komat and I will discuss matters."

Lando wondered whether to argue, but, truth was, he was . . . utterly exhausted. Physically. Mentally. Emotionally. He took the droid's hand and let himself be pulled up.

"Follow me," said KB-68, her electronic voice edged with annoyance. Lando couldn't resist a quiet chuckle as he followed the droid out of the room.

KB-68 led Lando down another of the tunnel-like, white-plastered passages. At the end of it was an empty, almost circular room, devoid of anything except a low wooden platform, crafted of the same stuff as the table in the other room. On this platform was another intricately embroidered cushion in red and gold thread—this one large enough to sleep on.

Lando turned to say thanks to the droid, but KB-68 was gone. With a shrug and a sigh, he sat on the bed for a moment, then he lay back, his hands locked behind his head as he stared at the ceiling.

A second later, he was out for the count.

CHAPTER 40

SOMEWHERE, SOMEPLACE
THEN

"**N**o, no, no, no!"

She disappeared around the corner, leaving nothing but her giggle lingering in the air, and a spotted trail of melted ice cream across the floor. A moment later there was a clatter of something light and plastic, and Lando felt his stomach flip.

"No, no, no, *no!*"

He rounded the corner, balancing his own ice cream, regretting now the two extra scoops he had ordered for himself and Kadara. But what had started as a simple game of hide-and-seek had now turned into an epic chase—and one that was about to end in tragedy.

Because Kadara was in Lando's cape closet. A two-year-old girl, high on sugar, holding a scoop of ice cream as big as her fist.

Things were about to get . . . messy.

Lando sprinted into the room, ice cream held high, just in time to see two capes slip from their hangers and hit the floor. Farther into the closet, more capes—a forest of silken colors and fine embroidery—shifted as Kadara tunneled into them in a desperate bid to win the game.

Lando's jaw worked, and he shook his head. Even as he stood there, his ice cream continued to melt, the sticky runoff now covering his knuckles.

So, okay, they'd had a nice day, and Kadara deserved a treat—and so did he, Lando thought—and sure, why not, ice cream was fun and sometimes you needed a little fun and the parlor was just on the concourse by the apartment and . . .

More giggles, muffled now by thousands of credits' worth of high-class fashion accessories, a good proportion of which were now covered with melted ice cream. Lando just shook his head again and absent-mindedly licked his triple-scoop double-chocolate special.

. . . and she liked hide-and-seek, because she liked Lando's closet. It was dark and full of mystery and full of color and all kinds of things that were silky and smooth, and it smelled like his cologne, and hide-and-seek also meant dress-up, and if there was anything Kadara liked more than hide-and-seek, it was wrapping herself in one of her father's capes and parading around the apartment.

Hell, she liked to sleep in his capes, too—once chosen, her costume piece would usually remain with the girl for the rest of the evening, unable to be extricated from her tiny hands until she was well and truly asleep.

Kadara laughed again, and then called out for her father to come find her. More capes moved, another fell from a hanger, and then there was a wet sound and . . .

"Uh-oh," came the girl's muffled voice.

And then Lando—

He grinned, and then that grin turned into a laugh, and then he took a big lick of his ice cream, wincing momentarily as brain freeze set in.

"Ready or not, here I come!" he said. He massaged his forehead with his free hand, and then, with a shake of his head as the discomfort cleared—and ice cream firmly in hand—he dived into the closet, disappearing into the forest of capes. A few more fell to the floor, then Kadara laughed again, and Lando laughed, too.

There was another wet sound.

"Uh-oh," came Lando's muffled voice.

And then Kadara Calrissian giggled, high and bright, and her father laughed with her.

CHAPTER 41

KOMAT'S HERMITAGE, POLAAR

NOW

Lando woke with a start, then gasped at his protesting muscles. He'd fallen into a deep sleep, one leg hooked under the other, his hands still locked behind his head. He extracted each limb in turn, wincing as the intense pins-and-needles sensation reached a crescendo, then he went to stand and nearly fell off the low bed. Looking around, the white plaster walls were cast in a faint blue glow, which was coming from the passageway.

Massaging his neck, Lando stood. He didn't know how long he had slept—the faint tracery of a dream lingered in his mind, but as soon as he realized, it faded into nothing—but he was very thirsty. He padded over to the doorway, then headed back down the passageway, toward the main room of Komat's compound, and toward the blue glow.

The glow was bright in the main room, although Lando immediately saw that the light source was *outside*, shining in through the large window-wall that looked out over the vast white grasslands.

It was raining—no, it was *snowing*—the air filled with a steady drifting fall of small, ashy particles. It was entirely silent, the room's only sound the quiet hum of the miniature moisture vaporators in the food preparation station.

Lando blinked, his eyes adjusting to the spooky blue glow. It was coming from over the crest of the nearby hills, the source a single pillar of blue light, bright at the center, radiating outward to form a soft column that shone directly into the sky, lighting the snow around it. The column of light seemed to be coming from somewhere a long, long way away—the crashed Mon Calamari cruiser, Lando realized.

Then Lando saw something else. It was a figure, standing out in the tall grass, facing the light, arms outstretched to the sky and, indeed, the head tilted back to let the snow fall on its face.

It was KB-68.

"Don't worry," said a voice behind him, "apparently she likes nights like this."

Lando turned and realized Luke was still sitting at the table, facing the window. He was in a cross-legged position, his ankles locked together in a pose Lando knew he'd never be able to emulate himself. Luke's hands rested, palms facing up, on his knees.

"How long have you been there?" asked Lando.

"A few hours," said Luke. He smiled. "You looked like you needed the rest."

Lando nodded, and, rubbing his temples, made his way to the table. "Like you wouldn't believe," he said. He moved around to the end of the table, and as he slowly lowered himself down, he became aware that Luke was watching his every move, his old friend making absolutely no attempt to hide his amusement at Lando's stiff joints.

"Hey, hey!" said Lando, waving at Luke as his backside finally hit the cushion with a bump. "I'm older than you, farmboy."

Luke laughed. "Yes, General, sir."

With a wince, Lando got himself more or less comfortable, then grinned. "Komat back yet?"

"Not yet."

"And I don't suppose you know how long it will take? Whatever it is she's doing."

"I'm afraid not."

Lando shook his head. "So until she comes back with our ship, we're stuck on a poison planet with a—" He gestured to the window, where KB-68 was still standing outside. "—with a droid that likes the snow."

Luke's grin widened. "That's not snow," he said, "it's lucanol-550. It's emitted from the melting reactor and condenses in the upper atmosphere at night, then falls to the ground."

"Oh, great, that makes me feel a lot better," said Lando. "Walk around outside during the day, you get slowly cooked by distronic radiation. One step outside at night and you get fried by lucanol fallout." He sighed. "I'm so glad we came here, Luke, I really am." But he said it with a laugh in his voice. "So what's her magic trick, anyway, this tracking thing? Did she tell you how it works?"

"She did," said Luke. "It's called hyperwave signal interception."

"Oh, of course, I should have known."

Luke frowned. "Do you want to know or not?"

Lando held up a hand in apology. "Sorry. It's just I thought hyperspace tracking was impossible."

"It is," said Luke. "The Empire was working on it before the Battle of Yavin, but their research came to a dead end. What Komat managed to learn from a decrypted data cache the Acolytes found is derived from that same project, but it's a different thing."

"I'm listening."

"Hyperwave signal interception," Luke explained, "involves mapping the energy signatures of ships as they enter and exit hyperspace." As he spoke, he gestured with his hands, miming the dipping and diving of ships as they jumped to lightspeed and then reentered realspace. "The Empire had a whole network of Imperial beacons seeded across the galaxy. Most of them are still operational, even if they aren't used for navigation. But part of their function is routine monitoring, including measurements of cosmic background radiation."

Lando frowned. "And this can tell you where a ship is?"

"It can," said Luke, "if you have the right data. If you know exactly what you're looking for, including the ionization rate and cycle frequency of the ship's hyperdrive motivator, you can theoretically filter the hyperwave data collected by the beacons and match it to the signature of the ship."

Lando squeezed the bridge of his nose with a forefinger and thumb, closing his eyes.

"So let me get this straight," he said. "With the right data, and a way to slice what's left of the Imperial network, you can pinpoint where a particular ship comes out of hyperspace?"

"That's it, exactly."

Lando opened his eyes. "That's some party trick. How come the Empire never found a way to use it?"

At that, Luke frowned. "From what Komat could discover, it seems they never cracked the filtering algorithm needed to make it work. The project was still of interest—Scarif housed the Imperial Center of Military Research—but it was put on ice."

"So this filter algorithm, that's what Komat figured out, and then it all just works?" Lando whistled. "Sounds like something the New Republic would be very interested in."

But Luke shook his head. "Even if Komat was willing to share her knowledge, hyperwave signal interception requires the beacon network. Those satellites weren't built to last, and according to Komat, a lot of them are failing already. Soon enough, there won't be enough of the old network left to use."

"That's a shame," said Lando. He stood—gingerly—and made his way over to the food station. He looked at one of the burbling moisture vaporators, wondering how he could extract a glass of water.

"Even without the hyperwave signal . . . *whatever it is* . . . it was worth coming here just to find out about Kiza," Lando called over his shoulder. "Does Artoo have enough data on her ship, the TIE Defender class? You said yourself, they never entered Imperial service, at least not officially. There can't be many still flying. Komat could use the hyperwave thing to get a bead on her location. Aha!" He pressed the side of the vaporator, revealing an internal compartment with a tap. Then he began looking around for one of Komat's tumblers to drink from. "If we can find both Kiza and the *Goldstone,* it might be worth splitting up. One of us could get back to Adelphi and call up some reinforcements, and we can go after them both."

"You think Commander Blacwood will be any more cooperative this time?"

"She will be when she hears we've discovered who was behind the attack on Halo Squadron."

Luke nodded. As Lando got himself a drink of distilled water, he glanced out the large windows. At the horizon, beyond the blue column of light, the sky was beginning to brighten, and the ashy fall of deadly lucanol snow had stopped. Of KB-68, there was no sign.

"It's nearly dawn," he said, and as he did, the peace of Komat's compound was broken by the dull roar of a starship engine. Lando joined Luke at the window, and the pair watched as the *Star Herald* came in from low orbit on a sharp trajectory, retro engines firing as Komat brought it in on a tight turn and landed it directly outside the windows. Lando winced as the landing gear only just extended for touchdown, the whole ship jolting as it dropped onto the planet's surface. He glanced at Luke, frowning. "She came in pretty fast."

"Something's wrong," said Luke.

Outside, the hooded form of Komat disembarked from the ship and ran toward the compound, disappearing from view. A moment later, there was a muffled clattering and hiss as the sealed workshop entrances were opened and closed.

Komat rushed into the main room. She was wearing her standard protective gear, her wide white hood billowing out. Lando noticed that the text scrawled across the front of her mirror mask was different from what it had been yesterday.

Luke moved around the bench of the food station and stopped in front of Komat.

"What is it? Did you locate the ship?"

Komat nodded. "I was indeed successful, Master Skywalker. But unidentified ships approach. If I had not been piloting the *Star Herald* in low orbit, they would have landed without our knowledge."

"An ambush?" Lando moved back to the window. He scanned the sky—

And then he saw them. Two ships, of types he didn't recognize, except for the fact that they were old models, the kind of crates often seen banging around starports and hangars, the last running old-timers from decades past, predating the Empire.

These crates, however, had been repaired, refurbished—they may have been old, but they were still perfectly serviceable. Komat and Luke joined Lando, and the three of them watched as the two ships turned in the air above the crest of the hill, their snub-nosed cockpits now pointing at the compound. A moment later, side doors swung open on each, like the unfurling of metal wings. Figures appeared—Lando counted five from one ship, six from another—and rappelled down cables to the ground.

Lando looked at the other two. Komat, not speaking, ducked away, running toward another exit.

Lando glanced down, and saw Luke's hand already curling around the hilt of his lightsaber. He gave Lando a curt nod, which Lando returned. Together, they ran out, following Komat.

Polaar was under attack.

CHAPTER 42

KOMAT'S HERMITAGE, POLAAR
NOW

Of Komat, there was no sign. Instead, Luke led Lando back down the main passageway and into the workshop. The space was dimly lit only by the flickering energy of the particle stills, but it was enough for the two men to rush over to the equipment locker and grab a mask and poncho each. Even as they were pulling the gear on, the sound of blaster-fire echoed from outside.

Luke and Lando didn't speak. They didn't need to. Both knew what they had to do, even if they had no idea what was happening.

Lando got a glimpse of Luke's face the split second before he slipped his mirror mask on. He didn't much like his friend's dark expression, but he thought he could probably guess what Luke was feeling—because he felt it himself.

They had disturbed Komat's peace, asked her to help them with something that had nothing to do with her, and now they had brought the enemy right to her door. Whether the *Star Herald* had somehow been tracked here, or Komat's subsequent trip into orbit had been detected, it didn't matter.

This was their fault.

Geared up, they raced out, Lando's blaster swinging in his hand, Luke's lightsaber unclipped from his belt, his thumb on the activator.

Outside, they followed the sounds of battle around the side of the workshop area and main loading door, following the white plaster curve of the building underneath the great sails, until they were facing the hillside. The *Star Herald* sat in front of them, the long, low-profile ship catching the rising dawn light.

But the fight was on the hillside. The two raiding ships had now landed on the crest of the hill, and the troop of eleven invaders was marching down the slope, sending a barrage of red blasterfire down the hill. From their position, with their view impeded by the *Star Herald*, Lando couldn't see Komat, but there were flashes of white blasterfire aimed back up at the invader. She was nearby, but terribly outnumbered.

"You take the left," said Lando, gesturing with his blaster. "I'll take the right. Use the *Star Herald* for cover. They're out in the open, we can pick them off."

Luke nodded his assent, and the pair ran out from the wall, peeling off in different directions, both heading for the cover of the *Star Herald*'s landing gear. Ducking down behind the nose gear, Lando peered over the rim and took aim with his blaster, then paused.

The invaders were droids—a mix of types, but all battle droids of some kind, antiques like the two landers they'd come in on. That was why they didn't need cover, their armored chassis providing protection from anything except a precise hit. Even as Lando watched, two white bolts of energy glanced off the shoulder of one of the larger machines, which paused to shift aim with its arm-mounted weapon before unleashing another few rounds of fire.

This was going to be difficult. The droids were marching in formation—they weren't exactly running, but they were approaching steadily and would overrun the *Star Herald* in moments.

Lando ducked down, squinting along the short barrel of his pistol. He was a good shot, but his blaster was designed for close-quarters fighting, not sniping on an advancing troop of battle droids. But . . . if he could just hit a weak spot—

A shower of sparks exploded in his face as an energy bolt collided with the landing gear Lando was hiding behind, dazzling him. He cried out in surprise and felt himself being pulled backward onto the ground. As purple stars spun in his vision, he saw that he'd been saved by KB-68, the droid's blue-visor optics staring down at him.

"Cover me," said the droid, before pulling her long blade from its magnetic scabbard and running toward the invaders.

Lando pushed himself up and fired wide shots around KB-68, watching in astonishment as the droid got within melee distance of the first battle droid and struck with her blade.

The battle droid put up a defense, blocking with armor-plated arms, retaliating with punches that would put a hole clean through the side of the *Star Herald*.

But KB-68 was . . .

Lando lowered his blaster, caught in the moment. Because what he was watching was *beautiful*.

KB-68 was fast, and she was agile, wielding her metal blade with a precision that was almost a dance, ducking and weaving to escape the slow hand-to-hand attacks of the battle droid, attacking with her own weapon, probing the droid's defenses.

And then Luke was with her, the green blade of his lightsaber swinging in to cut the droid down. Immediately, KB-68 and Luke moved in opposite directions, targeting different droids, their movements almost mirrored.

And equally effective. Luke dispatched his droid. KB-68, likewise, her attack taking only a few more seconds with her less powerful weapon.

Komat appeared, running out from her own cover underneath the *Star Herald*; at this, Lando snapped out of it, and let off some more shots as Komat added her own blasterfire, the pair distracting the remaining advancing droids while Luke and KB-68 pushed their way up the hill, one on each side, reducing the invaders to smoking parts.

Lando ran to Komat, kneeling beside her as the two laid down fire. One of Lando's shots hit the bull's-eye, lifting the head of a droid clean off its torso. As the body continued to march, the blaster now firing blindly at Lando and Komat's position, KB-68 swept in, first slicing off the arms holding the blaster, then cleaving the droid's torso in half with a two-handed downward cut.

Thirty seconds later, there was one droid left, at the top of the hill. A larger battle droid—perhaps a command unit of some kind? Lando had noticed it had ceased firing a few moments earlier, and now it turned, apparently keen to escape in one of the landers. But as Lando watched, the droid raised its weapon and took aim at one of the ships, opening fire. The small starship bucked under the hail of bolts, then sagged forward on its nose as the front landing gear failed. A second later, the front of the ship erupted in a gout of flame.

The droid turned, ready to disable the second lander to prevent it being taken by the enemies the squad had been sent to eliminate. But as it swung to take aim, another form appeared, rising clear over the crest of the hill, front legs stretched out and ready for the kill, long tail swishing in anger.

Sekhmet. The targon was bigger than the battle droid, and took it down under her own weight. As the pair hit the ground, Sekhmet lifted her head to roar, then bit down on the droid's neck. There was a sparking flash, and the thrashing droid fell still.

Komat stood and reached down a hand to help Lando up; he gratefully accepted. Up on the hill, Luke deactivated his lightsaber and walked down toward them. KB-68 remained where she was, scanning the area around her, blade held ready.

"I've never seen a droid like that," said Lando as Luke joined him and Komat. "It was incredible."

"KB-68 is a Duelist Elite droid," said Komat. "I found her on Mircapala, standing guard over the dead body of her master, who had programmed her to defend him against an attacker who never came. She had been standing guard for many years. I promised her a new home."

"I think I like her," said Lando, holstering his blaster.

Komat turned her mirror mask to Luke. "Do you know where these droids came from, Master Skywalker?"

Luke shook his head, then turned to look at the carnage on the hillside. "I have no idea—wait."

He reached out with his human hand. As Lando watched, Luke cocked his head. Lando could imagine his friend's face beneath the mirror mask—the closed eyes, the expression of intense concentration.

Lando knew exactly what Luke was doing.

"The Sith sent them, right?"

Luke turned his mask to Lando. But before he could answer, Komat's mouse droid scooted out from somewhere, shooting between Lando's legs as it chirped away, zooming toward the nearest defeated droid. M-1 rolled back and forth, back and forth, around the droid's head, then moved in close. There was a whirring sound, like a miniature electric saw, and then Lando realized it *was* a miniature electric saw, the little droid having severed the battle droid's head from its body. It then pulled it off the torso and began to pull it in reverse back toward the humans. It stopped, wheels spinning, as something seemed to snag. Then the droid leapt forward as the final vestige of connecting cable snapped, and it pulled its prize to them.

It had the droid's head—and the head was trailing a long cluster of cables and metal filaments, the mouse droid having pulled the entire spinal control column out of the other machine. In the mess of cables, something bright red glinted in the morning light.

Lando pointed. "Is that what I think it is?"

Luke crouched down beside the mouse droid and reached forward with his cybernetic hand, pushing the cables apart. Then he sat back on his haunches.

It was a red kyber crystal, a jagged, split shard, like the ones Luke was carrying.

Lando shook his head, trying to figure out why a droid would have a kyber crystal in it, when Komat walked over to another fallen droid. She hefted the machine over onto its back with her boot, then pulled out her blaster and fired seven shots at point-blank range into its chest plate. As the smoke cleared, Komat reached down and yanked the chest plate off, then worked at something else inside the chassis. A moment later, she lifted her hand—in it was another kyber crystal shard.

"What?" Lando asked nobody in particular as he looked around.

"They've all got kyber crystals in them? What is that even supposed to do?"

Luke stood. He had the kyber shard in his hand, and he turned it over, examining the geometry of the thing. Lando could see the broken edges of the shard, like it had been split from a larger piece.

"That's how they found us—that's how they found *me*," said Luke.

"You're saying they used the *crystals*?"

Luke nodded. "I think so. They're part of the same original crystal." He held the shard up again, to catch the light. Lando didn't like the way the blood-red color of the thing seemed to darken, rather than lighten, in the rays of the rising sun. "It's like . . ." Luke trailed off. Then he lowered the crystal. "It's like they're *connected*, somehow," he said.

Komat rejoined them, her own crystal shard in one hand. "This planet is protected by the energy field. No sensor can penetrate it."

"Not a sensor," said Lando. He looked at Luke. "You're talking about the Force, right? These crystals are all connected in the Force. These droids were drawn here—to the crystals you're carrying. That's how they found us."

Luke nodded.

Lando cocked his head in appreciation. "You gotta hand it to them, they're clever."

"And dangerous," said Komat. "If the Sith rise again, the entire galaxy will be cast in their shadow once more."

Luke and Komat looked at each other. Lando watched them a moment, then turned and looked at KB-68, who was still standing on the hillside, the devoted protector ever alert.

Just a droid, right?

Lando shook his head. He knew full well there was no such thing as "just" a droid. He felt the emotions stir inside him, and he turned to Luke.

"We have to get out there and find that family. They need our protection."

Luke looked at him but didn't answer. Lando knew why—there was conflict in Luke's mind. Their quest was to help the family. It was also to stop the Sith.

"Go," said Komat, and Lando realized she was talking to Luke. She nodded her mirror mask to the landers up on the hill. "Your astromech will be able to slice the navicomputer of the remaining droid lander to find its point of origin. I will take Lando Calrissian in my own starship to provide aid to the family you seek. I know where they are."

Luke's mirror mask stared at Komat's. Lando watched them a moment; he didn't need to see their faces to guess what they were thinking.

"You should go with him," said Lando, turning to Komat. "It's not just a dead Sith at the end of those coordinates. It's Kiza, too."

Komat tilted her mask at him. "As I have previously explained to you, Lando Calrissian, the Acolytes of the Beyond are no longer my concern. Kiza lost her way many years ago. There is little I could do to change that now. Master Skywalker is a Jedi Knight. This battle is his. The family, however, is in need of our aid." With that, she turned and headed back to the compound. "I will prepare the *Warglaive*."

Lando turned to Luke. "Okay, I guess she's the boss."

Luke reached out a hand, and Lando took it. "Safe travels, Lando."

"We'll send a transmission when we've got them, and we'll arrange a rendezvous. See you soon, Luke."

They parted company. Luke headed to the *Star Herald*, calling for R2-D2, before turning and walking up the hill toward the surviving lander.

Lando watched him a moment, then turned as an electronic burbling sounded from behind him. R2-D2 rolled down the *Star Herald*'s ramp. He turned his dome inquisitively to Lando.

"Hey, look after that guy, Artoo," said Lando. "He's the only Jedi we've got left, okay?"

R2-D2 whistled an affirmative, then rolled on after his master.

CHAPTER 43

TAW PROVODE IMPERIAL FUEL FACILITY
NOW

"This is going to work. Relax. We're going to be fine."

Dathan looked at his wife, but her attempt to ease his mind didn't quite work. He continued to pace around the *Goldstone*'s flight deck, arms tightly folded.

And . . . now he had doubts. And fears. And uncertainties. He wondered if it was too late to change his mind, to change his plan. Part of his brain screamed at him that he'd made a mistake and was leading his family—the family he was supposed to protect—into even greater danger.

The fact of the matter was . . . this was the truth. To say what they were about to do was a huge risk was an understatement like no other.

But if they could pull it off, stranding their pursuer—at least for a short while—while they escaped in his ship, then there was a chance they could get ahead of this whole situation.

Right now, that felt like a lot of *ifs*.

Rey sat on a big couch at the back of the flight deck, watching her father, the unease—the fear—on her face growing by the moment.

"Dathan," said Miramir, quietly, "you're scaring Rey."

At that, Dathan stopped exactly where he was and turned to his daughter.

"Hey, hey, hey," he said, scooting over to the couch next to Rey, drawing her in for a hug. "Sorry if I scared you. We're just trying to figure something out, okay?" He kissed the top of her head, his heart breaking—not for the first time, and not for the last time, he knew that all too well—for his child.

"So," said Dathan, looking up at Miramir, forcing a note of optimism into his voice—for his own benefit as much as for his wife and child. "This is going to work. We're going to do this."

But as he spoke the words, he . . . actually, he started to believe it. Especially when he looked into Miramir's hazel-green eyes, saw the smile on her face—saw the same optimism he had tried to fake but knew was there, somewhere, inside him.

You and me, he thought. *We're in this together and nothing can stop us. The only way out is through.*

Miramir nodded, just once, a very definitive yes.

"Okay, okay," said Dathan, with a nod. "Can we check on progress? I mean . . ."

Miramir smiled as her husband trailed off. "You mean," she said, "am I sure I knew what I was doing?" She turned and sat at the console, tapping a finger on the top of Zargo's medallion, still in its slot. "You were right—I mean, I *knew* you were right. The medallion gave us access to the refueling systems by sending a transmission to the fuel dump's control computer. That computer will check the medallion holder's authority and credit."

"A control computer that was highly honored to have such an illustrious guest as Zargo Anaximander pay a visit," said Dathan. "But it'll transmit that information on a wide-band, right?"

Miramir nodded. "With my modification, yes. I sliced the datachip and added in a new subroutine, making the control computer double-check everything. It keeps the transmission open longer. Not only that, I introduced a loop error. The transmission frequency will drift across the bands before the control computer can correct it. Any half-decent bounty hunter scanning for the *Goldstone*'s location will be able to pick it up."

"Which means we're leading them right to us," said Dathan.

There was a tone from the control console. At the sound, Rey looked up, and Miramir turned around to check the alert.

"It's worked," she said. "There're some other ships coming in. Three of them." She turned back around.

Dathan nodded. "All right, time to get ready for phase two."

CHAPTER 44

TAW PROVODE IMPERIAL FUEL FACILITY
NOW

Lando crouched behind the railing and looked down at the staging area. He counted twenty troopers—a full platoon—in a brown armor that he hadn't seen in some time, the regular soldiers joined by a handful of officers in their distinctive red helmets. Tightening his grip on his blaster, he glanced sideways at his companion, but her face was hidden behind the large, green-glass visor of her helmet.

Lando hadn't been familiar with the Taw Provode system, but as soon as they'd dropped out of hyperspace, the reason for that had become abundantly clear.

There was nothing here.

Well, no, scratch that. There was a *lot* here. Dust and rock and ionized gases, orbiting a small white star. Two of those rocks formed a system of their own: One qualified as the only planet in the system, the other, its solitary moon.

Truth was, there were more systems like this one in the galaxy than not—unremarkable footnotes in star charts, nothing more than catalog numbers linking points A to B to C. That Taw Provode actually had a name was due to the fact that, as uninhabited and barren as the planet was, a use had been found for it.

And Lando *had* seen these kinds of things before, because Taw Provode was home to an old Imperial fuel dump, a patch of a few square kilometers on the planet's equator flattened and turned into an artificial environment of black concrete and gray metal, filled with huge spherical tanks, arranged in clusters, covered in gantries and walkways, the streets that linked the large, square staging areas between fuel tank clusters and landing pads lined with pumps and other essential machinery. Industrial on a scale only the Empire had any interest in investing in, a completely automated facility that continued to be maintained, ready for use by anyone with the requisite credentials and credits, the simple service droids patiently monitoring systems, making repairs, refilling stocks.

Taw Provode was a dark world, its sun distant, its single moon almost as bright in the night sky. The environment of the fuel dump itself was artificially maintained, the place lit in the harsh glare of vast floodlights on high towers; the shadows thrown between the tanks and machinery were as dark as space.

Which, as Lando could see, made for an interesting, potentially useful, place to make a stand. If you got there first, got into a good position, you could pick off anyone who came by.

Problem was, they were not the first.

Lando signaled to Komat, and the pair shuffled back along the gantry, into the safety of the dark shadow cast by the tank they were halfway up.

"Corporate Sector Authority," said Lando, wincing as even his low voice echoed a little around the metal jungle they were in. "I'd heard they were back in play, building themselves up, but I haven't seen that many together, ever. Looks like the rumors were true, they've formed some kind of army." He paused. "They don't look like the Espos though. Not the regular ones, anyway."

"What is an Espos, Lando Calrissian?"

"CSA security police," said Lando, keeping his voice low. "But these have been seriously beefed up."

Komat nodded. She had swapped the hood and mirror mask for an unusual helmet—a sleek, angled metal mask underneath a large glare shroud, itself comprising a wide, wraparound cowling of dark-green glass, widening to two large triangular sections on either side, while a second, separate piece rose from the eyeline up over the top of the helmet. Gone, too, was her utilitarian work clothing. Now she wore a sleek, figure-hugging combat suit, armor-plated with more green glasslike material.

"If they have turned the Espos into an army," she said, her voice just a deep, electronic growl from behind her helmet, "that would be logical. This is an advanced operation. They arrived well before we did, but it might not have anything to do with the family you seek."

Lando frowned. "You sure your tracking system is accurate? I mean, this *is* the right place, right?"

"Of that," said Komat, "there is no doubt."

"Okay. So that means they're here, somewhere. Maybe the family is in more trouble than we thought, if the CSA are after them." Lando turned and lifted his head, risking a quick look at the staging area. The two rows of CSA troopers were standing at ease while the redcaps were in close discussion.

"They're waiting for something," said Lando. "That might give us some time." Hefting his blaster, he raised himself carefully up. "Come on, let's take a look around."

Plotting a path across the interconnected gantries and walkways high among the fuel tanks gave Lando and Komat a distinct advantage over the Espos. Up here, they could cover a much larger area, walking straight over the fuel dump's systems instead of having to circumnavigate them, and at a height that varied between twenty and thirty meters, they had the perfect position to see what was happening at ground level without being detected.

"There," said Komat, rounding a corner of a gantry, then ducking down to a crouch. She lifted her weapon—a heavy-duty, long-range blaster rifle that could have punched a hole in the armored side of an AT-ST—and lined its long scope up with the slotlike gap between the cowlings on her helmet. She played the rifle around a little, clearly scanning the way ahead with telescopic vision.

Lando didn't need the scope to see what was in front of and below them. It was a landing pad, identical to the one they'd come in on themselves. On it sat the polygonal form of a small, twin-engined starship, the landing ramp down. As Lando watched, a redcap walked down the ramp . . . followed by a familiar, black-clad hunter.

"That answers that question," said Lando, as Komat lowered her scope. "That's Ochi of Bestoon. Looks like he's working for the CSA." He frowned. It didn't feel right, but he wasn't sure it mattered. "Come on, let's keep searching."

They traveled the gantries for what felt like an hour—up and down ladders and walkways, all the while keeping a low profile, trying to stick to the shadows and, where that wasn't possible, taking routes directly across the top of the fuel tanks, where they figured they were unlikely to be seen from the ground, despite feeling like they were running under literal spotlights.

The layout of the fuel dump quickly became apparent—clusters of tanks, surrounded by their associated pumping machinery, interspaced with staging areas and landing pads, all repeated in a regular pattern. There were no pads they had yet seen that could accommodate anything larger than a midsized cargo freighter, but Lando presumed those facilities were located farther out, at the distant peripheries of the dump.

"Lando Calrissian," came Komat's voice from the darkness behind him. He stopped immediately and glanced over his shoulder. In the half shadow, her green visor flashed as it caught the light, and she pointed down with one armored hand.

Following her direction, Lando moved to the edge of the platform and peered carefully over the edge. Far below, at ground level, several Espos were creeping forward, blaster rifles raised.

"More."

Lando looked up as Komat spoke. From their high position, they could see through the gaps among several more clusters of fuel tanks. Shapes moved in the gaps—more CSA troopers, all of them moving forward slowly, heading in a different direction.

"Looks like a search to me," said Lando. "They're going to have the whole place covered soon. We have *got* to find them first."

Komat's helmet vocalizer clicked. "There should be another pad on the other side of these tanks," she said, then turned and led the way, not waiting for Lando's response. He followed, keeping close.

She was right—and they were ahead of the troopers. Komat lifted her blaster again and scanned the pad with the scope.

Zargo Anaximander's luxury yacht sat under the floodlights, its golden hull a beacon of bright color in the dark-gray world of Taw Provode. Lando was surprised the thing wasn't visible from orbit, it was so conspicuous.

"Any sign of life?"

Komat adjusted her scope. "I see nothing outside. The cockpit viewports have the blast shields down. I cannot see into the interior."

Lando moved to the other side of the gantry and looked down. The Espos were close, and getting closer. Any minute, they'd come around the corner and be face-to-face with their target.

He ducked down and shuffled back to Komat.

"Come on," he said. "We have to get down there and get them out."

This time, he led the way, Komat following close behind.

CHAPTER 45

TAW PROVODE IMPERIAL FUEL FACILITY
NOW

Moving at ground level was an entirely different experience, putting Lando and Komat at a distinct disadvantage. But they had no choice—the only way to reach the *Goldstone* was across open space. And, much to Lando's frustration, the only way down from the fuel tank gantries had led them quite a distance away from the landing pad.

Now they were in a race against time, them versus the CSA. He was determined to get to the *Goldstone* first, but he also knew he had to be cautious. It was just the two of them, versus who knew how many Espos.

He didn't like those odds.

For now, he was grateful for Komat's guidance. Clearly skilled in covert arts, she took point again, keeping to the deep shadows in and around the pump machinery that lined the open boulevards of the fuel dump. She moved with silent ease, her huge rifle raised up to her helmet, always scanning the way ahead.

Lando, for his part, wasn't just following her lead. He walked behind, covering their rear 180, his back touching hers. It was slow progress, but it was necessary—at each junction, they would split up, covering opposite corners, checking around machinery, ensuring the coast was clear and keeping each other covered as they moved on.

They fell into that pattern with some ease, and even as Lando's heart thumped in his chest, the blood rushing in his ears, he felt . . .

Actually, he felt *good.*

Here he was, doing something. He was engaged in the task at hand, mind and body, and the clarity with which his mind operated was like a blast of the freshest, cleanest, most recycled and purified Cloud City air.

Oh, he had needed this. He really did.

Komat stopped, suddenly, and Lando felt her pull away from him, one hand reaching behind to tap his side as she moved. In the shadow of a fuel tank, Lando dropped into a crouch and turned on the balls of his feet, blaster ready.

They had reached the edge of the landing pad. Ahead of them was open ground, the *Goldstone* shining brightly under the floodlights, looking less like a starship and more like an art installation in a high-class gallery.

Zargo would have liked the way his baby looked, Lando thought with a rueful smile.

That smile quickly faded as Lando realized the cost of their slow progress.

They were too late. The ship was surrounded by Espos, and now its entry ramp was down. Two redcaps stood at the base of the ramp. A trooper marched down and stopped in front of them, giving his report to his superiors, along with a shrug and sweep of an arm to indicate their quarry was, perhaps, somewhere else.

Komat waved Lando back, the pair retreating into the deep shadow.

"They are not there," said Komat. "It appears that ship is empty."

Lando shook his head. "Okay, okay, well . . . that's good, right? They're not there. They got out. That's one for our team."

Komat turned her helmeted face to Lando, but he just shrugged. "Hey, I'm just running the options. But if they're not in *there—*" He jerked a thumb back at the *Goldstone.* "—that means they're out *here* somewhere. Right?"

"This facility is occupied by the CSA." She glanced up. "We need to retake the high ground and find the family before they do."

Komat ducked back and the pair ran at a crouch, sticking to the shadows, until they found the ladder they had originally descended. As they climbed, Lando felt his stomach grow tighter, and tighter.

This was taking too long—but at the same time they needed to pause, take stock, make a plan.

He stopped on the ladder, wincing at his own indecision. He looked over his shoulder, and—

There. Two CSA redcaps were walking quickly away from the *Goldstone*'s landing pad, taking a path through the fuel dump that was leading them away from the rest of the company. One of the officers was wearing an equipment pack, the top of which was . . .

Moving?

Lando knocked gently, three times, with his blaster to get Komat's attention. She was several rungs higher, but she stopped and looked down.

Lando held one hand out to Komat. "Give me the scope."

Without question, Komat slid her rifle's telescopic sight off and dropped it down to Lando. He caught it, then brought it up to his eye. It took him a moment to get his bearing, but—

There.

He'd been right. Peering out from under the top flap of the backpack was a face—that of a young girl who couldn't be more than, what, five or six years old? As the pair of Espo officers walked on, Lando saw the one in front glance around, waving their hand for their companion to hurry up.

The parents, taking their daughter to safety.

Except Lando wasn't sure anywhere was safe, not here.

He lowered the scope. "It's them," he said. He looked up, and saw Komat watching the pair. "Come on," he said, looking around, spying the best route high above them. "We can get ahead of them that way." He pointed with his free hand. Komat glanced in that direction, then, without a word, started climbing.

As Lando followed, he found himself allowing a smile to creep over his face. The parents were actually pretty good at this. They seemed to always be one step ahead and there was a chance, Lando thought, just a chance, that there might be a happy ending after all.

CHAPTER 46

TAW PROVODE IMPERIAL FUEL FACILITY

NOW

Dathan flexed his shoulder, each movement sending a sharp bolt of pain down his arm. He'd expected to have to fight, and he had mentally prepared himself for a punch-up. What he hadn't expected was for the dull-brown plastoid armor the troopers were wearing to have been so remarkably hard. Dathan's intention had been to drop down from the *Goldstone*'s maintenance hatch directly onto the trooper's head, feetfirst, but at the last second the trooper had moved and it had been Dathan's shoulder that connected with the man's back, clipping the hard ridge of the trooper's backplate as the two men tumbled to the ground.

It had, however, worked—the trooper had been surprised, and before he'd been able to raise any kind of alarm, Dathan had torn his helmet off and rendered him unconscious with a solid punch.

That was part one. Part two had gone a little more according to plan. Slipping the trooper's helmet on, Dathan had sneaked to the edge of the landing pad and, picking his moment, quickly called another trooper over before ducking around to hide behind one of the ship's landing gears. Suspecting nothing—fortunately—the second trooper had walked right into Dathan's trap, and had gone down with a heavy blow to the back of the neck. Dathan had almost bitten his tongue as that attack sent another shock wave of agony up to his jarred shoulder, but he had managed to restrain himself from inadvertently calling out in pain.

Dathan suspected his fists would start to hurt a hell of a lot more than they did now once his nervous system had gotten over the pain in his shoulder. But his plan had worked, although he wasn't really sure if he'd been lucky or if the troopers were just sort of . . . *bad* at their jobs? But he wasn't going to argue with fate. He got the two unconscious troopers out of their armor, safe for the moment in the deep, black shadow-space cast by the hull of the *Goldstone* above him. He glanced up at the ship, where Miramir, following Dathan's plan, would now be jamming the *Goldstone*'s entry ramp before getting on with her other, more specialized task.

They'd done it. In fact, it couldn't have gone better. And now, the pair clad in two sets of armor, Rey hidden in the pack on Miramir's back, Dathan led them toward the landing pad that, according to the *Goldstone*'s systems, held the bounty hunter's own ship.

It was a risk. All of it. Dathan had no doubts about that. But then, everything they did now was a risk. There were no guarantees of success, only the knowledge that a single mistake and everything would be over in an instant.

Dathan pushed the dark thoughts out of his mind again as they hustled down a large thoroughfare, the landing pad ahead of them. Yes, they were in this because of him. But he was damn sure he was going to get his family out of it.

They got closer, and closer. Other troopers, some of whom wore red helmets—the officers, Dathan assumed—ran back and forth, paying them not the slightest bit of attention.

A small victory. Perhaps leading to a larger one. But the worst mistake, Dathan knew, was to become complacent, even cocky. A small victory could easily turn into a large failure.

Almost there, thought Dathan.

Almost. There.

CHAPTER 47

TAW PROVODE IMPERIAL FUEL FACILITY
NOW

Following the family from on high, Lando realized soon enough where they were heading.

Ochi's ship.

Which meant . . . what, exactly? That they were going to meet their pursuer, head-on, in one desperate last stand?

No, that didn't make any sense. But what *did* make sense was another thought that crept into Lando's mind. He almost wanted to run out into the open and cheer the family on.

Because if they were heading to Ochi's ship, disguised as redcaps, then there was only one other thing they could possibly be doing.

They were going to *steal* it.

And Lando was damned if he wasn't going to help them.

Racing across the tanks, Lando lost sight of the family down below, but he figured they had gotten far enough ahead. He signaled to Komat, pointing to an access ladder, and together they made their way down the zigzagged scaffold of gantries and walkways and platforms until they were back at ground level. They emerged into a narrow cut-through between two fuel tank clusters. The shadows here were deep indeed, rendering Lando and Komat completely invisible.

Lando took lead, holstering his blaster for speed, and ran forward. If Komat was behind him or not, it didn't matter. He was just meters away from getting to the family and seeing them to safety.

At the end of the cut-through, he emerged into the light of the main thoroughfare. The landing pad on which Ochi's ship was parked was just on the other side of the next tank cluster, and the path the family was taking was to Lando's north. They would be coming into view any . . . moment . . . *now*—

That was when the fuel dump reverberated to the earsplitting, high-pitched *tang* of a blaster bolt; Lando ducked just as the bolt impacted the ladder beside his head, twisting it into hot scrap that then fell with a hard clatter onto the concrete ground.

Blinking against the sudden flash of light, Lando found himself shoved to the ground; a split second later, all he could hear was a deep *doof-doof-doof-doof* as Komat returned fire with her heavy rifle. Each bolt—shell?—exploded on the other side of the thoroughfare in rapid succession; Lando looked up to see three Espos fly backward through the air, blown off their feet by Komat's high-velocity, high-impact bolts. Then she grabbed Lando by the collar and yanked him to his feet.

"I calculated my attack to bring the other Espos to us," she said. "The family appeared to be quite capable. They will be able to use the confusion as cover." Komat then looked in the other direction. "The Espos now approach."

Lando dropped to one knee, scooping his blaster from its holster and turning away from Komat's line of fire, ready to protect from the other side once more. He wasn't quite sure what quality of trooper the CSA were training, but the fact that the next three ran straight into Komat's line of fire instead of coming back around to approach from Lando's direction told him all he needed to know. He was grateful—not for the first time in his life—that it wasn't old-fashioned Imperial stormtroopers they were facing.

"We have to get to the ship, give them support," Lando yelled, not worried now about giving away their position.

Komat stood and cocked her head. Lando assumed her helmet gave her augmented hearing, but even he could hear the sound of rapidly approaching footfalls.

The rest of the troopers were on their way.

"Komat, come on!" Lando went to leave, but found Komat pulling him back again.

"Aiding the family will reveal their position, Lando Calrissian, and ours also," said Komat. "Better to draw the Espos away, so the family can make good their escape."

Lando stared at Komat, his jaw working as he followed her logic and . . .

And tried to find an argument against it. But she was right. They *could* help them get away. Just not directly.

It was for the best. They'd be safe off this rock.

That didn't stop Lando's wanting to run after them, to help them aboard, to pilot Ochi's ship away from Taw Provode himself.

But he couldn't do that. He knew he couldn't. He wasn't their protector. Hell, they didn't know *who* he was.

But he could still help them. They both could.

Lando nodded, and lifted his blaster. "Fine. Let's go."

The pair stepped out into the thoroughfare, immediately adopting the back-to-back, 360-degree cover pose as they crabbed forward. Komat led the way, her long rifle held out parallel to the ground, her helmet visor fixed to the scope, ready to clear the way for them. Lando held his trusty blaster firmly in his hand, covering their rear.

They proceeded at pace, crisscrossing junctions, stepping from shadow to light to shadow, the pair splitting, covering front, rear, sides, before rejoining and moving on. Lando was just grateful that the CSA redcaps hadn't realized their troopers could get clear shots if they ordered them up into the high gantries.

That progress soon ground to a halt, however, as the Espos began arriving on the scene, the first group of six running around a corner and nearly skidding to a halt when they saw Komat and Lando coming toward them. Before they even had a chance to fire, Komat unleashed a rapid burst from her rifle, Lando swinging out from behind her to add his own, carefully aimed shots to the mix. This succeeded in breaking the group of troopers up, individuals now running for the different pathways and the cover of the tanks and pumps.

This was bad. With the enemy splitting up, Lando and Komat were in very real danger of being surrounded, fast.

"We have to draw them away from Ochi's ship," said Lando, picking off a trooper, then ducking as the Espo's shots flew high. "We need to draw these guys deeper into the fueling area."

Komat nodded. As Lando spun around, loosing a few wide shots to give the Espos something to think about, Komat hefted her rifle and ran for the shadows again—as Lando followed, he could see it was another cutting, a space of deep darkness between two tank clusters. Just as he reached the entrance, he was nearly blinded by a flash of white energy as Komat cut down a trooper who had been coming in from the other side in a valiant attempt to surprise them from behind.

The thoroughfare fell quiet, the remaining Espos having apparently failed to work out where their quarry had gone. Looking around, Lando saw they were back on the main route to Ochi's ship—in fact, the landing pad, glowing under the brilliant lights, was just a hundred meters away. The ship's ramp was still down, but there was now no sign of Ochi himself or any of the CSA.

Then Lando saw the family—they were just a shape, a huddle in the shadow of a fuel pump, but he recognized the lump of the backpack one of them was carrying.

This was it.

"Cover me," Lando said, and he broke from the shadows, running toward the family. He was exposed, running in a direct line, an easy target. But he was going to make it.

He didn't know *how* he knew, but . . . he knew.

Behind him, the heavy *thud* of Komat's gun, the harsh *tang* of the CSA blasters.

In front, one part of the huddle broke away from the other, and moved out a little into the light, looking back at Lando. He wasn't sure who it was, mother or father, and it didn't matter.

All that mattered was that they get on that ship.

"Go! Go!" Lando yelled, waving both arms at the figure in a clear gesture to *get the hell out of here.* Responding, the figure waved, not at Lando, but at their partner, who emerged from the shadows and, hand in hand with the other, turned and ran toward the landing pad.

That was when a pair of Espos emerged from a side route. They stopped, apparently surprised to see two officers running, then they seemed to realize they weren't CSA and raised their weapons to take aim.

Lando yelled something—he wasn't entirely sure what—and opened fire in a desperate attempt to buy the family the little extra time they needed.

His wildly fired shots found their mark. The two Espos fell back, Lando's blaster bolts exploding directly against their breastplates. Lando paused just long enough to check that they weren't getting up again, then ran for the landing pad, his blaster already raised, ready to take out any opposition that might have stopped the family from getting aboard.

He needn't have worried. He made it just a few more meters before the twin engines of Ochi's ship roared into life and the vehicle turned on the pad, the exhaust pointed right at Lando. He ducked, covering his head in his hands, but even at this distance, the heat and engine wash were intense. He felt himself gently lifted up, like he was being scooped by a single, giant hand, and the moving air around him was first warm then suddenly very, very hot.

He hit the hard ground on his shoulder, and rolled with it, allowing his momentum and the engine wash to push him along the ground. His right shoulder jolted, sending electric arcs of pain up and down his side, but Lando gritted his teeth and did his best to stop himself hitting his head against the concrete.

As the roar of the ship's engines receded, Lando unfolded himself and flopped onto his stomach. At once, he pushed himself up with his hands, ignoring the way his entire nervous system sang in protest, and looked around.

Ochi's ship was a fast-disappearing dot of light, almost impossible to follow, even when Lando shaded his eyes against the glare of the floodlight towers. Around him, he counted bodies—twelve in all, CSA troopers and one redcap.

Of Komat, there was no sign.

CHAPTER 48

THE *STAR HERALD*, UNKNOWN REGIONS
NOW

The *Star Herald* leapt across the galaxy, the powerful engines of the prototype scout ship collapsing the endless gulfs of space, twisting the vessel through the hyperspace lanes with no effort at all.

Luke had arrived at his mystery destination.

He hadn't known what to expect. The coordinates taken from the droid lander's navicomputer were just that—numbers, referenced as standard from the galactic center. The *Star Herald*'s onboard databank was more up-to-date than the one in the *Lady Luck,* but Luke still found little information about where he was headed, even when he consulted charts from New Republic intelligence.

This truly was the Unknown Regions. And as soon as the *Star Herald* snapped back into realspace, Luke had a fair idea of just why this particular quadrant was so uncharted.

The entire forward view was occupied by a vast, red nebula, but unlike any Luke had seen on his travels. Far from a static cloud of ionized gas, this one roiled and curled, the jagged cloud layers moving and flashing with red energy. As Luke piloted the ship closer, he saw something else, too—something moving, something vast and unknown; a colossal, monstrous, living form, hinted at, but not actually seen.

Luke decided not to investigate. The sensor readings were all over the place, his navicomputer protesting at the scale of the interference emanating from the cloud.

Fortunately, the crimson nightmare was not his intended destination. Checking the coordinates again, Luke piloted the *Star Herald* to a large asteroid that floated on the edge of the nebula, from his current viewpoint nothing but a black, ragged outline silhouetted against the evil red glare of the impenetrable cloud behind it.

As they came in, skimming the asteroid's terrain, R2-D2 wailed mournfully, and Luke thought he knew exactly how the little droid felt.

The asteroid was just that—a rock, albeit one with enough mass for standard gravity—gravity that, it became apparent, had brought many ships crashing down to the surface.

The asteroid was a graveyard, the tumbling terrain littered with the shattered hulls of a thousand starships, big and small, one-person fighters and scouts to corvettes, cruisers, both military and civilian. The asteroid may not have had a sun, but the wrecks were all bathed in the malignant red light of the nebula.

R2-D2 bleeped again, quietly. Luke glanced down at the readout and laughed.

"Yes, Artoo," he said. "I have a bad feeling about this as well."

Ahead was what passed for a mountain range on the asteroid, the upper slopes of which were free of wreckage. As the *Star Herald* approached, R2-D2 twittered excitedly. One hand on the controls, Luke reached up and double-checked the sensors. They were still swamped by interference, but they were starting to pick up strong local readings that cut through the fog of noise.

"I see it," said Luke. "An energy signature. I think we're getting close."

They passed over the ridge of the mountain, and Luke couldn't help but gasp at the view ahead.

The shipwrecks continued on this side of the asteroid, but rising from the center was a massive curved shape, the broken shell of a huge ship that had once been almost spherical—a Separatist core ship, a relic from a war that had been fought before Luke had even been born. Here it sat, like a giant smashed eggshell, the surviving superstructure towering over the graveyard. It might have been not a starship, but a vast sculpture crafted by a forgotten, esoteric civilization.

Luke pulled the *Star Herald* in a tight arc around the core ship, and R2-D2 beeped again. The energy reading was stronger here, and a new indicator lit up on the *Star Herald*'s sensor bank. Glancing down to get a bearing, Luke then peered through the forward viewport as the structure swung by below them.

"This is it," he said.

From the cracked side of the core ship hull, a shimmering haze was clearly visible, rising from an exhaust port. Something was still active inside.

Kiza. This was the place.

"Okay, Artoo," said Luke. "Here we go."

He picked a spot that was clear enough of ship debris, and rotated the *Star Herald* for landing. Checking the readings once more, he saw that the asteroid had a thin atmosphere. All he would need was a basic rebreather.

Ship on firm ground, Luke unstrapped himself from his seat and stood to leave. R2-D2 chattered away, but Luke laid a gentle hand on his dome.

"This might be dangerous," he said. "You wait here. Have the ship ready for takeoff as soon as I give the signal."

With that, Luke headed out. R2-D2 whistled at his retreating back, and Luke laughed.

"Thanks," he said. "I might need it."

CHAPTER 49

THE SEPULCHRE, KIZA'S WORLD, UNKNOWN REGIONS

NOW

It wasn't hard to find his way into the core ship interior. Once inside, the environment seemed a little better—the air was stale, but breathable, and it was much warmer than the asteroid surface. It was also pitch black.

Luke pocketed the rebreather, nothing more than a simple silver cylinder with a mouthpiece, and unclipped his lightsaber. He held it above his head and activated the blade, the brilliant beam of green energy providing ample light for his journey onward.

Onward to . . . where, exactly? While the ship was a wreck, it was also still a truly mammoth structure. Luke knew he could walk for hours—days—inside the thing, without finding the source of the energy signature. Getting lost was easy.

He thought for a moment of calling R2-D2 to accompany him—the droid would be able to follow the energy signature easily—but dismissed the idea. He had been telling the truth when he said it was dangerous, and while the astromech was a capable little droid, Luke didn't want to do anything that would place him in deliberate danger.

So instead, Luke closed his eyes for a moment. He reached out, with one hand, feeling for a direction.

It was easy to find. That presence—or rather, that *absence*—in the Force was clear.

She was here, with the mask. And he knew exactly where to go.

Luke opened his eyes and, boots echoing on the metal walkways, proceeded to the heart of the ship.

After a short while, Luke stopped and lowered his lightsaber. The chamber ahead, while not exactly well lit, was certainly not the pitch dark of the rest of the core ship. He approached with caution—still following his instincts, tied to the disturbance in the Force that rang as clear as a bell in his mind, and while that meant he knew he'd reached the right place, he still had no real idea of what might be waiting for him in the room beyond.

Crossing the threshold, he found himself in a huge, vaulted chamber—it might have been the ship's main hangar, although it was hard to tell. Looking up, he saw that many interior floors had collapsed, enlarging the space beyond its original design, the curve of the ceiling disappearing up in the darkness. The structure groaned, just faintly. Luke wondered how stable the ruin truly was.

Various pieces of equipment and control consoles were dotted around the walls, their multicolored lights gently winking in the gloom. The light Luke had seen was a soft white glow emanating from the large object at the far end of the chamber: a multifaceted polyhedron, split horizontally across the middle, with the upper half suspended in the air. The opening between, from which the white light shone, had an edge that followed the lines of the object's many facets, making the whole thing look like a giant set of many-toothed jaws, ready to trap the unwary—a meditation chamber, perhaps. Not something that belonged in a Separatist core ship, but another relic retrieved by Kiza.

In front of this chamber, silhouetted by the white light from within, were ranks of deactivated droids. All were kneeling; all faced the light. Luke cautiously stepped around them, his lightsaber at the ready. Closer to the front, he saw marks on the floor where some droids had been removed.

Eleven empty spaces.

Eleven kyber-crystal-empowered droids, sent to Polaar to take the crystal shards Luke had found on Yoturba, and which were now very safely hidden inside R2-D2.

He stepped closer, lowering the lightsaber to illuminate the floor. From each empty position were drag marks, all of them converging into a single path that wound around the side of the central chamber.

Luke followed the trail, still wary, still aware that despite his discoveries—despite what he could feel in the Force—it seemed that Kiza and her mask weren't actually present.

Around the back of the chamber, a large bulkhead led through to another room, still huge but far smaller in scale than the main vault. Luke stepped through, noticing the heavy blast door sitting on a railing right over his head as he entered the room. He stopped in front of a raised, cylindrical structure that sat in the center of the room, to one side of it a large, carbonized slab of black iron and a worktable littered with tools that were likewise scorched. The cylindrical structure itself had a cover consisting of several panels, like the folded petals of a flower. The panels were ajar, allowing flickering tongues of blue-green flame to escape.

It took Luke a moment to recognize the chamber for what it was— a droid forge, albeit one of an old, long-since-discontinued design. Looking up, he scanned the curved ceiling and spotted the jutting square opening of the forge's exhaust port, which would lead to the external port on the ship's outer hull, which was the source of the energy signature Luke had seen from the *Star Herald*.

Luke turned in a circle, casting the glow of his lightsaber into every corner as he looked around. Satisfied the droid forge was empty, he headed back into the main vault.

There.

He circled the meditation chamber, peering into the white glow to see inside. As his eyes adjusted, he could see it had been turned into a nest. Bundles of cloth and blankets lay around scattered books—as with the small library he had managed to gather at his own temple, these looked like ancient and rare tomes and folios, bound in leather, their pages crafted from paper, vellum, leviahide, quartzleaf, and other archaic materials—while the interior walls of the chamber seemed to be covered with scrawled writing.

To one side of the meditation chamber's center stood a small plinth, the same burnished bronze as the ancient relic that sat on top of it.

The mask of Viceroy Exim Panshard.

As soon as that thought came to mind, Luke heard it. Whispers, indecipherable mutterings that were so close, it was like someone was standing at his shoulder, their lips brushing his ear.

Luke resisted the urge to turn and check, knowing that while the voices were very much real, there was nobody there with him.

The only person with him was Viceroy Exim Panshard, the spirit of the long-dead Sith Lord haunting the mask on the plinth.

Steeling himself, Luke stepped into the meditation chamber, not taking his eyes from the mask for a second. He could end it, here and now. One cut from his lightsaber and he could cleave the mask in two. Exim Panshard would be no more.

That was when Luke's head was filled with a single, endless scream, a cry of agony so immeasurably awful, so uncountably ancient, that Luke could do nothing to stop himself falling onto his knees, his deactivated lightsaber clattering away on the floor as he pressed both hands against the sides of his head.

Gritting his teeth against the pain, Luke looked up at the mask.

And he saw—

. . . a forest at night. The mist rising, the sky clear, and across it, a brilliant flare of light as a star falls, carving a path of red and white across the heavens. Luke feels the orbak kick beneath him, the animal rising up in fear, and feels his own hand tighten on the whip as he cruelly strikes his steed, driving it forward into the night, toward the place where the star fell . . .

And he saw—

. . . a great hall, filled with people, a mighty feast, a fire roaring, performers spinning and juggling and throwing knives for the entertainment of

their liege, their viceroy, who sits upon his jeweled throne. His heart is as black as his iron crown and his barked command causes a wave of panic to spread across the hall, noblemen and their guests frozen in fear, their lord and master displeased by their efforts. The viceroy stands, steps down from the throne, as his jesters kowtow and beg for their lives. The viceroy smiles, but it is a cruel smile, and he takes the black iron rod that hangs from his belt. Somebody screams as the red blade appears, long and curved, a scimitar made of the dying light of a red sun and of the hate of Viceroy Exim Panshard. He beheads the jester, then stands and laughs, and laughs, and laughs, and his court laughs with him . . .

And he saw—

. . . a blacksmith's hammer strikes again, and again, and again. The metal he pounds is white-hot, but it is not enough. He takes the sheet of meteoric metal and holds it to the plasma furnace. He closes his eyes, begging for more time, pleading for his life. Beside him, in his iron crown, Viceroy Exim Panshard smiles and lifts his weapon. The blacksmith cowers and closes his eyes, but when the red blade spits into terrible existence, the viceroy plunges it not into the blacksmith's body but into the plasma furnace. Sparks shower, catching the forge alight, the heat almost unbearable. But when the blacksmith pulls the metal back to the anvil, it is malleable, workable, as soft as silk. The blacksmith, his red face peeling from the blast of the fire, begins to work. Roughly shaped, still ablaze with sunlike intensity, the blacksmith holds the glowing metal up to the viceroy and asks again what his master desires he forge. And the viceroy takes the offering in one gloved hand, his gauntlet catching fire and falling away as the very flesh of his hand smolders and smokes, and he tells the blacksmith it is to be a mask. The blacksmith tries to move, but finds he cannot; he is held by some mysterious power, the pure force of the viceroy's will. The blacksmith's frozen body rises from the floor as the viceroy releases the metal, the two objects now held in the viceroy's grip as he completes his design. The blacksmith screams as the hot starstuff slowly, inexorably, floats toward his own face—screams that are cut short as the metal seals itself onto his face, molding itself in the twisted agonal form of a dying man . . .

And he saw—

... *the great hall, another feast, but the only sounds are the muted noises of eating, and the roar of the great fire in the hearth. Viceroy Exim Panshard sits upon his throne, his face hidden behind a mask of burnished bronze that fell from the stars. There is no nose, a line of rivets marks the mouth, the two eyes are black glass voids. He sits in silence. He does not eat. He does not drink. His court will not look at him. Finally, he demands they gaze upon his new face—the face of their master. The courtiers look at one another, afraid. Viceroy Exim Panshard stands from his throne, his red scimitar ablaze with a new rage they scarcely thought possible, the sound of the curved blade the sound of the end of the world. And the court members scream as he cuts them all down, and when they are all dead, he continues to cut, until there is nothing left but blood, ankle-deep, and the echoing screams of the dead inside his cold mask of meteoric metal . . .*

And he saw—

... *the town that huddles next to the great castle, where the lord, who once offered protection from the darkness, now offers only death. The town burns, the citizens huddled in rags, being driven in huge lines by soldiers in black metal masks of their own, crude facsimiles of the midnight gaze of their master, Viceroy Exim Panshard. The viceroy himself stands under the great castle gate, his red scimitar of light held aloft, as his subjects are marched into huge murder engines, machines of moving conveyors and churning blades built to do nothing but kill in numbers vast and terrible. And as the viceroy watches, he can hear nothing at all, except the scream-ing in his head, and the boil of blood in his own ears. And he can feel the power grow. The more he kills, the stronger he becomes, the screams of the dead adding to the others that echo inside the mask, their essence, their life force, adding to his own. Soon, he will be able to do the impossible. Soon, he will be able to transcend death itself. The reign of Viceroy Exim Panshard will be long and it will be terrible, and this is good, and he laughs, and laughs, and laughs . . .*

CHAPTER 50

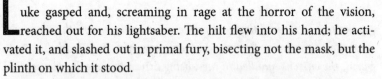

THE SEPULCHRE, KIZA'S WORLD, UNKNOWN REGIONS
NOW

Luke gasped and, screaming in rage at the horror of the vision, reached out for his lightsaber. The hilt flew into his hand; he activated it, and slashed out in primal fury, bisecting not the mask, but the plinth on which it stood.

The top half of the plinth slid, then toppled to the floor with a heavy, dead thud, the mask itself spinning into a corner, where it lay, facing away from Luke. As Luke heaved for breath, out of the corner of his eye he could see the darkness behind the mask roll like smoke. Quickly, he turned away, realizing now just how powerful the ancient Sith spirit truly was.

Relics, both of the Jedi and of the Sith, had power. True power. For some, this was literal, as well as symbolic—lightsabers, for example, were a particular prize sought by the Acolytes of the Beyond, and others. Some relics were useful less as weapons than as signs and sigils, reinforcing beliefs and seeding new ones. Others again held knowledge once lost—stories of other times and places, promises of secrets, and codes, and paths to power and glory and control, if only they could be understood.

But some relics held something else. Something truly terrible, the vestigial influence of those who had crafted them, or used them, or worn them. Those powerful in the Force could leave an impression.

Some could even leave something more.

Like Viceroy Exim Panshard.

"He's alive," came the voice. It was tired, and female, the accent from a moon of the Pantora system.

Still on his knees, Luke turned his head toward the source.

Kiza.

She was standing in the vault, in the space where one of the eleven droids had once stood. She was still in her tattered black robes, but without the cloak, revealing bare blue arms, streaked at the shoulders with golden tattoos, the marks of her family. Luke looked at her face, framed by long dark hair that was black in the gloom of the chamber. Her golden eyes matched the golden tattoos.

Neither of them moved.

"He is still here, with us now," said Kiza. "He has promised me many things. He has promised me power and glory. He has promised me the galaxy."

Luke narrowed his eyes. There was something about the way she said it, her voice flat, like it was something she had recited to herself again and again in an attempt to, somehow, believe it.

But Luke knew the truth. He stood and stepped out of the meditation chamber, slowly shaking his head.

"That isn't what you want, is it? Search your feelings. Exim Panshard's time has come and gone a long, long time ago."

Kiza snarled, the expression almost animalistic.

"You're wrong," she said. "He's here. He's with me. He is always with me. It is through me that his destiny will be fulfilled. He will rise again, through me. Together, we will become one, something more powerful than even the Jedi can imagine."

"It's not possible," said Luke. "The dead cannot rejoin the living. That power you can feel is nothing but an echo, a shadow from a long time ago. And that shadow is *using* you, Kiza. You know this. You know I speak the truth. You are being manipulated. You are a tool, obeying nothing but the dying echo of an evil that has long been vanquished. A shadow whose power *you* control, if you choose it."

Kiza's expression softened. In the light cast by the meditation chamber, her eyes looked wet. Luke could see the muscles of her jaw bunching. He couldn't imagine what was going through her mind.

"I serve my Master," she said. "I . . . I have to serve him."

Luke shook his head again.

"No, you don't."

"He has shown me many things."

"You are master to nobody but yourself, Kiza."

"He has shown me wonders."

"Listen to your feelings."

Kiza gave a half smile, and lifted her arms as she looked around. "We found all of this." She lowered her arms and glanced at the remaining rows of dead droids. "We built an army. Together. He showed me the way, and I was his hands . . ."

Luke gritted his teeth. He could feel something now, a pressure in the back of his mind, a presence again, growing stronger.

He didn't have much time.

"I can help you." He reached out with one hand, palm-up, ready to take hers. He took a single step forward. "I can free you."

Kiza turned to Luke. She looked at his hand, then looked at his face. Her expression flickered, her gaze distant and unfocused.

"I . . . I'm so tired," she said, softly. "All these years, I've worked so hard. He promised me . . . promised me . . ."

"Evil lies. It is what it does."

"I . . . I will be free. Soon. We are so close. So very, very close. And when we are done, I will be free."

Luke shook his head. "I can help you right now, Kiza. I can see what the mask has done to you. How it *feeds* off you, off your anger and your pain. The more you suffer, the stronger it gets. It will kill you, and then when you die, it will find someone else. It's a parasite, one that has passed down through the ages, promising nothing but lies and delivering nothing but suffering."

Kiza swayed a little on her feet. Luke lowered his outstretched hand and watched her. Had she even heard what he was saying?

"He has promised to take me there. He has promised me I will be healed. Rebirth. Glorious rebirth."

"Where, Kiza?"

At this, her eyes snapped up to his, her focus suddenly laser-sharp.

"To Exegol. To the place of rebirth. Both for him, and for me."

"There is nothing for you on Exegol."

"He promised me. The geometries of power can show the path, the parts connected to the whole, and together they can seek them out and be one."

Then she reached out, her fingers clawing the air, searching for—

"Where are they?" She looked back up at Luke's face, her own twisted in pain. "Where are the crystals?"

"They're somewhere safe. I can take you there." Luke held out his hand again. "Come with me. I can help you. Please."

Kiza looked at his hand. Luke took another step closer, their outstretched hands almost in touching distance. "I can get you out of this place, away from the mask. I can help you rid it from your mind, forever."

Kiza looked into his face.

"Exim Panshard is dead," Luke continued. "He has no power over you, not if you don't want him to."

She looked at his hand, and then—

She took it. Her skin was cool in Luke's grip. He gently closed his hand around hers. He looked at her, and gave a faint smile. He opened his mouth to speak—

And then she yanked him toward her, throwing Luke off balance as she spun sideways, out of his way, but still gripping his hand tightly. As she turned, she pulled her lightsaber from her belt and ignited it. The red blaze of the curved Sith blade cast a glow to the vault like the light of the nebula outside. Hissing in anger, Kiza pulled Luke back toward her and swung for the killing blow.

But Luke was faster. He yanked his hand up at an angle, slipping out of her grasp. Regaining his footing as Kiza lost hers, he had his lightsaber in his hand, the blade activated just as Kiza, recovered, snarled and aimed a two-handed strike directly at Luke's head. She swung down; Luke blocked Kiza's attack, the force of the impact jolting his entire body. Then he lifted a foot and shoved her in the stomach. Kiza reeled backward with a cry, tripping onto the floor, her lightsaber gouging the decking of the core ship in a shower of sparks.

Luke stood back and fell into a defensive position, but this time he was prepared to press his attack.

"Please," he said. "I was telling you the truth. I don't want to hurt you. I don't want to kill you." He adjusted his grip on his weapon. "But I will do what I have to."

The pressure in the back of his mind seemed to rise up. He watched as Kiza righted herself and stepped backward, the curved edge of her lightsaber bouncing on the decking, causing tiny, percussive bangs with every step. She was now by the side of the meditation chamber.

She reached toward it with her free hand.

"No!" Luke called out, but it was too late.

The mask of Viceroy Exim Panshard flew through the air, emerging from the meditation chamber. Luke, too far away to strike it, reached out with his hands and tried to grab the object with the Force, willing it to halt in midair. Anything to stop Kiza from getting it.

But as Luke tried to direct his will toward it, he heard the screams of the dead, now loud enough, real enough that they echoed around the entire vault, waves of sound like the rolling of an ocean tumbling around the interior of the sepulchral chamber. The mask itself slowed in the air, but it did not stop—in the Force, it was too heavy, too big, too *undefined*, a shadow of a dark power, cast long. For all his power, Luke could not stop it, only slow it. And as he watched, it floated with a smooth and easy grace until it was in front of Kiza's face. She stepped forward, *into* the mask, and Luke knew the battle for Kiza's soul was lost.

But he would not give up.

Luke Skywalker would *never* give up.

He concentrated, focusing his mind, listening now to the maelstrom of noise around him. They were the voices of the dead, the thousands of lives that Exim Panshard had ended, absorbing their life force to gain power, enough to survive in his last relic, his ritual mask of meteoric bronze.

Luke owed it to them. It was not revenge, or punishment, but . . .

Justice.

Kiza leapt forward, sailing high into the ruined space of the vault; at the top of her arc, she spun her red lightsaber so the curve of the blade was aimed at Luke, then she fell toward him, her tattered robes streaming out behind her, intent on landing a single, vicious killing blow.

But as she landed, Luke batted her blade away then instantly somersaulted up, tumbling head over heels right over the top of her, landing on his feet behind her. He swept his own weapon back and was met with a solid parry. Her riposte was strong, but his own defense stronger. They stood, trading blows, each perfectly aimed, each perfectly defended.

Luke didn't know who he was fighting. Kiza was no Sith, but Exim Panshard's ancient power flowed through her, guiding her actions as she fought with fierce determination, never pausing in her search for a gap in Luke's own defenses.

Luke, for his part, kept his attacks in check, withholding, but ready to unleash his power if needed.

But he really hoped it wouldn't come to that. Kiza was, literally, a woman possessed. Yes, she had trodden a dark path, even before she had been given the mask. She had been a criminal since an early age. A thief. A *murderer*. That she had to pay for her actions was never in question.

But she wasn't a Sith, and Luke knew, as he faced her now, that she wasn't in complete control of her actions.

Luke was sure he could save her, turn her toward the light, as he had done with Komat. The price Kiza would have to pay may be higher than her Acolyte sister, but it was better than a lifetime—a *short* lifetime—of pain and suffering under the thrall of the dark power that emanated from the evil relic.

Luke stepped back, and back again, deflecting Kiza's attacks, parrying with his own, but only to throw her off target, interrupting lightsaber blows and cutting off lines of attack.

But she seemed well aware of what he was doing. She picked up the pace, her swings far wider, far stronger, than the previous light work. Her blade hummed through the air, left and right, cutting swaths toward Luke.

Luke deflected each, feeling the steadily increasing violence of each blow as Kiza strengthened her attack. In their duel they had moved all across the great vault, and now, backing away as he reconsidered his tactics, Luke found himself standing among the remaining rows of dead droids.

This didn't stop Kiza. She swung, her blade bouncing from Luke's, slicing clean through the droids, their neatly divided forms falling to the floor, the cut edges glowing red hot. Kiza's attacks were getting ever wilder, her blade now gouging the floor, slicing even the fallen droid bodies, as she pushed Luke back and back again.

He had to stop this. But he also had to wait—he could see now that his moment of opportunity was approaching.

Kiza was tiring, the elemental evil that was the remaining will of Exim Panshard pushing the possessed body to its limit. She couldn't continue much longer.

Luke spun as he countered another blow, sliding his blade along hers, sending lightning flashes of energy strobing the dim night of the vault. He pushed, then turned on his feet, forcing Kiza to turn with him.

Now he began pushing her back, wearing down what strength she had remaining with a barrage of powerful, controlled strikes.

It was working. Kiza's blade was flung left and right, hitting the floor, hitting more droids. It was a noble effort, but she was now very much on the defensive.

The Jedi Master now controlled the duel.

They had made their way back behind the meditation chamber, and still Kiza would not yield. Instead, she screamed in fury, her voice augmented by the viceroy's mask, and she pushed Luke back with a flurry of attacks—high and low, high and low, each swing of her blade met with a bang as the two energy blades shorted against each other. Opening a gap between them, she turned and darted into the droid forge.

Luke followed, wary. The forge was comparatively small. A fight in there would be a close one, with limited room to maneuver.

Was that what she wanted? To end it? Was she merely seeking refuge, a moment to recover her strength?

Or did the mask have another strategy?

The furnace purred loudly behind Kiza. Luke moved into the doorway, his blade ready, his eyes on his opponent. Kiza's chest rose and fell heavily as she heaved for breath on the opposite side of the furnace. Then, blade raised, she began to stalk around it. Luke matched her every movement, keeping the heat of the machinery between them.

"You can stop this," he called out, over the sound of the furnace. "You say the mask has given you power. So use it. Use it to end your pain." Luke pointed to the center of the forge with his lightsaber blade. "You can destroy the mask. You can destroy the power that has a hold on you. You can end this." He paused, lowering his blade slightly, reaching out with his other hand. "*We* can end this."

Kiza stood watching him, her head tilted, her hair spilling out around the blank metal face, her shoulders rising and falling, rising and falling. Her red lightsaber was now hanging loosely from her hand, the curved tip of the energy blade buzzing near the floor.

"I can't stop it," she said, quietly. Her voice still echoed from behind the mask, but the deep resonance was different. This wasn't Exim Panshard speaking. It was Kiza, the kid from Pantora who had stolen a lightsaber so many years ago, who had been used by Yupe Tashu for his own sinister ends, who had killed first her lover Remi and then Yupe Tashu himself as she succumbed to the power of a relic she couldn't control and the curse of a future she'd never wanted. "He's too powerful," she said. "There's no way out for me."

"There is. With me."

She shook her head. "No. I have already made my choice. I follow my Master's will. Only when our task is complete shall I have my freedom."

And with that, she lifted the lightsaber of Darth Noctyss, and, yelling in rage, launched herself over the top of the furnace, the flame billowing as she flew through it and landed in front of Luke, so close he found himself face-to-face with the relic mask, separated from Kiza by only his green blade as he pushed with all his strength against her red one. He looked into the black glass of the mask's eyes, but could see nothing but a green light in one, a red light in the other.

With a yell, he pushed back. She fell against the side of the furnace, her lightsaber flailing. It sliced straight through the side of the furnace, down to the floor. As Kiza twisted to regain her footing, she pulled the blade back, cutting a parallel line through the furnace base before ripping the weapon out and stumbling back out through the door. Luke was right behind her, but he came to a crashing halt as Kiza turned on her heel and gestured with both hands, her lightsaber still lit.

There was a metallic crack as something broke above Luke's head. He looked up, and ducked back just as the blast door of the droid forge slid down, slamming shut and trapping Luke inside.

Behind him, the furnace roared, its flame guttering for a moment before exploding in a huge torch of fire, shattering the petals of its lid as the released energy of the furnace burst up to reach the ceiling of the chamber. As Luke watched, his back to the blast door, the lightsaber incisions on the side of the furnace base glowed brilliant blue and yellow, and then the structure buckled, then shattered, spilling glowing molten slag in a waist-high wave that sloshed and rolled toward him with surprising speed.

Luke deactivated his lightsaber and, using the Force, leapt up, as high as he could go, catching the edge of the forge's exhaust port. He gritted his teeth as the hot metal burned the fingers of his human hand, and let it go, allowing himself to swing only by his cybernetic one. Looking down, he saw the burning contents of the split furnace boil, the lethal, white-hot mix of molten elements bubbling and spitting as it continued to pour from the wrecked forge, channeled up from what Luke assumed was some vast reservoir beneath.

Luke didn't need the Force to sense what was coming next. The slag erupted into a geyser, rising high in the air; Luke swung himself toward the blast door, and just as the geyser hit the exhaust port he had just been holding on to, Luke let go, at the same time igniting his lightsaber and throwing it at the blast door mechanism high on the wall in front of him. The weapon spun, a wheel of blurring green energy, slicing through the rail that held the door in place. As his boots touched the top of the door, he gave himself another push using the Force and kicked the heavy door down with all the mass and momentum of a stampeding bantha bull. As his lightsaber boomeranged back into his outstretched hand, he continued his flight, landing with a roll on a patch of hot decking behind the meditation chamber. He quickly stood, patting the charred edge of his cloak, which had caught in the river of molten material that still flowed from the furnace and was now pouring out into the main vault itself.

Luke looked up. Kiza was standing on the upper half of the meditation chamber's roof, balanced with all the precision of a master of the Force, the hilt of her lightsaber held in a firm grip.

A river of molten slag made Luke sidestep as it flowed past him and began to pool around the base of the meditation chamber. The old ceramic structure cracked with a sharp series of retorts, the geometric tiles that made up its casing starting to disintegrate as the slag lapped around the edges, then finally found a way inside.

The effect was instantaneous, the entire contents of the chamber igniting in a *whoomph,* yellow flames now licking the jagged edges of the open chamber as the heat of the slag began to consume the contents.

Luke thought about the books and relics inside, things so rare and precious and important, thought about the knowledge that was about to be lost forever. He looked up, but Kiza had gone as the flames continued to grow.

Luke deactivated his lightsaber and dived forward, both arms across his face as a shield. Then, just as he was about to pass through the meditation chamber entrance and hit the wall of flame straight-on, he opened his arms, sweeping them across and to the side.

The wall of flame buckled, then parted as the huge gust of air, driven by Luke's use of the Force, temporarily sucked the life out of the fire. Luke didn't have much time—he knew that in just moments, his desperate action would stoke the fire rather than extinguish it—so he continued through the meditation chamber, not stopping to collect anything, instead sweeping his arms again, using the Force to drag the burning tomes out of the chamber and into the vault. The ancient papers scattered as some of the smoking bindings failed under the stress, filling the vault with a blizzard of drifting pages, the ones of paper and animal hide alight, others of quartzleaf and more hardy materials thankfully impervious to the heat. The storm of material spiraled up into the air before beginning to settle among the ruined droids.

Luke rolled on the floor as he exited the meditation chamber, and he remained curled as the fire reclaimed that which he had momentarily denied it. The heat washed over him—then suddenly intensified with an electric crackling. Luke moved himself forward, head still bowed, then risked a look behind him.

The fire was now an inferno, the entire meditation chamber ablaze as the material from which it was built now caught fire itself, burning with a fizzing white light. Within moments, it would be reduced to ash, and as Luke glanced around the debris in the vault, he saw he had at least managed to save some of the tomes and folios that Kiza had collected over the years.

Now he just had to save Kiza herself.

Shielding his face against the glare with one arm, he stepped toward it. Already his exposed skin was hot. He couldn't get much closer. Kiza had been standing on top of the chamber. Surely she must have been caught in the blast.

And then she appeared. Luke sensed the movement first, felt the air part, before he looked up and saw her falling toward him again from somewhere high in the vault, Sith lightsaber blade held downward, ready for a second attempt to slice through her target.

Luke dived to the left, and Kiza landed exactly where he had been standing, the impact of her fall driving her lightsaber into the decking up to the hilt. Luke activated his own weapon, sweeping the humming blade up just in time as Kiza pulled her lightsaber from the floor and, without pause, charged at him.

Luke deflected the first attack, then the second, allowing himself to be pushed back. But Kiza was once again possessed by the rage of Exim Panshard, the Sith spirit pushing his physical puppet body beyond endurance. Kiza wouldn't stop. She would continue until she fell.

Until the spirit of Viceroy Exim Panshard literally *broke* her.

Luke held her strikes at bay, taking a moment to study his opponent. While Kiza was not a Sith herself, and was not trained in the art of lightsaber combat, neither—Luke realized—was Exim Panshard. He fought with fury and rage and skill born of pure experience and the methods of older, lost forms of hand-to-hand, blade-to-blade combat, making the attacks unpredictable, but often ineffective against the mastery of a true Jedi.

Kiza began to falter, and Luke pressed his attack, carefully pushing her back, navigating his opponent through the wrecked droids. Her blade snapped left and right, cutting more of the machines down until just a few were left standing.

Then she stumbled, fell backward, and banged the back of her head hard on a fallen droid's carapace. The viceroy's mask fell off on impact, leaving Kiza's face exposed, the blood that smeared her mouth and chin reflecting the glare of the firelight as the meditation chamber continued to burn. Her lightsaber sparked against the floor, then the blade vanished, leaving a smoking gouge on the metal decking.

She blinked and looked up at Luke, her chest once again heaving for breath. Luke stood over her and deactivated his lightsaber. He held out his human hand.

"Join me."

Kiza didn't move. Her golden eyes flicked between Luke's outstretched hand and his face.

And then, still ignoring his hand, she pushed herself to her feet. Luke took a step back to give her room, aware now of the heat in the vault, of the way the metal of the entire structure was sounding a protest as the ruin itself began to weaken.

If Kiza was going to do this, it had to be on her terms. Luke knew that. That he had managed to get through to her at all was the real battle won. Now he had to tread carefully, show that her trust in him was not misplaced.

Kiza stood, her long blue-black hair, greasy with ash and sweat, framing her blue face. In the firelight, her golden tattoos seemed to glow.

"Join me," said Luke again.

Kiza looked up, and then she uttered just a single word in reply.

"No."

It happened fast. She reached out, not to Luke, but to her side. In a second, the mask of Viceroy Exim Panshard flew from the floor and into her hand, and this time she put it on herself, willingly. Mask in place, the black glass eyes flashed red as she ignited her lightsaber and once again swung at Luke.

Luke stepped to the side, avoiding her attack, his heart racing along with his mind, but he knew that she had made her decision. She was lost to the mask, to the endless night of Exim Panshard, and she knew it, and nothing he could say would make any difference.

There was a heavier groan from above; Luke glanced up quickly, scanning the curving shell of the dead ship's hull, lit by the burning meditation chamber, the white flames now reaching meters into the air, lapping at the already distressed metal of the wreck high above them.

Then it happened. Part of the upper hull failed, the superstructure collapsing in on itself, a huge panel at first folding, then falling. Kiza looked up, the panel coming straight down for her.

Luke reached out, shoving Kiza clear with the Force, but it was too late. There was a deafening crash as the hull panel came down, the floor bucking under the impact hard enough to throw Luke off his feet.

Luke turned off his lightsaber and raced toward the debris. The panel was huge, a giant triangular shard as long as the *Star Herald*. Luke had managed to push Kiza out of the way, but only just. Kiza lay on the floor, her lightsaber-arm trapped, and most certainly crushed, by the panel. The mask was gone, and her eyes were closed. Her mouth and jaw were covered in blood.

Luke knelt by her body, feeling for a pulse, finding none. Quickly searching her body, he pulled back her robes and immediately found the cause of death—a jagged metal shard had pierced her chest, straight through her heart.

Luke sank to the floor, his head bowed. Then he looked up at Kiza's face.

"There should have been another way," he muttered, to nobody.

Muffled explosions made him turn around. The river of molten slag had continued to flow during their fight and was now spreading out across the vault floor, causing the fallen droids to explode as it consumed them. All over the vault, the scattered items Luke had saved from the meditation chamber began to ignite as they were caught in its path, even the quartzleaf sheets stiffening, then shattering like tissue-thin glass panes in the heat.

Luke stood and looked around.

The mask was gone. He searched, first with his eyes, then he reached out and felt with the Force, but felt nothing.

More explosions. The vault rumbled and rocked. High above, more groans, and then the earsplitting shriek of metal tearing under its own weight.

Luke jumped aside as another, smaller portion of the upper hull crashed down. Before long, the entire structure would collapse.

Luke grabbed a handful of smoldering papers, his heart sinking as his failure to save Kiza was compounded by the imminent loss of the ancient texts he had tried to save. He gathered a few more scraps, and then he ran out as the remaining ceiling of the vault finally came crashing down behind him.

CHAPTER 51

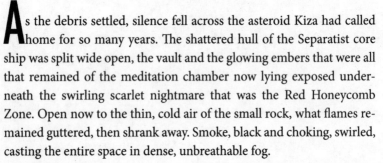

THE SEPULCHRE, KIZA'S WORLD, UNKNOWN REGIONS

NOW

As the debris settled, silence fell across the asteroid Kiza had called home for so many years. The shattered hull of the Separatist core ship was split wide open, the vault and the glowing embers that were all that remained of the meditation chamber now lying exposed underneath the swirling scarlet nightmare that was the Red Honeycomb Zone. Open now to the thin, cold air of the small rock, what flames remained guttered, then shrank away. Smoke, black and choking, swirled, casting the entire space in dense, unbreathable fog.

And then—

Movement, slow and steady, as the few droids that had remained standing during the lightsaber duel suddenly came to life, limbs stretching, bodies unfolding, like insects emerging from a long hibernation. In the swirling, red-lit murk, their eyes came alive, solid and unblinking, scarlet beacons shining through the curling smoke.

What power now activated them, now animated them, gave them their new programming, their new orders, the droids couldn't even begin to process, as every part of their antique systems were overwhelmed by a code as ancient as it was arcane.

A code of symbols, of power. One last projection of a shadow, cast long, from the past to the present.

The tide of power, flowing once more.

Nine droids, nine servants of the Sith, possessed, controlled by their master's will.

They marched, moving in unison, their electronic minds linked by this new power. They moved debris, pushing it to one side as they searched the wrecked landscape.

The mask was easy to find. It sat on the floor, safe beneath a fallen panel, the black glass eyes staring at the crimson storm above.

One droid picked it up, and then followed two others as they lumbered to the body trapped by the fallen panel.

The panel was lifted easily, the body dragged out. One arm was badly damaged, but the ancient lightsaber it held had been well protected. The second droid found the weapon and picked it up while the third lifted Kiza gently across its arms. The three droids then joined the others, the final nine now forming a line with the droid holding Exim Panshard's mask at the front, the droid carrying Kiza at the rear.

Together, the line marched back to the droid forge, a funereal procession through the shattered sepulchre. The forge chamber was still largely intact, the river of slag now a still, glowing path leading to the ruined furnace.

As the lead droid moved through the slag, it lifted the mask aloft even as its systems began to shut down, its legs melting from underneath it. As it began to collapse, the droid turned and passed the mask to the droid behind, then it fell into the slag. The second droid, now holding the mask high, led the train over their fallen brother, before the second droid stepped down into the slag. It made it a few meters before it began to fail, and, like the first droid, it turned and passed the mask back down the line, then it fell, sacrificing itself to form a bridge.

Three droids were left when they reached the broken furnace. In the smaller chamber, the heat was intense, and the tattered robes that clothed Kiza's dead body began to smolder. The lead droid knocked the worktable next to the electro-anvil over, the heavy ferrometal impervious to the heat of the slag, forming a safe surface to stand on. The droids carrying Kiza and the lightsaber stepped up onto it as the first hopped off the other side and into the furnace itself, the mask of Viceroy Exim Panshard held high in the air. In the center of the furnace, it stopped, and sank into the flames, taking the mask with it.

The bubbling surface of slag that rolled under the blue-green flame spat, the color darkening.

The droid holding the lightsaber turned to face its brother carrying Kiza. It stepped closer to it, feet clanking on the makeshift floor. Then it made a fist and smashed it through the chest plate of the other droid, reaching inside to tear out its red kyber heart. Then it did the same to itself, punching a hole in its own carapace, exposing the kyber crystal within. It yanked it out in a shower of sparks, then it turned and dropped the crystals into the furnace.

The liquid within rolled, and spat, and the color changed again.

Now it was red—the brilliant red of a Sith lightsaber, the brilliant red of a bled kyber crystal.

The droid holding Kiza's body remained still, while beside it, its mechanical brother placed Kiza's lightsaber hilt on the electro-anvil and, unfolding a set of delicate tools from the palm of its right hand, got to work, blue sparks showering the two droids as it disconnected its own left arm from the elbow down. As the work continued, the droid carrying Kiza's body laid it down on the electro-anvil.

The first droid, arm now disconnected, then turned its attention to Kiza. It lifted its unfolded hand, tools spinning and buzzing, and got to work. The task took mere minutes, the droid expertly obeying the whispered song in its circuits, but when it was complete, Kiza's body had a replacement arm for the one crushed by the fallen platform—crudely mechanical, but entirely functional.

The two droids stood impassively by the furnace. Then, at a silent order that echoed inside it, the now one-armed droid turned, plunged its remaining hand into the furnace, and pulled out the mask.

The mask had changed. It was still that of Viceroy Exim Panshard— the glassy eyes set in the sculpted face, the lost art of a civilization long dead.

But it was no longer burnished bronze. The mask was red, crystalline, a million tiny shards of gem covering the entire surface like the scales of a lizard, glittering in the flamelight.

The droid lowered the mask onto Kiza's face.

Then, in the heat of the forge, the two droids collapsed, their tasks performed, their function no longer required.

There was no movement.

Until the mechanical hand that had once belonged to a droid closed around the ancient lightsaber of Darth Noctyss, and a shadowed form left the chamber.

CHAPTER 52

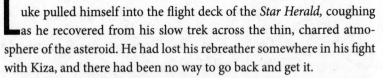

THE *STAR HERALD*, KIZA'S WORLD, RED SPACE PERIMETER
NOW

Luke pulled himself into the flight deck of the *Star Herald*, coughing as he recovered from his slow trek across the thin, charred atmosphere of the asteroid. He had lost his rebreather somewhere in his fight with Kiza, and there had been no way to go back and get it.

He dropped into the pilot's seat. R2-D2, still plugged into his workstation, bleeped and beeped. Luke turned to look down at the readout. The *Star Herald* was ready for takeoff, the hyperdrive motivator primed, the navicomputer ready for coordinates.

"Good work, Artoo."

Another chirp, another burble.

Luke got himself comfortable at the controls, and looked out at the curve of the Separatist core shipwreck. From here, remarkably, there was no sign that anything had happened, the hull on this side unchanged. He paused in his thoughts, and wondered if he should go back—the *Star Herald* had a locker full of protective equipment. He could gear up, and go back out, search the ruins properly, to find the mask or to confirm it had gone up with the rest of Kiza's relics.

That was when there was an alert from the comm deck—Luke knew who it would be before he even hit the button to open the channel.

"Lando, I found—"

"That's great, Luke," his friend's voice echoed tinnily across the comm. "Just great. You can tell me all about it. But we could really use your help here. We've got company. Lots of company. Sending coordinates now."

Luke nodded, his priority now reset. "Understood, we're on our way." As he busied himself with the takeoff procedure, he glanced over his shoulder. "Artoo, set a course. Let's see just how fast this ship can go."

R2-D2 whistled his affirmative, and a moment later the *Star Herald* powered off from the asteroid and headed out, ready to make the jump to lightspeed.

That's great, Luke. Just great.

That's great, Luke. Just great.

That's great, Luke. Just great.

Lando's voice echoed around another cockpit in another vessel, parked on the landing pad on the other side of the core ship. As the message repeated itself, over and over, a blue-fingered hand moved over the controls, twisting a dial as a masked red face read the trace, the lines converging, the coordinate readout scrolling as the data was intercepted.

There.

As the blue-fingered hand adjusted the tracer, a mechanical hand, black and greased and sooty, the mechanisms clicking, gripped the control yoke and the TIE Defender lifted up, the scream of its twin ion engines merging with the screams of the dead that echoed inside the mask, and inside the cockpit itself.

And there was a new voice, now, a new soul added to the collection. It was the cry of a woman, screaming in anguish, in rage.

Screaming in regret and in pain.

Viceroy Exim Panshard set course and made the jump.

CHAPTER 53

TAW PROVODE IMPERIAL FUEL FACILITY
NOW

Komat adjusted the scope of the rifle and the angle of the weapon's long barrel as she rested it on the railing. She was near the top of the highest gantry that surrounded the largest fuel tank in this cluster. It was the perfect place to sit and watch the land and watch the enemy, learn their movements, their numbers, in total invisibility.

Komat had missed this kind of work.

She was looking down at a staging area, where the Espos were regrouping around the landing pad that held the *Goldstone*. She had thinned their numbers considerably, along with their confidence; rather than engaging in a seek-locate-exterminate search mission typical of the old Imperial days, the CSA were content to merely regroup, lick their wounds, figure out what to do next.

They may have had the numbers, but they didn't have the training or experience. She didn't know how the CSA were involved with the family Luke Skywalker and Lando Calrissian were following, but one thing was certain: The only people the CSA had fooled into thinking they were a battle-ready army were themselves.

And now, things down in the staging area were getting interesting.

Ochi of Bestoon had joined the redcaps. But the way he was talking to the CSA officers, the way he seemed to be giving them orders, made one fact clear.

Ochi wasn't working for the CSA—they were working for *him*.

Komat could only observe, not overhear. What she needed to do was get to a better position, somewhere closer. There were plenty of inky black shadows nearby. They'd never know she was there.

Then there came a brilliant blue flash of light—Komat ducked instinctively behind the railing, the optics in her mask adjusted to compensate for the glare when, a second later, a ball of red-and-yellow flame erupted from the *Goldstone* as the entire ship exploded, sending a cloud of smoke into the air and destroying one of the huge floodlight towers that stood over the landing pad, the lamp and its framework crashing down on the spot where the CSA troopers had been assembled. Some were not so lucky; as the smoke began to clear, Komat's helmet adjusted for the suddenly changed lighting conditions, and she was able to count the bodies of those who had been a little too close.

Pulling back from the railing, Komat lifted her wrist and tapped the computer pad on it. Inside her mask, a smaller picture appeared in her eyeline, the helmet's computer rolling back through a recording of the explosion in slow motion.

There. She paused, rolled back, played it again, slower.

The initial blue flash had come from inside the ship's engine cowling, the vent cleverly hidden on the underside of the *Goldstone*'s delta wing. The explosion that followed was one of the ship's fuel cells going up. But the initial spark? That had been a rigged detonation.

Lando was right. The people in this family, whoever they were, were clever and capable.

Around the landing pad, the surviving Espos shielded themselves from the burning wreck as Ochi stood directly in the light, staring at it, those cybernetic eyes obviously providing as much protection as Komat's helmet. As she looked away, her helmet adjusted for the lighting again, and she saw the movement behind the troopers.

It was Lando. He was approaching the burning landing pad slowly, blaster held by his side, his other arm shielding his face from the glare.

Fool. He was going to walk right into the Espos, who were still rushing around in confusion. The blaze of the *Goldstone* had reduced the excellent shadow cover to mere scraps. They would find him.

Komat ducked down. It was too far away for her to call out, which would not only alert the troopers but reveal her own position, perhaps making the CSA finally realize that there was a viable, even preferable, vantage point over the whole facility from the top of the tank gantries.

Instead, she had a better idea. She dropped down onto her stomach and brought her rifle up, resting the bottom edge on the lip of the gantry. Adjusting the power setting on her weapon, she took careful aim through the scope.

She squeezed the trigger, slowly. The rifle bucked, the stock kicking powerfully into her shoulder, but the shot itself was almost silent. If any of the Espos had looked up and saw the glowing white bolt streak overhead, there was nothing they could have done to stop it.

The bolt struck the spherical fuel tank on the other side of the landing pad dead center. For a second, nothing happened.

Then the ground shook, knocking half of the still-standing CSA troopers to the ground. Komat stood and looked over the rail for Lando, and saw he was now crouching behind one of the ubiquitous fuel pumps.

And then the fuel tank exploded.

The sound it made was low, almost wet . . . a great *whump* of heavy gases igniting, the explosion itself falling *down,* a rolling tidal wave of flame spilling out across the landing platform, sending the Espos scurrying away.

Then there was a secondary explosion, and this one was a *bang* like no other, the pressure wave enough to knock Komat back onto the gantry. The fuel tanks must have had multiple internal compartments, separating volatile elements safely, preventing any dangerous cross-contamination.

Until Komat had punctured them.

Smoke rose in a mushroom cloud, brilliantly lit by the shaking floodlight towers that were still standing. Light flashed inside the cloud as the explosion seemed to go on for *seconds.*

Komat stood, surveying her handiwork. As far as distractions went, that was a particularly effective one.

Checking Lando's position, she turned and rattled down the gantries, rifle slung across her back as she slid down the ladders using the inside edge of her boots as brakes. At ground level, she glanced once at the landing pad, the CSA still in a state of confusion. She ran across the space behind them, to Lando.

Lando saw her and lowered his blaster. In the safety of the shadows, he nodded back at the landing pad.

"Your doing?"

"Only the tank," said Komat. "The other ship appears to have been rigged to detonate by the family. They are more ingenious than I have given them credit for."

Lando slapped Komat on the shoulder. "All right," he said, his grin glinting in the dark. "Let's get out of here while we can. The CSA is going to be busy with this lot. That should have bought them a head start. Do you think you can find them again in the other ship?"

Komat lifted her rifle, indicating the scope.

"Perhaps. I have a reading of its drive signature. But I will need Luke Skywalker's astromech."

"I called Luke earlier, he's on his way here. So, in the meantime—"

"Halt! Freeze! Don't move!"

Lando's eyes went wide, then he gasped as a bright spotlight was thrown on him. He winced, looking away, his hands already raised.

Komat turned slowly, her mask adjusting for the glare of the powerful flashlight mounted on the front of the CSA trooper's breastplate. Behind the Espo were another four, and all of them had their weapons aimed at the pair.

It seemed, thought Komat, her distraction hadn't quite had the outcome she'd intended.

CHAPTER 54

TAW PROVODE IMPERIAL FUEL FACILITY
NOW

Lando and Komat were marched out into the staging area, where what was left of the CSA company had regrouped.

The Espos were rattled. Lando could see it, could feel it. Yes, the CSA had won this one, but they'd been punished, and hard, by Lando and Komat—just two people—and a family with a small child.

He'd been right in his initial assessment. The CSA had soldiers, but while they were a step up from their old security police, they were still not disciplined, they were not battle-hardened. Nor were they brainwashed by propaganda and Imperial doctrine.

The CSA were running scared.

This was not a good thing. Because being surrounded by frightened Espos, led by redcaps who seemed to be running on gut instinct and adrenaline rather than tactical experience, was unlikely to end well. There were lots of blasters, and lots of nervous trigger fingers, all around them.

The troopers pulled Lando and Komat around to the front of the company, the brown-armored Espos watching them with some interest— a hint of nerves, a hint of power.

But, Lando thought, the family had gotten away. If this was it, then at least they'd given them the best chance they could.

"Interesting," said a voice. Lando looked toward it and saw Ochi of Bestoon approach, the hard black leather armor reflecting the dull-orange light from the flames that continued to flicker around the wreck on the landing pad—light that also shone on the dagger at his belt, a double-lobed blade, the dull metal inscribed with a dense, geometric text.

Lando glanced at Komat, but she was looking dead ahead, the green glass cowling of her helmet alive in the firelight.

Lando cleared his throat. "What is?" he called out. This elicited a shove from the Espo behind him; Lando went with the movement and stepped out of line, into the path of Ochi. The redcap beside Ochi lifted his blaster, but Ochi waved the man down. He stepped closer, his black electronic eyes gleaming.

"You are," said Ochi, looking first at Lando, then at Komat. "Very, very interesting." He slipped the dagger from his belt and pointed it at Komat's middle. "Where is the girl?"

Lando stiffened, the pang of adrenaline coursing through his body at those words, making him feel both alive and electric, tired and sick.

"Somewhere you'll never find her," said Lando, loudly, proudly, pushing as much calm and control into his voice as he could, making sure that everyone could hear him. "You've lost her for good this time, Ochi of Bestoon. Doesn't matter how many reinforcements you get from the Corporate Sector, it won't be enough."

Ochi cocked his head at Lando, then, pulling the blade away from Komat's stomach, he gestured with it.

Immediately, Lando felt heavy hands grab him from behind, a boot to the back of his knee, and he was brought crashing to the hard concrete ground beneath him. He gasped in pain as Ochi grabbed a handful of his hair and yanked his head back sharply.

"I asked you where the girl is," said Ochi, quietly. He put the blade to Lando's neck.

Lando's eyes went wide, his breath suddenly quick, fast, shallow, the ice cold of the blade against his skin a shock, a single, huge chilling wave spreading across his entire body. And—

He gasped again, like he couldn't get his breath. No, the blade wasn't cold, it was hot, red-hot, a superheated shard of metal, the slightest movement of which wouldn't just cut his throat, it would sever his head from his body entirely.

Ochi drew his face close to Lando's. Lando didn't dare move anything except his eyes, wide as they strained to look at the Jedi hunter's scarred, smooth face.

"You know where she is," Ochi whispered. "You sent her away. I thought they had been given help before; now I know who it was who helped them." Ochi turned his head, the skin of his neck stretching horribly in Lando's vision as the hunter looked at Komat, still standing impassively, under the guard of two CSA blaster barrels. "I don't know who you are," said Ochi, turning back to Lando, "and I don't care. But any who dare cross Ochi of Bestoon will regret the very moment of their birth." He pushed the blade, nicking Lando's neck, and leaned forward, until his mouth was brushing Lando's ear.

"Where is the girl?"

Lando fought to control the rising panic—it wasn't that he was being held at knifepoint. Hell, he'd been in this exact same position, oh . . . well, far more times than he would have liked, truth be told. And sure, Ochi was ugly as hell and a nasty piece of work, but no more or less unpleasant than a lot of people Lando had found himself at the displeasure of over the years.

No, this was different, this was different. Lando ran with the thought, allowing his mind to wander, distracting him from the way the blade felt against his skin, the trickle of blood from his neck, the strangest sensation—no, not sensation, *knowledge*, yes, that was it—the strangest knowledge that the blade was hungry, that it had tasted his blood and liked it.

Liked it . . . and wanted more.

Lando forced his eyes closed. A relic, that was it. The blade was some Sith relic. It was almost hilarious, really. Here they were, in an automated refueling dump for starships that could cross the galaxy, in a galaxy full of technological wonder and invention, and yet in some dark corners of that same galaxy there were things, objects—nothing more, nothing less—somehow imbued with dark power that was almost like magic.

"What's so funny?"

Lando opened his eyes and realized he was laughing. Ochi still had the blade to his neck, but he'd pulled back a little, like he was suddenly nervous of being so close to his prisoner.

"Oh, nothing," said Lando, then he chuckled again. "I like your dagger. Where'd you get it? I was thinking of getting one for myself."

At this, Ochi growled, the sound so primal, so animalistic that Lando's laugh died immediately. The hunter stood and lifted the dagger, which shone in the flamelight.

For a microsecond, Lando wondered who was in charge—Ochi, or the dagger—and then Ochi stabbed down, the fire dancing in his eyes and dancing along the blade.

And then Lando wondered what his final thought would be— something profound, deep, meaningful? Some observation of his own character, some sudden, regretful realization of his place in the galaxy, of the things he had learned—or should have learned?

Or would it just be a single moment of terror, a split-second recognition that he was alone and he was going to die, and there was nothing he could do about it.

Or perhaps one last memory of love.

Of the mother of his daughter. Of his daughter herself.

Of Kadara Calrissian, the little girl he couldn't save.

There was a sound and a rush of air, together—*boomph!*—and suddenly Ochi wasn't there. Lando blinked, saw nothing but firelight and something else, brilliant, green, moving quickly, filling his vision as a deep, whooshing buzz filled his ears. He fell sideways—it seemed prudent to get out of the way—and a single word formed on his lips.

"Luke?"

Blasterfire. Lando shuffled on the concrete and looked up at a sideways world as Luke Skywalker cut through the assembled Espos with his lightsaber, deflecting aimless blasterfire with single, precise strokes. Within moments, none were left standing, and Lando watched as Luke turned, his blade angled away from his body.

Lando sensed movement near and turned on the ground as Komat crouched beside him, helping him to his feet. Lando allowed himself to be lifted, then he spun around, one hand grasping for his empty holster as he saw Ochi of Bestoon square off against Luke, the two men meters apart, Luke with his lightsaber, Ochi with the dagger.

"Luke, be careful!" Lando called out. "That's no ordinary dagger. It's a Sith relic."

Luke glanced at his old friend, and gave a nod of acknowledgment.

Ochi, meanwhile, began to laugh.

"Of course," he said, "I should have known they had a Jedi as their protector." He took a step sideways; Luke matched the motion, the two now slowly circling a central point.

Lando looked around and saw the silver glint of his blaster on the ground, among the bodies of the CSA troopers. He grabbed it, then saw Komat's rifle. He pulled the long weapon out from underneath a body and tossed it to her.

"You know, I used to hunt Jedi," said Ochi. "In the days of the Clone Wars, and after. I was an assassin of the Sith, a tool wielded by the Emperor with precision."

"That was a long time ago," said Luke.

Lando lifted his blaster, taking aim at Ochi. Beside him, Komat didn't move, and was using her long rifle as a staff. "Hey, come on." Lando nudged her. "Little help here?"

"This is not our fight, Lando Calrissian."

"Some time for honor," muttered Lando, under his breath.

"Some things you never forget," Ochi said to Luke with a chuckle. "I look forward to adding another notch on my belt."

Ochi lunged with the dagger—just as Lando was about to squeeze off a well-aimed shot. Lando hissed in annoyance, lowering his weapon as Luke raised his lightsaber in defense.

But Luke didn't need his help, or Komat's. A Jedi and a lightsaber against, what, exactly?

Ochi didn't stand a chance.

Luke's blade hit Ochi's dagger—and Ochi sliced parallel to the glowing green blade, sending it skittering off. If Luke was surprised that the dagger was apparently impervious to the power of his weapon, he didn't show it, his face a still mask of concentration as he nimbly sidestepped and brought his lightsaber to bear again.

Ochi was fast, Lando had to give him that. Ochi spun to the side, once again allowing a glancing blow of the lightsaber blade on the dagger, using the strength of Luke's own attack to push the weapon away.

That was when Ochi pulled the blaster from his belt with his free hand. He hopped backward, blaster up and ready to fire.

But not at Luke.

As the lightsaber swung in again, Ochi dodged it, angling the attack away with the dagger before firing two blaster shots at one of the spherical fuel tanks on the side of the staging area. Both bolts deflected off the heavy armor side of the tank.

Beside Lando, Komat now swung into action as she saw what Ochi was trying to do. She dropped into a crouch, her rifle now up and aimed.

Ochi shot first—and it was third time lucky. The fuel tank exploded, debris shooting into the sky as the heavy burning gas rolled out from within, a surging wave that would incinerate every living being caught in its path.

Lando ran, one hand grabbing Komat under the armpit and wrenching her to her feet. Risking a glance over his shoulder, Lando saw Luke's lightsaber blade bobbing as he sprinted after them, the rolling inferno fast approaching behind. Of Ochi, there was no sign.

Then the scrap metal of the destroyed fuel tank began to rain down around them, and Lando, head ducked down, made for the safety of the next tank cluster, Komat and Luke close behind.

CHAPTER 55

TAW PROVODE IMPERIAL FUEL FACILITY
NOW

Lando could feel the heat from the raging fuel fire on his exposed skin, but in the dark space between two intact tanks, he and his friends were at least safe. He looked out as the inferno abated, leaving behind the smoking remains of the CSA troopers. Grimacing, Lando cast his eye over their bodies, but it didn't look like Ochi was among them.

"Did you reach the family?" asked Luke, brushing himself down.

Lando nodded. "They got away in Ochi's own ship," he said, then filled Luke in on what had happened in the fuel dump. Luke listened intently, nodding as he took the information in, then he gave an account of his own experience on Kiza's asteroid.

"So, she's dead," said Lando. "And the mask is gone, too."

Luke frowned. Komat inclined her cowled helmet.

Lando looked between the two of them. "She *is* dead, right?"

Luke's expression was dark. "I can't be sure," he said, "not until I go back."

"Wait, what?" asked Lando. "You want to go *back* there?"

"I have to," said Luke. "But I don't mean now. I need to investigate that asteroid properly and systematically. Kiza had spent years collect-ing relics—dangerous ones. Some of them might have survived, and I can't let them fall into the wrong hands."

"Fair enough," said Lando, "but we've got Ochi to deal with now. He can't have gotten far, and without his ship or the *Goldstone*, he's stuck here."

"I would not be so certain of this, Lando Calrissian," Komat intoned. "There were many more soldiers of the Corporate Sector Authority in this place. Ochi of Bestoon did not come to Taw Provode alone."

Right on cue, there came the sound of distant engines firing, which then increased in volume rapidly as a ship rose up from a nearby land-ing pad. Lando led the others out into the open, and they watched as a CSA transport sluggishly headed for space.

Komat was on one knee immediately, her long rifle aimed high. She pulled the trigger, sending a stream of glowing white bolts into the dark sky. But the small starship was already well out of range.

"We need to get after him," said Lando. "If he can call on the re-sources of the CSA, he'll be going after the family again."

Komat nodded. "Lando Calrissian speaks the truth. I believe our ac-tions here provided your family with a window of opportunity, but it will not stay open for very much longer, Master Skywalker."

"Agreed," said Luke. "But we have an advantage over Ochi."

Lando stroked his mustache with a thoughtful finger and thumb. "The *Star Herald*?"

"One of the fastest ships in the galaxy," said Luke with a nod. He pulled the comlink from his belt and pressed the button. "Artoo, is the *Star Herald* ready for takeoff?"

R2-D2's warbling tones signaled the affirmative—Lando recognized that much—but the little droid kept burbling, delivering a lot more in-formation.

Lando glanced at the others. "Little guy's trying to tell us something."

Then Komat stepped away, her masked face scanning the sky. "A ship approaches."

Lando and Luke split up, the three of them spacing out around the staging area as they tried to pick up on Komat's warning.

"Where?" asked Lando. "I don't see anything."

And then he heard it. Shrill, rasping, the all-too-familiar signature of an Imperial TIE fighter.

Luke spun around, lightsaber already in his hand. "Get behind me!" he yelled as his blade spat into life. He stood, legs spaced, lightsaber hilt clasped in both hands, as Lando and Komat moved in close.

The TIE Defender appeared to rise up from behind a distant fuel tank, although Lando knew it was just an optical illusion. Within moments, he could see the six angled wings, and he could make out the streaked paintwork that covered them and the central ball-like cockpit.

"So much for Kiza being dead," said Lando.

Luke didn't turn around to answer. "I said I wasn't sure."

"You were right to be doubtful, Master Skywalker," said Komat. "We must return to the *Star Herald* at once."

Lando went to move—and then realized that the TIE was headed straight for them, losing altitude all the time, the crosshatched cockpit viewport pointed right on target.

The TIE's cannons spat, sending two fast streams of heavy green blasterfire toward them. Luke pivoted, one arm now outstretched as he indicated for his charges to follow his movements, then turned and stood directly in the path of one stream of fire, both hands once again on his lightsaber.

The heavy fire caught Luke's lightsaber, the impact strong enough to send Luke sliding backward. He leaned into it, teeth gritted, as he shielded himself and his friends from harm.

Then the TIE shot above them, almost close enough to touch, before curving back up into the dark sky. Luke turned with it, his robes blowing in the ship's wake.

"She's coming back around," said Lando.

"Time to go," said Luke. He deactivated his lightsaber, then looked at Komat. "Lead the way."

The trio sprinted across the concrete as, high above, the TIE turned for another attack run.

Komat took them into the dead space that cut through a tank cluster, the trio vanishing into the darkness. Lando felt the hairs on the back of his neck rise as the screech of the TIE filled his ears, but the sound quickly passed as the fighter flew overhead and then began to gain altitude again, its targets now lost.

They ran through the shadows, ducking under pipework, jumping over cables, hoses, pump equipment. Komat moved with speed; Lando did nothing but keep his legs moving, figuring that Komat's sense of direction was far better than his own.

They emerged in another main thoroughfare. At first, Lando didn't recognize it—they all looked the same, the whole fuel dump laid out for automated efficiency—then realized he was looking at the ship he and Komat had come in, her *Warglaive*—the customized fighter a sleek crescent shape, the cockpit protruding like a spearhead from the center of the arc—and now, sitting beside it, the *Star Herald*. Standing between the two ships were two distinctive silhouettes—the unmistakable compact form of R2-D2, and beside him, the tall, powerful humanoid form of KB-68. The Duelist Elite droid had her blade in her hands and was standing guard over the *Warglaive* as Komat had instructed when they had first arrived.

KB-68 ran up to them, she and Komat greeting each other with a firm clasp of arms. "I suggest we move it, and fast," said the droid as they all grouped together. "That TIE will be back soon and we're easy to spot in the open."

Lando glanced at the two ships, then looked up as the distant sound of the TIE became audible. KB-68 was right, they didn't have much time—not only would the TIE be in range in seconds, but Ochi would be long gone by now. Likewise, the family. He only hoped that Komat could find them again.

But it was Luke who spoke first. He nodded at Lando, then lifted his chin at the *Star Herald*. "You and Komat, go after the family. You've got a good chance of reaching them before Ochi in the *Star Herald*." He turned to Komat. "I need to finish this."

Komat bowed. "You may take my *Warglaive*. But Kaybee Sixty-Eight and I will accompany you, Master Skywalker."

Lando held up both hands. "Whoa, whoa, whoa! Komat, I need you with me to . . . you know, do your thing, predict the ship's position."

"Master Skywalker's astromech has the correct programming," she said. She swung her rifle off her back and, fiddling with the scope on the top, pulled out a data card. She knelt by R2-D2 and inserted it into one of his reader slots. "This is all the data I recorded from Ochi's starship. Artoo-Detoo can do the rest aboard the *Star Herald*." She stood and looked up.

The TIE was now very close and getting closer.

"Come, Master Skywalker," said Komat. "Kaybee Sixty-Eight, with me."

With that, she turned and headed to her own ship, KB-68 sheathing her blade and following.

"Artoo?" Luke called. At his command, the droid trundled forward and, burbling, popped open a side panel on his chassis. In the tight space where an expansion data store could be plugged sat a small, wrapped bundle—the kyber crystal shards from Yoturba.

Lando eyed his friend. "You sure you want to take those with you, Luke?" He folded his arms. "Seems like we want to keep those as far away from Kiza as possible."

"I need to end this," said Luke, the bundle disappearing into his robes. "One way or another."

Lando sighed. "Okay, I guess you know what you're doing. Good luck, Luke. You know the drill."

Luke nodded. "I'll send a transmission. Happy hunting." He turned and ran to the *Warglaive*.

"I'll have a Declavian cognac ready on ice for you," Lando called out. "This time you might even try it!" Luke didn't stop, but he raised a hand in the air in acknowledgment.

Lando glanced once more at the sky, then headed for the *Star Herald*.

"Come on, Artoo. Let's go work a little magic."

CHAPTER 56

THE *STAR HERALD*,
TAW PROVODE SYSTEM
NOW

"All right," said Lando, dropping himself into position in front of the *Star Herald*'s controls. He hadn't flown the ship before—Luke seemed more than happy to have assumed that duty earlier, given the ship was theoretically in *his* care—but while it was a one-of-a-kind prototype, the flight controls were more or less standard. It took Lando just a few minutes to get the basic layout, while R2-D2 connected himself to the dataport in the console on the flight deck's portside workstation. Immediately, he began twittering and beeping; Lando glanced down at the translation on the readout in front of him, but was then distracted by the takeoff of Komat's ship, the *Warglaive*, which immediately banked and powered off after the TIE Defender, its engines ablaze.

Lando lifted the *Star Herald* off, then angled the ship over the vast fuel tanks of Taw Provode and headed up into a low orbit in roughly the same direction he'd seen Ochi pilot the CSA transport.

Not that it would make any difference. Ochi would be long gone by now.

Lando glanced over his shoulder at R2-D2. The dataport was spinning as the droid chirped, his primary red and blue indicator flashing as he turned his dome left and right, left and right, the astromech deep in his work. Outside, the *Star Herald* moved away from the glare of the fuel dump's giant floodlights, and soon they were in open space.

And . . . if that wasn't Ochi's CSA transport, dead ahead. The ship seemed to have stopped, the pilot perhaps trying to figure out what he was going to do next.

Perhaps, Lando thought, this was going to be easier than he thought. He glanced down, trying to decipher the *Star Herald*'s weaponry systems . . . only to discover the ship didn't have any, that particular module not currently installed.

"Well, isn't that just great," Lando muttered to himself.

And then he looked up just in time to see the CSA ship vanish into hyperspace, leaving nothing but a faintly glowing blue streak against the stars.

Lando banged a hand on the console in annoyance. But still, Ochi wasn't their target, not at the moment. Lando needed to find the family.

And he needed to find them before Ochi did.

"Artoo!" he called out over his shoulder. "How're we doing, little buddy? We ready to make the jump to lightspeed yet?"

The droid let out a long string of electronic burbles. With a frown, Lando turned to read the translation on his control panel.

"You have to do *what*?" Lando spun around in the pilot's seat. "You need to reconfigure the entire sensor bank and antenna array?"

R2-D2 chirped. The dataport on the workstation in front of him continued to turn.

"How long is that going to take?"

The response to this question was a low tone that Lando didn't like the sound of. He glanced down at the panel, then looked back up.

"You have got to be kidding me."

R2-D2 bleeped. Lando turned back around and, with a deep sigh, sank back into the seat, his hands linked behind his head. He closed his eyes in frustration.

Everything was now reliant on R2-D2 getting his sums right. Lando only hoped that Komat was right, that the astromech really did know what he was doing.

CHAPTER 57

THE *WARGLAIVE*, TAW PROVODE SYSTEM
NOW

Komat spun her starship out of Taw Provode's gravity well, the TIE Defender screaming away from them in a ragged, looping flight path. Luke wasn't sure if Kiza was trying to lose them or lead them, but it didn't matter. The *Warglaive* was faster, Komat maintaining a course that closed the gap steadily between the two ships.

"We're well within cannon range," said KB-68, sitting next to her mistress in the cockpit. "Give me the word and I'll vaporize them."

Sitting behind, Luke pulled himself forward, one hand on each of the seats in front. "No, hold fire, Kaybee," he said. "I have a plan." He peered ahead, then pointed. In the upper part of their view, the bright moon of Taw Provode shone, blotting out the starlight around it. "There," he said, then he glanced at Komat. Without needing further instruction, Komat nodded, then dipped the controls, sending the ship into a tight turn.

Luke sat back and watched as Komat expertly maneuvered the ship, almost sliding it sideways in space as she aligned their flight path with the erratic dance of the TIE, and the moon dead ahead.

Komat's skill as a pilot impressed even Luke as she eased the ship's control yoke, not matching the TIE's movements, but compensating.

Within moments, the Imperial fighter was a black silhouette against the circle of the moon, every detail outlined in perfect clarity.

Komat's right hand moved to a large lever, and she thrust it forward, leaning across the console with the movement. Luke felt the ship buck, and suddenly the moon was an awful lot closer than it had been.

Likewise, the TIE Defender. They were right on its tail.

"Acceptable, Master Skywalker?"

"Right on target," he said.

Komat inclined her head, then looked at her copilot. "Kaybee Sixty-Eight," she said, "disable that vehicle. We shall meet the pilot on the surface of the moon."

"Finally," said KB-68. "I wasn't sure you were ever going to let me shoot anything."

There was a buzz as KB-68 adjusted the targeting computer by her side, and then she squeezed the trigger on the small stick on her console. Two bolts of energy spat from the corner-mounted guns of the *Warglaive,* meeting at a point on one of the TIE's three main panel supports. There was a shower of spark and a roll of flame, and the TIE immediately veered as the targeted wing first twisted, then tore itself from the spherical central body. The whole TIE began to spin, then settled as the pilot managed to regain some modicum of control.

"Easy now," said Luke.

The TIE shrank as Komat eased back on the power, following at a safer distance while the surface of the moon came closer, and closer, shining brightly, with no surface features visible at all.

"I fear we may have miscalculated, Master Skywalker," said Komat in her forever-calm voice. "The TIE's entry approach is too fast."

"And the ground looks very hard," said KB-68. The droid leaned forward over a panel. "I'm reading density off the scale here." She turned to Komat. "Pull up or we're all going to meet the Maker today."

Komat nodded and reduced the power further. Ahead, the once stable TIE now began to spin again. They were mere kilometers from the surface of the moon.

KB-68 was right—the ground looked very hard. The surface was flat, almost polished, a deep snow white.

"It's too late," said Komat, slowing still further. "They will not survive the impact."

"Yes they will," said Luke. He leaned forward, reaching out. The TIE was a long way away, the distance increasing by the second, and there was nothing between their ship and the fighter but the vacuum of space.

But Luke had to try.

He closed his eyes, reaching out with his mind as well as his body. There. He found it. The TIE Defender was, like everything else in the galaxy, a presence in the Force. But it was a slippery one—its combined mass and velocity making it hard to even get a focus on, let alone a hold.

Luke concentrated. He gritted his teeth, willing the motion of the TIE to surrender to his will.

"They're slowing," said KB-68. "I just hope the Imps built those things strong."

Luke gasped, the effort of holding the ship now too great. He opened his eyes as it slipped away from him. Soaring low over the surface of the moon, the TIE suddenly dipped out of sight below them, and there was a flash of light.

"Komat," said Luke, but Komat was already turning the ship around, bringing it in to land. As they touched down, they could see their quarry ahead of them, a smoking black wreck on an impossibly flat, white surface.

Smoking . . . but intact.

Mostly.

"Come on," said Luke, unstrapping himself and heading to the exit ramp.

They approached on foot across a surface that was perfectly smooth, and perfectly treacherous. Luke warily glanced around with every footfall at the glass-like surface of the satellite, every breath of stale, dead air telling him that there may have been life here, once, but that life had long since fled, and rightly so.

Their footsteps sounded hollow against the ground—the surface of

Taw Provode's solitary moon was made of thin diamond sheets; glancing down, Luke could see motion beneath them, the sheets they walked on merely a firm, but thin, crust, held aloft by larger crystal bergs floating in a subterranean ocean. That he had managed to control the wild descent of the TIE enough for the diamond crust to remain intact on impact was a surprise, even knowing his own power. The sky above was a flat, featureless black, save for the curve of Taw Provode that filled half the sky, the lights of the fuel dump looking so close, like Luke could just reach up and pluck them down.

He had his lightsaber in his hand. On his left, Komat held her long rifle like a staff as she walked. On his right, KB-68's long deadblade was already drawn and held perfectly vertical in the Duelist Elite's mechanical hands.

The smoking TIE was a hundred meters away. And walking toward the trio was the pilot, black-clad, her tattered cloak sweeping around her boots as it hung limp in the still, ancient atmosphere.

Kiza lived. Luke didn't know how, but she had survived their encounter. He knew then that he had made a mistake—that he should have found a way to go back, to save her, turn her away from the evil that consumed her very being.

It was possible. More than possible. The path to the dark side was a choice, but far from an irrevocable one.

At that moment, Luke remembered his father, the dying man's final wish to see his son with his own eyes. And more recently, the vision of Anakin Skywalker, his warning, and his advice.

No matter how dark the night may grow, you are never alone.

Luke glanced to his right, to his left. He was not alone. He had his friends by his side. And out there, another friend, one of his oldest— Lando Balthazar Calrissian—was continuing their mission while Luke corrected his own mistake.

Let the Force guide you. Let it flow through you as it flows through me. Use that power, and your instincts, for they are one and the same.

As Anakin's words faded from Luke's mind, he sensed the true nature of the foe he now faced.

It wasn't Kiza. Luke could sense the eclipse in the Force, the invisible lines of power bending around Kiza, the mask of Viceroy Exim Pan-shard warping the Force, lensing it like the gravity of a giant star.

Luke stopped, and his companions stopped with him.

That mask was different now—the same shape, the same face of torment, of death, but instead of burnished bronze, it was brilliant red, as crystalline and shining as the ground beneath their feet, infused with the power of the kyber crystals.

Kiza was dead. Luke felt a sadness, an almost vertiginous rush as he realized the truth.

Viceroy Exim Panshard lived on, a Sith Lord from an eon past, inhabiting the mask, and now, inhabiting Kiza, taking full control of his dead host in a final, desperate attempt to resurrect himself into a galaxy he had no place being.

"We got company," KB-68 said, lowering the volume of her vocabulator. From the corner of his eye, Luke saw Komat turn to the droid, then look down.

And then he saw it, and he looked down himself, taking his eyes off Kiza for just a few seconds.

There was something moving underneath their feet, in the oceanic depths beneath the moon's diamond crust. It was long and dark, and it wove around beneath them. Then it was joined by another shape identical to the first, two huge, serpentine forms writhing.

The moon was not lifeless, after all. And now, sensing the intrusion into their domain, the monstrous inhabitants stirred.

Then Viceroy Exim Panshard spoke. His voice was metal and it was fire, the sound of a droid furnace spitting impossible words, shaped by an intelligence that was as dark as it was ancient as it was evil.

"SHOW ME THE WAY TO EXEGOL. SHOW IT TO ME!"

Luke stepped forward, his lightsaber hilt held out to one side, always ready.

"This won't work," he said. "You cannot sustain yourself like this. Whatever power you had, you are burning through it. Soon enough you will die, as you should have centuries ago."

Panshard took a step forward, the mask tilting, the mass of kyber crystal facets glittering.

"YOU, JEDI." He raised the cylinder of his lightsaber and pointed it at Luke, and Luke saw that the arm from the elbow down was now mechanical, transplanted from one of Kiza's droids. **"YOU WILL SHOW ME THE WAY TO EXEGOL, OR YOU SHALL DIE."**

Luke held his ground, not moving a muscle as he spoke. "The way to Exegol is lost," he said. "And that is how it will remain." Then he took another bold step forward. "Your power is failing. I can feel it. Let it go. Surrender to the Force, and you will have the peace you seek."

Exim Panshard laughed. **"I SEEK NOT PEACE, JEDI. I SEEK WAR. I SEEK POWER. I SEEK TO FEAST ON YOUR SOUL AND THE SOULS OF ALL THE GALAXY. THROUGH THEIR POWER I SHALL REACH EXEGOL, AND THROUGH EXEGOL I SHALL BE REBORN. NOW SHOW ME THE WAY."**

Panshard reached out with his other hand, a single, swift motion. Luke ducked back instinctively, his thumb over the activator of his lightsaber even as he felt the cloth of his robe tear. He stumbled backward, Komat catching him, KB-68 ready on his other side.

The bundle of kyber crystals ripped free from Luke's robe to float in the air between the two groups. Panshard twisted his hand of flesh and blood, and the cloth fell away, revealing the red shards rotating slowly over the diamond ground.

"I COMMAND THE ARCHITECTURES OF THE FORCE," said Panshard, **"AND THROUGH THEIR FEARFUL SYMMETRY I WILL BE GUIDED TO THE DARK WORLD OF THE SITH. THERE I SHALL BE REBORN."**

Panshard ignited his lightsaber. The red blade emerged, curving from the black hilt like a scimitar of hateful radiance. The crystal shards spun in the air, absorbing the glow of the lightsaber blade and shining it back out.

"AND THE SITH WILL BE REBORN WITH ME, ALL THOSE WHO LIVED AND DIED BETWEEN MY TIME AND THIS. AND ALL I NEED IS TO LISTEN TO THE RESONANCE OF THESE CRYSTALS AS THEY SING FOR THEIR WAY HOME."

Panshard snapped his fist closed, and the crystals shot through the air toward him. Luke ignited his own lightsaber and reached out, catching the crystals with the Force. The shards vibrated in the air, humming with power that steadily grew louder and louder.

Luke understood now how Panshard was going to do it. The kyber crystal source was on Exegol. These pieces, together with the fragments that had been subsumed into his mask, were part of the larger whole that remained on the hidden world.

That was how the lost pilot had hoped to reach the planet of the Sith centuries before, taking the crystal shards and making a desperate run for Exegol with only the barest navigational data held in their holocron, relying mostly on the Force resonance of the crystals to guide them through Red Space. They had failed, crashing on Yoturba, because the crystal shards they possessed did not have the required critical mass to interact fully, through the Force, with the Exegol source. That was also how the droids had found them on Polaar, the crystals within their systems resonating with the ones in Luke's possession, drawing the hunter droids in.

But where the ancient pilot had failed, Panshard could succeed. With all of the crystals together, they would have enough mass for the resonance to be strong. With them, he could reach Exegol.

Luke was determined to make sure that never happened.

He summoned his strength and increased his hold on the crystals. They spun and drifted toward him—only for Luke to find himself sliding on the diamond ground, the surface almost impossible to get a purchase on. He looked down and saw the serpent-shapes continue to slide beneath them.

"Enough. Enough!"

Komat. She stepped around Luke and tossed her rifle to KB-68, just as the droid likewise threw her deadblade to her mistress. Komat caught the weapon by the handle with one hand and then swung it around in a single swift, dancelike motion. The blade fell away at the hilt, and there was a sharp buzzing snap. Luke could taste ozone on his tongue as Komat swung now with one long lightsaber, the extended blade blazing white.

It was the lightsaber Luke had purified for her, all those years ago, when he helped her escape from the Acolytes of the Beyond. The white of the blade symbolized the purging of evil from her mind and from her soul.

Komat swept the blade before her, passing around Luke, and brought it to bear on the floating shards of kyber crystal. As the blade connected with them, the crystals shattered, exploding in a rain of tiny, razor-sharp fragments. His hold in the Force suddenly released, Luke spun around, flicking his hood up over his head as he ducked, protecting himself from the shower of crystal pieces.

Exim Panshard's scream was the roar of a hurricane, rage and pain blending in equal measure into an inhuman wall of sound. Then he leapt forward, red blade swinging.

Luke turned, his green blade ready. Panshard attacked with a strength born of pure hate and desperation, knocking Luke's blade back and then, turning, without pause, to parry an attack by Komat.

Red, green, white light flashed over the diamond ground as the trio fought. Komat let Luke lead the attack, offering support where needed, searching for gaps in Panshard's defense as Luke executed a series of tight, controlled motions with his blade, both defending himself and testing the abilities of his resurrected opponent.

In moments, the air was filled with a fine clear dust as Luke and Komat's attacks began to wear Panshard down, his red lightsaber slicing into the ground beneath them, nicking divots into the moon's hard crust, then carving huge gouges as Panshard pushed forward, his attacks as wild as they were fast.

Luke saw the opportunity first—Panshard's attacks were now falling into a pattern. He only hoped that Komat could see that pattern, too, because he would need her for what he planned to do next.

He readied himself, counting the seconds in his head.

Then Panshard roared again from behind the mask and threw a punch with his free hand, directing the motion at Komat. The two opponents were beyond striking distance, but Panshard's fist didn't need to connect.

Not physically, at least.

Komat doubled over and was then lifted into the air as Panshard channeled the Force into her. As she tumbled back onto the hard ground, her white lightsaber blade carved deeply into the surface. She rolled and righted herself, her free arm across her stomach as she heaved for breath, composing herself to rejoin Luke.

Then Panshard stepped backward and raised both hands in the air, curved lightsaber brilliant red against the black sky. The ground shook, forcing Luke to check his balance. Cracks appeared, shooting across the surface of the moon with loud bangs that sounded like a malfunctioning blaster, each fracture emerging from the jagged line cut by Komat's lightsaber. Then Panshard swung his arms down, and the ground erupted, tons of crystal carbon rising up into the air, held aloft by the will of the dead Sith Lord.

Luke looked up and braced himself, ready to deflect the rubble with the Force as best he could. The mass of debris was enormous, and it was going to not only crush him but fall on a large area around him, making it impossible to dive out of the way.

Then the ground erupted again. Luke fell and rolled over; he saw KB-68 fall, the disarmed droid having kept well away from the duel. In front of him, Exim Panshard staggered backward, the vast mass of crystal once held aloft now crashing onto the ground around him as he lost control.

Then Luke rolled again, and saw Komat vanish behind a huge, dark shape that emerged from the ground and shot into the black sky.

It was a serpent, fifty meters long, its green-black body slick and wet as it emerged from the underground sea, the muscles of its vast body propelling it up vertically.

It was joined by its mate a moment later, the two lithe forms twining together in the air, then twisting apart as they reached the apex of their climb and fell back toward the ground. Their heads were nothing but enormous jaws, wide open, filled with row upon row of triangular teeth the color of steel.

They were going for Komat, who had been closest to the now gaping maw in the ground. Luke stood and saw her scrambling backward, her hand and heels sliding hopelessly on the wet crystal ground as the underground sea lapped at the edges of the hole.

Luke pushed himself to his feet, and sprinted for Komat, pushing out with the Force as he raced toward her. The pressure wave of the Force hit the serpents, knocking them to the side as Luke reached Komat. He helped her to her feet, then, hardly stopping, dragged her toward the tear in the moon's crust, throwing her into the exposed portion of the hidden sea before diving in after her. Underwater, the pair found each other, then watched the flickering tails of the twin serpents shoot up past them as the creatures turned their attention elsewhere. Treading water, Komat nodded at Luke, and the pair swam to the surface, emerging at the hard edge of the hole, the rim as sharp as a razor.

Beyond the hole, Luke watched as the serpents coiled around each other as they slid toward Exim Panshard at frightening speed on the near-frictionless ground. Panshard swung with his lightsaber, but the blade merely glanced off the shining scales of the serpents, doing nothing but angering them further.

Panshard's rage echoed across the moon as one of the serpents wrapped its long body around his while the other rose up and then, jaws wide, came straight down, ready to swallow the prize. Panshard lifted his weapon again and slashed at the gaping maw. The creature roared with pain as its top row of teeth was severed, the triangular, knifelike objects skidding across the wet, glassy ground. The serpent backed away, then turned, heading now for the safety of the moon's new lake.

Luke saw the creature approach—apparently unaware of the two people in its path—and pulled himself up onto the surface, turning to grab Komat's arm and yank her up. His boots slipped on the surface and he nearly fell, but was caught by two metal arms.

KB-68 pulled Luke backward, her metal heels cracking into the ground as she created her own traction. Moments later, the droid lost her balance and fell backward, lifting Luke and Komat with her, just as the injured serpent dived into the water and was gone.

"Help me!"

Luke and Komat were on their feet at once. On the other side of the lake, Panshard was still held by the serpent. As Luke watched, he flailed with his lightsaber, but the blade bounced off the crest of the serpent's armored head, and the blade deactivated, the weapon flung away under the force of the impact.

But the voice cried out again—small, female, muffled by the heavy mask.

"Kiza!" Komat yelled. She ran for her former friend, using the slick surface of the moon to drop into a fast slide, a wave of water gushing around her boots as she grabbed Kiza's lightsaber, activating the blade even as she kept sliding, before using the weapon to gouge a foothold in the ground to arrest her movement. Getting back to her feet, she ran for Kiza.

Partway there, she froze, coming to an abrupt—and impossible— stop. Luke got to his feet and made for her, realizing now that Kiza's voice had been a trick, as Viceroy Exim Panshard held Komat in place with the Force even as he used that same power to tear the serpent that held him to pieces. Now freed, and standing on his own feet, Panshard reached out toward Komat, yanking the lightsaber from her grip. The red blade shot through the air—

—and into Luke's hand, his bare cybernetic fingers curling around the black metal with a series of clicks.

Panshard spun around as Luke lifted both the red blade and his own green one. The voice of the dead Sith Lord raging from behind the mask, he raised his arms, ready to use the Force once more against the Jedi Master.

Too slow. Luke used the same power to pull the mask from Kiza's face. As it flew toward him, he sensed Panshard using the Force on the mask himself, turning it in the air so the interior now faced Luke, ready to claim the Jedi Master as a new host.

Luke's reflexes were lightning-fast. Just before the mask made contact with his face, he raised both lightsabers and slashed down, crossing the green and red blades in front of him.

The mask, cut into four pieces, hit the ground, skittering along it until Luke called on the Force to make them stop.

Kiza's body collapsed, telescoping down onto the ground, a puppet with its strings suddenly cut.

Luke deactivated both lightsabers and stepped cautiously forward, his soaked robes heavy and cold. Kiza was lying facedown, her arms spread out, the mechanical replacement limb twitching, three blunt metal fingers tapping against the diamond surface as its energy pack discharged.

Luke bent down and was about to turn the body over when the injured serpent exploded out of the lake once more, its damaged jaw open and snapping. Luke allowed himself to fall backward, out of the way, as the creature grabbed Kiza's limp body then turned and carried it swiftly back into the churning waters.

Luke pushed himself up onto his elbows, and then onto his haunches. He sat, gasping for breath. Nearby, KB-68 helped Komat to her feet, and the two of them made their way over to Luke.

The moon was silent, save for the gentle lapping of the water.

It was over. Already, Luke's mind began to clear—it had not been clouded, exactly, but the disturbance in the Force, the malign presence of the spirit of Viceroy Exim Panshard, had been with him for weeks, he now realized. It was the source of his visions of Exegol, the source of his nightmares, his uncertainties.

The source of his fears.

Nearby, the pieces of the viceroy's mask smoked on the ground, leaving a black, sooty residue on the diamond surface.

Luke stared at them a long time, but they were nothing more than burned metal and shattered crystal, the power they once held extinguished now and, he hoped, forever.

CHAPTER 58

CSA CAPITAL SHIP *EMCHEN,*
DEEP SPACE RECONNAISSANCE
NOW

If there was one thing the Corporate Sector Authority excelled at, thought High Colonel Enric Pryde as he took another turn around the spacious bridge, it was *arrogance.*

That was, in fact, a very high compliment. The CSA had some lofty ambitions, and members who worked hard to achieve them. That was something to respect.

Take the capital ship they had essentially *given* to Pryde as his command while he was on this temporary . . . secondment. It was one of two command ships in the fleet—this one was the *Emchen,* sister of the *Kaywhite*—and it was . . . big. Very big, in fact. Perhaps not a Star Destroyer, more a midsized executive ship, a small frigate. An easier command, certainly, and somewhat more agile, responsive. And yet the CSA treated it as though it were some kind of planet-busting superweapon.

It was faintly ridiculous—it was no wonder the CSA needed people like Pryde to show them just how empires were forged—but there was something about the whole situation that Pryde actually admired. The CSA thought they were replacing the grandeur of the Empire. That they were entirely wrong was beside the point, but the fact that they, and their own officers like Viceprex Coromun, seemed to *genuinely* believe this, was an impressive feat of cognitive dissonance.

Pryde completed another lap of the bridge, the design of which even imitated the old Imperial architecture, with raised command dais, sunken technical pits, the brown-uniformed CSA crew all hard at work doing, as far as Pryde could see, very little.

Well, no change there.

He made his way slowly down the length of the bridge, enjoying the echo of his boots, enjoying the way he could look down his nose—literally, as well as figuratively—at the pit crews as he passed them. When he reached the arch of the bridge's huge forward viewports, he looked at, not the depths of space that stretched before them, but his own reflection in the transparisteel.

He shivered. He looked pale. Ill, even. Something from that blasted rock, Basta Core. Or maybe it was from that Ochi of *wherever.*

Aliens. You never knew where they'd been.

Pryde shivered again.

He'd never warmed up. He supposed he could send someone to his quarters to fetch his greatcoat. He frowned, stood taller, looked down his nose at *himself* in the reflection. Would that show weakness? Did that *matter?*

He glanced, in the reflection, at the nearest pit crew, and he swore as he did so that they all quickly looked away, like they'd been watching his back.

He sighed again. He was cold. He was thirsty. Abrax, that would warm him up. He muttered under his breath as he recalled where the flask of the precious liquor had ended up and how long it would be before he was on a planet where he could procure some more—all charged as a corporate expense, of course.

No, what he needed was embrocation. That would get him warm, at least until he was off this ship. He recalled, with a smile, the stuff the Ewoks of Endor had used, a concoction of the boiled fat of their enemies, emulsified with strong, almost mineralized oil of one of the species of giant tree that covered their moon. Now, *that* was a liniment. It had proved most useful on the cold Endor nights, awaiting the inevitable arrival of the rebels. Pryde remembered the tang of the stuff, the slight feeling of light-headedness the solventlike mixture produced.

The Ewoks had been very useful. Marvelous insulating fur, too. That greatcoat he had had made from the pelts of an entire family of the little creatures was one of the finest pieces of tailoring he'd ever owned. Worthy of an officer of the rank of high colonel.

Pryde's happy reminiscence was disturbed by the approach, in the reflection, of Viceprex Coromun, the lifelong CSA devotee marching down from the other end of the bridge. He stopped at Pryde's shoulder. The two men's eyes met in the reflection; Pryde frowned, more than a little annoyed that his CSA adjunct hadn't saluted him.

"Well?" he asked.

"Your *agent*," said Coromun, his face twitching as the little episode on Basta Core was remembered. "He demands you speak to him, immediately."

Pryde barked a small laugh. "That *thing* can demand all he likes. Our business was concluded on that wretched planet, and if I see Ochi of *Bestoon*"—he pronounced the word like he didn't believe it was a real place, not for an instant—"again, I will not be held responsible for my actions." He paused, his smile widening. "Or perhaps I should assign that particular duty to you, Viceprex?"

Coromun grinned. Pryde could see the struggle in the other man as he tried and failed, miserably, to control his emotions.

Yes, this was how you led. This was how you demonstrated authority. Give little people like Coromun just a bit of what they wanted, now and again, and soon enough they would be eating out of your hand.

An alert rang out across the bridge. Pryde and Coromun both turned, looking down into the comm pit.

"Incoming transmission, sirs," said the crew member. "Priority one channel."

Pryde and Coromun glanced at each other; Pryde shook his head wearily, but Coromun gave the nod anyway.

Priority one channel? Oh, *please*.

In the middle of the bridge, the blue, head-and-shoulders holographic form of Ochi of Bestoon materialized. His shimmering image leaned forward, and—to Pryde's annoyance—took a swig from Pryde's own Abrax flask.

"I need more men." Ochi's voice echoed out across the bridge, Pryde noting the slight slur behind the words.

Pryde straightened himself, running the flat of his hand across his greased-back hair almost self-consciously.

"*That,* my dear fellow," he said calmy, "is entirely your own affair. Our arrangement is at an end." Beside him, he could feel the viceprex rocking on his heels, enjoying the authority in Pryde's tone. "More to the point," the high colonel continued, "if you come within a parsec of the Corporate Sector, I will know about it, and it will be *your* turn to be hunted down across the galaxy."

With that, he waved a hand, and the hologram vanished. Then, one arm outstretched toward the comm pit, he snapped his fingers. "Get me a trace on his ship."

"Immediately, sir," came the response. As soon as the crew member spoke, there was another alert, this time from a different section.

"Proximity alert," called the officer at her station. "Hyperspace flux, very close."

"What?" Pryde and Coromun turned to face the viewport just as a ship lurched into existence outside. Pryde jerked back in reflex surprise, as the nose of the new arrival was barely a meter away from the bridge viewport.

Viceprex Coromun pointed down to the comm pit. "Hail that ship, mister!"

"Aye, sir."

Another tone, repeated, as the *Emchen* contacted the new arrival. Recovering his composure, Pryde moved back to the viewport. The other ship was a CSA transport, large enough to carry a contingent of troopers and their matériel. The forward viewports of the boat were large and steeply angled, allowing Pryde a view directly into the other flight deck.

"*Ochi,*" he breathed.

. . .

Ochi of Bestoon stood in the other ship, drinking from Steadfast's flask. There was a chime as contact was established.

"What are you doing?" Coromun's voice echoed around the bridge. "You could have killed us, and yourself."

Ochi's laugh was small and filled with menace. "But I didn't," he said. "You underestimate me. I think you underestimate a lot of things. I felt it was time we conducted these negotiations in person."

"There are no negotiations." Steadfast, now. "I will give you two minutes to plot an exit vector or I will blow your ship out of the system. *Now* who has been underestimated?"

Ochi laughed again. He stepped forward in his borrowed ship until he was as close to the viewport as he could get. In the capital ship, separated by a few centimeters of transparisteel and a meter of hard vacuum, Steadfast moved forward, too. Together, he and Ochi were almost as close as if they were face-to-face on the CSA capital ship's bridge.

"I need a full squadron of ships, plus a phalanx of troopers," said Ochi, sipping from the flask again. "You can keep your capital ship, but I will need something faster than this crate."

He watched as Coromun visibly bristled, but Steadfast held up a hand, quieting his subordinate.

"An entire squadron, Ochi of Bestoon? I thought you were supposed to be the best hunter in the galaxy. Don't tell me you've lost them? A mother and a father and a child? Hardly the most difficult bounty in the galaxy, I would have thought."

Ochi slammed his flask down on his control console. "A minor setback. They took the *Bestoon Legacy* and deactivated the transponder. I need ships to search. Lots of ships." He stabbed a finger at the other man. "And *you* will supply them."

Steadfast laughed. "You fail at one simple task, and you come crawling back for help."

"I am Ochi of Bestoon! I do not fail!"

"You are pathetic. I'd feel sorry for you if I could stand the sight of you."

Ochi lowered his hand. "You will regret those words one day, Steadfast."

The other man grinned.

Ochi didn't like the expression. He wanted to wipe it off Steadfast's face. Give the blade of the Sith Eternal a taste of the arrogant fool's blood. Already, he could feel the dagger singing in his head.

Steadfast lifted his chin. "I can tell you exactly where they are."

Ochi froze, then tilted his head, a curious tooka-cat listening to a curious sound.

"What?"

"It's really quite simple," said Steadfast, "but then I don't expect you to have thought of it. I had a tracker fixed to your ship." He turned and looked down at the technical pit. As Ochi watched, Steadfast clicked his fingers, and one of the officers sprang up the steps onto the bridge platform and handed him a datapad.

Steadfast glanced at the 'pad then stepped as close as he could to the viewport. The CSA patrol boat Ochi had commandeered was sitting a fraction lower than the *Emchen*'s bridge, the difference exaggerating the height difference between the two men.

"They are on Jakku," said Steadfast, then he frowned. "I mean, if you can't handle a simple job like this, you could always go to one of the gangs you used to run with. Or, no, did they all throw you out as well? Never mind, I'm sure you have some old drinking buddies who would be more willing to lend you support than the CSA."

"Jakku?" Ochi muttered. "You are sure of this?"

In the other ship, Steadfast handed the datapad to Coromun, then clasped his hands behind his back. "Of course," he said.

Ochi recognized the body language immediately—it was the conceit and superiority of the old Imperial officers. Maybe this Steadfast was a survivor of the old order. Suddenly his attitude started to make a lot of sense. Couldn't be easy, seeing all you worked for on fire, forced to work for second-rate wannabes like the CSA.

Ochi was starting to feel better already.

There was a click as the comm channel was closed. Pryde watched as, in the CSA transport, Ochi almost fell into the pilot's seat. Within moments the smaller craft reversed away from the *Emchen* and swung around to take a vector that would lead it to a safe jump distance.

Beside the high colonel, Viceprex Coromun sprang to life. He ran to the weapons pit and started barking instructions at the crew. A moment later, he looked up at Pryde. "We have him in range. Shall I fire?"

Pryde watched Ochi's boat begin to recede into the distance. He pursed his lips. "No," he said. "I've had enough of Ochi of Bestoon. It would be a waste of energy. Let him dig his own grave." He turned from the viewport and marched back down the bridge walkway.

Ochi of Bestoon? How pathetic.

One day, there would be no room for the likes of Ochi of Bestoon.

One day, thought Pryde, there would be a new order in the galaxy.

And one day, I will be in charge.

CHAPTER 59

NIIMA OUTPOST, JAKKU
NOW

Dathan sat in the shade of the awning, looking out into the desert. Niima Outpost was bustling, a hive of activity as traders, merchants, and scavengers all argued and haggled, bought and sold, had their disagreements, made friends. It was a place Dathan knew well—a place that, while he was never entirely comfortable in it, he had, at least, felt safe.

Dathan blinked at that thought. Safe? Really? He interrogated his feelings, but . . . yes, safe. That concept had entered his head, entirely unforced.

Safe. They had been safe here.

Until . . . they weren't. But that wasn't Niima Outpost, that was something else, the darkness that Dathan had brought here himself. Once that was removed from the equation, then . . .

He smiled, but only slightly. He decided not to dwell on his emotions right now, knowing full well he could just have been rationalizing, making this decision—*their* decision—as palatable as possible.

Safe.

That wasn't to say Jakku wasn't rough. It was. But it, or Niima Outpost, anyway, wasn't *lawless*, and not everybody in the town was a villain. There were good people here—it was just that sometimes, it took a while to learn who they were.

People like Unkar Plutt.

Quite how a Crolute had ended up in the desert of Jakku, Dathan had never discovered. Perhaps that contributed to his mood, because he had never known Plutt *not* to be angry about something. Plutt was not a person who made friends—he was not a person who *wanted* friendship, because that was a kind of deal where you were expected to contribute something without any requirement that you get something in return.

Which made friendship bad for business, according to Unkar Plutt. He lived by another creed entirely, one devoted to power and to profit. For Plutt, those were two sides of the same coin—power led to profit, profit bought power. He took no sides. He made no judgments. If you were useful to him, then you could do business. If you weren't, then you might as well not even have existed.

That's why they were here. Unkar Plutt was the most unpleasant, most obnoxious, most callous individual Dathan had ever met.

He was also the only person they could trust right now.

Dathan looked out at the desert stretching in front of him; Niima Outpost itself was to his back. He could see wrecked ships from here—on the horizon, the hull of a Star Destroyer was less a wreck and more a part of the landscape, the moving sands gathering around it but never being able to bury the gigantic thing. The sands did, however, make short work of the rest of the battlefield—sometimes salvage work on Jakku required more time excavating the wrecks than actually stripping them down. Ships like the Star Destroyer were a tempting target, but Dathan knew of too many people who had been killed trying to safely navigate the shattered hull.

A speeder crossed his vision, and he blinked out of his reverie. Miramir had been with Plutt for hours. And . . .

Dathan frowned, and rubbed his forehead. Yes, he felt guilty at letting his wife make the deal. Here they were, making the most important decision of their lives, and . . . he couldn't do it. Part of his mind mocked him, calling him a coward, berating him for running away and hiding, not merely unable to face the dangers ahead but unwilling to even try.

Worse, he feared that he was being a bad father—that he didn't even know what it was, to be a good parent. His own upbringing, his childhood, had been a living nightmare. How could he possibly have thought he could raise a child of his own? That he had put Rey through a short life of hardship before now striking a mercenary deal with Unkar Plutt was nothing short of criminal.

Dathan worked hard to control his breathing, to calm himself. Perhaps some of those thoughts were true, and he accepted those feelings, those emotions. Of course they would come, and he knew there would be worse yet. He had to be prepared for the hard road ahead, as much as he could be.

Because he knew, he honestly knew, that they were doing the right thing, and that their sole concern *was* for their daughter. They'd been lucky so far, and that luck could run out at any time. Rey didn't deserve that. If they were going to get to safety—if *he* was going to get them to safety—then he had to know Rey was safe. And, Dathan reminded himself, it was only temporary. An arrangement—a business deal—nothing more, nothing less. They would leave Rey in safety. They would . . . fix things. Escape their pursuers. Make contact with the Jedi. Get the help they so desperately needed.

And then they would come back.

And that was it.

The sound of boots on a dusty floor made Dathan stand and turn around. Miramir appeared in the rear entrance of the large tent which formed a rear extension to Plutt's store, pushing aside the flap of heavy fabric. He locked eyes with his wife, and then she stepped down into the Jakku dust. They didn't speak. They didn't need to. Miramir moved forward and held her husband in an embrace that lasted for a long, long time.

Eventually, they pulled apart. Miramir wiped the tears from her cheeks, and then, looking into Dathan's eyes, wiped the tears from his.

"Where's Rey?" Dathan asked.

"Inside," whispered Miramir. She glanced down. Dathan took her hands. She was trembling—her whole body was shaking. Then she choked back a sob and, pulling away from her husband, she turned and ran back inside.

Dathan moved to the entrance and looked inside. Rey stood, alone, in the middle of the space. Miramir didn't stop, she fell to her knees, sweeping her daughter up, the hood of her blue cloak falling back, her face hot, the tears stinging in her eyes.

This beautiful woman, tears in her wide eyes, hugged her beautiful daughter.

"My love," she said, and then she looked at Rey's tiny face, held in her hands. "Rey, be brave."

Dathan ran in. He knelt beside his wife, his daughter. He looked at Rey. "You'll be safe here," he said, his voice cracking with emotion. "I promise."

Rey burst into tears, crying now with her mother.

Dathan's heart broke, the sobs of his wife and his child a dagger to his own heart.

But all that mattered now was that Rey would be safe, for as long as she needed to be. As he drew Miramir and Rey into a tight hug, he buried his face in their hair.

Miramir's voice was a whisper.

"Stay here. I'll come back for you. *We'll* come back for you, Rey. We need to go and do something. I'll come back, sweetheart. I promise. And dad will be here, too. We'll all be together again. You'll be safe here until then. I know Unkar shouts a lot, but he doesn't mean it. It's just how he is. But he'll keep you safe. I promise, I promise."

Dathan screwed his eyes tight shut. He wanted to stay like this forever, to have his family in his arms, to have Rey close and Miramir close and for them all to be together, safe.

Safe, and free.

Heavy footfalls announced the return of their unlikely protector, Unkar Plutt, from his store proper. Dathan opened his eyes and stood. Miramir looked up, clutching Rey to her chest.

Plutt held up one meaty paw. In it dangled the hex charm amulet. He looked at it, and sniffed, loudly.

"Analysis complete," he said. "It is songsteel, like you said. Of course I had to check. I wouldn't take kindly to our arrangement starting off with an untruth, now would I?"

Dathan walked around to put himself between his family and the Crolute. He nodded at the amulet and chain.

"It should be more than enough."

Plutt grunted. "No such thing as *more* than enough. But it will do. For now."

Dathan sighed and held up both hands. "It's only temporary. We'll be back before the end of the season."

Plutt stuffed the amulet down the neck of his tunic. "You'd better." He pointed a thick finger at Rey. "Any longer and her ledger will be in the red, and she'll have to start working to pay the debt."

"Don't worry," said Dathan, "don't worry."

"Oh, but I do worry, Dathan," said Plutt, taking a step forward. "I worry a very great deal." He paused and closed one eye as he peered down at the human. "I don't know what kind of trouble you are in, but I don't want you to bring it back here. I had enough trouble out at your farmstead."

At this, Miramir stood. "We won't bring you trouble," she said, wiping her face with the heel of each hand. "And we're grateful for your business, truly."

Plutt made a sound that was part snort, part belch. Dathan knew that sound well—the junk boss was uncomfortable about something.

"I just hope you know what you're doing," said Plutt.

Dathan nodded. "We know what we're doing."

Plutt's bass-drum *hrmm* rattled the collection of junk in the tent around him. Miramir glanced around at the noise. Dathan watched as she moved to a table where a string of loosely threaded beads had fallen off the top of a squat ceramic urn.

"What is it?" asked Dathan as Miramir, still holding Rey by the hand, went over to the urn and picked up the beads.

"I know these," she said, perhaps more to herself than the others.

Plutt was watching her, too. "Aki-Aki beads," he said.

Miramir nodded slowly. "From Pasaana, aren't they?" Holding the beads up, she moved closer to Plutt. Plutt, meanwhile, was scratching the side of his stomach.

"Good place to lose someone, Pasaana," said Plutt. He then looked sideways at Dathan and actually *winked* at him. "If you have someone to lose, that is."

Seeing the confusion on Dathan's face, Plutt continued. "Pasaana is a desert world, but one that is full of surprises. And hazards. Sinking sands. Sarlaccs. Forbidden valleys." Plutt paused and shrugged. "The Aki-Aki can be a bit too literal, you ask me."

Miramir nodded, clearly deep in thought. She held the beads up, and Plutt *hrmm*ed again, then nodded. Miramir slipped them into her cloak.

"Your ship is refueled," said Plutt. "Sooner you go, the sooner you'll be back."

Miramir and Dathan both froze, then slowly looked at each other.

"Mum? What's happening? Dad?"

Miramir looked down at her daughter and squeezed her hand so hard, Rey gasped.

"We'll be back, Rey. I love you."

Dathan took Rey's other hand. "You'll be safe. See you soon. Love you."

Then Dathan and Miramir glanced at each other, and let go of their daughter. Unkar Plutt took Rey's hand.

As Rey started crying again, Dathan and Miramir turned and left, in a hurry.

Outside, they ran to their stolen ship.

"What was that with the beads?" asked Dathan. He didn't know, and he didn't actually care, right now, but the question was a useful distraction from the pain in his heart that threatened to fell him like a tree, right there and then.

"Insurance," said Miramir, and then she picked up speed, springing ahead of her husband.

The ship blasted off with a roar, the twin engines burning with blue fire as it headed into the hot desert sky. Far below, standing outside Plutt's tent, a little girl screamed, her arm held firm by the junk boss.

"Come back! No!" cried Rey. She pulled against the hand holding her, but it was no good, and as she watched, the ship grew smaller, and smaller, and smaller.

And then it was gone.

CHAPTER 60

Lando Calrissian flopped onto the padded seat that curved around the table in the *Star Herald*'s mess, rubbing his face with both hands.

It had not gone well. Not in the slightest.

R2-D2 had been hard at work—*still was* hard at work, the little astromech standing in front of the workstation, data coupling spinning, dome twitching, the droid chirping and beeping to himself as he ran the algorithms again and again, making adjustments, correcting the angle of the scout ship's sensor array, rerouting power to boost the primary antenna dish—and nearly blowing every power conduit in the ship in the process—and all for . . . ?

Nothing. Not. A. Thing.

Whatever Komat's secret was, R2-D2 didn't seem to know it. Lando knew better than to take his frustration out on the droid, of course—right now, R2-D2 was a hell of a lot more use than he was, even if their attempt to replicate hyperwave signal tracking had, so far, come up short.

And as every second passed, their task was getting more and more difficult, the chances of finding Ochi's ship diminishing in a mathematical sequence of probability that Lando really, really didn't care to think about.

With a sigh, Lando dropped his hands and leaned on the table, staring into nothing but the middle distance, wondering just what they were going to do next.

He was a general. A leader. Before that, baron administrator of an entire city. Before that, trader (a good one, too), smuggler (even better), scoundrel (sometimes), gambler (often).

And now? A lost father, an aging hero getting older by the second.

He shook his head. He knew these thoughts, knew how dangerous they were. He'd wrestled with them a lot over the past six years.

But . . . had he really lost it? Was he really getting too old?

Or did he just need to remember how to unlock that fire, that spirit, within himself?

He lifted his arm and looked down at his wrist link. He tapped a sequence, then held his arm out, hand facing the table, as the tiny holoprojector in the device snapped into life.

He sighed, deeply.

"The Calrissian Chronicles," said the ghostly blue image of his younger self. "Chapter seventy-three. Double Jeopardy—or, as I like to call it, the terrible secret of the planet Lahsbane, for reasons that you, fellow sentient being, are about to discover. If you dare!"

Lando chuckled. Had he really recorded up to chapter seventy-three? He cringed as the recording went on, both embarrassed and, actually, slightly impressed at the hubris of his younger self.

Was that younger self still inside him, somewhere? That charm, that cocky self-assuredness. Even the way the little hologram slouched as he related his adventure—to be perfectly honest, Lando couldn't quite remember the details of the planet Lahsbane, and he stopped the playback quickly, perhaps unwilling to recall just how far his younger self had turned adventure into legend.

But those were the days, right? His whole life ahead of him, the future as bright and as open as the galaxy.

Lando sat back again, lost for a moment in melancholic nostalgia. Glancing down, he then noticed there was a cupboard underneath the table. The table itself had a checkerboard surface, ready to be used for tabletop gaming to pass the long hours in hyperspace.

On a whim, Lando slid the compartment's door open. Inside was a stack of games—something called *Naboo Kingmaker,* something else called *Lavorgna's Age of Dragons,* and sandwiched between the boxes, a battered deck of sabacc cards.

He grabbed the cards and leaned over the table, idly shuffling them. They were greasy and sticky, the edges brown with years of play.

A perfect deck, in other words.

That was when an alert sounded from the flight deck. Lando looked up sharply.

"Artoo?"

The astromech's whistle was loud and clear.

Reassembling the deck in his hands, Lando got up from the table and ran to the flight deck. Inside, R2-D2 had disconnected himself from the main workstation and was trundling across to the flight positions. He installed himself next to the pilot's chair and accessed the dataport there.

Lando watched him, his eyes wide.

"Wait, did you get something?"

R2-D2's dome spun around, and his indicator flashed as he gave a shrill but happy whistle.

Affirmative.

"Yes. *Yes!*" Lando made a fist in the air as he swung himself around and sat in the pilot's seat. He dumped the sabacc deck on the console, then looked over the readouts. "Okay, show me what you got, little buddy."

Lando's heart raced, his hopes soaring—

And then crashing.

Lando turned to R2-D2. "Twenty-three? You found *twenty-three* locations for Ochi's ship?"

R2-D2 bleeped. Lando read the response on the console panel, and he sighed.

"Yeah, okay, I know it's difficult, but I thought you helped Komat out last time? Didn't you learn how to do it?"

Another chortled response. Lando frowned at the readout.

"I'm sure it is hard, but—"

More beeps, staccato.

"I agree, Komat should be here with us, but—"

A final string of electronic tones, ending with a whistle and rasping buzz.

Lando sat back and held both hands up. "All right, all right, all right!" Then he let his hands drop in his lap. "But . . . twenty-three?" He shook his head. "We gotta do better than that. There's no way we can search all those vectors," he said, sitting back. "I mean, twenty-three? That's pure sabacc, a winning hand . . ."

Lando trailed off, his eyes on the deck of cards sitting on the console.

He thought about his younger self—about the charm and the charisma and the sheer barefaced *arrogance*, like Lando junior thought the universe owed him something.

Well. Maybe it did.

"Artoo," he said, pointing over at the navicomputer. "Plot the destinations."

R2-D2 whistled inquiringly.

"Yes, *all* of them."

The droid beeped, and the dataport began to rotate again.

Lando picked up the sabacc deck and began to shuffle. For a microsecond, he felt foolish, then he pushed that thought to one side.

No, not foolish. Desperate, yes. Foolish, no.

He held his breath, then turned the first card over onto the console.

"You have gotta be kidding me."

It was the Idiot—card value, zero. Completely useless.

What was that about the universe owing me something?

Lando flipped the next card. Two.

Well, okay.

And the next.

Three.

Lando blinked in surprise.

Zero-two-three. *The idiot's array.* The perfect, unbeatable hand in the game.

Lando opened his mouth, then snapped it shut. He breathed out slowly. "Okay, you have *got* to be kidding me." He turned in his chair. "Artoo, twenty-third location, program it in."

R2-D2 whistled that the task was complete.

"What have we got?" Lando asked, peering at the navicomputer display. "Jakku?" He paused. Jakku. There was an itch, somewhere at the back of his mind. "Huh."

Jakku.

Of course. That was where the family were from—or at least, where they had picked up their original starship, the old freighter, according to Dina Dipurl's report.

The best place to hide, Lando knew full well from experience, was the last place the hunter would look. And *sometimes,* that meant going right back to the place where they'd found you originally.

Lando felt his smile grow. "Okay, Jakku it is. Time to fly."

With that, Lando confirmed the coordinates in the main system, then took a firm grip of the hyperdrive activator and slid the lever forward. Through the angled front viewports of the *Star Herald,* the stars of the galaxy first swelled, then turned into rapidly elongated streaks, then disappeared into a spinning vortex of light.

They were on their way. Lando just hoped that his famous luck was going to hold out.

CHAPTER 61

CSA TRANSPORT, JAKKU SYSTEM
NOW

"Boss. Hey, boss."

Ochi jolted awake, banging the back of his skull on something very hard. He winced, then pushed the other man away as he tried to remember just where he was. And then, slowly, it came back to him.

Where he was, was on the floor of the CSA transport, leaning against a protruding bulkhead at the back of the troop compartment, his legs outstretched, the silver flask of Abrax on his lap. He looked down at the flask, his electronic eyes struggling to focus on the shiny metal.

Abrax was strong stuff, it seemed.

He needed more. He tipped the flask up to his lips and found it was empty. He snarled and let his arm drop, the flask banging against the decking.

"You okay, boss?"

Ochi looked up. Standing in front of him was Bosvarga, his brother Cerensco at his shoulder. The two were looking down at him but keeping their distance—as they had been for the whole journey, since Ochi had stopped to pick them up after leaving his final meeting with Steadfast.

He snarled again.

Ochi of Bestoon was awake, and he was in a bad mood.

"What is it?" he said, his voice a little slurred. He leaned forward to get up; Bosvarga went to help, but Ochi shrugged him off. "Don't touch me! Never touch Ochi of Bestoon. Never." He slipped on the floor, then used the bulkhead to help push himself upright. Standing, he felt a little better.

"We've arrived at Jakku," said Cerensco. He gestured in the direction of the transport's cockpit, and through the bulkhead door, Ochi could see the yellow globe of the planet looming large through the front viewports.

Ochi nodded. "About time," he said. He pushed off from the wall and headed to the cockpit, his head clearing with every step. As he settled in to pilot the ship, his minions behind him, an alert sounded. Ochi ignored it, leaving Bosvarga to reach over to the panel and activate the sensor array.

"Got a ship coming in," he said. Then he paused and glanced at his brother.

"So?" Ochi asked, as he unlocked the autopilot.

"It's the *Bestoon Legacy.*"

Ochi turned sharply to him. Standing behind, Cerensco laughed. "Like shaaks to the slaughter."

Ochi tapped his fingers on the console as he studied the simple but unfamiliar controls of the CSA ship. Beside him, Bosvarga dropped into the copilot's seat. "Better hurry," he said, pointing ahead. "Looks like they're about to jump to lightspeed."

"Everything is under control," said Ochi, and then he yanked the transport's control yoke. The ship banked, sharply, throwing Cerensco off his feet.

"I can fly this if you want," said Bosvarga, clutching the edge of the console as Ochi swung the ship again. Ahead, they were now directly in the path of the *Bestoon Legacy.* "That's close, Ochi, that's close!"

"Shut up," said Ochi. "I know what I'm doing." With that, he reached forward and activated a control. There was a muffled thud, and outside, two cables shot out from the front of the transport, their heavy mag-

netic clamps sticking fast to the side of the *Legacy* as whoever was piloting it banked around to try to find an escape vector.

"Got 'em," said Ochi. "Cerensco, prep the boarding tube. I'll line us
up."

Cerensco pushed himself to his feet and left the cockpit at a run. Bosvarga laughed, watching as Ochi manipulated the controls, using the
magnetic cables to hold the *Legacy* in place and turn it so the entry
ramp was now facing the transport. A mechanical whine sounded, and
at the bottom of the cockpit viewports a square, telescopic metal tube
could be seen extending toward the other ship.

"Come on," said Ochi. "Time to collect."

Locking off the controls, he leapt out of the seat. Behind him, Bosvarga stood and, pulling his blaster, followed his boss.

This is how it ends.

A simple fact, one she knew as soon as the other ship appeared in
space in front of their stolen one. It was a CSA transport—distant, shining in Jakku's sun, the reflective glare making it impossible to see the
pilot through the viewport, but Miramir knew who was at the controls.

It couldn't be anyone else.

She'd disabled the *Bestoon Legacy*'s transponder even as they blasted
off from Taw Provode. There was no way of following the ship. No way
of finding them.

And yet, Ochi of Bestoon had done it.

Sitting next to her, Dathan just stared and shook his head. "Time to
go, time to go," he said, finally.

Miramir worked at the console, setting short coordinates again, just
another quick jump, enough to lose the trail. Studying the readouts, she
waved a hand at her husband.

"There's another tracker somewhere, there must be." She looked up.
She felt dizzy, the rush of adrenaline almost too much. "Go look. Pull
the ship apart. We have to find it."

Dathan stood, but as he turned to leave the flight deck there came a
metallic clang, and the ship shook. Dathan spun back around, and there

was a second clang. The ship rocked hard enough this time for him to fall against the back of the pilot's seat.

"What was that?"

Miramir shook her head. "Grapples." She looked up just in time to see the CSA transport disappear underneath them. "They're going to board us."

This is how it ends.

She tried to jam the entry ramp, but the control embedded in the support pillar exploded under Miramir's fingers, the *Bestoon Legacy*'s owner overriding the command from outside. Dathan grabbed Miramir and pushed her behind him, then they backed away.

Ochi of Bestoon stormed up the ramp of his ship. In his hand he held a strange blade. Miramir felt her eyes drawn to it, could almost feel its presence, like it was alive, like *it* was wielding the hunter, not the other way around.

She held her husband, one arm wrapped around his waist. In the other, she held the beads from Unkar Plutt's store.

Ochi stopped at the top of the ramp. He looked at them, saying nothing, Miramir watching as his chest rose and fell, rose and fell. She could feel the anger, the hate radiating off him.

Then he turned and marched into the flight deck. Dathan shuffled around, keeping Miramir behind him. Then two more people walked up the ramp—a pair of identical beings, with wide skulls and long snouts. They were wearing the same gray armor and they held the same gray blasters, both of them now aimed at Miramir and Dathan.

There was a clatter from the flight deck, then Ochi reemerged. He walked slowly toward Dathan. He held up his blade.

"Where is she?"

The girl's father pulled away from his wife, pushing her back a little as he placed himself between her and Ochi.

The hunter took another step forward. "I said, *where is she?*"

Dathan said nothing. He raised his chin and met Ochi's dead electric gaze.

It was Miramir who spoke. She leaned forward over Dathan's shoulder, the defiance swelling inside her.

She would not show Ochi any fear. She would not give him the satisfaction.

"She isn't on Jakku," she said. "She's gone."

Ochi closed the gap between himself and her husband in a single fast movement—and plunged the dagger into Dathan's stomach, right to the hilt.

Dathan gasped, his body sagging against Ochi.

"No!" Miramir backed away as Dathan's body slid to the decking.

This is how it ends.

Miramir thought of Rey. She wished her daughter to have a good life, that one day someone would take her from Jakku, even if Miramir knew now it would not be her. Because

this is how it ends, and it ends now, but at least Rey you are safe, and maybe one day you will remember me and you will remember your father, and feel our love for you forever, but now you are safe and you must be patient but you are safe, my love, you are safe, you are safe, you are safe, you are

She didn't feel the dagger, but she did feel the pain, and she felt something else, too.

Hunger.

Thirst.

She looked into the eyes of Ochi of Bestoon and as the light went out in her own, she smiled at him, one final act of defiance, one final gesture of non-compliance. Ochi of Bestoon had killed her, but he hadn't won.

He would never win.

The blade drank the spilled blood. Ochi held the woman upright, her face close to his, her mouth twisted into a cruel smile.

The rage inside him was a supernova and in his cybernetic ears was nothing but a wall of endless white noise, so loud he wanted to rip his implant out right there and then.

No one makes a fool of Ochi of Bestoon. No one.

He pushed the blade, pushed again, and then he slowly, almost gently, let the woman's body down onto the deck. He kept his hand on the dagger's hilt, the blade still buried inside her. She lay on the decking, her eyes still open, the smile frozen on her cooling lips.

Ochi stayed like that for a second, two, three. Behind him, Bosvarga and Cerensco shuffled, the twins glancing at each other.

"You okay, boss?" asked Cerensco.

"You want to go down and search Jakku?"

"Boss?"

Finally Ochi pulled the blade out, then he stood, accidentally knocking the woman's hand with his boot. It fell open, revealing the string of beads that she had been clasping tightly as she died.

Ochi glanced down, then nudged the hand again and turned around. He stood and stared at the wall, the dagger still in his hand.

Cerensco and Bosvarga glanced sideways at each other again, then Bosvarga looked down at the two bodies.

"Hey," he said. He reached down and plucked the beads from the woman's hand. "These are Aki-Aki beads."

Ochi turned around. He didn't speak, he just stared at Bosvarga.

Bosvarga held the beads up. "From Pasaana."

Still Ochi didn't speak.

"Pasaana," said Bosvarga again. He gestured to the beads in his outstretched hand.

"You know where these came from?"

Cerensco nodded. "Pasaana. That's what we're say—"

Ochi snatched the beads with his free hand. He brought them close to his optics, and turned them over.

"That's where she is," he whispered. "They've hidden the girl on Pasaana."

His two minions looked at each other but didn't answer. Ochi stood, frozen to the spot, listening to the new sound inside his head, the song of the Sith blade now loud and clear as the white noise receded.

The blade was happy. It had been fed, and fed well.

But it needed more.

Ochi's task was nearly complete. And then the blade would tell—the blade would show him the way to Exegol, where he would bring the girl, collect his reward.

Ochi snapped back into life. He pocketed the beads, then gestured to the bodies with the dagger.

"Get rid of these." He glanced around, then pointed to an empty weapons crate. "Dump them in that." He hissed, a new, amusing thought entering his mind. He turned to the other two. "And find the tracking beacon. Put it in with them, then eject the crate into space."

"I'll go," said Cerensco, quickly holstering his blaster and heading back to the ramp, eager, perhaps to remove himself from Ochi's presence.

As Ochi went to the cockpit, Bosvarga dragged the bodies into the empty crate. As soon as Cerensco reappeared with the tracking beacon pulled from the lower lip of the ship's entry ramp, he tossed the small device into the crate and sealed the lid. Moments later, as the *Bestoon Legacy* pulled away from the now empty CSA transporter, the crate drifted out into space.

Back in the cockpit, Ochi pulled the Abrax flask and then cursed as he remembered it was empty. He turned and threw the flask out of the cockpit, where it clipped D-O's head, sending the droid scuttling away.

"You want a little help there, Ochi?" Bosvarga leaned over the back of Ochi's seat, pointing a heavy finger at the navicomputer. "Pasaana is the Middian system, out in the Ombakond sector—"

"I don't need your help!" yelled Ochi. Bosvarga backed away with a shrug, but then Ochi pushed himself out of the seat and advanced on him.

"You think I don't know how to fly my own ship, Cerensco?"

"It's Bosvarga, and I don't—"

"Don't correct me! Nobody ever corrects Ochi of Bestoon, do you hear me? Do you hear me?"

Bosvarga gave a low whistle. "I think the whole galaxy can hear you, Ochi."

Ochi stepped forward, the static in his eyes now matching the static that grew once more in his head, the blade hot and light and demanding more and more and more.

Bosvarga glanced down. "What are you doing?" he asked, then ducked around, trying to get out of the way, then realized he had his back to the ship's nose, the control console pressing into the small of his back.

"What's going on?"

Ochi turned as Cerensco entered the cockpit, blade pointing right at him. Cerensco lifted his hands, then shuffled around to join his brother.

Ochi froze, yet again, and this time he swayed on his feet, his head spinning, his cybernetic implants using every available processing cycle to isolate the interference, figure out what was going on, all the while rejecting the concept that the blade in Ochi's hand was somehow responsible.

Was somehow . . . alive.

Alive, and hungry.

Bosvarga's hand twitched over his blaster, ready to pull when the moment was right.

It was the last thing he ever did, and the last thing he ever heard was Ochi screaming as he stabbed the blade, over and over again, and the scream of Cerensco, as the two brothers died together, their blood splattering against the front viewports as Ochi surrendered himself to the primal need of the Sith blade one more time.

CHAPTER 62

THE *STAR HERALD*, JAKKU SYSTEM
NOW

Jakku materialized in front of the *Star Herald* as the ship dropped out of hyperspace, the yellow-orange world large and smooth as it hung in space.

Lando gave the planet a quick glance, but he was more interested in the instruments as his fingers flew across buttons, switches, and dials as the pilot turned up every sensor bank the ship had in an attempt to find . . .

Lando sighed. Find something. Anything. Jakku was a big planet—and he wasn't even sure it was the right one.

But just as he began to feel that odd mix of foolishness and guilt again, R2-D2 bleeped, calling Lando's attention to a new reading on the scanners. Immediately, Lando sat up, his back straight, as he focused his attention on the readout.

"I got it," he said, as he adjusted the trackers, homing in on the signal. "It's a tracking beacon." He frowned.

R2-D2 beeped and whistled, and Lando nodded.

"I know, but it's close. I say we take a look."

Lando set the controls and steered the ship along the new vector, one eye on the console readout, the other on the view ahead.

He had a—

Actually, he wasn't quite sure what kind of feeling he had about this. Good? Bad? Somewhere in the middle?

But whatever the case, he certainly had a feeling.

R2-D2 chortled, and Lando pointed ahead.

"There it is." He dropped his hand and leaned forward. "Looks like one of the Corporate Sector transport ships." He grinned, just a little, then his brow furrowed in thought and he began to absentmindedly rub a finger along the underside of his mustache.

The CSA ship meant they were in the right place, assuming it was the one Ochi had taken. But the transport was drifting, the engines dead, according to the *Star Herald*'s readout.

Something was wrong. And as for the tracking beacon, why would it be attached to the dead transporter anyway?

R2-D2 bleeped and whistled. Lando glanced, distracted, at the droid. "What?" Then he looked at the readout and cocked his head. "*What?*"

The tracking signal wasn't coming from the ship, it was coming from a small object that was now just visible, floating near the craft—as Lando carefully brought the *Star Herald* closer, he could see it was an equipment crate, lazily turning end over end.

There was a soft thud from somewhere above. Lando glanced up, wondering what he'd hit that the ship's sensor banks hadn't detected— something low mass, low density?—when a shape drifted over the top of the *Star Herald*'s front viewports, then tumbled down the long nose of the scout craft.

Lando grimaced. It was a body, frozen in the cold vacuum of space. One of Ochi's minions, one of the pair Lando had first seen at Boxer Point Station.

Lando blinked, quite unsure what to make of the situation. Had the family actually done it? Had they finally confronted their pursuers . . . and won? There was no sign of Ochi's ship, the CSA transporter had no lifesigns, and at least one of Ochi's men had met his end.

"Artoo, is there a way we can scoop that crate into the hold?"

R2-D2 whistled the affirmative, then continued with a long string of Binary, the translation of which filled the display panel on Lando's console. Lando held up his hands. "Great, just show me what to do."

R2-D2 chirped, then disconnected himself from the dataport and wheeled off out of the cockpit. Lando unclipped the belt on his flight seat, then stood and took another look at the drifting debris outside.

"Let's see what we got here," he said to himself, before following R2-D2 out.

CHAPTER 63

THE FORBIDDEN VALLEY, PASAANA
NOW

Ochi set the *Bestoon Legacy* down on a bluff overlooking a vast stretch of desert that cut between two jagged mountain ranges. According to the navicomputer, this was the so-called Forbidden Valley on the planet Pasaana.

Ochi shook his head and took a swig from his flask, refilled not with Abrax but a sickly blue liquid he had tapped from the coolant system of his hyperdrive motivator. It was thick and sweet, and it did extremely pleasant things to his other senses as it coated his tongue and mouth, the burn in his throat mixing with the hot metal taste of blood.

"Master. Don't go. Don't go. Master. Don't go."

Ochi lurched in the flight seat, swinging a fist toward D-O but missing by meters.

"Don't tell Ochi of Bestoon what to do. Nobody tells Ochi of Bestoon what to do!"

He pushed himself up and marched into the main cabin, taking one more mouthful of distilled coolant before tossing the flask into a corner.

His vision crackled with black sparks as he looked around, his cybernetic implants sounding a warning about the toxic compounds they had now detected in Ochi's system.

Ochi hissed a wet, snakelike laugh. It was strong stuff, all right. Nothing but the best for Ochi of Bestoon.

He began searching the cabin, sweeping equipment aside until he found what he was looking for—his old pair of quadnocs, which were sitting in their charging cradle. He picked them up, knocking the cradle to the floor, and then he headed for the exit ramp.

Outside it was hot and bright. Ochi's optics struggled a little against the glare, the neuro-electronic interface between the implants and his biological brain impaired by his drinking. He swayed a little, sliding on the rocks as he found a good lookout position, then raised the quadnocs to his electronic eyes and scanned the land ahead.

It was a desert, like hundreds Ochi had seen before. Tall mountains, sand dunes that shifted, exposing more pale-orange rock. Ahead, as the twin mountain ranges seemed to converge on the valley, the sand looked darker—ore deposits, probably, Ochi thought. He adjusted the quadnocs, trying to get a better look.

And then he saw him—the man, over in the dark sand fields. He stood there, still, watching the *Bestoon Legacy*—watching Ochi.

Ochi lowered the quadnocs, his blue-stained tongue running over his lipless slit of a mouth. He could see nothing now, just the valley, the dark sand, devoid of life.

Of course he was imagining it. It was his optical circuits, or his head implant, malfunctioning. Throwing up a vision of the man he had killed, the father of the child he sought—a glitch, a distraction, a false memory presented as visual hallucination thanks to his impaired neurons.

He raised the quadnocs again. There was nothing there but dark sand and rock and

a woman in a blue hooded cloak

and Ochi stumbled, his balance failing him as he fell to his knees on the hard rock and

a woman in a blue hooded cloak watching his ship, watching him

and he stood up, his shout of anger echoing around the valley as he raised the quadnocs and saw

a woman in a blue hooded cloak and a man beside her and

Nothing.

Ochi of Bestoon yelled again. It was a . . . trick. Some kind of illusion, deliberate. They were taunting him. Teasing him. Telling him he had failed already, that he would never get the girl, he would never get to Exegol.

He fell to his knees again, the quadnocs on the rock beside him. He stared at the valley, at the dark sands, while his hand crept closer and closer to the dagger hanging on his belt.

When he touched it, he felt its chill, he felt its fire, and his head cleared, suddenly, like someone had turned on a light. Pasaana shone brightly under its blazing sun, the mountains that shaped the Forbidden Valley casting shadows deep and wide.

Ochi got to his feet and climbed back up the outcrop and into the *Bestoon Legacy*. D-O moved forward, inquiring as to the health of his master, and Ochi turned. He picked the tiny droid up and threw it with all his might against the wall before heading to his speeder, parked at the rear of the ship. Climbing aboard, he activated the repulsors and revved the engine. Then he took the Sith blade out and held it tightly in one hand as he lowered the speeder on its lifter, then exited through the *Legacy*'s rear cargo doors. He headed out into the desert, the speeder bumping down the near-vertical side of the outcropping, threatening to throw its driver out over the vehicle's hood.

But Ochi held tight with one hand, riding it out, and as the speeder hit the ground, its repulsors firing and throwing a wall of sand behind it as they adjusted themselves to the terrain, Ochi stood in the driver's seat, the throttle locked on full, the speeder's nose pointed into the valley.

The vehicle rocketed onward, Ochi's short cape streaming out behind him, the dagger held in front of him. Over the wind and the sand, he could hear the dagger. It was singing to him, telling him a story about Exegol, about the Sith, about Ochi's own destiny.

The child was here. Ochi knew it. She'd been hidden. Her parents were so stupid, keeping the Aki-Aki beads, thinking that they had succeeded, delivering their precious daughter to safety. They had been so stupid, vastly overestimating their own intelligence. That was not a problem Ochi ever suffered from.

Ochi was different. He was a hunter. The best in the galaxy. Nobody was better than Ochi of Bestoon.

The speeder bumped underneath him, then slowed, suddenly. Ochi, still balanced on the front seat, rocked forward and grabbed hold of the speeder's low windshield to keep himself upright as the vehicle came to a slow stop. He dropped down into the seat and checked the controls, gunning the accelerator.

As his foot operated the pedal, the rear corner of the speeder sank; looking behind, Ochi saw a spray of heavy black sand arc into the air at the back of the vehicle. Ochi slammed his foot down on the accelerator again, but all this did was make the rear of the speeder sink even further, the front of the vehicle now lifting a clear meter into the air, the repulsorlift engines whining horribly as they began to overheat, unable to compensate for the unstable terrain.

Ochi stood again, realizing now that the speeder was beached. He swung himself over the side of the vehicle, dagger still clutched firmly in his hand.

Fine. He would proceed on foot. He was so close to the girl, he could feel it.

What he could also feel was the way his feet were sinking into the dark sand underneath him. He glanced down and pulled his foot up and out of the dry mire.

But all this did was make his other leg sink further, up to the knee. Ochi pushed down with his free foot, trying to step up and out, but then that leg disappeared into sand and became trapped by the sucking sensation that was rapidly growing stronger.

Ochi managed to turn, both arms held up, as he now realized he was waist-deep in the dark sand. Beside him, there was a stony roar, like someone pouring a load of ferro-ceramics from a huge hopper, and his speeder tipped back, hex charm emblem to the sky, then vanished straight down into the sinking sands.

Ochi felt himself being pulled downward. Now he was buried to his armpits. He pushed down on the black sand, which had a smooth, almost seedlike consistency, but his arm disappeared and he couldn't pull it back up.

For a moment, Ochi wondered if he had made a mistake. Why would they have hidden the girl here? Why would the mother have kept the beads? He tried to recall her last words, but he couldn't, so loud was the song of the blade in his head, then and now, scrambling any logical thoughts as his cybernetic implant scrambled for coherence.

He remembered the father. And he remembered the mother. Her name was Miramir, and now, as the world disintegrated around him, he remembered her face. He had thought she was afraid of Ochi of Bestoon, the greatest hunter the galaxy had ever known.

But no. She wasn't afraid of him. She wasn't even thinking of him as he pushed the blade into her body, letting it drink of her blood. She was thinking of her daughter. The child Ochi had been tasked to find.

The child that was still out there, somewhere.

Hidden.

Safe.

And then Ochi of Bestoon held his head back, optics to the sky, as his head sank beneath the surface. The Sith dagger, held high, flashed in the desert sun, then it, too, was gone as the sinking sands of the Forbidden Valley of Pasaana claimed another unwary traveler to their suffocating depths.

CHAPTER 64

NEFTALI, SOCORRO SYSTEM, OUTER RIM
NOW

Neftali was a cold, frozen world, a planet of tundra and glacier, of ice floes and crystal seas. Barren, the surface scoured by a biting wind that never dropped, reducing the ambient temperature in half again.

Barren, but not lifeless. Deep beneath the surface, at the end of tunnel-like caves, there was warmth, and there was even light, as glowing mosses and ferns illuminated the secret underground world in a rainbowlike cascade of color.

Lando Calrissian had been to Neftali before. In the old days, Neftali had been a useful stopping point for criminal cartels, the underground caves the perfect place to hide illicit goods and to conduct illegal business—Lando knew that because he had been one of those criminals, once upon a time, doing deals in the glowing yellow and red and purple and blue light of the caverns.

But that was the old days, and while the cartels were still around— old and new alike—Neftali had fallen into disuse. Business was done differently now. The remoteness of the planet and the secrecy of the caves were now an inconvenience.

Nobody came to Neftali now.

That was why Lando and Luke, and Komat and R2-D2 were there.

They stood together in the cavern. Around them, the ferns and mosses glowed softly, casting their gentle light over the two cairns of deep-blue slate that occupied the center of the chamber.

It was Lando who had suggested Neftali. Luke remembered his old friend's transmission, pleading with Luke to hurry, as he described what he had found inside the crate floating in orbit above Jakku, his voice cracking with a pain and sorrow that Luke didn't wish on anyone. Neftali was a good choice, Luke knew that. Nobody would find the bodies here. They could rest in peace, free from the clutches of Ochi of Bestoon.

Wherever he was.

The trio stood by the cairns, heads bowed, Komat's mirror mask reflecting the light of the plants. There was new writing across her mask—a new prayer, this time not one for herself, but for a woman and a man that they had never known, but that they had tried to help, nonetheless.

After several minutes of silent reflection, R2-D2 gave a low, uncertain tone. Luke glanced at his trusty droid and gave him a soft smile. R2-D2's indicator flashed blue, and he turned his dome back to the cairns, leaning forward as he balanced on his two primary legs.

It was Lando who spoke first.

"She's out there, somewhere," he said, quietly. Luke looked at him. Lando was watching the cairns, the tears on his cheeks reflecting the colored light. As he spoke, his whole body shivered, his voice in danger of breaking up altogether.

"She's out there on her own. We failed. I failed her. I tried, and I failed."

He looked at Luke, his bottom lip trembling as he fought to control his emotions. He didn't say any more.

He didn't need to. Luke knew that he was talking about the daughter of the people they had just buried, but also that Lando's words reflected the search for his own child.

Luke turned back to the cairns. Yes, they'd failed. They'd gotten so close to saving the family, only for their mission to end in tragedy.

The child was missing.

But Luke had hope. He didn't know where it came from, but he knew himself well enough to trust those feelings, the intuition that came unbidden, a gift of the Force.

She was alive. He could feel it. Not only alive, but Ochi hadn't found her.

And now, as Lando looked at him—looked at him for support, for an answer, for hope—he wanted to say again what he had said earlier, but he thought better of it. And even as he thought it, Lando shook his head.

"Don't Luke, don't," he said, turning back to the cairns, shaking his head, wiping his face. "I want to trust you, I really do, but you can't know she's safe. You can't know that Ochi didn't find her."

Then Komat lifted her mirror mask to Luke.

"Lando Calrissian speaks the truth, Master Skywalker. Until we find Ochi of Bestoon, we cannot know for certain that he did not complete his task and take the girl to Exegol."

Luke frowned, and then he nodded.

"Then we keep looking," he said. "We keep looking until we find him."

At this, Lando choked back a sob, and started to cry, unable to hold it back any longer. Luke moved over to his friend, and they embraced, Lando burying his face in Luke's shoulder.

"We must rest if we are to resume the search, Master Skywalker," said Komat. Her mask tilted as she observed the two men. "Lando Calrissian has lost much and needs time to recover. I suggest the solitude of Polaar, where I will look after him."

Luke nodded, and Lando pulled away, shaking his head, wiping his face once more.

"No, no," said Lando. He pointed toward the cavern entrance. "We gotta get out there, right now. We gotta keep looking." He dropped his arm. "She's out there. Their daughter. And mine. They're out there and we have to get them back."

Luke nodded. "And we *will* keep looking. But Komat is right, you need time to recover. Go with her to Polaar. I'll work on finding some new leads on Ochi. The trail has gone cold, but we'll find him."

Lando stared at Luke, then dropped his head and cleared his throat. "Okay," he said, then he laughed, softly. "I'm sorry."

"There is nothing to apologize for, Lando Calrissian," said Komat. "Come, I will take you." She turned to Luke. "We will await your transmission, Master Skywalker."

Luke nodded as Komat, her arm around Lando's shoulder, led him from the cavern.

R2-D2 whistled a low tone. Luke moved over to the astromech, and crouched beside him, his cybernetic hand resting on the droid's dome.

Together, they watched the cairns for a few minutes more, and then Luke stood and left, R2-D2 close behind.

CHAPTER 65

THE JEDI TEMPLE OF MASTER LUKE SKYWALKER, OSSUS
NOW

Luke sat on the grass, eyes closed, the warm sun on his back, half listening to the sounds of the younglings as they worked with their training blades in the central plaza of the temple.

"Master Skywalker?"

Luke's eyes snapped open, and he made a deliberate effort to soften his expression—too late, it seemed.

"Are you okay?" Ben Solo asked as he folded his gangly form down into a cross-legged position, mirroring his Master's meditative pose, without asking permission.

That was when the corner of Luke's mouth rose—ever so slightly—in a smile. His Padawan knew just what he could get away with with his uncle—Jedi Master or not.

"I'm fine, Ben, fine. Actually, it's good to see you. I know we haven't spent much time together since I got back yesterday."

"Right!" said Ben, almost bouncing on the ground in excitement. He leaned forward, long arms waving. "You have got to tell me what happened out there. Lor San Tekka said you were on a sacred quest." He paused and grinned. "But then he says that even when you're doing your laundry." At this, Ben glanced over Luke's black robes, which he hadn't changed out of since returning in his X-wing the previous afternoon.

"And we will talk, and soon," said Luke, "but I still have . . . matters to attend to."

"I can help!"

Luke's smile returned. "A Padawan offering to help his Master is an honorable gesture, but an unnecessary one."

Ben rocked back, his hands clasped under the front of his long legs. "Now you sound like Lor San Tekka again."

Luke laughed, and Ben joined him, and then the two fell silent, happy in each other's company. Luke knew he should be more focused with his Padawan, toning down the familiarity that came with family, instilling something more formal. But right now, Luke was just glad to be back, and he allowed himself this one moment of peace.

"Something's still wrong, isn't it?" Ben said at last, and Luke realized he had allowed his thoughts to show on his face again.

Truth was, something *was* still wrong. The disturbance in the Force was gone, fading rapidly with the fall of Viceroy Exim Panshard and the destruction of his mask, the evil shadow of the Sith cast out into the void where it belonged.

But there was still business left unfinished—and Luke, despite his best efforts, couldn't sense it.

Actually, he couldn't sense anything.

It wasn't that the Force had left him. That was an impossibility. But the power Exim Panshard had managed to trap in his mask had been a power unlike anything Luke had encountered before. The shadow it had cast in the Force had been long and dark, and now that it was gone, Luke's connection with the Force was clear and pure and also . . .

Empty, like the disturbance had been the tolling of a great bell, and now that it was gone, the silence it left behind was almost more deafening.

Luke knew it would pass. A disturbance like that would leave a wake that stretched long and wide, and would take time to fully dissipate.

But it still unsettled him. He felt both at one with the Force and apart from it, like he was straining all his senses to hear something, but there was only the echo of his thoughts in his own mind.

"Uncle Luke?"

Luke blinked, realizing once again he had allowed his focus to drift, his concentration not on the here and now as it should be.

"Padawan," he said, injecting what he hoped was a friendly reminder into that word. It worked, as Ben's expression flickered for a moment, and he glanced at the ground.

"Sorry, *Master* Skywalker."

Luke smiled. "I think I'm the one who should be sorry," he said, sheepishly. "I'm not a good teacher today. And besides," he added as he stood, Ben standing with him, "you should go back to the younglings. Give them another session with the training blades."

Ben nodded, pushing his black hair out of his eyes. Luke wondered if he should have insisted his Padawan cut his hair in the traditional manner, but it was a little late for that kind of decision. Ben Solo was becoming a fine apprentice, regardless of how messy he liked to keep his hair.

Ben turned to leave, then stopped and turned back. "Just . . . let me know if I can help, okay? I might not be a Jedi Knight, but I'm stronger than you think."

With that, he jogged off between two huts and rejoined the group of younglings, who all turned, faces alive with delight, as he returned and told them they could have another round with the training blades.

Luke watched them work for a moment, then headed back into his own hut. Inside, he laid out his flight suit and helmet again, then sat and considered his next move before standing and walking to the other side of the room. There, he knelt by a secure box and waved a hand over it, the hidden lock accessible only with the Force.

The box's lid opened. Inside, the fragments of Exim Panshard's mask sat in a row, the red crystalline surface dull and blackened, pieces of the kyber already splitting off, revealing the carbonized metal beneath.

Luke looked at the pieces for a moment. He hadn't decided what to do with the mask fragments, whether they were something to be studied, or something to be destroyed. He would need to consult with Lor San Tekka.

Closing the strongbox, Luke stood and, moving now to the small table by his bunk, picked up his comlink.

He had work to do—lots of work. Ochi of Bestoon was still out there. And so, too, perhaps, was the wayfinder he was looking for.

And so, too, was the girl. Luke had to find her. He owed her that much.

Luke thumbed the button on the comlink. "Artoo, get ready for take-off."

R2-D2's affirmative bleep came over the comlink as Luke tossed it onto the bunk and began pulling on his flight suit.

CHAPTER 66

KOMAT'S HERMITAGE, POLAAR
NOW

Lando Calrissian padded across the living area of Komat's homestead, then sat carefully down on a cushion by the table. His hips still protested, just a little, but otherwise he felt . . .

Actually, he felt pretty great. Luke and Komat had been right. A week of total rest had done him a world of good.

It hadn't started well. He'd spent the whole journey from Neftali pacing around the flight deck of Komat's ship as KB-68 flew them back to Polaar. Of Komat herself, Lando saw little, but then, in retrospect, he knew he hadn't been paying attention to anything but his own thoughts anyway. All he could do was run the events of the past several days over, and over, and over again in his mind—analyzing his own actions, trying to figure out where he'd gone wrong, what they could have done differently, how their mission could have had a different outcome.

It was futile, of course, although it had taken him another day to be able to look back and realize that. On Polaar, he'd collapsed into a deep sleep as soon as he'd returned to the cool, quiet sleeping chamber at the heart of Komat's homestead compound. When he'd woken on the first day, he'd found himself alone. The *Warglaive* was still on the pad, but the truck was gone from the workshop—she was out in the particle array, working with her droid, no doubt enjoying time spent with Sekhmet, leaving Lando be.

That had made him . . . angry, actually. He spent the next few hours sitting, staring at the window, his mind just a fog of rage, not even a single coherent thought forming. At some point he'd gone back to his room, and he must have fallen asleep, because the next thing he remembered was waking in the blue light of the starship wreck, with Komat sitting beside him on the floor. As Lando had pushed himself up onto one elbow, Komat placed a full tumbler of water on the floor in front of him, told him to drink, then rose and left him to it.

Lando drank the water, then realized how thirsty he was, how hungry he was. He drank several more tumblers from the vaporator at the food station, and helped himself to Komat's well-stocked pantry.

The next day, he went out with Komat and KB-68, and the three of them worked all day, harvesting plates from the particle array. When Lando slept that night, it was less a collapse of total mental and physical exhaustion, more the happy, deep slumber after a day of hard work.

He sipped his water now, knowing just how important this time had been. Yes, they still had a job to do. Ochi was out there. So was the child.

So was his daughter.

But if there was anything Komat had taught him, it was patience—something he knew he had never really been capable of. When the Lando Calrissian of old wanted something, he got it—there and then. Later, when he found his interests aligned more with the Rebel Alliance, he wanted results, and he wanted them fast.

That trait was not, however, a virtue.

But here on Polaar, the exquisitely beautiful, exquisitely poisonous planet?

Well . . . Lando had learned a lot. He had learned that there were some things you couldn't control; that some things had to happen and there was nothing you could do about it, and beating yourself up over failures to prevent the inevitable was a waste of time.

Not that the death of the child's mother and father had been inevitable. No way, no how. *That* was a failure, and one Lando knew he would live with for the rest of his life. He remembered their voices, back on Nightside. They were the first things he heard when he woke, the last things he heard when he fell asleep, and he suspected it would remain that way for a long, long time.

Days passed; Lando tracked them at first, then he stopped. Life with Komat was simple. They worked, they ate, they slept. Komat never initiated conversation, instead always waiting for Lando to speak first. Perhaps that was her culture, or perhaps that was part of what she was doing for Lando. She seemed to be able to understand his moods, maybe even his thoughts and emotions, more than he did.

It was another morning; Lando, clad in one of Komat's own short robes, looked up from his quiet contemplation of the window view as his host appeared. Her own robe, like Lando's, did little to hide her lithe, muscular bare limbs, but Lando found himself completely relaxed in her presence—both attracted to her and not. It was a pleasant balance, he thought—this was a powerful warrior and a beautiful woman. He couldn't think of any better company right now.

But he also knew that his time with Komat was coming to an end. He felt . . . healed, he supposed, was the right word. The time spent here, as it had been when he'd first visited with Luke, was time invested for the future.

And now it was time to start looking to that future.

He put down his tumbler and opened his mouth to speak, but Komat spoke first.

"Yes."

Lando pursed his lips. "Uh, okay. Thanks. I think." He paused, took a drink, put the tumbler back down. "What did you just agree to?"

"You wish to take my ship beyond the energy field, Lando Calrissian. You wish to contact Master Skywalker and recommence your search for Ochi of Bestoon."

Of course she had figured it out. She was Komat.

Lando spread his hands. "I can't tell you how much I have appreciated your hospitality. I wish I could stay here forever, I really do." He looked out toward the window and watched as the white grass rustled in the breeze. He shook his head. "There's just something about this place. I don't know what it is, but I like it." He laughed. "I can't go outside without a protective suit, but I like it."

"This planet is a desert," said Komat, following Lando's gaze. "The product of a war, a planet that will remain as a terrible warning forever. But it is also a place of peace, the knowledge of its past centering the mind, helping you to understand what you must do now and what you can let sleep in your mind." She turned back to him. "The desert helps you forget."

The two sat in silence for a moment. Then Lando cleared his throat.

"I'll bring your ship back, of course."

"I assumed this would be so."

"Because I know you've got a lot of . . . uh, particles to sell, right?"

"You are correct, Lando Calrissian."

Lando turned. "Can I borrow your armor?" He gestured with his hands around his face. "It might be useful."

"The armor of a Wind Raider of Taloraan is not something that can be borrowed."

"Oh," said Lando, holding his hands up. "Of course. Sorry. I thought I recognized it but I wasn't sure. You're from Taloraan?" He paused, then laughed. "All this time, and I still don't know much about you, Komat of Taloraan."

"I will give you my armor as a gift."

"Oh," said Lando again. He dropped his hands, and he grinned. "Well, I can't thank you enough, honestly, and—"

"But if you do not return my ship, there will be consequences, Lando Calrissian."

Lando blinked. "Um, of course," he said. He stood, and drained the last of his water. He pointed to the passageway leading to his room. "I'm just . . . going to . . . you know . . . get ready."

Komat nodded. "All will be prepared for you."

Lando gave a bow, then headed for the door.

· · ·

As soon as the ship was outside Polaar's interfering energy field, Lando locked the controls into a geostationary orbit and got to work on the comm deck. His first instinct was to call Luke, but he felt so . . . out of it. After so much time spent incommunicado with Komat, Lando at least felt like he needed to reconnect, catch up on what was happening in the galaxy, find some new starting point for his trail, maybe put together what he had heard with what Luke might have learned. It was a broad approach, untargeted, the kind of thing Lando had done when he'd started the search for his daughter six years ago, but Lando knew he needed to ease himself back into his mission.

A few hours later, Lando tapped the final few notes on the datapad he'd found stowed in the cockpit of Komat's ship, then flicked the switch on the comm deck again.

"You sure about this, Nikka?"

"Seems to fit, Lando," came a female voice. "I'll send a holoimage. Hold on."

Lando sat back and waited. He'd been talking for hours, crossing the channels, calling up anyone and everyone he could think of.

And he'd found something. Or rather, Nikka had. She'd been a commander in the Bespin Wing Guard, back when Lando had been baron administrator of Cloud City, and they'd kept in touch—somewhat loosely, it had to be said—over the years after she left and started running her own private security service, building up a small fleet of fighters that traders could hire to escort them on dangerous runs.

It was on one of these runs that one of her crew had seen something strange, and now, as the holoimage came through and the three-dimensional picture assembled itself in the air in front of Lando's face, he knew it was exactly what he was looking for.

He snapped forward in his seat as he stared at the image.

"That the ship?" asked Nikka.

"It most certainly is the ship," said Lando with a wide grin. "Nikka Xizen, I should never have let you go."

Nikka laughed. "Well, now you owe me, okay?"

"Just name your price, Nikka. Name your price."

"I'll think about it. You need any muscle, you know who to call."

With that, the two ended the transmission. Lando sat and looked at the image of Ochi's ship as it sat on the rocky bluff. He stroked his mustache, then locked his hand behind his head. Progress, and so soon.

He leaned forward, fingers flying across the comm deck. Now it was time to call his old friend.

"Lando, it's so good to hear from you. How are you feeling?"

Lando's grin was wide as he replied. "Doing well, Luke, doing well. But listen. I have a lead. I think I've found Ochi's ship."

There was a pause, then Luke said. "What? Really?"

"Really," said Lando. "It's on a planet called—" He checked the data stamp on the holoimage transmission. "—called Pasaana. Middian system, according to my navicomputer."

There was a faint bleeping sound over the comm, as, somewhere across the galaxy, R2-D2 checked the coordinates and relayed the information to Luke.

"We've got it," said Luke. "Setting a course now."

"See you there."

Lando killed the comm, then leapt up, heading to the pilot's position, his hands moving over the control panels that lined the cockpit ceilings, readying Komat's ship to make the jump.

Destination: Pasaana.

CHAPTER 67

THE FORBIDDEN VALLEY, PASAANA

NOW

"What a mess," said Lando, his voice resonating with a deep, metallic echo as he cast an eye around the interior of the *Bestoon Legacy*. He slipped off the Wind Raider's helmet, and placed it carefully on a stack of crates.

"You're telling me," said Luke, pulling back his hood, joining his friend as they surveyed the main cabin.

It was dirty and dusty, the entry ramp having been left open, along with a wide cargo door at the rear of the ship, the ramp of which angled down below the ship's twin engines. Lando moved to peer down at the lowered section of floor in the main cabin. Something had clearly been unloaded, but when, he couldn't guess. The ship had been lying open for days, the interior being slowly filled with dust and sand. In the cockpit area, the front viewports were covered with something sticky and brown that Lando took one look at and decided he didn't want to investigate further.

Sand and dirt aside, the ship was a mess. The rear section was stacked with equipment crates, some of which were empty, the full ones revealing themselves to be filled with guns. Around the walls, other weapons were slung in webbing, as though Ochi had begun to unload the cargo and then given up when he ran out of room in his ship.

Across the floor were scattered papers, leaves from ancient, crumbling texts. Luke bent down and gathered a few up. Examining the top page, he moved to Lando.

"Look at this."

The page was inscribed with a lot of text, crowding around a hand-drawn picture of a polygonal object, a kind of tall pyramid with a thick, black frame around a core that looked like it was inscribed with a symbolic rendering of a star chart.

"What am I looking at?" asked Lando, brushing the sand from the page as Luke held it.

Luke tapped the drawing with his finger. "*That* is a wayfinder. That's what Ochi was looking for."

Lando looked around. "I don't see a wayfinder. But I don't see Ochi, either." He turned back to Luke. "Something's not right here. If Ochi found the girl, he'd be on Exegol by now. Look around. This ship hasn't moved in quite a while."

Luke nodded. He took the pages and carefully rolled them before stowing them inside his robe's inner pocket. Then he moved over to the rear of the cabin, where the floor plate was lowered. He dropped down into the space behind the cargo door and crouched. There was a layer of sand on the decking, but something else, too. He reached down and brushed it off, revealing a long black mark on the decking.

"He left in a speeder."

"With a faulty rear repulsorlift," said Lando, crouching at the edge of the cargo lift and pointing at the black mark. "Carbon scoring from where the projector got dragged along."

Luke nodded, and stood. "Let's take a look," he said. He pulled his hood up and stepped out through the cargo door.

Lando grabbed his helmet and left to join his friend via the main ramp.

Luke stood on the outcropping, scanning the terrain with a pair of quadnocs. Lando slipped his helmet on, then adjusted the green glass cowling on the front to essentially do the same thing. In his vision, the valley ahead crawled with text as the Komat's helmet painted data over the landscape.

He pointed. "Sinking fields," he said. "Looks like they're all over the valley."

Luke lowered his quadnocs. "Let's take a look. We can be careful if we go on foot." Pulling his hood back over his head, he picked out a path on the steep side of the outcrop and headed down, Lando close behind.

The pair walked for an hour or more, Lando grateful for the protection his borrowed helmet offered against the intense glare and heat of the sun. A few steps ahead of him, Luke marched on. Lando wasn't sure how he hadn't even broken out into a sweat, clad in black as he was.

They'd been right about the sinking fields. At close range, they were easily distinguishable from the regular desert surface, consisting as they did of a different kind of sand altogether. At the edge of one field, Lando picked up a handful of the stuff to take a look, and found the grains were large and smooth, almost like polished seeds. But without the aid of the computer in his helmet, he knew the true nature of the fields would be difficult to spot until you were almost on top of them—and, he thought, when it was too late to do anything about it.

Ahead now, as the valley narrowed, the black sinking sands seemed to spread all the way across the path ahead.

"Luke," he called out. Luke stopped and turned as Lando caught up with him.

"Not sure we can go much farther," said Lando, pointing ahead. "This whole area is one natural booby trap." He shook his head then pulled his helmet off, wincing against the sudden heat of the day on his face. "And so far, I've not seen any trail of a speeder, with or without a faulty repulsor. We have no idea if we're even looking in the right direction."

Luke nodded and turned in a circle, gazing out at the land around them.

"Agreed," he said. "If we're going to search the valley, we need to do it properly." He frowned then cocked his head, his eyes narrowing like he was listening to something far away.

"What is it?" asked Lando, only for Luke to wave at him to be quiet.

Luke closed his eyes fully, then turned around. He held out his human hand, palm-down, and spread his fingers.

Lando watched, wanting to ask Luke what he was doing, knowing full well that he wasn't sure he'd understand the answer. But it was like he'd, what, heard something in the Force? Not *heard* heard, not with his ears, but with his . . . mind?

Lando frowned and decided to leave Luke to it.

A moment later, Luke sighed. He dropped his arm and turned back around to Lando, shaking his head.

"What is it? You feel something out here?"

"I thought I did," said Luke, "then it was gone. But I am sure there is no life out here. At least, nothing significant."

"You mean, no Ochi of Bestoon?"

Luke shrugged. "Wherever he is, it's not here." He paused. "There was something else, too, but . . ."

Lando gestured for Luke to continue. "Come on, Luke, give me something to work with here."

Luke closed his eyes and cocked his head again. He stood, silent, as the seconds passed. Then he sighed again and opened his eyes.

"Anything?"

"That's just it," said Luke. "Nothing. It's like . . . I can't explain it. There's nothing. The feeling I get is like . . ." He grimaced as he tried to put it into words. "Like we're not going to make any headway, not here."

Lando lifted an eyebrow. "You trying to tell me the Force says we're wasting our time?"

Luke's smile twitched to life. "Would you believe me if I said yes?"

Lando barked a single, short laugh, then he batted Luke on the shoulder with one hand and turned, slipping his helmet back on.

"Let's head back," he said. "Maybe there's a clue we missed at the ship."

·   ·   ·

Night had fallen, the air now pleasantly cool.

Lando sat on a flat rock on the side of the outcropping, Ochi's ship to his back. He looked out at the vast plain on the opposite side of the valley. Pasaana's moon was rising, bright white, surrounded by a faint violet halo.

It was still and peaceful. It reminded Lando of Polaar—the landscape was different, certainly, and on Pasaana he could actually stay outside without any protective gear other than something to guard against the sun.

But the feeling, that was the same. He thought about it, wondering whether it was the planet, or if it was him. His time with Komat had certainly given him a new perspective. He'd learned a lot from her— a lot about himself.

That's what she'd meant by rest—true rest. Not just sleep, not just relaxation. Something far more fundamental, primal, even.

"The desert makes you forget," he said, to himself.

"What was that?"

Lando looked up as Luke joined him.

"Just something Komat taught me," he said as Luke settled onto the rock beside him. "Find anything?"

Luke shook his head. On their return from the valley, they'd spent several hours practically dismantling the interior of the ship, but had found nothing that gave any clue as to where Ochi had gone, only some custom novelty droid with a drained battery crumpled in one corner, a tiny thing that was nothing more than a cone-shaped head on a single wheel. While Luke had sat in the cockpit, scanning through the navicomputer log, Lando had tried, and failed, to find the droid's charging dock.

"You think maybe he's watching us?" asked Lando. He pointed out to the plain. "He's nearby, hiding, waiting for his moment?"

Luke shrugged. "Maybe. But I think I would have sensed his presence." He paused. "I didn't feel anything out there at all."

"Well, this place *would* be an easy spot to hide," said Lando. "Those settlements we saw on the way in were big but sparsely spread. Nobody would know you were here." He raised his arms to take in the vast landscape that stretched out around them. "What did Artoo say this place was called?"

"The Forbidden Valley," said Luke.

Lando pursed his lips. "Good name." He looked back out at the plain. He thought about Ochi; he thought about the girl.

He thought about Kadara.

Then he turned to Luke. "I'm going to stay and search."

Luke looked at him for a moment but didn't answer.

"Look," said Lando, "you have your temple to look after. The trail has gone cold—and you said it yourself, you don't . . . I don't know, you don't *feel* anything here. Could be Ochi is here. Could be he isn't. But if he is, then he's going to come back for that." He pointed up at the ship above them.

"You're going to keep a watch on this ship yourself?"

Lando shrugged. "Sure. But not just watch. If he's here, I'll find him. Maybe he did go to one of those settlements, try to recruit some locals. I'll go and take a look."

He stopped talking and stared out into the distance.

Luke watched him a moment, then asked, "There's something else, isn't there, Lando?"

Lando nodded, but he didn't answer. Instead, he pointed a finger up at the sky.

"I haven't searched this quadrant for my daughter," he said. "Pasaana will make a good base." He nodded, to himself this time. "You know, I think I have a good feeling about this."

Luke nodded, then laid a hand on Lando's shoulder. "I'll take another look through the computer logs, see if there is anything I missed, and I'll take a copy for Artoo to analyze."

"Hey, sounds good, sounds good."

As Luke headed back into the ship, Lando looked out at the plain, then he leaned back, looked at the stars, and made a new promise to himself, and to his daughter.

Kadara Calrissian.

She was out there, somewhere. They both were—his daughter, and the child.

He lifted his hand and tapped at the wrist link.

"The Calrissian Chronicles, chapter . . . next." He laughed. "And maybe let's stick to an audio log for this one, I'm not sure anyone wants to look at my ruggedly handsome yet decidedly middle-aged face right now.

"As the night fell on Pasaana, I looked out across the Forbidden Valley, the deadly sinking sands now veiled in the dark of night. Our quarry was Ochi of Bestoon, an infamous Jedi hunter who had in his possession a clue to the location of a wayfinder.

"And what's a wayfinder? you may ask yourself. Well, let's go back to the beginning.

"I was on Boxer Point Station, in the Janx system, playing the best game of sabacc in my entire life in Sennifer's Beam and Balance, when all of a sudden . . ."

ACKNOWLEDGMENTS

My thanks to the incredible team at Del Rey/Penguin Random House, not only for their sterling editorial work and endless support and advice, but for the incredible opportunity to contribute to the greatest storytelling mythos in popular culture with a book like . . . this! Elizabeth Schaefer was my brilliant, insightful editor and is completely wonderful. Thanks also to Tom Hoeler (also wonderful) for comments and suggestions. You are both the best in the business, and it's a pleasure to work with you. The pink drinks are on me!

To the team at Lucasfilm/Disney—Jen Heddle, Pablo Hidalgo, Matt Martin, Mike Siglain—thanks for your keen editorial eye, your comments and suggestions, and discussions of the minutiae of the *Star Wars* saga. Thanks also to Kristin Baver for early notes and being a great sounding board, and to Rae Carson for those interesting chats on the ins and outs of *The Rise of Skywalker*. My thanks also to Lauren Kretzschmar, and to Kasim Mohammed and Daisy Saunders at Penguin Random House UK.

Writing is a peculiar profession—we work alone and yet rely an awful lot on the support of others. To Team Trash Compactor!—Kiersten White and Mike Chen!—2022 is a year we're going to remember for a long, long time. Thanks so much for the long-distance friendship and endless, ongoing discussions of what it means—and how much fun it is—to be a *Star Wars* author.

Luke's Sith-possessed adversary in this book (see, I know you're reading this first, so no spoilers from me) was created by Chuck Wendig. My thanks to Chuck for the years of friendship and for his blessing in using his marvelous creation. *Star Wars* is a weird and wonderful thing, and I'm glad you were there to lend a guiding hand. Thanks also to Cavan Scott and George Mann for the friendship, support, and advice offered to this newbie. And to Jock, superstar artist, thanks so much for your kind words and your keen eye for design.

This book took a long time to write, and whenever I needed a sympathetic ear, I had my team with me. My thanks to Michaela Gray, Bria LaVorgna, and Jen Williams for being on hand whenever I needed you.

To Mark Newbold and Eric Trautman, my thanks for information, data, and deep, deep *Star Wars* nerdery that was so much fun to dig into. Thanks also to Diane Douglas, Michael Haswell, Tina Mairi Kittelty, Greg Manchess, Joshua Ziegler, and to Juan Esteban Rodriguez for *that* cover, and thanks to Kristen Hersh, Sarah Blackwood, and members of the bands Blushing and No Joy.

Star Wars has a long and glorious legacy in literature. To add to this ever-growing body of work is an honor, and I have to salute those who have gone before me. In particular, my thanks to Michael A. Stackpole for his support and encouragement, and for some of the best *Star Wars* adventures ever written. Likewise, thanks to Matthew Stover for his superb body of work; the warning from a darker time that opens this book is taken from his superlative *Revenge of the Sith* novelization.

To Stacia Decker, my long-time agent and friend—we did it! Thank you for . . . everything, everywhere, all at once.

Finally, thanks to my mum and dad for endless support and love, and to my wife, Sandra, who knows exactly how hard this job is and also exactly what it means to me. I love you.

May the Force be with you, always.

ABOUT THE AUTHOR

ADAM CHRISTOPHER's debut novel, *Empire State*, was *SciFiNow*'s Book of the Year and a *Financial Times* Book of the Year. The author of *Made to Kill, Standard Hollywood Depravity,* and *Killing Is My Business,* Christopher's other novels include *Seven Wonders, The Age Atomic,* and *The Burning Dark.*

Author of the official tie-in novels for the hit CBS television show *Elementary* and the award-winning Dishonored videogame franchise, Christopher is the co-creator of the twenty-first-century incarnation of the Archie Comics superhero The Shield. He has also contributed prose fiction to the world of Greg Rucka and Michael Lark's *Lazarus* series from Image Comics.

Adam is also a contributor to the internationally bestselling *Star Wars: From a Certain Point of View* anniversary anthology series and has written for IDW's all-ages *Star Wars Adventures* comic.

adamchristopher.me
Twitter: @ghostfinder

Read on for an excerpt from

THE PRINCESS AND THE SCOUNDREL

BY BETH REVIS

PROLOGUE

LEIA

The fires had all died down, smoke trailing in the night sky, dissipating long before it could reach any of the countless glittering stars twinkling through the tree canopy. Leia's hand trailed over the white and black helmets of the stormtroopers and Imperial fighters that the Ewoks had turned into an impromptu drum set. She had laughed and danced along with everyone else when the fires were bright and the drinks had flowed freely.

But now her hand lingered over the scratches and dents on a previously gleaming-white helmet.

A person, a living being, had been under this helmet.

The enemy.

Someone who would have shot to kill—any rebel, of course, but Leia knew that her death would have been the highlight of a stormtrooper's career. Someone shot this person before they could shoot her. And then the dead trooper's helmet had been plucked from their head and banged on like a drum.

She wondered who the trooper had been. Someone indoctrinated as a child, perhaps? That happened often enough. Someone from an occupied world, pressed into service? Had this stormtrooper chosen the path that led to their death and derision on a forest moon, or had they simply been unlucky?

Her fingers slid over the scuffed surface of the helmet, but her hand froze before she touched the next one.

Black.

It wasn't *his* helmet, she knew. The night made the gray-green of the AT-ST operator's helmet appear darker than it was, and the shape was similar but still distinctly different.

A hand fell on Leia's left shoulder, fingers firm, pulling her back. Leia sucked in a harsh breath—the touch was too familiar. The hand pulled her back with the same pressure as before, the same spacing of fingers, one painfully on her clavicle, and when she shuddered at the touch, the same soft, almost gentle rub of a thumb against her shoulder blade.

"It's just me," Luke's voice said, concern etched on his face when she jerked away and turned toward him.

Just Luke. Her brother.

Darth Vader's son.

"You smell like . . ."

"Smoke?" Luke guessed. "We all do." He attempted a smile, but Leia didn't return it. Because the scent that clung to Luke's black tunic was not the same as the smoke that still lingered throughout the Ewok village of Bright Tree. The stench of it made her sick to her stomach—that, and the idea that while she'd danced, he had gone to give Darth Vader a funeral pyre.

Still, when she looked in his eyes, she saw only Luke. And he was sad.

"The whole galaxy celebrated while you mourned," Leia said softly.

Luke shook his head. "I wasn't the only one mourning."

Leia glanced at the stormtrooper's helmet. "No, I suppose not."

"How are you?" Luke's voice was sincere, but Leia wasn't sure how to answer him. This was supposed to be a triumph, but all she really felt was confused. Not just about what Luke had told her about her lineage— their connection was something she'd felt for some time, and it had been easy to accept Luke as her brother. She would not think what that meant about her biological father. No—it wasn't just that.

"It's the Force, isn't it?" Luke asked.

Leia nodded. She had told Luke that she didn't—couldn't—understand the power he had, but he seemed eerily calm and confident that she *could* actually wield the Force as he did. Leia might not have any real experience with the Force, but there was no denying the power Luke had . . . the power she felt, too, like a fluttering of flitterfly wings just on the edge of her consciousness. Waiting for her to seize it.

"He told me to tell you—" Luke started, but Leia's head whipped up, eyes fierce as she glared at him.

"Don't," she warned.

"They were his last words. He wanted me to tell you—"

"I don't care."

"He *was* good," Luke insisted. "There was still good in him, after all . . ."

My father was good, Leia thought, but in her mind she pictured Bail Organa, not Darth Vader. Thinking of Bail made her think of Breha, her mother. Of her home. Of everything she had lost.

When she had spoken to Luke earlier this night, Leia had told him that she remembered the mother they shared, their birth mother. It had been vague images, feelings, really, nothing more. But she *did* have a memory—of love, of closeness, of things she could not describe. It was impossible to put her feelings into words, but there was no denying their truth. It felt like . . . a connection, a bond made of light.

Yet Luke, who was a Jedi Knight, strong in the Force, had no memory of the woman who had birthed them both.

Did he have memories of their father? Was that why he was so capable of forgiving the monster that was Darth Vader? They had been separated at birth, not just from each other but from their biological parents. Maybe Leia had a connection with their mother, and Luke had a connection with their father.

Leia bit back a bitter laugh. Perhaps it wasn't as deep as that. Perhaps it was merely that Luke had never been tortured by their biological father the way she had.

"What happens next?" Luke asked.

Leia looked at him. Since becoming a Jedi Knight, he always seemed so calm, so sure of his direction.

He wasn't sure now. His eyes searched hers. *He's waiting for me to decide my fate before he chooses his own,* she realized. Their blood connection may be new knowledge, but he was also her friend. The threads of fate that had pulled them in separate directions could be rewoven.

Beyond Luke, in the shadows, Leia saw the outline of someone else. Han was backlit by a lingering torch, but she recognized his shoulders, his stance. Cocky, even when no one was looking. When his eyes settled on her, he strode directly toward her, his feet loud on the rickety boards of the walkway between the treetop dwellings.

Leia had no idea what would happen tomorrow or the next day or the next. But as she left Luke in the shadows and met Han on the bridge, she knew exactly what would happen tonight.

CHAPTER 1

HAN

TWO DAYS LATER

"It's not over yet."

That's what Han had told the rebel Pathfinders after he'd left the Imperial base they'd uncovered on the other side of Endor. While the Death Star had been constructed in orbit around the forest moon, a separate communications base had been built on the surface, undamaged in the aftermath of the Death Star's destruction—until Han and his troops had arrived. Signal intelligence had decrypted some of the messages the base had been sending out, transmitting throughout the galaxy. Blowing up the Death Star may have been fun, but it wasn't enough. Imperials occupied countless worlds, and they weren't just rolling over. The Pathfinders had gone in blasters blazing, but they hadn't been quick enough to stop the signal.

Data, comms, plans. All that info scattered across the galaxy. And it all came down to Emperor Palpatine still giving orders despite being nothing but ash and space debris now. He had calculated for his legacy to live on even if he exploded in space, and that was exactly what they'd been too late to prevent.

One night. They'd all had one night to celebrate and pretend that the war was over. But . . .

It wasn't over yet.

Han cursed. The debriefing with the generals—the other generals, because he now held that rank, too—had been quick and dirty, just a relay of information followed by the others scattering in various directions to make new plans. Time for the brains to work. No one had invited Han to stay and concoct a strategy to round up the Imperials that still remained and hadn't gotten the message that they'd lost. That was fine. They just needed to tell him where to fly and what to shoot. He was good at that part. The best. Sure, he'd had some decent ideas in the past. But now that the blasting was over, it made sense for the others . . .

Beside him, Chewbacca roared.

"Yeah, I get you," Han muttered. It never seemed to end. But then he paused, turning to look up at his old friend. "I haven't forgotten, though, you know that, right? We're heading back to Kashyyyk as soon as possible, kicking the Imperials off your world. You've got a family to take care of."

Chewie started to grumble, but Han cut him off. "No. We stick to *our* plan, and it was always for you to go home as soon as we had a break."

Han grabbed the rung of one of the ladders leading up into the tree village. While the leaders of the Rebellion had set up a base on the ground in order to be closer to the ships in the clearing and the immediate action they anticipated, it was little more than a large tent with a few smaller ones nearby to handle the overflow of quartering pilots and ground troops. The Ewok huts were far more comfortable living quarters. Beneath him, the ladder swung as Chewie followed Han up, his added weight throwing Han off balance for a moment before he could adjust.

Leia hadn't been at the debriefing.

Han knew she'd been elsewhere, recording messages for allies, and he knew that the others would catch her up to speed. But . . .

He wanted to see her.

Han's track record with love wasn't necessarily the best. But this thing with Leia—it felt like more than . . . He couldn't quantify it. It just felt *more*. He'd tried to walk away, more than once. Maybe, if he'd been able to leave Hoth when he'd planned . . .

Han had meant it when he'd told Leia he'd exit her life if she wanted. Of course, that was before he knew Luke and Leia were siblings, before he knew a lot of things. But he'd meant his words. He would have left, not for his own benefit, but for hers. Every other time in Han's life, when he walked away, he did it for himself. But not that time.

Instead of letting him leave, though, she'd come to him.

And Han didn't know if he could let her go again.

Especially not after how much time he'd already lost. He'd been frozen on Bespin and by the time he'd woken up again—blind and disoriented with hibernation sickness—so much time had passed. Leia had loved him for nearly a whole year, and Vader had stolen that year from him. Han wasn't going to let more time slip through his fingers.

Distantly, he became aware that Chewie had been talking to him. Han hooked his leg over the top of the ladder and landed with a thud of his boots on the wooden walkway of the village. "Yeah, buddy?" he asked.

Chewie swung himself up, big arms balancing before he landed fully. He roared, half in amusement, half in discontent at being ignored.

"Sorry!" Han said, throwing up his hands. "I've got things on my mind."

"Oh, am I just a thing?" Leia's voice sliced through Han's brain.

"Hey, now, you don't occupy my *every* thought, Princess," Han snapped back, but the warm smile in his eyes belied the statement.

"You sure about that?" she asked, smirking, her rosy lower lip just begging to be kissed, and Han blanked for several moments, incapable of doing anything more than blink at her.

Chewie chuckled.

"Yeah, yeah," Han grumbled, reorienting himself.

"I was just looking for you," Leia said. Her tone slid from playful to business. "Mon told me about the plans discovered on the Imperial base, and I wanted to check in with the general who made the discovery."

Right. That was him.

Leia kept speaking, unaware that Han wasn't focused on her words. "The timing of that base's communication—even if we haven't been able to decrypt most of the encoded contents yet—indicates that there's far more at play than we originally thought."

Grumbling, Chewie left the two of them alone, heading deeper into the village. Han was far too focused on Leia to really register his friend walking off, though. His mind raced with the impossibility of his thoughts—him, and a *princess*? It couldn't possibly work in the long term.

"We've been monitoring a lot of traffic in the Anoat system in particular, and I wanted to see if any of the transmissions you intercepted indicated that," Leia continued. "Or perhaps you saw something in the base—not everything needs to be online, physical transportation of sector codes could indicate—"

Since when did Han care about the long term, though?

"Han?" Leia asked, her head tilted up at him.

"I want you," he stated flatly.

"Me?" She looked around—although the base below had been bustling with activity, this part of the village was remarkably quiet. "For what?"

"Forever," Han said.

Leia's confusion shifted to something else, something he couldn't quite read. He never could tell everything going on in her mind, and he loved that about her.

He loved her.

She was a princess, the face of the Rebellion, the new government's greatest hope, a symbol more than a person. But she was also just Leia. And she was his. Han needed her the same way he needed the *Falcon*— sure, he could fly without her, but what was the point?

"Marry me," Han said.

Leia, usually so calm and collected, with the ability to face down Vader himself, could not hide her shock in that moment. Her eyes widened, her lips parted, and the rest of her body stilled, frozen in surprise. Han felt the corner of his lips twisting up, watching as Leia didn't try to hide her shock. She didn't hide her desire, either. He was hers, too.

But she had a grander destiny than he could comprehend. Elbows-deep in politics and someone who would always be doing, doing, doing.

Even now, even though neither of them had physically moved, Han could see Leia spinning away from him, out of his grasp.

So he reached out to her. He took her hand. Rubbed the place on her finger where a ring could go.

Han was sure the same questions flying through his mind were in hers as well. How many people were already discussing marriages and settling down with folk they'd only known in combat? It was a common enough thing—emotions ran high after battle, people felt the need to grasp at life when faced with the death of war. The flip side of fighting was loving, and there was a hell of a lot of energy that needed to be redirected somewhere.

This was the part where Han was supposed to tip his chin, laugh, say it was all a joke.

But he didn't.

He didn't flinch as he watched doubt cloud Leia's face. He stood there, and he waited for her to realize the same truth he knew.

They were better together.

And marriage? Well, it was a formality. But it was also a promise.

One he intended to keep.

"Yes," she said. Just that word, but with a smile that went along with it that lit up the entire galaxy.

Something inside of Han eased, invisible bands loosening around his lungs. The days coming were not going to be easy; the Empire would see to that. He and Leia *would* eventually have to separate—there would be battles she couldn't fight, political machinations he couldn't play a role in, worlds and trials and issues that would divide them.

But . . .

It wasn't over yet.

CHAPTER 2

LEIA

Leia should be questioning this, him, everything. But they'd already stolen one night—why not steal a lifetime more? As chaotic as it was, she knew that she would never regret this decision. She was making her happiness an indelible part of her own history, and that was worth the risk.

As Han whooped before sweeping her into his arms and twirling her around the wooden platform above the trees, Leia could do no more than laugh in joy. So much of her life had always been planned. What to wear, what to say, when to work, how to dress her hair, even the meals she ate. She'd never liked ruica, but by the stars she ate it, just as a good princess of Alderaan should.

For so long, everything in her life had been a part of a greater plan, but love could not be scheduled.

Han set Leia down again, his grin wider than she'd ever seen it before. "Wait till I tell Chewie," he said, laughing ruefully. "He always said I'd settle down one day."

Leia raised an eyebrow. "Why does marriage have to mean settling down?"

"See?" Han said, shaking a finger at her playfully. "That's why I'm marrying you."

I need to tell Luke, Leia thought. He was the only family she had left. Her breath caught, but Han, still elated, didn't notice. Leia put her smile back on, a mask.

Han froze. "What's wrong?" he asked.

A bubble of emotion burst out of her. "Am I that easy to read?" She shook her head, her eyes sliding away from his.

"Second-guessing this scoundrel already?" Han asked gently.

"No, it's just . . ." Her voice trailed off. Han put a finger on her chin, pulling her gaze back to him. "I wish my family could meet you."

"Oh, I don't need their disapproval." It was a joke, and Leia appreciated it, weak as it was. His gaze darkened as his teasing smile shifted to a worried frown. "What aren't you telling me?"

Leia's breath came out shaky. If he was going to marry her, he needed to know the truth. She would not entangle him with lies. "When I say family, I mean my mother Breha and my father Bail."

"I know—"

Leia held her hands up to stop him; if she didn't speak now, she was worried she'd never muster the courage to do it. "They adopted me. They're my parents. I love them. But my blood is . . ."

"Luke," Han said, nodding, clearly still confused.

"Not just Luke," Leia said softly. "He found out about our biological father." Han's brow creased in confusion. "Vader." She whispered the word like a confession.

Han blinked several times, the only reaction that revealed he'd heard her. He swallowed, hard, and Leia watched the bump in his throat rise and sink. "Well," he said finally, shaking his head. "Good thing he's dead."

"You . . ." Leia's heart stuttered. "You don't care?"

"Why would I?"

Leia's eyes rounded in disbelief. Han cut her a sharp look. "You care," he said in a voice so low that Leia wasn't sure if it was a statement or a question.

"Of course I do."

Han paused, clearly thinking through what to say next. Finally he settled on, "Are you okay?"

She wasn't. She didn't think she would ever be okay with the knowledge of her bloodline. But she also didn't want to mar this moment any more with the shadow of his memory. "I will be," she said.

When he looked at her, he seemed to know everything she wasn't able to put into words. "Okay then," he said, nodding once, that trademark smirk twitching on his lips. "We're gonna get married."

"Seems so."

"I've gotta go tell Chewie the good news. And you've gotta tell . . ." Han nodded his head at someone behind Leia. She turned and saw Luke approaching, a tentative smile on his face but worry lines between his eyes.

Han smirked. "I can't wait to tell Lando. I'm pretty sure there's an old bet he made with me that I could cash in right now . . ." He headed off, clasping Luke's shoulder as he passed the other man, leaving the explanations to Leia.

"You and Han, huh?" Luke asked her.

Leia felt a twist of nerves in her stomach as she waited for his response. What if he didn't approve, what if this soured their friendship, what if—

"*Finally!*" Luke shouted, elation spread over his face.

"Really?" Relief flooded her senses.

Luke pulled her into a hug. "You should know," he said with a chuckle in his voice, "that Chewie was already threatening to kidnap you two and drop you off on some deserted planet until you could both figure out how right you were for each other."

Leia's shoulders shook with laughter. "Wookiees aren't exactly known for subtlety, I suppose."

"Not at all." Luke stepped back, eyes sparkling. "Seriously, I'm happy for you both."

"I told him," Leia said. "I told him what you told me, and he didn't care."

"Of course he didn't. Han's one of the good ones."

Are we? Leia wanted to ask. How did the knowledge of their parentage not disturb Luke the way it did her? For that matter, how had Han's reaction been so calm? He should have been disgusted; he should have been—

Concern washed over Luke's features, but Leia ignored him, wrapping her arms around herself. A part of her wondered at how quickly Luke had come to this deserted landing. She'd sought out Han earlier, intent on reuniting with him after his mission with the Pathfinders. But Luke had seemed to arrive almost as soon as she'd thought of him. Had she somehow unconsciously reached out to him—or did he control their connection? She wasn't sure how she felt about that. Luke had told her that she could have the same power he did, but . . .

Her brother's eyes searched hers, and she knew he didn't need the Force to see the conflicted emotions coursing through her. "How do you feel?" he asked.

He was so different now from when she'd first met him. Years had passed, of course, but the boy she'd met on the Death Star, proclaiming he'd come to save her, had been boisterously excited, full of optimism and opportunities. This man before her now was the same Luke, but . . . calmer. He moved with purpose rather than crashing around, bursting through doors or bumbling across the galaxy. Leia almost mourned the change. She had seen it before, of course, over the years of the war— bright hopefuls who became jaded when they realized they were no longer shooting at inanimate targets. Luke held a deeper sort of stillness within him, like a tree growing on a moon with no air, no wind to shift the branches.

Leia walked away from him and stepped to the edge of the platform. Railings circled the landing, but they were built for the Ewoks' diminutive stature. More than one pilot drunk on jet juice in the celebrations after the destruction of the Death Star had toppled over the barriers that hit them around knee height. Now Leia let the sturdy rails press against her legs as her toes, covered in leather slippers, curled over the edge of the wooden platform. "I feel like I'm on a precipice," Leia answered Luke as she forced herself to look down, through the tree branches to the distant ground below.

She glanced over her shoulder. "I feel like that for all three of us. You, me, Han. This moment, right now, it feels like . . ." She turned back to the railing, but this time her eyes were on the tree-dappled horizon. "It feels like one step, and we'll all scatter in different directions. Right now, we're together. Right now, we're safe."

And I just want to make this moment last forever, she thought, although she guessed that Luke understood her unspoken sentiment.

Luke didn't move toward her; he stayed in the center, near the place where the fires had burned. "When you think of the future . . ."

"I don't want to think of that," she said, her tone pleading. "I want *this* moment to last. When we've won. When we're all together." And, if she were honest with herself, getting married right now would give the moment permanence. To her, if nothing else. Endor was not just the place where the war ended . . . because, after all, the fighting wasn't over yet. The war wasn't over. It might never be over, not if the Empire continued operating despite the Emperor's death. But getting married now, here, turned the battle-that-wasn't-actually-the-end into the day she forgot about the war and chose love instead.

"I think . . ." Luke's voice trailed off. Leia searched his eyes. His brow crinkled in a smile that belied the gravity of the moment. "I think you're forgetting that the end of the war didn't just buy the galaxy peace. It bought you time."

Leia shook her head, confused. In answer, Luke took her hand, pulling her away from the edge. "You *are* right," he conceded. "The three of us have many different paths we could take. And this moment is a deciding one. The choices we make now will . . . linger." He paused. "But following this path doesn't mean you can't follow others. You have the freedom now to pursue any route you want to explore."

"I don't know if I want . . ." Leia's voice trailed off. She knew what Luke was offering, but as much as she was curious about what the Force could offer her, she also knew that every step closer to it was a step closer to the power that had twisted Darth Vader into a monster.

Pain flashed over Luke's face, and Leia realized she had missed the point Luke was making. He wasn't thinking about power at all. He was thinking about her. She wasn't the only one who'd lost family. Luke had, too. He had told her about his aunt and uncle. Leia's heart lurched—had they been *her* aunt and uncle as well? Luke's home had burned, and with it, everything that had represented his past. Tatooine still existed, but to Luke, it was as gone as Alderaan.

Leia leaned in, tucking a lock of Luke's hair behind his ear. Always scruffy, these boys.

"I can help you learn," Luke said, taking her movement to mean acceptance. "After you've had some time with Han, you and I can start training. I have heard of places where I can find more Jedi lore. Yoda is gone, but I can train you as he trained me. And there's so much I still don't know. Yoda called me a Jedi Knight, but I know in the past, Jedi trained from the time they were younglings. There's more for me to learn, too. We can do it together."

His voice trailed off as Leia shook her head. "I don't care about the Force," she said softly. "I would want to go with you because I would like to be with *you*. I would like to get to know my brother as my brother."

Luke kept telling her that she had time to decide, that it wasn't one or the other. But it *felt* like she had a choice to make. Go with Luke and choose a family of a sibling pair, exploring the unknown elements of the galaxy, discovering the Force and all it meant. Or go with Han and choose a family of her own making, discovering nothing more than herself.

"We could do such great things together," Luke said, his eyes unfocused, as if he could see a different future from the one Leia envisioned.

How lonely it must be, she thought. She was among the last Alderaanians, but he *was* the last Jedi. "You could come with us," she offered.

Luke snorted. "On your honeymoon with Han?"

"No." Leia laughed. "I mean you could help us form the new government. My father told me how the Jedi once served alongside the Senate, how they were a part of politics, too. When the new republic is fully formed, you could work with me at the capital. We could build something together." *You don't have to be alone.* For one shining moment, Leia allowed herself the fantasy of a capital city, gleaming and new, with a glorious Senate Hall. She could advocate and bring peace through politics, and then come home to her husband and—perhaps—a youngling or two. Dinner with her children's uncle. A home for them all to center on.

She didn't need to plan every moment of her life as she had on Alderaan, but that stability had enabled love and families to flourish together. It would be nice.

"There's so much left to learn and discover," Luke said, his words shattering her fantasy. "I don't know where I'll be going, but I do know I'll be gone." It was like when he'd disappeared after Hoth, chasing Yoda on a far-flung planet, unable even to comm and let them know he was safe. He searched her eyes, trying once more: "You could go with me."

"I don't think I can," Leia said gently. Luke might believe she could choose multiple paths, but Leia wasn't so sure. Following him would mean chasing power, and that power could help shape the type of galaxy she'd worked her entire life to build. But if she had to choose between power and happiness, she would choose happiness.

Because that was what the choice really was. Going with Luke, becoming a Jedi—it would be an adventure. It might give her the power he tempted her with.

But she had given her whole life to power.

And she was ready to choose, for the first time, what she wanted for herself.

ABOUT THE TYPE

This book was set in Minion, a 1990 Adobe Originals typeface by Robert Slimbach (b. 1956). Minion is inspired by classical, old-style typefaces of the late Renaissance, a period of elegant, beautiful, and highly readable type designs. Created primarily for text setting, Minion combines the aesthetic and functional qualities that make text type highly readable with the versatility of digital technology.